About the Authors

Cathy Williams can remember reading Mills & Boon books as a teenager, and now that she is writing them she remains an avid fan. For her, there is nothing like creating romantic stories and engaging plots, and each and every book is a new adventure. Cathy lives in London, and her three daughters – Charlotte, Olivia and Emma – have always been, and continue to be, the greatest inspirations in her life.

Maya Blake's hopes of becoming a writer were born when she picked up her first romance book aged thirteen. Little did she know her dream would come true! Does she still pinch herself every now and then, to make sure it's not a dream? Yes, she does!

Feel free to pinch her too, via Twitter, Facebook or Goodreads! Happy reading!

Chantelle Shaw lives on the Kent coast and thinks up her stories while walking on the beach. She has been married for over thirty years and has six children. Her love affair with reading and writing Mills & Boon stories began as a teenager, and her first book was published in 2006. She likes strong-willed, slightly unusual characters. Chantelle also loves gardening, walking and wine!

Ruthless Revenge
COLLECTION

July 2018 · August 2018 · September 2018

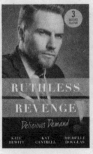

October 2018 · November 2018 · December 2018

Ruthless Revenge: Passionate Possession

CATHY WILLIAMS

MAYA BLAKE

CHANTELLE SHAW

MILLS & BOON

Published in Great Britain 2018
by Mills & Boon, an imprint of HarperCollins*Publishers*
1 London Bridge Street, London, SE1 9GF

Ruthless Revenge: Passionate Possession © 2018 Harlequin Books S.A.

A Virgin for Vasquez © 2016 Cathy Williams
A Marriage Fit for a Sinner © 2015 Maya Blake
Mistress of His Revenge © 2016 Chantelle Shaw

ISBN: 978-0-263-26812-6

09-0818

MIX
Paper from
responsible sources
FSC™ C007454

This book is produced from independently certified FSC™ paper to ensure responsible forest management.

For more information visit: www.harpercollins.co.uk/green

Printed and bound in Spain
by CPI, Barcelona

A VIRGIN FOR VASQUEZ

CATHY WILLIAMS

CHAPTER ONE

JAVIER VASQUEZ LOOKED around his office with unconcealed satisfaction.

Back in London after seven years spent in New York and didn't fate move in mysterious ways…?

From his enviable vantage point behind the floor-to-ceiling panes of reinforced rock-solid glass, he gazed down to the busy city streets in miniature. Little taxis and little cars ferrying toy-sized people to whatever important or irrelevant destinations were calling them.

And for him…?

A slow, curling smile, utterly devoid of humour, curved his beautiful mouth.

For him, the past had come calling and that, he knew, accounted for the soaring sense of satisfaction now filling him because, as far as offices went, this one, spectacular though it was, was no more or less spectacular than the offices he had left behind in Manhattan. There, too, he had looked down on busy streets, barely noticing the tide of people that daily flowed through those streets like a pulsing, breathing river.

Increasingly, he had become cocooned in an ivory tower, the undisputed master of all he surveyed. He was thirty-three years old. You didn't get to rule the concrete jungle by taking your eye off the ball. No; you kept focused, you eliminated obstacles and in that steady, onward and upward march, time passed by until now...

He glanced at his watch.

Twelve storeys down, in the vast, plush reception area, Oliver Griffin-Watt would already have been waiting for half an hour.

Did Javier feel a twinge of guilt about that?

Not a bit of it.

He wanted to savour this moment because he felt as though it had been a long time coming.

And yet, had he thought about events that had happened all those years ago? He'd left England for America and his life had become consumed in the business of making money, of putting to good use the education his parents had scrimped and saved to put him through, and in the process burying a fleeting past with a woman he needed to consign to the history books.

The only child of devoted parents who had lived in a poor *barrio* in the outskirts of Madrid, Javier had spent his childhood with the driving motto drummed into him that to get out, he had to succeed and to succeed, he had to have an education. And he'd had to get out.

His parents had worked hard, his father as a taxi driver, his mother as a cleaner, and the glass ceiling had always been low for them. They'd managed, but only just. No fancy holidays, no flat-screen tellies for the house, no chichi restaurants with fawning waiters. They'd made do with cheap and cheerful and every single penny had been put into savings for the time when they would send their precociously bright son to university in England. They had known all too well the temptations waiting for anyone stupid enough to go off the rails. They had friends whose sons had taken up with gangs, who had died from drug overdoses, who had lost the plot and ended up as dropouts kicked around on street corners.

That was not going to be the fate of their son.

If, as a teenager, Javier had ever resented the tight controls placed on him, he had said nothing.

He had been able to see for himself, from a very young age, just what financial hardship entailed and how limiting it could be. He had seen how some of his wilder friends, who had made a career out of playing truant, had ended up in the gutter. By the time he had hit eighteen, he had made his plans and nothing was going to derail them: a year or two out, working to add to the money his parents had saved, then university, where he would succeed because he was bright—brighter than anyone he knew. Then a high-paying job. No starting at the ground level and making his way up slowly, but a job with a knockout financial package. Why not? He knew his assets and he had had no intention of selling himself short.

He wasn't just clever.

Lots of people were clever. He was also sharp. Sharp in a streetwise sort of way. He possessed the astuteness of someone who knew how to make deals and how to spot where they could be made. He knew how to play rough and how to intimidate. Those were skills that were ingrained rather than learnt and, whilst they had no place in a civilised world, the world of big business wasn't always civilised; it was handy having those priceless skills tucked up his sleeve.

He'd been destined to make it big and, from the age of ten, he had had no doubt that he would get there.

He'd worked hard, had honed his ferocious intelligence to the point where no one could outsmart him and had sailed through university, resisting the temptation to leave without his Master's. A Master's in engineering opened a lot more doors than an ordinary degree and he wanted to have the full range of open doors to choose from.

And that was when he had met Sophie Griffin-Watt.

The only unexpected flaw in his carefully conceived life plan.

She had been an undergraduate, in her first excitable year, and he had been on the last leg of his Master's, already considering his options, wondering which one to take, which one would work best for him when he left university in a little under four months' time.

He hadn't meant to go out at all but his two housemates, usually as focused as he was, had wanted to celebrate a birthday and he'd agreed to hit the local pub with them.

He'd seen her the second he'd walked in. Young, impossibly pretty, laughing, head flung back with a drink in one hand. She'd been wearing a pair of faded jeans, a tiny cropped vest and a denim jacket that was as faded as the jeans.

And he'd stared.

He never stared. From the age of thirteen, he'd never had to chase any girl. His looks were something he'd always taken for granted. Girls stared. They chased. They flung themselves in his path and waited for him to notice them.

The guys he'd shared his flat with had ribbed him about the ease with which he could snap his fingers and have any girl he wanted but, in actual fact, getting girls was not Javier's driving ambition. They had their part to play. He was a red-blooded male with an extremely healthy libido—and, as such, he was more than happy to take what was always on offer—but his focus, the thing that drove him, had always been his remorseless ambition.

Girls had always been secondary conquests.

Everything seemed to change on the night he had walked into that bar.

Yes, he'd stared, and he'd kept on staring, and she hadn't glanced once at him, even though the gaggle of girls she was with had been giggling pointing at him and whispering.

For the first time in his life, he had become the pursuer. He had made the first move.

She was much younger than the women he usually dated. He was a man on the move, a man looking ahead to bigger things—he'd had no use for young, vulnerable girls with romantic dreams and fantasies about settling down. He'd gone out with a couple of girls in his years at university but, generally speaking, he had dated and slept with slightly older women—women who weren't going to become clingy and start asking for the sort of commitment he wasn't about to give them. Women who were experienced enough to understand his rules and abide by them.

Sophie Griffin-Watt had been all the things he'd had no interest in and he'd fallen for her hook, line and sinker.

Had part of that driving obsession for her been the fact that he'd actually had to try? That he'd had to play the old-fashioned courting game?

That she'd made him wait and, in the end, had not slept with him?

She'd kept him hanging on and he'd allowed it. He'd been happy to wait. The man who played by his own rules and waited for no one had been happy to wait because he'd seen a future for them together.

He'd been a fool and he'd paid the price.

But that was seven years ago and now...

He strolled back to his chair, leant forward and buzzed his secretary to have Oliver Griffin-Watt shown up to his office.

The wheel, he mused, relaxing back, had turned full circle. He'd never considered himself the sort of guy who would ever be interested in extracting revenge but the opportunity to even the scales had come knocking on his door and who was he to refuse it entry...?

* * *

'You did what?'

Sophie looked at her twin brother with a mixture of clammy panic and absolute horror.

She had to sit down. If she didn't sit down, her wobbly legs would collapse under her. She could feel a headache coming on and she rubbed her temples in little circular movements with shaky fingers.

Once upon a time, she'd been able to see all the signs of neglect in the huge family house, but over the past few years she'd become accustomed to the semi-decrepit sadness of the home in which she and her brother had spent their entire lives. She barely noticed the wear and tear now.

'What else would you have suggested I do?' There was complaint in his voice as he looked at his sister.

'Anything but that, Ollie,' Sophie whispered, stricken.

'So you went out with the guy for ten minutes years ago! I admit it was a long shot, going to see him, but I figured we had nothing to lose. It felt like fate that he's only been back in the country for a couple of months, I just happen to pick up someone's newspaper on the tube and, lo and behold, who's staring out at me from the financial pages…? It's not even as though I'm in London all that much! Pure chance. And, hell, we need all the help we can get!'

He gestured broadly to the four walls of the kitchen which, on a cold winter's night, with the stove burning and the lights dimmed, could be mistaken for a cosy and functioning space but which, as was the case now, was shorn of any homely warmth in the glaring, bright light of a summer's day.

'I mean…' His voice rose, morphing from complaint to indignation. 'Look at this place, Soph! It needs so much work that there's no way we can begin to cover the cost.

It's eating every penny we have and you heard what the estate agents have all said. It needs too much work and it's in the wrong price bracket to be an easy sell. It's been on the market for two and a half years! We're never going to get rid of it, unless we can do a patch-up job, and we're never going to do a patch-up job unless the company starts paying its way!'

'And you thought that running to...to...' She could barely let his name pass her lips.

Javier Vasquez.

Even after all these years the memory of him still clung to her, as pernicious as ivy, curling round and round in her head, refusing to go away.

He had come into her life with the savage, mesmerising intensity of a force-nine gale and had blown all her neat, tidy assumptions about her future to smithereens.

When she pictured him in her head, she saw him as he was then, more man than boy, a towering, lean, commanding figure who could render a room silent the minute he walked in.

He had had presence.

Even before she'd fallen under his spell, before she'd even spoken one word to him, she'd known that he was going to be dangerous. Her little clutch of well-bred, upper-middle-class friends had kept sneaking glances at him when he'd entered that pub all those years ago, giggling, tittering and trying hard to get his attention. After the first glance, she, on the other hand, had kept her eyes firmly averted. But she hadn't been able to miss the banging of her heart against her ribcage or the way her skin had broken out in clammy, nervous perspiration.

When he'd sauntered across to her, ignoring her friends, and had begun talking to her, she'd almost fainted.

He'd been doing his Master's in engineering and he

was the cleverest guy she'd ever met in her life. He was so good-looking that he'd taken her breath away.

He'd been also just the sort of boy her parents would have disapproved of. Exotic, foreign and most of all… unashamedly broke.

His fantastic self-assurance—the hint of unleashed power that sat on his shoulders like an invisible cloak—had attracted and scared her at the same time. At eighteen, she had had limited experience of the opposite sex and, in his company, that limited experience had felt like no experience at all. Roger, whom she had left behind and who had been still clinging to her, even though she had broken off their very tepid relationship, had scarcely counted even though he had been only a couple of years younger than Javier.

She'd felt like a gauche little girl next to him. A gauche little girl with one foot poised over an unknown abyss, ready to step out of the comfort zone that had been her privileged, sheltered life.

Private school, skiing holidays, piano lessons and horse riding on Saturday mornings had not prepared her for anyone remotely like Javier Vasquez.

He wasn't going to be good for her but she had been as helpless as a kitten in the face of his lazy but targeted pursuit.

'We could do something,' he had murmured early on when he had cornered her in that pub, in the sort of seductive voice that had literally made her go weak at the knees. 'I don't have much money but trust me when I tell you that I can show you the best time of your life without a penny to my name…'

She'd always mixed with people just like her: pampered girls and spoilt boys who had never had to think hard about how much having a good night out might cost.

She'd drifted into seeing Roger, who'd been part of that set and whom she'd known for ever.

Why? It was something she'd never questioned. Oliver had taken it all for granted but, looking back, she had always felt guilty at the ease with which she had always been encouraged to take what she wanted, whatever the cost.

Her father had enjoyed showing off his beautiful twins and had showered them with presents from the very second they had been born.

She was his princess, and if occasionally she'd felt uneasy at the way he'd dismissed people who were socially inferior to him, she had pushed aside the uneasy feeling because, whatever his faults, her father had adored her. She'd been a daddy's girl.

And she'd known, from the second Javier Vasquez had turned his sexy eyes to her, that she was playing with fire, that her father would have had a coronary had he only known...

But play with fire she had.

Falling deeper and deeper for him, resisting the driving desire to sleep with him because...

Because she'd been a shameless romantic and because there had been a part of her that had wondered whether a man like Javier Vasquez would have ditched her as soon as he'd got her between the sheets.

But he hadn't forced her hand and that, in itself, had fuelled her feelings towards him, honed and fine-tuned them to the point where she had felt truly alive only when she'd been in his company.

It was always going to end in tears, except had she known just how horribly it would all turn out...

'I didn't think the guy would actually agree to see me,' Oliver confessed, sliding his eyes over to her flushed, distressed face before hurriedly looking away. 'Like I said, it was a long shot. I actually didn't even think he'd remember who I was… It wasn't as though I'd met him more than a couple of times…'

Because, although they were twins, Oliver had gone to a completely different university. Whilst she had been at Cambridge, studying Classics with the hope of becoming a lecturer in due course, he had been on the other side of the Atlantic, going to parties and only intermittently hearing about what was happening in her life. He'd left at sixteen, fortunate enough to get a sports scholarship to study at a high school, and had dropped out of her life aside from when he'd returned full of beans during the holidays.

Even when the whole thing had crashed and burned a mere few months after it had started, he had only really heard the edited version of events. Anyway, he had been uninterested, because life in California had been far too absorbing and Oliver, as Sophie had always known, had a very limited capacity when it came to empathising with other people's problems.

Now she wondered whether she should have sat him down when he'd eventually returned to the UK and given him all the miserable details of what had happened.

But by then it had been far too late.

She'd had an engagement ring on her finger and Javier had no longer been on the scene. Roger Scott had been the one walking up the aisle.

It didn't bear thinking about.

'So you saw him…' *What did he look like? What did he sound like? Did he still have that sexy, sexy smile that could make a person's toes curl?* So much had happened over the years, so much had killed her youthful dreams about love and happiness, but she could still remember, couldn't she?

She didn't want to think any of those things, but she did.

'Didn't even hesitate,' Oliver said proudly, as though

he'd accomplished something remarkable. 'I thought I'd have to concoct all sorts of stories to get to see the great man but, in fact, he agreed to see me as soon as he found out who I was...'

I'll bet, Sophie thought.

'Soph, you should see his office. It's incredible. The guy's worth millions. More—billions. Can't believe he was broke when you met him at university. You should have stuck with him, sis, instead of marrying that creep.'

'Let's not go there, Ollie.' As always, Sophie's brain shut down at the mention of her late husband's name. He had his place in a box in her head, firmly locked away. Talking about him was not only pointless but it tore open scabs to reveal wounds still fresh enough to bleed.

Roger, she told herself, had been a learning curve and one should always be grateful for learning curves, however horrible they might have been. She'd been young, innocent and optimistic once upon a time, and if she was battle-hardened now, immune to girlish daydreams of love, then that was all to the good because it meant that she could never again be hurt by anyone or anything.

She stood up and gazed out of the patio doors to the unkempt back garden which rolled into untidy fields, before spinning round, arms folded, to gaze at her brother. 'I'd ask you what he said...' her voice was brisk and unemotional '...but there wouldn't be any point because I don't want to have anything to do with him. He's...my past and you shouldn't have gone there without my permission.'

'It's all well and good for you to get sanctimonious, Soph, but we need money, he has lots of it and he has a connection with you.'

'He has no connection with me!' Her voice was high and fierce.

Of course he had no connection with her. Not unless

you called *hatred* a connection, because he would hate her. After what had happened, after what she had done to him.

Suddenly exhausted, she sank into one of the kitchen chairs and dropped her head in her hands for a few moments, just wanting to block everything out. The past, her memories, the present, their problems. *Everything.*

'He says he'll think about helping.'

'What?' Appalled, she stared at him.

'He seemed very sympathetic when I explained the situation.'

'*Sympathetic.*' Sophie laughed shortly. The last thing Javier Vasquez would be was sympathetic. As though it had happened yesterday, she remembered how he had looked when she had told him that she was breaking up with him, that it was over between them, that he wasn't the man for her after all. She remembered the coldness in his eyes as the shutters had dropped down. She remembered the way he had sounded when he had told her, his voice flat and hard, that if he ever clapped eyes on her again it would be too soon… That if their paths were ever to cross again she should remember that he would never forget and he would never forgive…

She shivered and licked her lips, resisting the urge to sneak a glance over her shoulder just to make sure that he wasn't looming behind her like an avenging angel.

'What exactly did you tell him, Ollie?'

'The truth.' He looked at his twin defensively. 'I told him that the company hit the buffers and we're struggling to make ends meet, what with all the money that ex of yours blew on stupid ventures that crashed and burned. He bankrupted the company and took us all down with him.'

'Dad allowed him to make those investments, Oliver.'

'Dad…' His voice softened. 'Dad wasn't in the right place to stop him, sis. We both know that. Roger got away with everything because Dad was sick and getting sicker,

CATHY WILLIAMS 19

even if we didn't know it at the time, even if we were all thinking that Mum was the one we had to worry about.'

Tears instantly sprang to Sophie's eyes. Whatever had happened, she still found it hard to blame either of her parents for the course her life had eventually taken.

Predictably, when her parents had found out about Javier, they had been horrified. They had point-blank refused to meet him at all. As far as they were concerned, he could have stepped straight out of a leper colony.

Their appalled disapproval would have been bad enough but, in the wake of their discovery, far more than Sophie had ever expected had come to the surface, rising to the top like scum to smother the comfortable, predictable lifestyle she had always taken for granted.

Financial troubles. The company had failed to move with the times. The procedures employed by the company were cumbersome and time-consuming but the financial investment required to bring everything up to date was too costly. The bank had been sympathetic over the years as things had deteriorated but their patience was wearing thin. They wanted their money returned to them.

Her father, whom she had adored, had actually buried his head in his hands and cried.

At the back of her mind, Sophie had stifled a spurt of anger at the unfairness of being the one lumbered with these confidences while her brother had continued to enjoy himself on the other side of the world in cheerful, ignorant bliss. But then Oliver had never been as serious as her, had never really been quite as responsible.

She had always been her father's 'right-hand man'.

Both her parents had told her that some foreigner blown in from foreign shores, without a penny to his name, wasn't going to do. They were dealing with enough stress, enough financial problems, without her *taking up with someone who will end up being a sponge, because you know what these foreigners can be like... The man probably figures he's onto a good thing...*

Roger was eager to join the company and he had inherited a great deal of money when his dear parents had passed away. And hadn't they been dating? Wasn't he already like a member of the family?

Sophie had been dumbstruck as her life had been sorted out for her.

Yes, she had known Roger for ever. Yes, he was a perfectly okay guy and, sure, they had gone out for five minutes. But *he wasn't the one for her* and she'd broken it off even before Javier had appeared on the scene!

But her father had cried and she'd never seen her dad in tears before.

She had been so confused, torn between the surging power of young love and a debt of duty towards her parents.

Surely they wouldn't expect her to quit university when she was only in her first year and loving it?

But no. She'd been able to stay on, although they hoped that she would take over the company alongside Roger, who would be brought on board should they cement a union he had already intimated he was keen on.

He was three years older than her and had experience of working for a company. He would sink money into the company, take his place on the board of directors...

And she, Sophie had read between the lines, would have to fulfil her obligations and walk up the aisle with him.

She hadn't been able to credit what she had been hearing, but seeing her distraught parents, seeing their shame at having to let her down and destroy her illusions, had spoken so much more loudly and had said so much more than mere words could convey.

Had Roger even known about any of these plans? Was

that why he'd been refusing to call it quits between them even though they'd been seeing one another for only less than eight months before she had left for university? Had he already been looking to a future that involved her parents' company?

She had called him, arranged to see him, and had been aghast when he had told her that he knew all about her parents' situation and was keen to do the right thing. He was in love with her, always had been...

With no one in whom to confide, Sophie had returned to university in a state of utter confusion—and Javier had been there. She had mentioned nothing but she had allowed herself to be absorbed by him. With him, she could forget everything.

Swept along on a heady tide of falling in love, the panic she had felt at what was happening on the home front had been dulled. Her parents had not mentioned the situation again and she had uneasily shoved it to the back of her mind.

No news was good news. Wasn't that what everyone said?

She surfaced from the past to find a drink in front of her and she pushed it aside.

'I've got another appointment to see the bank tomorrow,' she said. 'And we can change estate agents.'

'For the fourth time?' Oliver gave a bark of laughter and downed his drink in one gulp. 'Face it, Soph. The way things are going, we'll be in debt for the rest of our lives if we're not careful. The company is losing money. The house will never sell. The bank will take it off our hands to repay our overdraft and we'll both be left homeless. It's not even as though we have alternative accommodation to return to. We don't. You bailed university to get married and moved into the family pile with Roger. I may have stayed on to get my diploma, but by the time I got back here everything had changed and we were both in it together. Both here, both trying to make the company work...' His voice had acquired the bitter, plaintive edge Sophie had come to recognise.

She knew how this would go. He would drink away his sorrows and wake up the following morning in a blurry, sedated haze where all the problems were dulled just enough for him to get through the day.

He was, she had been forced to accept, a weak man not made for facing the sort of situation they were now facing.

And she hated that she couldn't do more for him.

He was drinking too much and she could see the train coming off the tracks if things didn't change.

Did she want that? Wasn't there too much already on her conscience?

She shut down that train of thought, shut down the deluge of unhappy memories and tried hard to focus on the few bright things in her life.

She had her health.

They might be struggling like mad trying not to drown but at least Mum was okay, nicely sorted in a cottage in Cornwall, far from the woes now afflicting herself and her brother.

It might have been a rash expenditure given the dire financial circumstances, but when Gordon Griffin-Watt had tragically died, after a brief but intense period of absolute misery and suffering, it had seemed imperative to try to help Evelyn, their mother, who was herself frail and barely able to cope. Sophie had taken every spare penny she could from the scant profits of the company and sunk it all into a cottage in Cornwall, where Evelyn's sister lived.

It had been worth it. Her mother's contentment was the brightest thing on the horizon, and if she was ignorant about the extent of the troubles afflicting her twins, then that was for her own good. Her health would never be able to stand the stress of knowing the truth: that they stood to lose everything. One of the sweetest things Gordon Griffin-Watt had done had been to allay her fears about their financial situation while dealing with his own disastrous health problems, which he had refused to tell his wife about. She had had two strokes already and he wasn't going to send her to her grave with a third one.

'Vasquez is willing to listen to what we have to say.'

'Javier won't do a thing to help us. Trust me, Ollie.' *But he would have a merry time gloating at how the mighty had fallen, that was for sure.*

'How do you know?' her brother fired back, pouring himself another drink and glaring, challenging her to give him her little lecture about staying off the booze.

'Because I just do.'

'That's where you're wrong, sis.'

'What do you mean? What are you talking about? And should you…be having a second drink when it's not yet four in the afternoon?'

'I'll stop drinking when I'm not worrying 24/7 about whether I'll have a roof over my head next week or whether I'll be begging in the streets for loose change.' He drank, refilled his glass defiantly, and Sophie stifled a sigh of despair.

'So just tell me what Javier had to say,' she said flatly. 'Because I need to go and prepare information to take with me to the bank tomorrow.'

'He wants to see you.'

'He…*what*?'

'He says he will consider helping us but he wants to discuss it with you. I thought it was pretty decent of him, actually…'

A wave of nausea rushed through her. For the first time

ever, she felt that at the unseemly hour of four in the afternoon she could do with a stiff drink.

'That won't be happening.'

'You'd rather see us both living under a bridge in London with newspapers as blankets,' Oliver said sharply, 'rather than have a twenty-minute conversation with some old flame?'

'Don't be stupid. We won't end up *living under a bridge with newspapers as blankets…*'

'It's a bloody short drop from the top to the bottom, Soph. Can take about ten minutes. We're more than halfway there.'

'I'm seeing the bank tomorrow about a loan to broaden our computer systems…'

'Good luck with that! They'll say no and we both know that. And what do you think is going to happen to that allowance we give Mum every month? Who do you think is going to support her in her old age if we go under?'

'Stop!' Never one to dodge reality, Sophie just wanted to blank it all out now. But she couldn't. The weight of their future rested on her shoulders, but Oliver…

How could he?

Because he didn't know, she thought with numb defeat. What he saw was an ex who now had money and might be willing to lend them some at a reasonable rate for old times' sake. To give them a loan because they had nowhere else to turn.

She could hardly blame him, could she?

'I told him that you'd be at his office tomorrow at six.' He extracted a crumpled piece of paper from his pocket and pushed it across the table to her.

When Sophie flattened it out, she saw that on it was a scribbled address and a mobile number. Just looking at those two links with the past she had fought to leave behind made her heart hammer inside her.

'I can't make you go and see the man, Sophie.' Oliver stood up, the bottle of whisky in one hand and his empty glass in the other. There was defeat in his eyes and it pierced her heart because he wasn't strong enough to take any of this. He needed looking after as much as their mother did. 'But if you decide to go with the bank, when they've already knocked us back in the past and when they're making noises about taking the house from us, then on your head be it. If you decide to go, he'll be waiting for you at his office.'

Alone in the kitchen, Sophie sighed and rested back in the chair, eyes closed, mind in turmoil.

She had been left without a choice. Her brother would never forgive her if she walked away from Javier and the bank ended up chucking her out. And her brother was right; the small profits the company was making were all being eaten up and it wouldn't be long before the house was devouring far more than the company could provide. It was falling down. Who in their right mind wanted to buy a country mansion that was falling down, in the middle of nowhere, when the property market was so desperate? And they couldn't afford to sell it for a song because it had been remortgaged...

Maybe he'd forgotten how things had ended, she thought uneasily.

Maybe he'd changed, mellowed. Maybe, just maybe, he really would offer them a loan at a competitive rate because of the brief past they'd shared.

Maybe he'd overlook how disastrous that brief past had ended...

At any rate, she had no choice, none at all. She would simply have to find out...

CHAPTER TWO

SOPHIE STARED UP at the statement building across the frenzied, busy street, a soaring tower of glass and chrome.

She'd never had any driving desire to live in London and the crowds of people frantically weaving past her was a timely reminder of how ill-suited she was to the fierce thrust of city life.

But neither had she ever foreseen that she would be condemned to life in the tiny village where she had grown up, out in rugged Yorkshire territory. Her parents had adored living there; they'd had friends in the village and scattered in the big country piles sitting in their individual acres of land.

She had nothing of the sort.

Having gone to boarding school from the age of thirteen, her friends were largely based in the south of England.

She lived in a collapsing mansion, with no friends at hand with whom she could share her daily woes, and that in itself reminded her why she was here.

To see Javier.

To try to pursue a loan so that she could get out of her situation.

So that she and her brother could begin to have something of a life free from daily worry.

She had to try to free herself from the terror nibbling away at the edges of her resolute intentions and look at the bigger picture.

This wasn't just some silly social visit. This was...*a business meeting*.

She licked her lips now, frozen to the spot while the crowds of people continued to swerve around her, most of them glaring impatiently. There was no time in London to dawdle, not when everyone was living life in the fast lane.

Business meeting. She rather liked that analysis because it allowed her to blank out the horrifying personal aspect to this visit.

She tried to wipe out the alarming total recall she had of his face and superimpose it with the far more manageable features of their bank manager: bland, plump, semi-balding...

Maybe he had become bland, plump and semi-balding, she thought hopefully as she reluctantly propelled herself forward, joining the throng of people clustered on the pavement, waiting for the little man in the box to turn green.

She had dressed carefully.

In fact, she wore what she had planned to wear to visit the bank manager: black knee-length skirt, crisp white blouse—which was fine in cool Yorkshire, but horribly uncomfortable now in sticky London—and flat black pumps.

She had tied her hair back and twisted it into a sensible chignon at the nape of her neck.

Her make-up was discreet and background: a touch of mascara, some pale lip gloss and the very sheerest application of blusher.

She wasn't here to try to make an impression. She was here because she'd been pushed and hounded into a corner and now had to deal with the unfortunate situation in a brisk and businesslike manner.

There was no point travelling down memory lane because that would shatter the fragile veneer of self-confidence she knew she would need for this...*meeting*.

Another word she decided she rather liked.

And, at the end of the day, Oliver was happy. For the first time in ages, his eyes had lit up and she'd felt something of that twin bond they had shared when they'd been young but which seemed to have gone into hiding as their worries had begun piling up.

She took a deep breath and was carried by the crowd to the other side of the road as the lights changed. And then she was there, right in front of the building. Entering when most of the people were heading in the opposite direction because, of course, it was home time and the stampede to enjoy what remained of the warm weather that day was in full swing.

She pushed her way through the opaque glass doors and was disgorged into the most amazing foyer she had ever seen in her entire life.

Javier, naturally, didn't *own* the building, but his company occupied four floors at the very top and it was dawning on her that when Oliver had labelled him a 'billionaire' he hadn't been exaggerating.

You would have to have some serious money at your disposal to afford to rent a place like this, and being able to afford to rent four floors would require *very* serious money.

When had all that happened?

She'd reflected on that the evening before and now, walking woodenly towards the marble counter, which at six in the evening was only partially staffed, she reflected on it again.

When she'd known him, he hadn't had a bean. Lots of

ambition, but at that point in time the ambition had not begun to be translated into money.

He had worked most evenings at the local gym in the town centre for extra cash, training people on the punching bags. If you hadn't known him to be a first-class student with a brain most people would have given their right arm for, you might have mistaken him for a fighter.

He hadn't talked much about his background but she had known that his parents were not well off, and when she had watched him in the gym, muscled, sweaty and focused, she had wondered whether he hadn't done his fair share of fighting on the streets of Madrid.

From that place, he had gone to...*this*: the most expensive office block in the country, probably in Europe... A man shielded from the public by a bank of employees paid to protect the rich from nuisance visits...

Who would have thought?

Maybe if she had followed his progress over the years, she might have been braced for all of this, but, for her, the years had disappeared in a whirlpool of stress and unhappiness.

She tilted her jaw at a combative angle and squashed the wave of maudlin self-pity threatening to wash away her resolve.

Yes, she was told, after one of the women behind the marble counter had scrolled down a list on the computer in front of her, Mr Vasquez was expecting her.

He would buzz when he was ready for her to go up.

In the meantime...she was pointed to a clutch of dove-grey sofas at the side.

Sophie wondered how long she would have to wait. Oliver had admitted that he had had to wait for absolutely ages before Javier had deigned to see him and she settled in for the long haul. So she was surprised when, five minutes later, she was beckoned over and told that she could take the private lift to the eighteenth floor.

'Usually someone would escort you up,' the blonde woman told her with a trace of curiosity and malicious envy in her voice. 'I suppose you must know Mr Vasquez…?'

'Sort of,' Sophie mumbled as the elevator doors pinged open and she stepped into a wonder of glass that reflected her neat, pristine, sensible image back at her in a mosaic of tiny, refracted detail.

And then, thankfully, the doors smoothly and quietly shut and she was whizzing upwards, heart in her mouth, feeling as though she was about to step into the lion's den…

She was on her way up.

Javier had never been prone to nerves, but he would now confess to a certain tightening in his chest at the prospect of seeing her in a matter of minutes.

Of course he had known, from the second her brother had entered his offices with a begging bowl in his hand, that he would see Sophie once again.

As surely as night followed day, when it came to money, pride was the first thing to be sacrificed.

And they needed money. Badly. In fact, far more badly than Oliver had intimated. As soon as he had left, Javier had called up the company records for the family firm and discovered that it was in the process of free fall. Give it six months and it would crash-land and splinter into a thousand fragments.

He smiled slowly and pushed his chair back. He linked his fingers loosely together and toyed with the pleasurable thought of how he would play this meeting.

He knew what he wanted, naturally.

That had come as a bit of a surprise because he had

truly thought that he had put that unfortunate slice of his past behind him, but apparently he hadn't.

Because the very second Oliver had opened his mouth to launch into his plaintive, begging speech, Javier had known what he wanted and how he would get it.

He wanted *her*.

She was the only unfinished business in his life and he hadn't realised how much that had preyed on his mind until now, until the opportunity to finish that business had been presented to him on a silver platter.

He'd never slept with her.

She'd strung him along for a bit of fun, maybe because she'd liked having those tittering, upper-class friends of hers oohing and aahing with envy because she'd managed to attract the attention of the good-looking bad boy.

Didn't they say that about rich, spoilt girls—that they were always drawn to a bit of rough because it gave them an illicit thrill?

Naturally, they would never *marry* the bit of rough. That would be unthinkable!

Javier's lips thinned as he recalled the narrative of their brief relationship.

He remembered the way she had played with him, teasing him with a beguiling mixture of innocence and guileless, sensual temptation. She had let him touch but he hadn't been able to relish the full meal. He'd been confined to starters when he had wanted to devour all courses, including dessert.

He'd reached the point of wanting to ask her to marry him. He'd been offered the New York posting and he'd wanted her by his side. He'd hinted, saying a bit, dancing around the subject, but strangely for him had been too awkward to put all his cards on the table. Yet she must have suspected that a marriage proposal was on the cards.

Just thinking about it now, his insane stupidity, made

him clench his teeth together with barely suppressed anger.

She was the only woman who had got to him and the only one who had escaped him.

He forced himself to relax, to breathe slowly, to release the cold bitterness that had very quickly risen to the surface now that he knew that he would be seeing her in a matter of minutes.

The woman who had…yes…*hurt him*.

The woman who had used him as a bit of fun, making sure that she didn't get involved, saving herself for one of those posh, upper-class idiots who formed part of her tight little circle.

He was immune to being hurt now because he was older and more experienced. His life was rigidly controlled. He knew what he wanted and he got what he wanted, and what he wanted was the sort of financial security that would be immune to the winds of change. It was all that mattered and the only thing that mattered.

Women were a necessary outlet and he enjoyed them but they didn't interrupt the focus of his unwavering ambition. They were like satellites bobbing around the main planet.

Had he only had this level of control within his grasp when he'd met Sophie all those years ago, he might not have fallen for her, but there was no point in crying over spilt milk. The past could not be altered.

Which wasn't to say that there couldn't be retribution…

He *sensed* her even before he was aware of the hesitant knock on the door.

He had given his secretary the afternoon off. He'd been in meetings all afternoon, had returned to his offices only an hour previously, and something in him wanted to see Sophie without the presence of his secretary around.

He had brought Eva back with him from New York.

A widow in her sixties, originally from the UK anyway with all her family living here, she had been only too glad to accompany him back to London. She could be trusted not to gossip, but even so...

Seeing Sophie after all this time felt curiously *intimate*.

Which was something of a joke because *intimacy* implied some level of romance, of two people actually wanting to be in one another's company...

Hardly the case here.

Although, if truth be told, he was almost *looking forward* to seeing the woman again, whilst she...

He settled back in his leather chair and mused that *he* was probably the last person in the world *she* wanted to see.

But needs must...

'Enter.'

The deep, controlled tenor of that familiar voice chilled Sophie to the bone. She took a deep breath and nervously turned the handle before pushing open the door to the splendid office which, in her peripheral vision, was as dauntingly sophisticated as she had mentally predicted.

She had hoped that the years might have wrought changes in him, maybe even that her memory might have played tricks on her. She had prayed that he was no longer the hard-edged, proud, *dangerous* guy she had once known but, instead, a mellow man with room in his heart for forgiveness.

She'd been an idiot.

He was as *dangerous* as she remembered. More so. She stared and kept on staring at the familiar yet unfamiliar angles of his sinfully beautiful face. He'd always been incredibly good-looking, staggeringly exotic with finely chiselled features and lazy dark eyes with the longest eyelashes she had ever seen on a guy.

He was as sinfully good-looking as he had been then,

but now there was a cool self-possession about him that spoke of the tough road he had walked to get to the very top. His dark, dark eyes were watchful and inscrutable as she finally dragged her mesmerised gaze away from him and made her way forward with the grace and suppleness of a broken puppet.

And then, when she reached the chair in front of his desk, it dawned on her that she hadn't been invited to sit down, so she remained hovering with one hand on the back of the chair, waiting in tense, electric silence...

'Why don't you sit down, Sophie?'

He looked at her, enjoying the hectic colour in her cheeks, enjoying the fact that she was standing on shaky legs in front of him, in the role of supplicant.

And he was enjoying a hell of a lot more than that, he freely admitted to himself...

She was even more beautiful than the image he had stored in his mind carefully, as he had discovered, wrapped in tissue paper, waiting for the day when the tissue paper would be removed.

He couldn't see how long or short her hair was but it was still the vibrant tangle of colour it had been when he had first met her. Chestnut interweaved with copper with strands of strawberry blonde threaded through in a colourful display of natural highlights.

And she hadn't put on an ounce over the years. Indeed, she looked slimmer than ever. Gaunt, even, with smudges of strain showing under her violet eyes.

Financial stress would do that to a person, he thought, especially a person who had been brought up to expect the finest things in life.

But for all that she was as beautiful as he remembered, with that elusive quality of hesitancy that had first attracted him to her. She looked like a model, leggy, rangy and startlingly pretty, but she lacked the hard edges of someone with model looks and that was a powerful source of attraction. She had always seemed to be ever so slightly puzzled when guys spun round to stare at her.

Complete act, he now realised. Just one of the many things about her that had roped him in, one of the many things that had been fake.

'So...' he drawled, relaxing back in his chair. 'Where to begin? Such a long time since we last saw one another...'

Sophie was fast realising that there was going to be no loan. He had requested an audience with her *because he could*, because he had *known* that she would be unable to refuse. He had asked to see her so that he could send her away with a flea in her ear over how he thought he had been treated by her the last time they had been together.

She was sitting here in front of him simply because revenge was a dish best served cold.

She cleared her throat, back ramrod-straight, hands clutching the bag on her lap, a leftover designer relic back from the good old days when money, apparently, had been no object.

'My brother informs me that you might be amenable to providing us with a loan.' She didn't want to go down memory lane and, since this was a business meeting, why not cut to the chase? He wasn't going to lend them the money anyway, so what was the point of prolonging the agony?

Though there was some rebellious part of her that was compelled to steal glances at the man who had once held her heart captive in his hand.

He was still so beautiful. A wave of memories washed over her and she seemed to see, in front of her, the guy who could make her laugh, who could make her tingle all over whenever he rested his eyes on her; the guy who had lusted after her and had pursued her with the sort of intent and passion she had never experienced in her life before.

She blinked; the image was gone and she was back in the present, cringing as he continued to assess her with utterly cool detachment.

'Tut-tut-tut, Sophie. Don't tell me that you seriously expected to walk into my office and find yourself presented with a loan arrangement all ready and waiting for you to sign, before disappearing back to…remind where it is… the wilds of Yorkshire?' He shook his head with rueful incredulity, as though chastising her for being a complete moron. 'I think we should at least relax and chat a bit before we begin discussing…*money*…'

Sophie wondered whether this meant that he would actually agree to lend them the money they so desperately needed.

'I would offer you coffee or tea, but my secretary has gone for the day. I can, of course…' He levered himself out of the chair and Sophie noted the length and muscularity of his body.

He had been lean and menacing years ago, with the sort of physical strength that can only be thinly hidden behind clothes. He was just as menacing now, more so because he now wielded power, and a great deal of it.

She watched as he made his way over to a bar, which she now noticed at the far side of his office, in a separate, airy room which overlooked the streets below on two sides.

It was an obscenely luxurious office suite. All that was missing was a bed.

Heat stung her cheeks and she licked her lips nervously. For all she knew, he was married with a couple of kids, even though he didn't look it. He certainly would have a woman tucked away somewhere.

'Have a drink with me, Sophie…'

'I'd rather not.'

'Why not?'

'Because...' Her voice trailed off and she noted that he had ignored her completely and was now strolling towards her with a glass of wine in his hand.

'Because...what?' Instead of returning to his chair, he perched on the edge of his desk and looked down at her with his head tilted to one side.

'Why don't you just lay into me and get it over and done with?' she muttered, taking the drink from him and nursing the glass. She stared up at him defiantly, her violet eyes clashing with his unreadable, dark-as-night ones. 'I knew I shouldn't have come here.'

'Lay into you?' Javier queried smoothly. He shrugged. 'Things happen and relationships bite the dust. We were young. It's no big deal.'

'Yes,' Sophie agreed uneasily.

'So your brother tells me that you are now a widow...'

'Roger died in an accident three years ago.'

'Tragic. You must have been heartbroken.'

'It's always tragic when someone is snatched away in the prime of their life.' She ignored the sarcasm in his voice; she certainly wasn't going to pretend to play the part of heartbroken widow when her marriage had been a sham from beginning to end. 'And perhaps you don't know but my father is also no longer with us. I'm not sure if Ollie told you, but he suffered a brain tumour towards the end. So life, you see, has been very challenging, for me and my brother, but I'm sure you must have guessed that the minute he showed up here.' She lowered her eyes and then nervously sipped some of the wine before resting the glass on the desk.

She wanted to ask whether it was okay to do that or whether he should get a coaster or something.

But then, really rich people never worried about silly little things like wine glass ring-marks on their expensive wooden desks, did they?

'You have my sympathies.' Less sincere condolences had seldom been spoken. 'And your mother?'

'She lives in Cornwall now. We...we bought her a little cottage there so that she could be far from... Well, her health has been poor and the sea air does her good... And you?'

'What about me?' Javier frowned, eased himself off the desk and returned to where he had been sitting.

'Have you married? Got children?' The artificiality of the situation threatened to bring on a bout of manic laughter. It was surreal, sitting here making small talk with a guy who probably hated her guts, even though, thankfully, she had not been subjected to the sort of blistering attack she had been fearing.

At least, not yet.

At any rate, she could always walk out...although he had dangled that carrot in front of her, intimated that he would indeed be willing to discuss the terms and conditions of helping them. Could she seriously afford to let her pride come in the way of some sort of solution to their problems?

If she had been the only one affected, then yes, but there was her brother, her mother, those faithful employees left working, through loyalty, for poor salaries in the ever-shrinking family business.

'This isn't about me,' Javier fielded silkily. 'Although, in answer to your question, I have reached the conclusion that women, as a long-term proposition, have no place in my life at this point in time. So, times have changed for you,' he murmured, moving on with the conversation. He reached into his drawer and extracted a sheet of paper, which he swivelled so that it was facing her.

'Your company accounts. From riches to rags in the space of a few years, although, if you look carefully, you'll see that the company has been mismanaged for somewhat longer than a handful of years. Your dearly departed husband seems to have failed to live up to whatever promise there was that an injection of cash would rescue your family's business. I take it you were too busy playing the good little wife to notice that he had been blowing vast sums of money on pointless ventures that all crashed and burned?'

Sophie stared at the paper, feeling as though she had been stripped naked and made to stand in front of him for inspection.

'I knew,' she said abruptly. *Playing the good little wife?* How wrong could he have been?

'You ditched your degree course to rush into marriage with a man who blew the money on...oh, let's have a look...transport options for sustainable farmers...a wind farm that came to nothing...several aborted ventures into the property market...a sports centre which was built and then left to rot because the appropriate planning permission hadn't been provided... All the time your father's once profitable transport business was haemorrhaging money by the bucketload. And you knew...'

'There was nothing I could do,' Sophie said tightly, loathing him even though she knew that, if he were to lend them any money, he would obviously have to know exactly what he was getting into.

'Did you know where else your husband was blowing his money, to the tune of several hundred thousand?'

Perspiration broke out in a fine, prickly film and she stared at him mutinously.

'Why are you doing this?'

'Doing what?'

'Hanging me out to dry? If you don't want to help, then please just say so and I'll leave and you'll never see me again.'

'Fine.' Javier sat back and watched her.

She had never lain spread across his bed. He had never seen that hair in all its glory across his pillows. He had felt those ripe, firm breasts, but through prudish layers of clothes. He had never tasted them. Had never even *seen* them. Before he'd been able to do any of that, before he'd been able to realise the powerful thrust of his passion and his *yearning*, she had walked away from him. Walked straight up to the altar and into the arms of some little twerp whose very existence she had failed to mention in the months that they had been supposedly going out.

He had a sudden vision of her lying on his bed in the penthouse apartment, just one of several he owned in the capital. It was a blindingly clear vision and his erection was as fast as it was shocking. He had to breathe deeply and evenly in an attempt to dispel the unsettling and unwelcome image that had taken up residence in his head.

'Not going to walk out?' Javier barely recognised the raw lack of self-control that seemed to be guiding his responses.

He'd wanted to see her squirm but the force of his antipathy took him by surprise because he was realising just how fast and tight she had stuck to him over the years.

Unfinished business. That was why. Well, he would make sure he finished it if it was the last thing he did and then he would be free of the woman and whatever useless part of his make-up she still appeared to occupy.

'He gambled.' Sophie raised her eyes to his and held his stare in silence before looking away, offering him her averted profile.

'And you knew about that as well,' Javier had a fleeting twinge of regret that he had mentioned any of this. It had been unnecessary. Then he remembered the way she had summarily dumped him and all fleeting regret vanished in a puff of smoke.

She nodded mutely.

'And there was nothing you could have done about that either?'

'I don't suppose you've ever lived with someone who has a destructive addiction?' she said tightly. 'You can't just sit them down for a pep talk and then expect them to change overnight.'

'But you *can* send them firmly in the direction of professional help.' Javier was curious. The picture he had built of her had been one of the happily married young wife, in love with Prince Charming, so in love that she had not been able to abide being away from him whilst at university—perhaps hoping that the distraction of an unsuitable foreigner might put things into perspective, only for that gambit to hit the rocks.

Then, when he had inspected the accounts closely, he had assumed that, blindly in love, she had been ignorant of her loser husband's uncontrolled behaviour.

Now...

He didn't want curiosity to mar the purity of what he wanted from her and he was taken aback that it was.

'Roger was an adult. He didn't want help. I wasn't capable of manhandling him into a car and driving him to the local association for gambling addicts. And I don't want to talk about...about my marriage. I... It's in the past.'

'So it is,' Javier murmured. When he thought about the other man, he saw red, pure jealousy at being deprived of what he thought should have been his.

Crazy.

Since when had he considered any woman *his possession*?

'And yet,' he mused softly, 'when is the past ever *really* behind us? Don't you find that it dogs us like a guilty conscience, even when we would like to put it to bed for good?'

'What do you mean?'

'You ran out on me.'

'Javier, you don't *understand*...'

'Nor do I wish to. This isn't about understanding what motivated you.' And at this point in time—this very special point in time when the tables had been reversed, when she was now the one without money and he the one with the bank notes piled up in the coffers—well, she was hardly going to tell the whole truth and nothing but the truth when it came to motivations, was she? Oh, no, she would concoct some pretty little tale to try to elicit as much sympathy from him as she could...

'I'm not asking you to give me money, Javier. I...I'm just asking for a loan. I would pay it all back, every penny of it.'

Javier flung back his head and laughed, a rich, full-bodied laugh that managed to lack genuine warmth. 'Really? I'm tickled pink at the thought of a Classics scholar, almost there but never graduated, and her sports scholarship brother running any company successfully enough to make it pay dividends, never mind a company that's on its last legs.'

'There *are* directors in the company...'

'Looked at them. I would ditch most of them if I were you.'

'You *looked at them*?'

Javier shrugged. His dark eyes never left her face. 'I probably know more about your company than you do. Why not? If I'm to sink money into it, then I need to know exactly what I will be sinking money into.'

'So...are you saying that you'll help?'

'I'll help.' He smiled slowly. 'But there's no such thing as a free lunch. There will be terms and conditions...'

'That's fine.' For the first time in a very long time, a cloud seemed to be lifting. She had underestimated him. He was going to help and she wanted to sob with relief. 'Whatever your terms and conditions, well, they won't be a problem. I promise.'

CHAPTER THREE

'Perhaps we should take this conversation somewhere else.'

'Why?' The suggestion of leaving with him for *somewhere else* sent little shivers of alarm skittering through her.She could scarcely credit that she was sitting here, in this office, facing this man who had haunted her for years. All the things that had happened ever since that first tentative step as a young girl falling hopelessly in love with an unsuitable boy lay between them like a great, big, murky chasm.

There was just so much he didn't know.

But none of that was relevant. What was relevant was that he was going to help them and that was enough.

'Because,' Javier drawled, rising to his feet and strolling to fetch his jacket from where it lay slung over the back of one of the expensive, compact sofas in the little sitting area of the office, 'I feel that two old friends should not be discussing something as crass as a business bailout within the confines of an office.'

Two old friends?

Sophie scrutinised the harsh angles of his face for any inherent sarcasm and he returned her stare with bland politeness.

But his bland politeness made her feel unaccountably uneasy.

He'd never been polite.

At least, not in the way that English people were polite. Not in the middle-class way of clinking teacups and saying the right things, which was the way she had been brought up.

He had always spoken his mind and damned the consequences. She had occasionally seen him in action at university, once in the company of two of his lecturers, when they had been discussing economics.

He had listened to them, which had been the accepted polite way, but had then taken their arguments and ripped them to shreds. The breadth and depth of his knowledge had been so staggering that there had been no comeback.

He had never been scared of rocking the boat. Sometimes, she wondered whether he had privately relished it, although when she'd once asked him that directly, he had burst out laughing before kissing her senseless—at which point she had forgotten what she had been saying to him. Kissing him had always had that effect on her.

A surge of memories brought a hectic flush to her cheeks.

'Is this your new way of dressing?' he asked and Sophie blinked, dispelling disturbing images of when they had been an item.

'What do you mean?'

'You look like an office worker.'

'That's exactly what I am,' she returned lightly, following him to the door, because what else could she do? At this point, he held all the trump cards, and if he wanted to go and have their business chat sitting on bar stools in the middle of Threadneedle Street, then so be it. There was too much at stake for her to start digging her heels in and telling him that she felt more comfortable discussing business in an office.

She had come this far and there was no turning back now.

This floor was a sanctum of quiet. It was occupied by CEOs and directors, most of whom were concealed behind opaque glass and thick doors. In the middle there was a huge, open-plan space in which desks were cleverly positioned to allow for maximum space utilisation and minimum scope for chatting aimlessly.

The open space was largely empty, except for a couple of diligent employees who were too absorbed in whatever they were doing to look up at them as they headed for the directors' lift.

'But it's not exactly where you wanted to end up, is it?' he asked as the lift doors quietly closed, sealing them in together.

It didn't matter where she looked, reflections of him bounced back at her.

She shrugged and reluctantly met his dark eyes.

'You don't always end up where you think you're going to,' she said tersely.

'You had big plans to be a university lecturer.'

'Life got in the way of that.'

'I'm sure your dearly departed husband wouldn't like to be seen as someone who got in the way of your big plans.'

'I don't want to talk about Roger.'

Because the thought of him no longer being around was still too painful for her to bear. That thought struck Javier with dagger-like precision. The man might have been a waste of space when it came to business, and an inveterate gambler who had blown vast sums of money that should have been pumped into saving the company, yet she had loved him and now would have nothing said against him.

Javier's lips thinned.

He noted the way she scurried out of the lift, desperate to put some physical distance between them.

'When did you find out that the company was on the brink of going bust?'

Sophie cringed. She wanted to ask whether it was really necessary to go down that road and she knew that she had to divorce the past from the present. He wasn't the guy she had loved to death, the guy she had been forced to give up when life as she knew it had suddenly stopped. That was in the past and right now she was in the company of someone thinking about extending credit to the company. He would want details even if she didn't want to give them.

But there was a lot she didn't want to tell him. She didn't want his contempt or his pity and she knew she would have both if she presented him with the unadorned truth. That was if he believed her at all, which was doubtful.

'I knew things weren't too good a while back,' she said evasively. 'But I had no idea really of just how bad they were until…well, until I got married. '

Javier felt the dull, steady beat of jealousy working its poisonous way through his body.

He was painfully reminded of the folly of his youth, the naivety of imagining that they would have a future together. The poor foreigner working his way up and the beautiful, well-spoken, impeccably bred English girl who just so happened to be the apple of her father's adoring and protective eye.

At the time, he had thought himself to be as hard as nails and immune to distraction.

He'd set his course and he had been cocky enough to imagine that no ill winds would come along to blow him off target.

Of all the girls on the planet, he had found himself blown off target by one who had set her course on someone else and had been playing with him for a bit of fun, stringing him along while her heart belonged to someone else.

'And then...what?'

'What do you mean?' She nervously played with her finger, where once upon an unhappy time there had been a wedding ring.

She hadn't paid much attention to where they were going, but when he stood back to push open a door for her, she saw that they were at an old pub, the sort of pub that populated the heart of the City.

She shimmied past him, ducking under his outstretched arm as he held the door open for her. She was tall at five foot ten, but he was several inches taller and she had a memory of how protected he had always made her feel. The clean, masculine scent of him lingered in her nostrils, making her feel shaky as she sat down at a table in the corner, waiting tensely while he went to get them something to drink. She knew she should keep a clear head and drink water but her nerves were all over the place. They needed something a little stronger than water.

Outside it was hot and she could glimpse a packed garden but in here it was cool, dark and relatively empty.

The sun worshippers were all drinking in the evening sun.

Trying to elicit details about her past was not relevant. Javier knew that and he was furious with himself for succumbing to the desire to know more.

Just like that, in a matter of minutes, she had managed to stoke his curiosity. Just like that, she was back under his skin and he couldn't wait to have her, to bed her, so that he could rid himself of the uncomfortable suspicion that she had been there all along, a spectre biding its time until it could resurface to catch him on the back foot.

For a man to whom absolute control was vital, this slither of susceptibility was unwelcome.

He realised that when he tried to think of the last woman he had slept with, a top-notch career woman in New York with legs to her armpits, he came up blank. He couldn't focus on anyone but the woman sitting in front of him, looking at him as though she expected him to pounce unexpectedly at any minute.

She had the clearest violet eyes he had ever seen, fringed with long, dark lashes, and the tilt of them gave her a slightly dreamy look, as though a part of her was on another plane. He itched to unpin her neat little bun so that he could see whether that glorious hair of hers was still as long, still as unruly.

'Well?' Javier demanded impatiently, hooking a chair with his foot and angling it so that he could sit with his long legs extended. He had brought a wine cooler with a bottle of wine and one of the bartenders placed two glasses in front of them, then simpered for a few seconds, doe-eyed, before reluctantly walking back to the bar.

'Well...what?'

'What was the order of events? Heady marriage, fairy-tale honeymoon and then, lo and behold, no more money? Life can be cruel. And where was your brother when all this was happening?'

'In America.' She sighed.

'By choice, even though he knew?' With the family company haemorrhaging money, surely it would have been an indulgence for Oliver to have stayed in California, enjoying himself...

'He didn't know,' Sophie said abruptly. 'And I don't know why...how all this is relevant.'

'I'm fleshing out the picture,' Javier said softly. 'You've

come to me with a begging bowl. What did you think I was going to do? Give you a big, comforting hug and write out a cheque?'

'No, but…'

'Let's get one thing straight here, Sophie.' He leant forward and held her gaze. She couldn't have said a word even if she had wanted to. She could hardly breathe. 'You're here to ask a favour of me and, that being the case, whether you like it or not, you don't get to choose what questions to answer and what questions to ignore. Your private life is your business. Frankly, I don't give a damn. But I need to know your levels of capability when it comes to doing business. I need to know whether your brother is committed to working for the company, because if he was left to enjoy four years of playing sport in California, then I'm guessing he wouldn't have returned to the sick fold with a cheerful whistle. Most of the directors of the company aren't worth the money they're being paid.'

'You know how much they're being paid!'

'I know everything worth knowing about your crippled family company.'

'When did you get so…so…*hard*?'

Roughly around the same time I discovered what sort of woman I'd been going out with, Javier thought with the sour taste of cynicism in his mouth.

He leant back and crossed his legs, lightly cradling the stem of the wine glass between his long fingers.

'You don't make money by being a sap for sob stories,' he informed her coolly, keen eyes taking in the delicate bloom of colour in her cheeks. 'You've come to me with a sob story.' He shrugged. 'And the bottom line is this— if you don't like the direction this conversation is going, then, like I said before, you're free to go. But of course, we both know you won't, because you need me.'

He was enjoying this little game of going round the houses before he laid all his cards on the table, before she knew exactly what the terms and conditions of her repayment would be.

It wouldn't hurt her to realise just how dangerously close the company was to imploding.

It wouldn't hurt her to realise just how much she needed him...

'If you knew about your husband's hare-brained schemes and addiction to gambling, and you allowed it to go under the radar, then are you a trustworthy person to stand at the helm of your company?'

'I told you that there was nothing I could do,' she said with a dull flush.

'And if your brother was so clueless as to what was happening on the home front, then is *he* competent enough to do what would need to be done should I decide to help you out?'

'Ollie...doesn't have a huge amount of input in the actual running of things...'

'Why?'

'Because he's never been interested in the company and, yes, you're right—he's always resented the fact that he had to finally return to help out. He's found it difficult to deal with not having money.'

'And you've found it easy?'

'I've dealt with it.'

Javier looked at her narrowly and with a certain amount of reluctant admiration for the streak of strength he glimpsed.

Not only had she had to face a tremendous fall from the top of the mountain, but the loss of her husband and the father she had adored.

Yet there was no self-pity in the stubborn tilt of her chin.

'You've had a lot to deal with, haven't you?' he murmured softly and she looked away.

'I'm no different from loads of people the world over who have found their lives changed in one way or another. And, now that you've got the measure of the company, will you lend us some money or not? I don't know if my brother told you, but the family house has been on the market for over two years and we just can't seem to sell it. There's no appetite for big houses. If we could sell it, then we might be able to cover some of the expenses...'

'Although a second mortgage was taken out on it...'

'Yes, but the proceeds would go a little way to at least fixing certain things that need urgent attention.'

'The dated computer systems, for example?'

'You really did your homework, didn't you? How did you manage that in such a small amount of time? Or have you been following my father's company over the years? Watching while it went downhill?'

'Why would I have done that?'

Sophie shrugged uncomfortably. 'I know you probably feel... Well, you don't understand what happened all those years ago.'

'Don't presume to think that you know what goes on in my head, Sophie. You don't. And, in answer to your preposterous question, I haven't had the slightest clue what was going on in your father's company over the years, nor have I cared one way or the other.' He saw that the bottle was empty and debated whether or not to get another, deciding against it, because he wanted them both to have clear heads for this conversation.

When he knew that he would be seeing her, he had predicted how he would react and it hadn't been like this.

He'd thought that he would see her and would feel nothing but the acid, bilious taste of bitterness for having been played in the past and taken for a chump.

He'd accepted that she'd been in his head more than he'd ever imagined possible. A Pandora's box had been opened with her brother's unexpected appearance at his office. Javier had recognised the opportunity he had been given to put an end to her nagging presence, which, he now realised, had been embedded in him like a virus he'd never managed to shake off.

He would have her and he had the means to do so at his disposal.

She needed money. He had vast sums of it. She would take what was offered because she would have no choice. His *terms and conditions* would be met with acquiescence because, as he had learned over the years, money talked.

He had slept with some of the world's most desirable women. It had followed that whatever she had that had held him captive all those years ago, she would lose it when he saw her in the flesh once again. How could she compete with some of the women who had clamoured to sleep with him?

He'd been wrong.

And that was unbelievably frustrating because he was beginning to realise that he wanted a lot more from her than her body for a night or two.

No, he *needed* a lot more from her than her body for a night or two.

He wanted and needed *answers* and his curiosity to pry beneath the surface enraged him because he had thought himself above that particular sentiment when it came to her.

Nor, he was discovering, did he want to take what he knew she would have no choice but to give him in the manner of a marauding plunderer.

He didn't want her reluctance.

He wanted her to come to him and in the end, he reasoned now, if revenge was what he was after, then wouldn't that be the ultimate revenge? To have her want him, to take her and then to walk away?

The logical part of his brain knew that to want revenge was to succumb to a certain type of weakness, and yet the pull was so immensely strong that he could no more fight it than he could have climbed Mount Everest in bare feet.

And he was enjoying this.

His palate had become jaded and that was something he had recognised a while back, when he had made his first few million and the world had begun to spread itself out at his feet.

He had reached a place in life where he could have whatever he wanted and sometimes having everything at your fingertips removed the glory of the chase. Not just women, but deals, mergers, money…the lot.

She wasn't at his fingertips.

In fact, she was simmering with resentment that she had been put in the unfortunate position of having to come to him, cap in hand, to ask for his help.

He was a part of her past that she would rather have swept under the carpet and left there. He was even forced to swallow the unsavoury truth that he was probably a part of her past she bitterly regretted ever having gone anywhere near in the first place.

But she'd wanted him.

That much he felt he knew. She might have played with him as a distraction from the main event happening in her life somewhere else, or maybe just to show off in front of her friends that she had netted the biggest fish in the sea—which Javier had known, without a trace of vanity, he was.

But perhaps she hadn't actually banked on the flare of physical attraction that had erupted between them. She had held out against him and he had seen that as shyness, youthful nerves at taking the plunge… He'd been charmed by it. He'd also been wrong about it, as it turned out. She'd held out against him because there had been someone else in her life.

But she'd still fancied him like hell.

She'd trembled when he'd traced his finger across her collarbone and her eyes had darkened when their lips had touched. He hadn't imagined those reactions. She might have successfully fought that attraction in the end and scurried back to her comfort zone, but, for a brief window, he'd taken her out of that comfort zone...

Did she imagine that she was now immune to that physical attraction because time had passed?

He played with the thought of her opening up to him like a flower and this time giving him what he had wanted all those years ago. What he wanted now.

He wondered what she would feel when she found herself discarded.

He wondered whether he would really care or whether the mere fact that he had had her would be sufficient.

He hadn't felt this *alive* in a long time and it was bloody great.

'I was surprised when your brother showed up on my doorstep, so to speak, in search of help.'

'I hope you know that I never asked him to come to see you.'

'I can well imagine, Sophie. It must cut to the quick having to beg favours from a man who wasn't good enough for you seven years ago.'

'That's not how it was.'

Javier held up one hand. 'But, as it happens, to see you evicted and in the poorhouse would not play well on my conscience.'

'That's a bit of an exaggeration, don't you think?'

'You'd be surprised how thin the dividing line is between the poor and the rich and how fast places can be swapped. One minute you're on top of the world, the ruler of everything around you, and the next minute you're lying on the scrap heap, wondering what went wrong. Or I could put it another way—one minute you're flying upwards, knocking back all those less fortunate cluttering your path, and the next minute you're spiralling downwards and the people you've knocked back are on their way up, having the last laugh.'

'I bet your parents are really sad at the person you've become, Javier.'

Javier flushed darkly, outraged at her remark, and even more outraged by the disappointed expression on her lovely face.

Of course, in those heady days of thinking she was his, he had let her into his world, haltingly confided in her in a way he had never done with any woman either before or since. He had told her about his background, about his parents' determination to make sure he left that life behind. He had painted an unadorned picture of life as he had known it, had been amused at the vast differences between them, had seen those differences as a good thing, rather than an unsurmountable barrier, as she had. If she'd even thought about it at all.

'I know you've become richer than your wildest dreams.' She smiled ruefully at him. 'And you always had very, very wild dreams…'

The conversation seemed to have broken its leash and was racing away in a direction Javier didn't like. He frowned heavily at her.

'And now here we are.'

'You once told me that all your parents wanted was for you to be happy, to make something of your life, to settle down and have a big family.'

Javier decided that he needed another drink after all.

He stood up abruptly, which seemed to do the trick, because she started, blinked and looked up at him as if suddenly remembering that she wasn't here for a trip down memory lane. Indeed, that a trip down memory lane was the very last thing she had wanted.

He'd forgotten that habit of hers.

He was barely aware of placing his order for another bottle of wine at the bar and ordering some bar snacks because they were now both drinking on fairly empty stomachs. He hadn't a clue what bar snacks he ordered, leaving it to the guy serving him to provide whatever was on the menu.

She was filling up his head. He could feel her eyes on him even as he stood here at the bar with his back to her.

Whatever memories he'd had of her, whatever memories he'd kidded himself he'd got rid of and had buried, he was now finding in a very shallow grave.

She'd always had that habit of branching out on a tangent. It was as if a stray word could spark some improbable connection in her head and carry her away down unforeseen paths.

There were no unforeseen paths in this scenario, he thought grimly as he made his way back to the table, where she was sitting with the guarded expression back on her face.

The only unforeseen thing—and it was something he could deal with—was how much he still wanted her after all this time.

'I should be getting back,' she said as he poured her a glass of wine and nodded to her to drink.

'I've ordered food.'

'My ticket...'

'Forget about your ticket.'

'I can't do that.'

'Why not?'

'Because I'm not made of money. In fact, I'm broke. There. Are you satisfied that I've said that? I can't afford to kiss sweet goodbye to the cost of the ticket to get me down here to London. You've probably forgotten how much train tickets cost, but if you'd like a reminder, I can show you mine. They cost a lot. And if you want to do a bit more gloating, then go right ahead.' She fluttered her hand wearily. 'I can't stop you.'

'You'll need to pare down the staff.'

'I beg your pardon?'

'The company is top-heavy. Too many chiefs and very few Indians.'

Sophie nodded. It was what she had privately thought but the thought of sitting down old friends of her parents and handing them their marching orders had been just too much to contemplate. Oliver couldn't have done that in a million years and, although she was a heck of a lot more switched on than he was, the prospect of sacking old retainers, even fairly ineffective old retainers, still stuck in her throat.

Few enough people had stuck by them through thin times.

'And you need to drag the business into this century. The old-fashioned transport business needs to be updated. You need to take risks, to branch out, to try to capture smaller, more profitable markets instead of sticking to having lumbering dinosaurs doing cross-Channel deliveries. That's all well and good but you need a lot more than that if your company is to be rescued from the quicksand.'

'I…' She quailed at the thought of herself and Oliver, along with a handful of maybe or maybe not efficient directors, undertaking a job of those proportions.

'You and your brother are incapable of taking on this challenge,' Javier told her bluntly and she glared at him even though he had merely spoken aloud what she had been thinking.

'I'm sure if you agree to extend a loan,' she muttered, 'we can recruit good people who are capable of—'

'Not going to happen. If I sink money into that business of yours, I want to be certain that I won't be throwing my money into a black hole.'

'That's a bit unfair.' She fiddled with the bun which, instead of making her feel blessedly cool in the scorching temperatures, was making her sweaty and uncomfortable. As were the formal, scratchy clothes, so unlike her normal dress code of jeans, tee shirts and sneakers.

She didn't feel like the brisk, efficient potential client of someone who might want to extend a loan. She felt awkward, gauche and way too aware of the man looking at her narrowly, sizing her up in a way that made her want to squirm.

This wasn't the guy she had known and loved. He hadn't chucked her out of his office but, as far as feelings went, there was nothing there. There wasn't a trace of that simmering attraction that had held them both mesmerised captives all those years ago. He wasn't married but she wondered whether there was a woman in his life, someone rich and beautiful like him.

Even when he'd had no money, he could have had any woman he wanted.

Her mind boggled at the thought of how many women would now fall at his feet because he was the guy who had the full package.

A treacherous thought snaked into her head...

What if she'd defied her parents? What if she'd carried on seeing Javier? Had seen where that love might have taken them both?

It wouldn't have worked.

Despite the fact that she had grown up with money,

had had a rich and pampered life, money per se was not what motivated her. For Javier, it was the only thing that motivated him.

She looked at him from under her lashes, taking in the cut of his clothes, the hand-tailored shoes, the mega-expensive watch around which dark hair curled. He *breathed* wealth. It was what made him happy and made sense of his life.

She might be stressed out because of all the financial worries happening in her life, but if those worries were removed and she was given a clean slate, then she knew that she wouldn't really care if that slate was a rich slate or not.

So, if she'd stayed with him, she certainly wouldn't have been the sort of woman he'd have wanted. She might talk the talk but her jeans, tee shirts and sneakers would not have been found acceptable attire.

They'd had their moment in time when they'd both been jeans and tee shirts people but he'd moved on, and he would always have moved on.

The attraction, for him, would have dimmed and finally been snuffed out.

The road she'd taken had been tough and miserable and, as things had turned out, the wrong one. But it would be silly to think that she would have been any happier if she'd followed Javier and held the hand he'd extended.

'We can go round the houses discussing what's fair and what's unfair,' he said in a hard voice. 'But that won't get us anywhere. I'm prepared to sink money in, but I get a cut of the cake and you abide by my rules.'

'Your rules?' She looked at him in bewilderment.

'Did you really think I'd write a cheque and then keep my fingers crossed that you might know what to do with the money?' He'd had one plan when this situation had first arisen—it had been clean and simple—but now he didn't want clean and simple. He needed to get more immersed in the water…and he was looking forward to that.

'I will, to spell it out, want a percentage of your business. There's no point my waiting for the time when you can repay me. I already have more money than I can shake a stick at, but I could put your business to some good use, branch out in ways that might dovetail with some of my other business concerns.'

Sophie shifted, not liking the sound of this. If he wanted a part of their business, wouldn't that involve him *being around*? Or was he talking about being a silent partner?

'Does your company have a London presence at all?' Javier was thoroughly enjoying himself. Who said the only route to satisfaction was getting what you wanted on demand? He'd always been excellent when it came to thinking outside the box. He was doing just that right now. Whatever he sank into her business would be peanuts for him but he could already see ways of turning a healthy profit.

And as for having her? Of course he would, but where was the rush after all? He could take a little time out to relish this project…

'Barely,' she admitted. 'We closed three of the four branches over the years to save costs.'

'And left one open and running?'

'We couldn't afford to shut them all…even though the overheads are frightening.'

'Splendid. As soon as the details are formalised and all the signatures are in place, I will ensure that the office is modernised and ready for occupation.'

'It's already occupied,' Sophie said, dazed. 'Mandy works on reception and twice a week one of the accountants goes down to see to the various bits of post. Fortunately nearly everything is done by email these days…'

'Pack your bags, Sophie. I'm taking up residence in your London office, just as soon as it's fit for habitation, and you're going to be sitting right there alongside me.'

Not quite the original terms and conditions he had intended to apply, but in so many ways so much better…

CHAPTER FOUR

'I DON'T KNOW what you're so worried about. His terms and conditions seem pretty fair to me. In fact, better than fair. He's going to have a percentage interest in the company but at least it'll be a company that's making money.'

That had been Oliver's reaction when she had presented him, a fortnight ago, with the offer Javier had laid out on the table for her to take or reject.

He had been downright incredulous that she might even be hesitating to eat from the hand that had been extended to feed her. In a manner that was uncharacteristically proactive for him, he had called an extraordinary meeting of the directors and presented them with Javier's plan, and Sophie had had to swallow the unpalatable reality that her past had caught up with her and was now about to join hands with her present.

Since then, with papers signed and agreements reached at the speed of light, the little office they had kept open in Notting Hill had been awash with frantic activity.

Sophie had refused to go. She had delegated that task to her brother, who had been delighted to get out of Yorkshire for a couple of weeks. He had reported back with gusto at the renovations being made and, inside, Sophie had quailed at the way she felt, as though suddenly her life was being taken over.

She knew she was being ridiculous.

Javier had agreed to see them because of their old connection but there had been nothing there beyond that historic connection. He had made no attempts to pursue any conversations about what had happened between them. He had been as cool as might have been expected given the circumstances of their break-up and she was in no doubt that the only reason he had agreed to help them was because he could see a profit in what was being offered.

Money was what he cared about and she suspected that he would be getting a good deal out of them. They were, after all, in the position of the beggars who couldn't be choosers.

Hadn't he greeted her with all the information he had accumulated about the company?

He had done his homework and he wouldn't be offering them a rescue package if he wasn't going to get a great deal out of it.

She brushed her skirt, neatened her blouse and inspected herself in the mirror in the hallway, but she wasn't really seeing her reflection. She was thinking, persuading herself that his attitude towards her made everything much easier. For him, the past was history. What he had with her now was a business deal and one that had fallen into his lap like a piece of ripe fruit that hadn't even needed plucking from the tree.

Maybe in some distant corner of his mind there was an element of satisfaction that he was now in a position to be the one calling the shots, but if that was the case, he would have to have cared one way or another about her and he didn't.

The effect he still had on her was not mutual. And even her responses to him were an illusion, no more than a reminder of the power of nostalgia, because truthfully her heart was safely locked away, never again to be taken out to see the light of day.

She blinked and focused on the tidy image staring back at her. Everything in place. In a few minutes the taxi would come to take her to the station. A month ago, she would have hit the bus stop, which was almost a mile away, but he had deposited a large advance of cash in the company account to cover expenses and to ensure that everyone on the payroll was compensated for the overtime which they had contributed over the months and which had not been paid.

She would take the taxi to the station and then the train down to London so that she could see the final, finished product, the newly refurbished offices in which she would be stationed for as long as it took to get things up and running.

'How long do you think that's going to take?' she had asked Javier on day one, heart thumping at the prospect of being in an office where, on a whim, he could descend without warning.

He had shrugged, his dark-as-night eyes never leaving her face. 'How long is a piece of string? There's a lot of work to do with the company before it begins to pull its weight. There's been mass wastage of money and resources, expenditures that border on criminal and incompetent staff by the bucketload.'

'And you're going to…er…be around, supervising…?'

His eyes had narrowed on her flushed face. 'Does the prospect of that frighten you, Sophie?'

'Not in the slightest,' she had returned quickly. 'I would just be surprised if you managed to take time off from being the ruler of all you surveyed to help out an ailing firm. I mean, don't you have minions who move in when you take over sick companies?'

'I think I might give the minions a rest on this particular occasion,' he had murmured softly.

'Why?' Sophie had heard the thread of desperation in her voice. She couldn't be within five feet of him without her body reliving the way he had once made it feel, playing stupid games with her mind.

'This is a slightly more personal venture for me, Sophie,' he had told her, leaning across the boardroom table where both of them had remained after the legal team had exited. 'Maybe I want to see that the job is done to the highest possible standard given our…past acquaintanceship.'

Sophie hadn't known whether to thank him or quiz him, so she had remained silent, her eyes helplessly drifting down to his sensual mouth before sliding away as heat had consumed her.

With a little sigh, she grabbed her handbag as she heard the taxi circle the gravelled forecourt, and then she was on her way, half hoping that Javier wouldn't be there waiting at the office when she finally arrived, half hoping that he might be, and hating herself for that weakness.

She had no idea what to expect to find. The last time she had visited this particular office had been two years previously, when she and Oliver had been trying to decide which of the offices to shut. She remembered it as spacious enough but, without any money having been spent on it at all, it had already been showing telltale signs of wear and tear. That said, it had been the biggest and the least run-down, so they'd been able to amalgamate the diminishing files and folders there from the other offices.

Not for the first time, as she was ferried from north to south, she thought about how clueless she had been about the groundbreaking changes that had been happening right under her nose.

Ollie, at least, had had the excuse of being abroad, because he had left on his sports scholarship two years before she had gone to Cambridge. He'd been a fresh-faced teenager wrapped up in his own life, with no vision of anything happening outside it.

But she had still been living at home, in her final years at school. Why hadn't she asked more probing questions when her mother's health had begun to fail? The doctor had talked about stress, and now Sophie marvelled that she hadn't dug deeper to find out what the stress had been all about, because on the surface her mother could not have been living a less stressed-out life.

And neither had she questioned the frequency with which Roger's name had cropped up in conversations or the number of times he'd been invited along to the house for various parties. She had been amused at his enthusiasm and had eventually drifted into going out with him; she had never suspected the amount of encouragement he had got from her parents.

All told, she had allowed herself to be wrapped up in cotton wool. So when that cotton wool had been cruelly yanked off, she had been far more shell-shocked than she might otherwise have been.

Everything had hit her at once. She had been bombarded from all sides and, in the middle of this, had had to wise up quickly to the trauma of discovering just how ill her father was and the lengths he had gone to to protect them all from knowing.

She should have been there helping out long before the bomb had detonated, splintering shrapnel through their lives.

If she had been, then perhaps the company could have taken a different direction. And, if it had taken a different direction, then she wouldn't be here now, at the mercy of a guy who could still send her senses reeling, whatever her head was telling her.

Once in London, Sophie took a black cab to the premises of the office in Notting Hill.

Oliver had told her that things were coming along brilliantly but he had undersold just how much had been done in the space of a few days. It wasn't just about the paint job on the outside or the impressive potted plants or the newly painted black door with its gold lettering announcing the name of the company.

Standing back, Sophie's mouth fell open as she took in the smart exterior. Then the door opened and she was staring at a casually dressed Javier, who, in return, stared back at her as he continued to lounge indolently against the door frame. Arms folded, he was already projecting the signs of ownership so that, as she took a few tentative steps towards him, she felt herself to be the visitor.

'Wow.' She hovered, waiting for him to step back, which he did after a couple of seconds, taking his time to unfold his gloriously elegant body and then stand aside so that she had to brush past him, immediately turning around and establishing a safe physical distance between them. 'It's completely changed on the outside.'

'There's no point having an office that repels potential clients,' Javier said drily.

Yet again, she was in work attire. The sort of clothes that drained her natural beauty.

'Why have you shown up wearing a suit?' he asked, strolling past her and expecting her to follow, which she duly did. 'And where is your bag? You do realise that you will be relocating to London for the foreseeable future?'

'I've been giving that some thought…'

Javier stopped and turned to look at her. 'Forget it.'

'I beg your pardon?'

'Remember the terms and conditions? One of them is that you relocate down here so that you can oversee the running of the London arm of the business.'

'Yes, but—'

'No *buts*, Sophie.' His voice was cool and unyield-ing. He hooked his fingers on the waistband of his black jeans, which sat low on his lean hips, and held her stare. 'You don't get to dip in and out of this. You're on the let-terhead, along with your brother, and of course myself. Don't think that you're going to reap the rewards without doing any of the hard graft. I intend to oversee proceed-ings initially but I need to be assured that you and your brother won't run the company back into the ground the second my back's turned. Don't forget, this isn't a char-ity gesture of goodwill on my part. I'm not parting with cash if I don't think that there will be a decent return on my investment.'

Sophie thought that she'd been right. It was all about the money for him. Yes, there was a personal connection, but the animosity of their break-up wasn't paramount in his decision to help them. What mattered was that he was being handed a potentially very profitable business with an age-old reputation at a very cheap price because she and Oliver were desperate.

She imagined that, once the company was sorted, its reputation would not only be repaired but would ensure gold-plated business and a return of all the customers they had sadly lost over the years.

Right now, Oliver had an interest in a third of the com-pany, but he would quickly lose interest and, she foresaw, would cash in his shares, take the money and head back to California, where he could continue his sporting career in a teaching capacity.

In due course, Javier would have invested in a very worthwhile project at a very good price.

And their past history did not figure in the calcula-tions. In fact, she wondered whether he felt anything at all about what had happened between them.

'I thought I might commute down.'

Javier burst out laughing before sobering up to look at her with a gimlet-eyed warning. 'I wouldn't even entertain that notion if I were you,' he informed her in the sort of voice that did not expect contradiction. 'In the first few weeks there will probably be a great deal of overtime, and hopping on and off a train to try to get the work done just isn't going to cut it.'

'I have nowhere to stay here.' Once upon a time, there had been a snazzy apartment in Kensington but, she had discovered, that had been mortgaged up to the hilt when the company had started shedding customers and losing profit. It had been sold ages ago.

'Your brother has stayed in a hotel when he's been down.' Javier's eyes roved over her flushed face. 'But,' he mused with soft speculation, 'as you're going to be here for considerably longer, I have already made arrangements for you to have use of one of my apartments in Notting Hill. You'll be within convenient walking distance of the company. No excuse for slacking off.'

'No!' She broke out in clammy perspiration.

'Reason being…?'

'I…I can't just decamp down here to London, Javier!'

'This isn't something that's open to debate.'

'You don't understand.'

'Then enlighten me.' They hadn't even stepped foot into the renovated office and already they were arguing.

He couldn't credit that he had originally played with the thought of helping her in return for having her. He couldn't think of anything less satisfying than having her blackmailed into coming to him as a reluctant and resentful partner when he wanted her hot, wet and willing…

He also couldn't credit that he had simplistically imagined that one scratch would ease this itch that had surfaced with such surprising speed the second her brother had opened that door back into the past. The more he saw of her, the more he *thought* of her, the more dangerously deep his unfinished business with her felt. One or two nights wasn't going to be enough.

'I have to keep an eye on the house,' she said with obvious reluctance.

'What house?'

'The family home.'

'Why? Is it in imminent danger of falling down if you're not at hand with some sticking plaster and masking tape?'

Bitter tears sprang to her eyes and she fought them down as a red mist of anger swirled through her in a tidal rush.

'Since when did you get so arrogant?' she flung at him. They stared at one another in electric silence before she broke eye contact to storm off, out of the beautiful reception area, which she had barely noticed at all, and into the first set of offices.

It took a couple of seconds before Javier was galvanised into following her.

Being accused of *arrogance* was not something he was accustomed to. Indeed, being spoken to in that accusatory, critical tone of voice was unheard of. He caught her arm, tugging her to face him and then immediately releasing her because just the feel of her softness under his fingers was like putting his hand against an open flame. It enraged him that she could still have this effect on him. It enraged him that, for the first time in living memory, and certainly for the first time in many, many years, his body was refusing to obey his mind.

'Are you sure it's the house you need to be close to?' he growled.

'What are you talking about?'

'Maybe there's a man lurking in the background...'

Javier was disgusted to realise that he was fishing. Did he care whether there was some lame boyfriend in the background? She wasn't married and that was the main thing. He would never have gone near any woman with a wedding ring on her finger, but if she had a boyfriend somewhere, another one of those limp ex–public school idiots who thought that a polished accent was all that it took to get you through life, well…

All was fair in love and war…

Sophie reddened. The dull prickle of unpleasant memories tried to surface and she resolutely shoved them back where they belonged, in the deepest corners of her mind.

'Because, if you have, then he'll just have to take a back seat for…however long it takes. And word of warning— my apartment is for sole occupation only…'

'You mean if there was a guy in my life, and I happened to be living in one of your apartments, I wouldn't be allowed to entertain him?'

Javier looked at her appalled expression and swatted away the uncomfortable feeling that he was being pigeon-holed as some kind of dinosaur when that couldn't have been further from the truth. Having reached the soaring heights the hard way, he made a conscious effort to ensure that the employees of his company were hand-picked for all the right reasons: talent, merit and ability. He made sure that there were no glass ceilings for women, or for those who had had to struggle to find their way, as he had.

He was not the sort of guy who would ever have dreamt of laying down pathetic rules about men being kept apart from women, like teenagers in boarding schools overseen by strict house masters.

So what was he doing right now? And how was it that he had no intention of doing otherwise?

'I mean you're probably going to be working long hours. The distraction of some man who wants you back home to cook his meal by five-thirty isn't going to work' was the most he would offer.

Sophie laughed shortly. If only he knew...

'There's no man around to distract me,' she said in a low voice. 'And, yes, as a matter of fact the house *is* falling down, and Oliver won't be there because he's been dispatched to France to see what's happening to the company over there...'

'Your house is falling down?'

'Not literally,' Sophie admitted. 'But there's a lot wrong with it and I'm always conscious of the fact that if it springs a leak and I'm not there to sort it out, well...'

'Since when has your house been falling down?'

'It doesn't matter.' She sighed and began to run her fingers through her hair, only to realise that she had pinned it up, and let her hand drop to her side. She looked around her but was very much aware of his eyes still on her, and even more aware that somehow they were now standing way too close for comfort.

'You've done marvellous things with the space.' She just wanted to get away from the threat of personal quizzing. She took a few steps away from him and now took time really to notice just how much *had* been done. It was not just a paint job; everything seemed very different from what she remembered.

It seemed much, much larger and that, she realised, was because the space within the first-floor office block had been maximised. Partitions had been cleverly put in where before there had been none. The dank carpeting had been replaced with wooden floors. The desks and furniture were all spanking new. She listened and nodded as he explained the dynamics of the place being manned and who should be working the London office. The client list would have to be updated. The sales team would need to be far more assertive. He had identified useful gaps in the market that could be exploited.

Everything was perfect. There were two private offices and she would be occupying one. Again she nodded because, like it or not, she was going to be here, in London.

'But,' she said when the tour had been concluded and they were in the pristine, updated kitchen, sitting at the high-tech beaten metallic table with cups of steaming coffee in front of them, 'I still don't feel comfortable leaving the house and I don't want to live in one of your apartments.' *He would have a key... He would be able to walk in unannounced at any given time... She could be in the shower and he could just stroll in...*

Her nipples tightened, pushing against her lacy bra and sending tingles up and down, in and out and through her from her toes to her scalp. She licked her lips and reminded herself that if he felt anything towards her at all it would be loathing because of what had happened between them in the past. Although, in reality, he couldn't even be bothered to feel such a strong emotion. What he felt was…indifference.

So if he were to let himself in, which he most certainly wouldn't, the shower would be the last place he would seek her out. Her responses were all over the place and it wouldn't be long before he started to realise that she wasn't as immune to him as she was desperately trying to be.

'I'll bring your brother back over.'

'No! Don't…'

'Why not?' Javier raised his eyebrows expressively, although he knew the reason well enough. Oliver didn't want to be stuck in Yorkshire and he didn't see his future with the family business. He resented the penury into which they had been thrust and, although he recognised the importance of rebuilding what had fallen into disrepair, he really thought no further than what that personally meant for him. Given half a chance, he would have cashed in his shares and headed for the hills. In due course he would, which would be interesting should Javier decide he wanted more than he had. That was unlikely, because once he was done with getting what he wanted, he would be more than happy to disappear and leave the running of the business to an underling of his choice.

'He's enjoying being in Paris.'

'And that's how it's always been, isn't it?' Javier asked softly and Sophie raised translucent violet eyes to look at him with a frown.

'What do you mean?'

'I remember how you used to talk about your twin.' He had resolved not to go down any maudlin, reminiscing roads but now found that he couldn't help himself. 'The party animal. Off to California while you stayed behind to do your A levels. Praised for being sporty and indulged at a time when most kids that age would have had their head in textbooks to make sure they passed exams. When he came down to see you, he barely stayed put. He managed to make friends in five seconds and then off he went to see what nightclubs there were. He had his fun, enjoyed Mummy and Daddy's money and never had to face up to any grim realities because by then he was in California on his sports scholarship...

'I bet no one ever filled him in about the reality of the company losses, not even you...not even when they were glaringly obvious. I'll bet he only found out the extent of the trouble when you couldn't hide it from him any longer. Did your beloved ex-husband likewise conspire to keep your immature brother in the dark?'

'I told you.' Sophie stiffened at the mention of her ex-husband. 'I don't want to talk about Roger.'

Javier's lips tightened. The more she shied away from

all mention of her ex, the more his curiosity was piqued. He was bitterly reminded of his pointless *wondering* when she had dumped him, when she had told him that she was destined to marry someone else... When she had married a guy whom he had found himself researching on the Internet even though it had been an exercise in masochism.

He had learned strength from a very young age. It had taken a great deal of willpower to avoid the pitfalls of so many of his friends when he had been growing up in poverty in Spain. The easy way out had always been littered with drugs and violence, and that easy way had been the popular route for many of the kids he had known. He had had to become an island to turn his back on all of that, just as he had had to develop a great deal of inner strength when he had finally made it to England to begin his university career. He had had to set his sights on distant goals and allow himself to be guided only by them.

Sophie had taken his eye off the ball, and here she was, doing it again.

The sooner he got her out of his system, the better.

'So your brother stays in Paris,' he said, with the sort of insistence that made her think of steamrollers slowly and inexorably flattening vast swathes of land. 'I could get someone to house-sit and daily look for walls falling down...'

'You might think it's funny, Javier, but it's not. You might live in your mansion now, and you might be able to get whatever you want at the snap of a finger, but it's just not funny when you have to watch every step you take because there might just be a minefield waiting to explode if you put your foot somewhere wrong. And I'm surprised you have no sympathy at all, considering you... you were...'

'I was broke? Penniless? A poor immigrant still trying to get a grip on the first rung of that all-important ladder? I feel it's fair to say that our circumstances were slightly different.'

'And, in a way, you probably have no idea how much worse it makes it for me.' She swung her head away. Her prissy, formal clothes felt like a straitjacket and her tidy bun nestled at the nape of her neck was sticky and restricting.

Without thinking, she released it and sifted restless fingers through the length of her tumbling hair.

And Javier watched. His mouth went dry. Her hair cascaded over her shoulders and down her back, a vibrant wash of colour that took his breath away. He had to look away but he knew that he was breathing fast, imagining her naked, projecting how her body would feel were he to run his hands along its shapely contours.

'You're right. Oliver has always been protected,' she told him bluntly. He might very well be the first person she was telling this to. It was a truth she had always kept to herself because to have voiced it would have felt like a little betrayal. 'He only found out about…everything when Dad's illness was finally revealed, and even then we didn't tell him that the company was on its last legs. In fact, he returned to California and only came back after the…the accident when… Well, he came back for Dad's funeral, and of course Roger's, and by then he had to be told.

'But his heart isn't in getting the company up and running. His heart isn't in the house either. Mum's now living in Cornwall and, as far as Ollie is concerned, he would sell the family home to the highest bidder if there was anyone around who was in the slightest bit interested. He doesn't give a hoot if it all falls down in a pile of rubble just so long as we got some money for the rubble. So, no, he wouldn't be at all happy to leave Paris to house-sit.'

She took a deep, shaky breath. 'The house hasn't been maintained for years. It always looked good on the outside, not that I ever really *looked*, but it turned out that there were problems with the roof and subsidence that had never been sorted. There's no money left in the pot to sort that stuff out, so I keep my eyes peeled for anything that might need urgent attention. The worse the house is, the less money we'll get, if we ever manage to sell at all. I can't afford for a leak to spring in the cellar and start mounting the stairs to the hallway.' She sighed and rubbed her eyes.

'Why did you let him get away with it?' It was more of a flat, semi-incredulous statement than a question and Sophie knew exactly who he was talking about even though no name had been mentioned.

'I don't want to talk about that. It's in the past and there's no point stressing about the stuff you can't change. I just have to deal with the here and now...'

'Oliver,' Javier ploughed on, 'might be indifferent and clueless when it comes to business, but you clearly have the capacity to get involved, so why didn't you? You knew what was happening.'

'Mum wasn't in good health. Hadn't been for ages. And then Dad's behaviour started getting weird...erratic... Suddenly everything seemed to be happening at the same time. We found out just how ill he was and then, hard on the heels of that, the full repercussions of...of Roger's gambling and all the bad investments began coming to light. There was no one at the helm. All the good people were leaving. Lots had already left, although I didn't know that at the time, because I'd never been involved in the family business. It was...chaos.'

Even in the midst of this tale of abject woe, Javier couldn't help but notice that there was no condemnation of her scoundrel husband. Loyalties, he thought with a sour taste, were not divided.

'So I'll get a house-sitter,' he repeated and she shook

her head. He had already infiltrated her life enough. She wasn't sure she could cope with more.

'I'll come here,' she conceded, 'and go home at the weekends.' She breathed in deeply. 'And thank you for the use of an apartment. You have to let me know…I don't have a great deal of disposable income, as you can imagine, but please let me know how much rent I will owe you.'

Javier sat back and looked at her from under sinfully long lashes, a lazy, speculative look that felt like a caress.

'Don't even think of paying me rent,' he told her silkily. 'It's on the house…for old times' sake. Trust me, Sophie, I want you…' he paused fractionally '…there at the helm while changes are taking place, and what I want, I usually get…whatever the cost.'

CHAPTER FIVE

SOPHIE LOOKED AROUND her and realised guiltily that, after two weeks' living in the apartment Javier had kindly loaned her, refusing to countenance a penny in payment, she was strangely *happy*.

The apartment was to die for. She still found herself admiring the décor, as she was doing right now, having just returned from the office and kicked off her stupid pumps so that she could walk barefoot on the cool, wooden floor.

She had expected minimalist with lots of off-putting glossy white surfaces, like the inside of a high-tech lab. Images of aggressive black leather and chrome everywhere had sprung to mind when she had been handed the key to the apartment by his personal assistant, who had accompanied her so that the workings of the various gadgets could be explained.

She had assumed that she would be overwhelmed by an ostentatious show of wealth, would be obliged to gasp appropriately at furnishings she didn't really like and would feel like an intruder in a foreign land.

The Javier of today was not the teasing, warm, sexy, funny guy she had once known. The today Javier was tough, rich beyond most people's wildest dreams, ruthless and cutting edge in his hand-tailored suits and Italian shoes. And that would be reflected in any apartment he owned.

She'd been surprised—shocked, even—when she was shown the apartment.

'It's had a makeover,' the personal assistant had said in a vaguely puzzled voice, but obviously far too well-trained to comment further. 'So this is the first time I'm seeing the new version...'

Sophie hadn't quizzed her on what it had been like previously. Tired and in need of updating, she had assumed. He'd probably bought a bunch of apartments without even seeing them, the way you do when you have tons of money, and then paid someone handsomely to turn them into the sort of triple-A, gold-plated investments that would rent for a small fortune and double in value if he ever decided to sell.

Whoever had done the interior design had done a great job.

She padded towards the kitchen, which was cool, in shades of pale grey with vintage off-white tiles on the floor and granite counters that matched the floor.

Everything was open-plan. She strolled into the living room with a cup of tea and sank into the cosy sofa, idly flicking on the television to watch the early-evening news.

It was Friday and the work clothes had been dumped in the clothes hamper. Javier had told her that it was fine to dress casually but she had ignored him.

Keep it professional; keep it businesslike... she had decided.

Jeans and tee shirts would blur the lines between them...at least for her...

Not, in all events, that it made a scrap of difference how she dressed, because, after the first day, he had done a disappearing act, only occasionally emailing her or phoning her for updates. A couple of times he had visited the branch when she had been out seeing customers, trying to drum up business, and she could only think that he had timed his arrivals cleverly to avoid bumping into her.

He didn't give a passing thought to her, whilst she, on the other hand, couldn't stop thinking about him.

She didn't think that she had ever really stopped thinking about him. He'd been in her head, like the ghost of a refrain from a song that wouldn't go away.

And now she couldn't stop thinking about him. Worse than that, she spent every day at the office anticipating his unexpected arrival and was disproportionately disappointed when five-thirty rolled round and he'd failed to make an appearance.

Her heart skipped a beat when she opened up her emails and found a message from him waiting for her.

Her throat went dry when she heard the deep, sexy timbre of his voice on the end of the line.

She was in danger of obsessing over a guy who belonged to her past. At least, emotionally.

He'd suddenly reappeared on the scene, opening all sorts of doors in her head, making her think about choices she had made and bringing back memories of the horror story that had followed those choices.

He made her think about Roger. He was curious about her ex. She sensed that. Perhaps not curious in a personal way, but mildly curious, especially because so many things didn't quite add up. Why, he had asked her, hadn't she intervened when she'd known that he was blowing vast sums of money gambling? When she'd discovered the scale of the financial problems with the company? Why hadn't she acted more decisively?

But, of course, that was the kind of person he was. Someone who was born and bred to act decisively. He could never begin to understand how easy it was just to get lost and find yourself in a fog, with no guiding lights to lead you out.

She had grown up a lot since then. She had had to. And, in the process of taking charge, she had realised just how feeble her brother was when it came to making decisions and taking difficult paths.

When she looked back at herself as she had been seven years ago, it was like staring at a stranger. The carefree girl with a life full of options was gone for ever. She was a woman now with limited options and too many bad memories to deal with.

Was that why she was now obsessing over Javier, someone she had known for such a short space of time? Was it because he reminded her of the girl she used to be? Was it obsession by association, so to speak?

He made her think things she would rather have forgotten but he also made her heart skip a beat the way it once used to when she'd been with him.

And more than that, he made her body feel alive the way it hadn't for years. Not since him, in fact. He made her feel young again and that had a very seductive appeal.

With an impatient click of her tongue, she raised the volume of the television, determined not to waste the evening thinking about Javier and remembering what life had been like when they had been going out.

She almost didn't hear the buzz of the doorbell, and when she did, she almost thought that she might have made a mistake because no one could possibly be calling on her.

Since she had moved to London, she had kept herself to herself. She knew a couple of people who had relocated from the northern branch but the London crew, all very able and super-efficient, were new and she had shied away from making friends with any of them.

For starters, although it wasn't advertised and in all

probability none of them knew, she was more or less their boss. And also…did she really want anyone knowing her backstory? It was just easier to maintain a healthy distance, so there was no way whoever had buzzed her from downstairs was a colleague on the hunt for a Friday night companion.

She picked up the intercom which allowed her to see her unexpected visitor and the breath left her in a whoosh.

'You're in.' Javier had come to the apartment on the spur of the moment. Since she'd started at the London office, he had seen her once, had spoken to her six times and had emailed her every other day. He had purposefully kept his distance because the strength of his response to her had come as a shock. Accustomed to having absolute control over every aspect of his life, he had assumed that her sudden appearance in his highly ordered existence would prove interesting—certainly rewarding, bearing in mind he intended to finish what had been started seven years previously—and definitely nothing that he wouldn't be able to handle.

Except that, from the very minute he had laid eyes on her, all that absolute certainty had flown through the window. The easy route he had planned to take had almost immediately bitten the dust. He'd had every intention of coolly trading his financial help for the body he had been denied, the body he discovered he still longed to touch and explore.

She'd used him and now he'd been given a golden opportunity to get his own back.

Except, he'd seen her, and that approach had seemed worse than simplistic. It had seemed crass.

There was no way he was going to pursue her and showing up at the workplace every day would have smelled a lot like pursuit, even though he had every right to be there, considering the amount of money he was sinking into the failing company.

He wanted her to come to him but staying away had been a lot more difficult than he'd dreamed possible.

Like someone dying of thirst suddenly denied the glass of ice-cold water just within his reach, he had found himself thinking about her to the point of distraction, and that had got on his nerves.

So here he was.

Sophie frantically wondered whether she could say that she was just on her way out. His unexpected appearance had brought her out in a nervous cold sweat. She had been thinking about him, and here he was, conjured up from her imagination.

'I…I…'

'Let me in.'

'I was just about to…have something to eat, actually…'

'Perfect. I'll join you.'

That wasn't what she'd had in mind. What she'd had in mind was a lead-up to a polite excuse and an arrangement to meet when she had some sort of defence system in place. Instead, here she was, hair all over the place, wearing jogging bottoms and an old, tight tee shirt bought at a music festival a dozen years ago and shrunk in the wash over time.

'Come on, Sophie! I'm growing older by the minute!'

'Fine!' She buzzed him in, belatedly remembering that it was actually *his* apartment, so he had every right to be here. And not only was it *his* apartment, but she wasn't paying a penny towards the rent, at his insistence.

She scrambled to the mirror by the front door, accepted that it was too late to start pinning her hair back into something sensible, and even though she was expecting him, she still started when he rapped on the door.

He'd obviously come straight from work, although, *en*

route, he had divested himself of his tie, undone the top couple of buttons of his shirt and rolled his sleeves to his elbows. Her eyes dipped to his sinewy forearms and just as quickly back to his face.

'You look flustered,' Javier drawled, leaning against the door frame and somehow managing to crowd her. 'I haven't interrupted you in the middle of something pressing, have I?' This was how he remembered her. Tousled and sexy and so unbelievably, breathtakingly *fresh*.

And *innocent*.

Which was a bit of a joke, all things considered.

Dark eyes drifted downwards, taking in the outline of her firm, round breasts pushing against a tee shirt that was a few sizes too small, taking in the slither of flat belly where the tee shirt ended and the shapeless jogging bottoms began. Even in an outfit that should have done her no favours, she still looked hot, and his body responded with suitable vigour.

He straightened, frowning at the sudden discomfort of an erection.

'I haven't managed to catch much of you over the past couple of weeks.' He dragged his mind away from thoughts of her, a bed and a heap of hurriedly discarded clothes on the ground. 'So I thought I'd try you at home before you disappeared up north for the weekend.'

'Of course.'

There was a brief pause, during which he tilted his head to one side, before pointedly looking at the door handle.

'So...' He looked around him at his apartment with satisfaction. He'd had it redone. 'How are you finding the apartment?'

Some might say that he'd been a little underhand in the renovating of the apartment, which had been in perfectly good order a month previously. He'd walked round it, looking at the soulless, sterile furnishings, and had been able to picture her reaction to her new surroundings: disdain. He had always been amused at her old-fashioned tastes, despite the fact that she had grown up with money.

'I imagine your family home to be a wonder of the most up-to-the-minute furnishings money can buy,' he had once teased, when she'd stood staring in rapt fixation at a four-poster bed strewn with a million cushions in the window of a department store. She'd waxed lyrical then about the romance of four-poster beds and had told him, sheepishly, that the family home was anything but modern.

'My mum's like me,' she had confessed with a grin. 'She likes antiques and everything that's old and worn and full of character.'

Javier had personally made sure to insert some pieces of character in the apartment. He, himself, liked modern and minimalist. His impoverished family home had been clean but nearly everything had been bought second-hand. He'd grown up with so many items of furniture that had been just a little too full of character that he was now a fully paid-up member of all things modern and lacking in so-called character.

But he'd enjoyed hand-picking pieces for the apartment, had enjoyed picturing her reaction to the four-poster bed he had bought, the beautifully crafted floral sofa, the thick Persian rug that broke up the expanse of pale flooring.

'The apartment's fine.' Sophie stepped away from him and folded her arms. 'Better than fine,' she admitted, eyes darting to him and then staying there because he was just so arresting. 'I love the way it's been done. You should congratulate your interior designer.'

'Who said I used one?' He looked at her with raised eyebrows and she blushed in sudden confusion, because to picture him hand-picking anything was somehow... *intimate*. And of course he would never have done any such thing. What über-rich single guy would ever waste time hunting down rugs and curtains? Definitely not a guy like Javier, who was macho to the very last bone in his body.

'I'm afraid there's not a great deal of food.' She turned away because her heart was beating so fast she could barely breathe properly. His presence seemed to infiltrate every part of the apartment, filling it with suffocating, masculine intensity. This was how it had always been with him. In his presence, she'd felt weak and pleasurably helpless. Even as a young guy, struggling to make ends meet, he'd still managed to project an air of absolute assurance. He'd made all the other students around him seem like little boys in comparison.

The big difference was that, back then, she'd had a remit to bask and luxuriate in that powerful masculinity. She could touch, she could run her fingers through his springy, black hair and she'd had permission to melt at the feel of it.

She'd been allowed to want him and to show him how much she wanted him.

Not so now.

Furthermore, she didn't *want* to want him. She didn't *want* to feel herself dragged back into a past that was gone for good. Of course, foolish love was gone for good, and no longer a threat to the ivory tower she had constructed around herself that had been so vital in withstanding the years spent with her husband, but she didn't want to feel that pressing, urgent *want* either...

She didn't *want* to feel her heart fluttering like an adolescent's because he happened to be sharing the same space as her. She'd grown up, gone through some hellish stuff. Her outlook on life had been changed for ever because of what she'd had to deal with. She had no illusions now and no longer believed that happiness was her right. It wasn't and never would be. Javier Vasquez belonged to a time when unfettered optimism had been her constant companion. Now, not only was the murky past an unbreachable wall between them, but so were all the changes that had happened to her.

'I wasn't expecting company.' She half turned to find him right behind her, having followed her into the kitchen.

The kitchen was big, a clever mix of old and new, and she felt utterly at home in it.

'Smells good. What is it?'

'Just some tomato sauce. I was going to have it with pasta.'

'You never used to enjoy cooking.' Yet again, he found himself referring to the past, dredging it up and bringing it into the present, where it most certainly did not belong.

'I know.' She shot him a fleeting smile as he sat down at the table, angling his chair so that he could extend his long legs to one side. 'I never had to do it,' she explained. 'Mum loved cooking and I was always happy to let her get on with it. When she got ill, she said it used to occupy her and take her mind off her health problems, so I never interfered. I mean, I'd wash the dishes and tidy behind her, but she liked being the main chef. And then...'

She sighed and began finishing the food preparation, but horribly aware of those lazy, speculative eyes on her, following her every movement.

Javier resisted the urge to try to prise answers out of her. 'So you learned to cook,' he said, moving the conversation along, past the point of his curiosity.

'And discovered that I rather enjoyed it.' She didn't fail to notice how swiftly he had diverted the conversation from the controversial topic of her past, the years she had spent after they had gone their separate ways. His initial curiosity was gone, and she told herself that she was very thankful that it had, because there was far too much she could never, would never, tell him.

But alongside that relief was a certain amount of disappointment, because his lack of curiosity was all wrapped up with the indifference he felt for her.

She suddenly had the strangest temptation to reach out and touch him, to stroke his wrist, feel the familiar strength of his forearm under her fingers. What would he do? How would he react? *Would he recoil with horror or would he touch her back?*

Appalled, she thrust a plate of food in front of him and sat down opposite him. She wanted to sit on her treacherous hands just in case they did something wildly inappropriate of their own accord and she had to remind herself shakily that she was a grown woman, fully in control of her wayward emotions. Emotions that had been stirred up, as they *naturally* would be, by having him invade her life out of the blue.

She heard herself babbling on like the village idiot about her culinary exploits while he ate and listened in silence, with every show of interest in what she was saying.

Which was remarkable, given she had just finished a lengthy anecdote about some slow-cooked beef she had tried to cook weeks previously, which had been disastrous.

'So you like the apartment,' Javier drawled, eyes not leaving her face as he sipped some wine. 'And the job? Now that the work of trying to repair the damage done over the years has begun?'

'It's…awkward,' Sophie told him truthfully.

'Explain.'

'You were right,' she said bluntly, rising to begin clearing the table, her colour high. 'Some of the people my father trusted have let the company down badly over the years. I can only think that employing friends was a luxury my father had when he started the company, and he either continued to trust that they were doing a good job or he knew that they weren't but found it difficult to let them go. And then…'

'And then?' Javier queried silkily and Sophie shrugged.

'Getting rid of them never happened. Thankfully the majority have now left, but with generous pension payments or golden handshakes…' Yet more ways money had drained away from the company until the river had run dry.

'The company is in far worse shape than even I imagined…'

Sophie blanched. She watched as he began helping to clear the table, bringing plates to the sink.

'What do you mean?'

'Your father didn't just take his eye off the ball when he became ill. I doubt his eye had ever really been fully on it in the first place.'

'You can't say that!'

'I've gone through all the books with a fine-tooth comb, Sophie.' He relieved her of the plate she was holding and dried it before placing it on the kitchen counter, then he slung the tea towel he had fetched over his shoulder and propped himself against the counter, arms folded.

Javier had always suspected that her father had been instrumental in her decision to quit university and return to the guy she had always been destined to marry. Even though she had never come right out and said so; even though she had barely had the courage to look him in the face when she had announced that she'd be leaving university because of a family situation that had arisen.

He had never told her that he had subsequently gone to see her parents, that he had confronted her father, who had left him in no doubt that there was no way his precious daughter would contemplate a permanent relationship with someone like him.

He wondered whether the old man's extreme reaction

had been somehow linked to his decline into terminal ill health, and scowled as he remembered the heated argument that had resulted in him walking away, never looking back.

This was the perfect moment to disabuse her of whatever illusions she had harboured about a father who had clearly had little clue about running a business, but the dismay on her face made him hesitate.

He raked his fingers uncomfortably through his hair and continued to stare down at her upturned face.

'He was a terrific dad,' she said defensively, thinking back to the many times he had taken the family out on excursions, often leaving the running of the company to the guys working for him. 'Life was to be enjoyed' had always been his motto. He had played golf and taken them on fantastic holidays; she recognised now that ineffective, relatively unsupervised management had not helped the company coffers. He had inherited a thriving business but, especially when everything had gone electronic, he had failed to move with the times and so had his pals who had joined the company when he had taken it over.

In retrospect, she saw that so much had been piling up like dark clouds on the horizon, waiting for their moment to converge and create the thunderstorm of events that would land her where she was right now.

Javier opened his mouth to disabuse her of her girlish illusions and then thought of his own father. There was no way he would ever have had a word said against him, and yet, hadn't Pedro Vasquez once confessed that he had blown an opportunity to advance himself by storming out of his first company, too young and hot-headed to take orders he didn't agree with? The golden opportunity he had walked away from had never again returned and he had had to devote years of saving and scrimping to get by on the low wages he had earned until his retirement.

But Javier had never held that weak moment against him.

'Your father wouldn't be the first man who failed to spot areas for expansion,' he said gruffly. 'It happens.'

Sophie knew that he had softened and something deep inside her shifted and changed as she continued to stare up at him, their eyes locked.

She could scarcely breathe.

'Thank you,' she whispered and he shook his head, wanting to break a connection that was sucking him in, but finding it impossible to do so.

'What are you thanking me for?'

'He was old-fashioned, and unfortunately the people he delegated to were as old-fashioned as he was. Dad should have called a troubleshooter in the minute the profits started taking a nosedive, but he turned a blind eye to what was going on in the company.'

And he turned a blind eye to your ex as well...

That thought made Javier stiffen. Her father had been old-fashioned enough to hold pompous, arrogant views about *foreign upstarts*, to have assumed that some loser with the right accent was the sort of man his daughter should marry.

But that wasn't a road he was willing to go down because it would have absolved Sophie of guilt and the bottom line was that no one had pointed a gun to her head and forced her up the aisle.

She had *wanted* to take that step.

She had *chosen* to stick with the guy even though she knew that he was blowing up the company with his crazy investments.

She had *watched* and *remained silent* as vast sums of vitally needed money had been gambled away.

She had *enabled*. And the only reason she had done that was because she had loved the man.

He turned away abruptly, breaking eye contact, feeling the sour taste of bile rise to his mouth.

'The company will have to be streamlined further,' he told her curtly. 'Dead wood can no longer be tolerated.' He remained where he was, hip against the counter, and watched as she tidied, washed dishes, dried them and stayed silent.

'All the old retainers will end up being sacked. Is that it?'

'Needs must.'

'Some of the old guys have families… They're nearing retirement—and, okay, they may not have been the most efficient on the planet, but they've been loyal…'

'And you place a lot of value on loyalty, do you?' he murmured.

'Don't you?'

'There are times when common sense has to win the battle.'

'You're in charge now. I don't suppose I have any choice, have I?'

Instead of soothing him, her passive, resentful compliance stoked a surge of anger inside him.

'If you'd taken a step back,' he said with ruthless precision, 'and swapped blind loyalty for some common sense, you might have been able to curb some of your dear husband's outrageous excesses…'

'You truly believe that?' She stepped back, swamped by his powerful, aggressive presence, and glared at him.

The last thing Javier felt he needed was to have her try to make feeble excuses for the man who had contributed to almost destroying her family business. What he really felt he needed right now was something stiff to drink. He couldn't look at her without his body going into instant and immediate overdrive and he couldn't talk to her without relinquishing some of his formidable and prized self-control. She affected him in a way no other woman ever had and it annoyed the hell out of him.

'What else is anyone supposed to believe?' he asked with rampant sarcasm. 'Join the dots and you usually get an accurate picture at the end of the exercise.'

'There was no way I could ever have stopped Roger!' Sophie heard herself all but shout at him, appalled by her outburst even as she realised that it was too late to take it back. 'There were always consequences for trying to talk common sense into him!'

The silence that greeted this outburst was electric, sizzling around them, so that the hairs on the back of her neck stood on end.

'Consequences? What consequences?' Javier pressed in a dangerously soft voice.

'Nothing,' Sophie muttered, turning away, but he reached out, circling her forearm to tug her back towards him.

'You don't get to walk away from this conversation after you've opened up a can of worms, Sophie.'

There were so many reasons this was a can of worms that she didn't want to explore. On a deeply emotional level, she didn't want to confront, yet again, the mistakes she had made in the past. She'd done enough of that to last a lifetime and she especially didn't want to confront those mistakes aloud, with Javier as her witness. She didn't want his pity. She didn't want him to sense her vulnerability. He might no longer care about her, but she didn't want to think that he would be quietly satisfied that, having walked out on him, she had got her comeuppance, so to speak.

'It's not relevant!' she snapped, trying and failing to tug her arm out of his grasp.

'Was he…? I don't know what to think here, Soph…'

That abbreviation of her name brought back a flood of memories and they went straight to the core of her, burning a hole through her defence mechanisms. Her soft mouth trembled and she knew that her eyes were glazing over, which, in turn, made her blink rapidly, fighting back the urge to burst into tears.

'He could be unpredictable.' Her jaw tightened and she looked away but he wouldn't allow her to avoid his searching gaze, tilting her to face him by placing a finger gently under her chin.

'That's a big word. Try breaking it down into smaller components...'

'He could be verbally abusive,' she told him jerkily. 'On one occasion he was physically abusive. So there you have it, Javier. If I'd tried to interfere in his gambling, there's no accounting for what the outcome might have been for me.'

Javier was horrified. He dropped his hand and his fingers clenched and unclenched. She might have fancied herself in love with the guy but that would have been disillusionment on a grand scale.

'Why didn't you divorce him?'

'It was a brief marriage, Javier. And there is more to this than you know...'

'Did you know that the man had anger issues?' Javier sifted his fingers through his hair. Suddenly the kitchen felt the size of a matchbox. He wanted to walk, unfettered; he wanted to punch something.

'Of course I didn't, and that certainly wasn't the case when... You don't get it,' she said uneasily. 'And I'd really rather not talk about this any more.'

Javier had been mildly incredulous at her declaration that her descent into penury had been tougher to handle than his own lifetime of struggle and straitened circumstances. She, at least, had had the head start of the silver spoon in the mouth and a failing company was, after all, still a company with hope of salvation. The crumbling family pile was still a very big roof over her head.

Now there were muddy, swirling currents underlying

those glib assumptions, and yet again, he lost sight of the clarity of his intentions.

He reminded himself that fundamentally nothing had changed. She had begun something seven years ago and had failed to finish it because she had chosen to run off with her long-time, socially acceptable boyfriend.

That the boyfriend had failed to live up to expectation, that events in her life had taken a fairly disastrous turn, did not change the basic fact that she had strung him along.

But he couldn't recapture the simple black-and-white equation that had originally propelled him. He wondered, in passing, whether he should just have stuck to his quid pro quo solution: 'you give me what I want and I'll give you what you want'.

But no.

He wanted so much more and he could feel it running hot through his veins as she continued to stare at him, unable to break eye contact.

Subtly, the atmosphere shifted. He sensed the change in her breathing, saw the way her pupils dilated, the way her lips parted as if she might be on the brink of saying something.

He cupped her face with his hand and *felt* rather than heard the long sigh that made her shudder.

Sophie's eyelids felt heavy. She wanted to close her eyes because if she closed her eyes she would be able to breathe him in more deeply, and she wanted to do that, wanted to *breathe him in*, wanted to touch him and scratch the itch that had been bothering her ever since he had been catapulted back into her life.

She wanted to kiss him and taste his mouth.

She only realised that she was reaching up to him when she felt the hardness of muscled chest under the palms of her flattened hands.

She heard a whimper of sheer longing which seemed to come from her and then she was kissing him…tongues entwining…exploring…easing some of the aching pain of her body…

She inched closer, pressed herself against him and wanted to rub against his length, wanted to feel his nakedness against hers.

She couldn't get enough of him.

It was as if no time had gone by between them, as if they were back where they had been, a time when he had been able to set fire to her body with the merest of touches. Nothing had changed and everything had changed.

'No!' She came to her senses with horrified, jerky panic. 'This is…I am *not* that girl I once was. I… *No!*'

She'd flung herself at him! She'd practically assaulted the man like a sex-starved woman desperate to be touched! He didn't even care about her! She'd opened up and on the back of that had leapt on him and had managed to surface only after damage had been done!

Humiliation tore through her. She went beetroot-red and stumbled backwards.

'I apologise for that.' She immediately went on the attack. 'It should never have happened and I don't know what came over me!' She ran her fingers through her hair and tried to remain calm but she was shaking like a leaf. 'This isn't what we're about! Not at all.'

Javier raised his eyebrows and her colour deepened.

'There's only business between us,' she insisted through clenched teeth. 'I must have had…I don't normally drink…'

'Now, isn't that the lamest excuse in the world?' Javier murmured. 'Let's blame it on the wine…'

'I don't care what you think!' How could he be so *cool and composed* when she was all over the place? Except, of course, she knew how. Because she was just so much more affected by him than he was by her and she could see all her pride and self-respect disappearing down the plug hole if she didn't get a grip on the situation *right now.*

She cleared her throat and stared, at him and through him. 'I… We have to work alongside one another for a while and…this was just an unfortunate blip. I would appreciate it if you never mention it again. We can both pretend that it never happened, because it will never happen again.'

Javier lowered his eyes and tilted his head to one side as if seriously considering what she had just said.

So many challenges in that single sentence. Did she really and truly believe that she could close the book now that page one had been turned?

He'd tasted her and one small taste wasn't going to do. Not for him and not for her. Whatever her backstory, they both needed to sate themselves with one another and that was what they would do before that place was inevitably reached where walking away was an option.

'If that's how you want to play it.' He shrugged and looked at her. 'And from Monday,' he said with lazy assurance, 'bank on me being around most of the time. We both want the same thing, don't we…?'

'What?' Confused, the only thought that came to her was *each other*—that, at any rate, was the thing that *she* wanted, and she could *smell* that it was what he wanted as well.

'For us to sort out the problems in this company as quickly as possible,' he said in a voice implying surprise that she hadn't spotted the right answer immediately. 'Of course…'

CHAPTER SIX

'No.'

'Give me three good reasons and maybe I'll let you get away with that response.'

Sophie stared at Javier, body language saying it all as she supported herself on her desk, palms flattened on the highly polished surface, torso tilted towards him in angry refusal.

True to his word, he had more or less taken up residence in the premises in Notting Hill.

He wasn't there *all* the time. That would actually have been far easier for her to deal with. No, he breezed in and out. Sometimes she would arrive at eight-thirty to find him installed at the desk which he had claimed as his own, hard at it, there since the break of dawn and with a list of demands that had her on her feet running at full tilt for the remainder of the day.

Other times he might show up mid-afternoon and content himself with checking a couple of things with members of staff before vanishing, barely giving her a second glance.

And there had been days when he hadn't shown up at all and there had been no communication from him.

After six weeks, Sophie felt as though she had been tossed in a tumble dryer with the speed turned to high. She had been miserable, uncertain and fearful when she had had to deal with the horrendous financial mess into which she had been plunged. After her marriage, that had just felt like a continuation of a state of mind that had become more or less natural to her.

Now, though…

She was none of those things. She was a high-wire walker, with excitement and trepidation fighting for dominance. She leapt out of bed every morning with a treacherous sense of anticipation. Her pulses raced every time she took a deep breath and entered the office. Her blood pressure soared when she glanced to the door and saw him stride in. Her heart sang when she saw him stationed at his desk first thing, with his cup of already tepid black coffee on the desk in front of him.

Life was suddenly in technicolor and it scared the living daylights out of her. It had become obvious that she'd never got him out of her system and she seemed to have no immunity against the staggering force of his impact on all her senses. Her heart might be locked away behind walls of ice but her body clearly wasn't.

'I don't have to give you any reasons, Javier.' She was the last man standing and had been about to leave the office at a little after six when Javier had swanned in and stopped her in the act of putting on her jacket.

'Quick word,' he had said, in that way he had of presuming that there would be no argument. He'd then proceeded to lounge back in his chair, gesturing for her to drop what she was doing and take the seat facing him across his desk.

That had been half an hour ago.

'You do, really.' He looked at her lazily. Despite the fact that the largely young staff all dressed informally, Sophie had stuck it out with her prissy work outfits, which ranged from drab grey skirts and neat white blouses to drab black skirts and neat white blouses, all worn with the same flat black pumps. The ravishing hair which he had glimpsed on the one occasion when he had surprised her weeks ago at the apartment had gone back into hiding. Woe betide she actually released it from captivity between the hours of eight-thirty and five-thirty!

'Why?'

'Because I think it would work.'

'And of course, because *you* think it would work, means *I* have to agree and go along with it!'

'How many of the programmes that I've set in motion over the past couple of months have failed?'

'That's not the point.'

'Any? No. Is the company seeing the start of a turn-around? Yes. Have the sales team been reporting gains? Yes.' He folded his hands behind his head and looked at her evenly. 'Ergo, this idea makes sense and will generate valuable sales.'

'But I'm not a model, Javier!'

'That's the point, Sophie. You're the face of your company. Putting your image on billboards and in advertising campaigns will personalise the company—half the battle in wooing potential customers is making them feel as though they're relating to something more than just a name and a brand.'

She stared at him mutinously and he gazed calmly back at her.

The waiting game was taking longer than he had anticipated and he was finding that he was in no rush to speed things up. He was enjoying her. He was enjoying the way she made him feel and it wasn't just the reaction of his body to her. No, he realised that the years of having whatever he wanted and whoever he chose had jaded him. This blast from the past was...*rejuvenating*. And who didn't like a spot of rejuvenation in their lives? Of course, he would have to hurry things along eventually, because bed was the conclusion to the exercise before normal service was resumed and he returned to the life from which he had been taking a little holiday.

But for the moment…

He really liked the way she blushed. He could almost forget that she was the scheming young girl who had played him for an idiot.

'So we just need to talk about the details. And stop glaring. I thought all women liked to show off their bodies.'

Sophie glared. 'Really, Javier? You really think that?'

'Who wouldn't like to be asked to model?'

'Is that the message you've got from…from the women you've been out with?'

Javier looked at her narrowly because this was the first time she had ventured near the question of his love life. 'Most of the women I've been out with,' he murmured, 'were already catwalk models, accustomed to dealing with the full glare of the public spotlight.'

She'd wondered. Of course she had. Now she knew. Models. Naturally. He certainly wouldn't have dated normal, average women holding down normal, average jobs. He was the man who could have it all and men who could have it all always, but always, seemed to want to have models glued to their arm. It was just so…*predictable*.

'You've stopped glaring,' Javier said. 'Which is a good thing. But now there's disapproval stamped all over your face. What are you disapproving of? My choice of woman?'

'I don't care what your choice of girlfriends has been!'

'Don't you?' He raised his eyebrows. 'Because you look a little agitated. What's wrong with models? Some of them can be relatively clever, as it happens.'

'*Relatively clever…*' Sophie snorted. Her colour was high and the look in his sinfully dark eyes was doing weird things to her, making her feel jumpy and thrillingly excited.

Making her nipples tighten…stoking a dampness between her thighs that had nothing to do with her scorn for his choice of dates, whoever those nameless dates had been.

Instant recall of that kiss they had shared made her breath hitch temporarily in her throat.

Just as she had stridently demanded, no mention had been made of it again. It was as though it had never happened. Yes, that was exactly what she had wanted, but it hadn't stopped her constantly harking back to it in her head, reliving the moment and burning up just at the thought of it. How could a bruised and battered heart take second billing to a body that seemed to do whatever it felt like doing?

'You used to tell me that you liked the fact that I had opinions!'

'Many models have opinions—admittedly not of the intellectual variety. They have very strong opinions on, oh, shoes…bags…other models…'

Sophie felt her mouth twitch. She'd missed his sense of humour. In fact, thinking about it, he'd been the benchmark against which Roger had never stood a chance. Not that he had ever been in the running…

In fact, thinking about it, wasn't he the benchmark against which every other man had always been set and always would be? When would that end? How could she resign herself to a half-life because she was still wrapped up in the man in front of her? Because that intense physical reaction just hadn't died and could still make itself felt through all the layers of sadness and despair that had shaped the woman she was now.

She hadn't looked twice at any guy since she'd been on her own. Hadn't even been tempted!

Yet here she was, not only wanting to look but wanting to touch…

Why kid herself? Telling herself to pretend that that kiss had never happened didn't actually mean that it had disappeared from her head.

And telling herself that she should feel nothing for a guy who belonged to her past, a guy who wasn't even interested in her, didn't actually mean that she felt nothing for him.

Lust—that was what it was—and the harder she tried to deny its existence, the more powerful a grip it seemed to have over her.

And part of the reason was because…he *wasn't* indifferent, was he?

Heart racing, she looked down and gave proper house room in her head to all those barely discernible signals she had felt emanating from him over the past few weeks.

For starters, there had been *that kiss*.

She'd felt the way his mouth had explored hers, hungry and greedy and wanting more.

And then, working in the same space, she'd lodged somewhere in the back of her head those accidental brushes when he had leant over her, caging her in in front of her computer so that he could explain some detail on the screen.

She'd committed to memory the way she had occasionally surprised his lazy dark eyes resting on her just a fraction longer than necessary.

And sometimes…didn't he stand just a little too close? Close enough for her to feel the heat from his body? To smell his clean, masculine scent?

Didn't all of that add up to something?

She didn't know whether he was even aware of the dangerous current running between them just beneath the surface. If he was, then it was obvious that he had no intention of doing anything about it.

And then, one day, he would no longer be around.

Right now, he was making sure that his investment paid off. He had sunk money into a bailout, and he wasn't going to see that money flushed down the drain, so he was taking an active part in progressing the company.

But soon enough the company would be on firmer ground and he would be able to retreat and hand over the running of it to other people, herself included.

He would resume his hectic life running his own empire.

And she, likewise, would return to Yorkshire to take up full-time residence in the family home, which she would be able to renovate at least enough to make it a viable selling proposition.

They would part company.

And she would be left with this strange, empty feeling for the rest of her life.

She felt guilty enough about the way they had broken up. On top of that, he would remain the benchmark against which no other man would ever stand a chance of competing for ever.

She should have slept with him.

She knew that now. She should have slept with him instead of holding on to all those girlish fantasies about saving herself for when that time came and she knew that they would be a permanent item, for when she was convinced that their relationship was made to stand the test of time.

If she'd slept with him, he would never have achieved the impossible status of being the only guy capable of turning her on. If she'd slept with him, she might not feel so guilty about the way everything had crashed and burned.

Was it selfish now to think that, if she righted that oversight, she might be free to get on with her life? Things were being sorted financially but what was the good of that if, emotionally, she remained in some kind of dreadful, self-inflicted limbo?

She wasn't the selfish sort. She had never thought of herself as the kind of pushy, independent type who took what she wanted from a man to satisfy her own needs.

The opposite!

But she knew, with a certain amount of desperation, that if she didn't take what she wanted now she would create all sorts of problems for herself down the line.

She wondered whether she could talk to her mother about it and immediately dismissed that thought because, as far as Evelyn Griffin-Watt was concerned, Javier was a youthful blip who had been cut out of her life a long time ago, leaving no nasty scars behind.

Besides, her mother was leading an uncomplicated and contented life in Cornwall; was it really fair to bring back unpleasant memories by resurrecting a long, involved conversation about the past?

'Okay.'

'Come again?'

'I'll do it.'

Javier smiled slowly. In truth, the whole modelling idea had sprung to mind only the day before, and he had anticipated defeat, but here she was…agreeing after a pretty half-hearted battle. At least, half-hearted for her.

'Brilliant decision!'

'I was railroaded into it.'

'Strong word. I prefer *persuaded*. Now, I have a few ideas…'

Sophie peeped through a crack in the curtains and looked down into the courtyard which had been tarted up for the day into a vision of genteel respectability.

The shoot had been arranged in the space of a week, during which time Sophie had spoken to various media types and also to various stylists. She imagined that they were being paid a phenomenal amount for the day because they had all bent over backwards to pay attention to what she had said.

Which hadn't been very much because she had no idea what questions to ask other than the obvious one: *How long is it all going to take?*

Javier hadn't been at any of those meetings, choosing instead to delegate to one of the people in his PR department, but that hadn't bothered Sophie.

In a way, she'd been glad, because she had a plan and the element of surprise was a big part of the plan.

Except, the day had now arrived and the courtyard was buzzing with cameramen, the make-up crew, the director, producer and all the other people whose roles were, quite frankly, bewildering. And where was Javier? Nowhere to be seen.

It was today or it was not at all.

She dropped the curtain and turned to the full-length mirror which the stylist had installed in the bedroom because the small one on the dressing table *'just won't do, darling!'*

The brief which she had agreed on with Javier would have her standing next to a gleaming articulated lorry bearing the company logo, in dungarees, a checked shirt and a jaunty cowboy hat on her head.

Sophie had decided to take it up a notch and the reflection staring back at her had dumped the dungarees in favour of a pair of shorts with a frayed hem. The checked shirt remained the same, but it was tied under her breasts so that her flat stomach was exposed, and there was no jaunty cowboy hat on her head. Instead, she had slung it on her back so that her hair was wild and loose.

Javier had vaguely aimed for something wholesome and appealing, a throwback to the good old days of home-baked bread and jam, which was some of the cargo transported in the lorries. He'd suggested that it would be a nice contrast to the new face of the business, which was streamlined and fully up to spec on the technological front, which it hadn't been before. Something along the lines of the home-baked bread getting from A to B before it had time to cool from the oven and Sophie's image was going to sell the absolute truth of that.

She had taken it up a notch from wholesome to wholesome *and sexy*.

It had been her brainwave when she had sat there, numbly recognising that she would never, ever get over him if she didn't sleep with him, if she didn't seduce him into bed. He'd been in her head for years and she couldn't think of another way to make sure that he was knocked off the position he occupied there.

She'd never seduced anyone in her life before. Just thinking about doing something like that was terrifying, but when it came to her emotions, she had to be proactive. As proactive as she had been dealing with the mess she'd been left to clear up in the company.

She wasn't a simpering teenager any more, seeing the future through rose-tinted specs and believing in happy-ever-after endings.

She was an adult, jaded by experience, who would be left nursing regret for the rest of her life if she didn't give this a shot. And so what if she failed? What if he looked at her get-up and burst out laughing? So, she might have a moment's humiliation, but that would be worth the life-time she would have had thinking about an opportunity that had passed her by, an opportunity to claim what she knew could have been hers all those years ago.

The time had come to take a chance.

Except, it didn't look as though the wretched man was going to show up!

Her nerves were shot, her pulses were racing and she hadn't eaten since lunchtime the previous day because of the shot nerves and the racing pulses...

She was a mess and it was all going to be for nothing because Javier had obviously had his brainwave and then allowed his minions to realise it while he stepped back from the scene of the action.

She slunk down to the courtyard with a white bathrobe over her screamingly uncomfortable outfit and was immediately appropriated by a host of people whose only function seemed to be to get her ready for *the shoot*.

She allowed herself to be manoeuvred while disappointment cascaded through her in waves.

No Javier. No big seduction. It had taken absolutely everything out of her. And there was no way she was going to do this again. She wasn't going to set herself the task of staging seductive scenes in the hope of igniting something that probably wasn't there for him anyway, whatever stupid signals she thought she'd read!

A mirror was brought for her to inspect herself. Sophie barely glanced at the fully made-up face staring back at her. After the tension of the past couple of days, and the nervous excitement of earlier this morning as she had got dressed, she now felt like a balloon that had been deflated before it had made it to the party.

She was aware of orders being shouted and poses she was being instructed to adopt.

No one had questioned the slight change in outfit. She was Javier's personal pet project and no one dared question her for fear that she would report unfavourably back to their boss.

She was supposed to turn up in denim and a checked top with a cowboy hat and they knew what the direction of the shoot should be. The outfit was daring, though, and the poses were therefore slightly more daring than perhaps originally choreographed.

She had her back to the camera team, one hand resting lightly on the shining lorry, looking over her shoulder with a smile, when she heard his roar from behind her.

She'd given up on Javier coming.

But before she'd clocked his absence, she had somehow imagined him standing amongst the crew, goggle-eyed as he looked at her, wanting her as much as she wanted him and knowing that he had to have her. She'd pictured him waiting impatiently until the crew had packed up and gone and then...

Her wanton thoughts had not formulated much beyond that point. There would be a lot of ground to cover before the scene shifted from impatient seduction to the satisfied aftermath.

'What the hell is going on here?'

Sophie stumbled back against the lorry and the entire assembled crew stared at Javier in growing confusion, aware that they had done something wrong but not quite sure what.

Javier strode forward through them like a charging bull, face as black as thunder.

'You!' He pointed to the director of the shoot, who jumped to attention and began stammering out his consternation, puzzled as to what the problem was. The shoot was going very well. Indeed, if Javier wanted, he could see what was already in the bag. It was going to do the job and sell the business like hot cakes straight from the oven. Sophie was a brilliant model. No temper tantrums and no diva pouting. She was perfect for the job and the fact that she was part-owner of the company was going to be a nice touch. They'd make sure they got that in in the backdrop...

Javier held up one cold, imperious hand. 'This was not what I wanted!' he snapped. He looked across to Sophie with a scowl and she folded her arms defensively.

'They have no idea what you're going on about, Javier,' she said sweetly, strolling towards him although she was quaking inside, unable to tear her eyes away from his strident masculinity. He dominated the space around him, a towering, forbidding figure who clearly inspired awe, fear and respect in equal measure.

It was an incredible turn-on to think that this was the guy who had once teased her, told her that she made him weak, the guy whose eyes had flared with desire whenever they had rested on her.

The guy she wanted so much that it hurt.

The guy she was prepared to risk humiliation for.

'Consider this shoot over for the day.' He directed the command at the director but his eyes were focused on Sophie as she moved to stand right in front of him.

He cursed the overseas phone call that had held him up and then the traffic on the motorways and B-roads that wound their way to her family home. If he'd arrived when he had originally planned, he would have…

Made sure that she didn't step one delicate foot out of the house dressed in next to nothing.

He was shocked by his sudden regression to a Neanderthal, which was the very opposite of the cool composure he prided himself on having.

Hands thrust deep into his pockets, he continued to stare at her with ferocious intent while the entire assembled crew hurriedly began packing their equipment and disappearing fast.

Sophie heard the gravelly chaos of reversing cars and SUVs but she was locked into a little bubble in which the only two people who existed were herself and Javier.

'That wasn't the outfit we agreed on.' His voice was

a low, driven snarl and she tilted her chin at a mutinous angle.

'Checked shirt...*tick*. Denim...*tick*. Stupid cowboy hat...*tick*. Trainers...*tick*...'

'You know what I mean,' Javier gritted, unable to take his eyes off her.

'Do I?' She hadn't realised how chilly it was and she hugged herself.

'You're cold,' he said gruffly, removing his jacket and settling it around her shoulders. For a second, she just wanted to close her eyes and breathe in the scent from it.

And this was what it was all about. This *hunger* that had never gone away, but which *had* to go away, because if it didn't it would eat away at her for ever. And there was only one way of it just *going away and leaving her alone*.

'Tell me,' she pressed huskily. 'Why are you so furious? It wasn't fair of you to send all those poor people packing. They were only doing their job.'

'That's not the way I see it,' Javier growled. The jacket, way too big, drowned her and it was really weird the way that just made her look even sexier. He shifted in an attempt to ease the discomfort of his erection. Was she wearing a bra? He didn't think so and that made him angry all over again.

'How do you see it?'

'The brief was for you to look wholesome!' He raked his fingers through his hair and shook his head. This was the first time he had ventured to her family home but he hadn't noticed a single brick. His entire focus was on her. She consumed him. 'The attractive girl next door! Not a sex siren out to snag a man! How the hell is *that* supposed to sell the company?'

'I thought that sex sold everything?'

'Is that why you did it? Was that your concept of positive input? Dressing up in next to nothing and draping yourself over that lorry like a hooker posing in a motor-bike shot?'

'How *dare you*?' But she flushed and cringed and knew that there was some justification for that horrible slur. She barely stopped to think that in summer there were many, many girls her age who went out dressed like this and thought nothing of it. She just knew that it wasn't *her*.

'The entire crew,' he delineated coldly, 'must have had a field day ogling you. Or maybe that was what you had in mind. Is that it? Has living in London kick-started an urge to push the limits? Have you realised how much tamer your life up here was?'

'I didn't do this so that any of the crew could *ogle me*.' She fought to maintain his cool, disapproving stare and took a deep breath. 'I did this so that…' Her voice faltered. Her hands were clammy and she licked her lips as the tension stretched and stretched between them.

'So that…?' Javier prompted softly.

'So that *you* could ogle me…'

CHAPTER SEVEN

THIS WAS WHAT he had been waiting for, the slow burn until the conflagration, because he knew that it would be a conflagration. She oozed sex appeal without even realising it. And she had come to him. He hadn't been mistaken about those invisible signals his antennae had been picking up and he marvelled that he had ever doubted himself.

Of course, he would have to make it clear to her that this wasn't some kind of romance, that whatever they did would be a purely physical animal act. They'd had their window for romance once and she'd put paid to that. Romance was definitely off the cards now.

He smiled slowly, his beautiful, sensuous mouth curving as he lazily ran his eyes over her flushed face, taking in everything from the slight tremor of her hands to the nervous tic in her neck, a beating pulse that was advertising what she wanted as loud and as clear as if it had been written in neon lettering over her head.

Him.

She wanted him.

The wheel had turned full circle, and having walked away from him, she was now walking back.

That tasted good and it would taste even better when he laid down his conditions.

'Is that so?' he breathed huskily, his erection threatening to hamper movement.

Sophie didn't say anything in response to that. She read the satisfaction in his gleaming eyes and a primal lust that was so powerful that it easily swept aside any nagging doubt that she might be embarking on the wrong course of action.

He caught the lapels of his jacket and drew her a few inches towards him. 'There were less complicated ways of getting my attention, Soph...' he murmured. 'A simple *I want you* would have done the trick.'

The fact that he made no attempt to kiss her or touch her acted as an unbearably powerful aphrodisiac. Her heart was beating so fast that it felt as though it was going to explode and she was melting everywhere. She licked her lips and Javier followed that tiny movement with such intense concentration that it made her blood heat up even further.

'That would have been...too much,' she breathed. 'It was tough enough...' She gestured down to her lack of outfit and Javier half-smiled, remembering how shy she had once been, despite the fact that she had the face and figure that could turn heads from a mile away.

'Getting into your skimpy little get-up? Let's go inside. It's getting breezier out here.' He kept his distance but the electricity crackled between them. He wasn't touching her and he hardly dared because one touch and he would have to have her at once, fast and hard, up against a wall.

He didn't want that. He wanted slow and leisurely. He wanted to explore every inch of the woman who had escaped him. Only then would he be able to walk away satisfied.

Walking towards the house, he really noticed the signs of disrepair which he had failed to see when he had arrived earlier. He paused and looked critically at the façade and Sophie followed the leisurely and critical inspection, marvelling at the damage that had been done over a handful of years.

She longed to reach out and touch him. She longed to link her fingers through his in the same careless gesture of ownership to which she had once been privy. She reminded herself that times had changed since then. This was something quite, quite different.

'You're right,' Javier said drily, stepping back as she pushed open the front door. 'The place is falling down.'

'I know.' Sophie looked around her, seeing it through his eyes. He was now used to the best that money could buy. The apartment loaned to her was pristine, like something from the centre pages of a house magazine. This house, on the other hand...

They were in a cavernous hall. Javier could see that this would have been an enormous and elegant country estate once upon a time but the paint was peeling, the once ornate ceiling was cracked and he was sure that further exploration would reveal a lot more problems.

'I'm sorry,' he said gravely and Sophie looked at him, startled.

'What for?'

'You told me that penury was harder for you than it ever had been for me and you were probably right. I knew no better and things could only go up. You knew better and the journey down must have been swift and painful. But...' he tilted his head to one side and looked at her '...you coped.'

'I didn't have a choice, did I?' She suddenly felt shy. Should they be heading up to the bedroom? What was the etiquette for two people who had decided that they are going to sleep together? Not in the 'clutching one another while stumbling up the stairs' kind of way, but in the manner of a business transaction. At least that was what it felt like—two people putting an end to their unfinished business.

They wanted each other but neither of them liked it.

'Show me the rest of the place.'

'Why?' She was genuinely puzzled.

'I used to wonder what it was like. You talked about your home a lot when we were…going out. At the time, it had sounded like a slice of paradise, especially compared to where I had grown up.'

'And I bet you're thinking, *how the mighty have fallen*…' She laughed self-consciously because all of a sudden she was walking on quicksand. This was the man she had fallen in love with—a man who was interested, warm, curious, empathetic… For a minute, the cynical, mocking stranger was gone and she was floundering.

'No. I'm not,' he said quietly. 'I'm thinking that it must have taken a lot of courage not to have cracked under the strain.'

Sophie blushed and began showing him through the various rooms on the ground floor of the house. There were a lot of them and most of them were now closed with the heating off so that money could be saved. When she and Oliver had realised the necessity of putting the house on the market, they had made an effort to do a patch-up job here and there, but not even those dabs of paint in some of the rooms could conceal the disintegrating façade.

The more she talked, the more aware she was of him there by her side, taking it all in. If this was his idea of foreplay, it couldn't have been more effective, because she was on fire.

Talking…who would have thought that it could have changed the atmosphere between them so thoroughly?

Her nipples were tight and tingling and the ache between her thighs made her want to moan out loud. She could *feel* him, could feel herself warming to him, and she had to fight the seductive urge to start mingling the past with the present, confusing the powerful, ruthless man he had become with the man she had once known.

When they were through with the ground floor, she gazed up the sweeping staircase before turning to him and clearing her throat.

'The bedrooms are upstairs.' She wanted to sound controlled and adult, a woman in charge of a situation she had engendered. Instead, she heard the nervous falsetto of her voice and inwardly cringed.

Javier lounged against the door frame, hoping that it wouldn't collapse under his weight from dry rot or termites. He folded his arms and looked at her as she fidgeted for a few seconds before meeting his gaze.

'Why are you so nervous?' he enquired, reaching out to adjust the collar of the jacket which she was still clutching around her, and then allowing his hands to remain there, resting lightly on her. 'It's not as though you haven't felt the touch of my lips on yours before…'

Sophie inhaled sharply.

She had got this far and now realised that she hadn't actually worked out what happened next. Yes, on the physical level, terrifying and exciting though that was, her body would simply just take over. She knew it would. She remembered what it had felt like to be touched by him, the way he had made her whole body ignite in a burst of red-hot flame.

How much more glorious would it feel to actually *make love* with him…?

She was nervous, yes, thrillingly so at the prospect of making love with him. But there were other things… things that needed to be discussed…and now that the time had come she wondered whether she would be able to open up to him.

'I'm… I'm not nervous about…about…'

'Going to bed with me? Being touched all over by me? Your breasts and nipples with my tongue? Your belly…?' He loved the fluttering of her eyes as she listened, the way her tongue darted out to moisten her lips and the way she was breathing just a little faster; tiny, jerky breaths that were an unbelievable turn-on because they showed him what she was feeling. He doubted that she could even put into words what she was feeling because...

Because of her inherent shyness. It almost made him burst out laughing because she was far from shy. She was a widow who had been through the mill.

'I'm not nervous about any of that!' Sophie glared at him. 'Not really.'

'You're as jumpy as a cat on a hot tin roof, Sophie. If that's not nerves, then I don't know what is.'

'I need to talk to you,' she said jerkily and watched as the shutters instantly came down over his beautiful eyes.

'Is this the part where you start backtracking?' he asked softly. 'Because I don't like those sorts of games. You did a runner on me once before and I wouldn't like to think that I'm in line for a repeat performance...'

Sophie chewed her lip nervously. To open up would expose so much and yet how could she not?

How else would she be able to explain away the fact that she was still a virgin?

A virgin widow. It wasn't the first time that she'd wanted to laugh at the irony of that. Laugh or cry. Maybe both.

Would he even notice that she was a virgin? He would know that she lacked experience but would he really notice just how inexperienced she truly was?

Could she pretend?

'I'm not backtracking.' She glanced up the stairs and then began heading up, glancing over her shoulder just once. At the top of the staircase, she eased the jacket off and slung it over the banister. 'If I didn't want to do this...' she half-smiled '...would I be doing *this*?'

Javier looked at her long and hard and then returned that half-smile with one of his own.

'No, I don't suppose you would be,' he murmured, taking the steps two at a time until he was right by her, crowding her in a way that was very, very sexy.

He curved his big hand behind the nape of her neck and kissed her.

With a helpless whimper, Sophie leant into him. She undid a couple of his shirt buttons and slipped her hands underneath the silky cotton and the helpless whimper turned into a giddy groan as she felt the hard muscle of his chest.

This was what she had dreamed of and it was only now, when she was touching him, that she realised just how long those dreams had been in her head, never-ending versions of the same thing...*touching him.*

Javier eventually pulled back and gazed down at her flushed face.

'We need to get to a bed.' He barely recognised his own voice, which was thick with desire, the voice of someone drunk with *want*. 'If we don't, I'm going to turn into a caveman, rip off your clothes right here on the staircase and take you before we can make it to a bedroom...'

Sophie discovered that she was wantonly turned on by the image of him doing that.

'My bedroom's just along the corridor,' she whispered huskily, galvanising her jelly-like legs forward.

There were numerous bedrooms on the landing and most of the doors were shut, which led Javier to assume that they were never used. Probably in as much of a state of disrepair as some of the rooms downstairs which had been sealed off.

Her bedroom was at the very end of the long, wide corridor and it was huge.

'I keep meaning to brighten it up a bit,' she apologised,

nervous all over again because, now that they were in the bedroom, all her fears and worries had returned with a vengeance. 'I've had some of the pictures on the walls since I was a kid and now, in a weird way, I would feel quite sad to take them down and chuck them in the bin...'

He was strolling through the bedroom, taking in absolutely everything, from the books on the bookshelf by the window to the little framed family shots in silver frames which were lined up on her dressing table.

Eventually he turned to face her and began unbuttoning his shirt.

Sophie tensed and gulped. She watched in fascination as his shirt fell open, revealing the hard chest she had earlier felt under her fingers.

He shrugged it off and tossed it on the ground and her mouth went dry as he walked slowly towards her.

'There's...there's something I should tell you...' she stammered, frozen to the spot and very much aware of the great big bed just behind her.

Javier didn't break stride.

Talk? He didn't think so. The marriage she had hoped for and the guy she had ditched him to be with hadn't gone according to plan. That changed nothing. She still remained the same woman who had strung him along and then walked away because, when you got right down to it, he had not been good enough for her.

'No conversation,' he murmured, trailing his finger along her collarbone until she sighed and squirmed and her eyelids fluttered.

'What do you mean?'

'No confidences, no long explanations about why you're doing what you're doing. We both know the reason that we're here.' He hooked his fingers under the checked shirt and circled her waist, then gently began to undo the buttons on the shirt. 'We still want one another,' he murmured, nibbling her ear.

'Yes…' Sophie could barely get the word out. Her body tingled everywhere and his delicate touch sent vibrations racing through her. She rubbed her thighs together and heard him laugh softly, as if he knew that she was trying to ease the pain between them.

'This is all there is, Soph.' There was a finality to stating the obvious which, for some reason, set his teeth on edge, although he didn't quite understand why when it was pretty straightforward a situation. He was propelling her very gently towards the bed; she realised that only when she tumbled back, and then he leant forward, propping himself up on either side of her, staring down at her gravely.

Sophie couldn't have uttered a word if she'd tried. She was mesmerised by the compelling intensity of his expression, the soft, sexy drawl of his voice, the penetrating, opaque blackness of his eyes.

Somehow he had managed to undo every last button of her shirt and the cool air was a sweet antidote to the heat that was consuming her.

He stood up and paused for a few seconds with his fingers resting loosely on the zipper of his trousers.

She could see the bulge of his erection and half closed her eyes when she thought about the mechanics of something so impressively large entering her.

But no talking, he'd said…

No talking because he wasn't interested in what she had to say.

As though reading the anxious direction of her thoughts, he dropped his hand and joined her on the bed, manoeuvring her onto her side so that they were lying stomach to stomach, then she flopped over onto her back and stared up at the ceiling.

'Look at me, Soph.' He framed her face with his hand so that she was forced to look at him. His breath was warm on her cheek and she wanted to evade the deadly seriousness of his gaze. 'Whatever it is you want to tell me, resist, because I'm not interested.' He felt a sharp jab of pain deep inside him but pressed on, because this had to be said, and wasn't this all part of that wheel turning full circle? That she'd come to him and now, with her in the palm of his hand, he could reduce her to humility? That he could let her know, without even having to vocalise the obvious, that the shoe was firmly on the other foot?

That he was the one calling the shots?

He had the uncomfortable feeling that it should have felt more satisfying than it did.

'This is something we both have to do, wouldn't you agree? If you hadn't ended up back in my life in a way neither of us could ever have predicted, well, we wouldn't be here now. But we're here and...' He smoothed his hand over her thigh and felt her shudder, wishing she wasn't wearing clothes because he was itching to feel all of her, naked, supple and compliant. 'We have to finish this. But finishing it doesn't involve tender sharing of our life histories. This isn't a courtship and it's important for you to recognise that.'

Sophie felt the hot crawl of colour seep into her cheeks. Of course, he was just being honest. Of course, this was just about the sex they should have had all those years ago. Nothing more. If she could, she would have slid off the bed, looked at him with haughty disdain and told him to clear off, but what her body wanted and *needed* was calling the shots now.

'I know that,' she assured him in a calm voice which was not at all how she was feeling inside. 'I'm not on the lookout for a courtship! Do you really think that I'm the same idiotic young girl you knew all those years ago,

Javier? I've grown up! Life has…flattened me in ways you couldn't begin to understand.' Right now, she didn't feel very grown up. Indeed, she felt as unsure and uncertain as a teenager.

But she really wasn't the same girl she had once been. That much, at least, was true.

Javier frowned. Her words were the words of a cynic altered by circumstance, but the tenor of her voice…the soft tremble of her mouth…seemed to be saying something different, which was, of course, ridiculous.

'Good,' he purred. 'So we understand one another.'

'A one-night stand,' she murmured, flattening her hand against his chest as a tingle of unbridled excitement rippled through her. She'd never been a one-night stand kind of girl but a one-night stand with this man would be worth the final demolishing of all her girlhood, or whatever remnants remained in some dark closet at the very back of her mind.

Javier was a little piqued at the speed with which she had accepted the brevity of what they were about to embark on but he was done with thinking.

His erection was so rock-hard it was painful and he took her hand and guided it to his trousers.

'If you don't hold me hard,' he muttered, 'I'm not going to be able to finish what's been started the way it should be finished.'

'What do you mean?'

'I mean it's time to stop talking.'

He stood up in one fluid movement and began undressing. She marvelled at his utter lack of self-consciousness. He looked at her and held her fascinated gaze as he removed his trousers, tossing it on the ground, where it joined his shirt, leaving him in his low-slung silk boxers, which did nothing to conceal the evidence of his arousal.

She did this to him!

Hard on the heels of that thought came another, less welcome one.

How many other women had done this to him? How many women had lain on a bed and watched him with the same open-mouthed fascination with which *she* was now watching him?

He wouldn't have slept with any of *them* because they had started something years ago that needed *to be finished*. He wouldn't have slept with any of them because he'd been *driven to*. He would have slept with them *because he'd wanted to*. The difference felt huge but it was good that she was aware of that, because it would make it easy to walk away when they were finished making love.

It would make it easy to detach.

'I'm really surprised you never got married,' she blurted out and he grinned and slipped onto the bed alongside her.

His erection butted against her thigh and then against her stomach as he angled her to face him.

Javier was accustomed to women who couldn't wait to strip off so that they could show him what was on offer and it was weirdly erotic to be naked and in bed with a woman who was still fully clothed. He couldn't wait to get those clothes off, yet he was reluctant to undress her, wanting to savour the thrill of anticipation.

Once they'd made love, once he'd had her, it would signal the end and where was the harm in delaying that inevitable moment? They had the night to make love and in the morning, with that itch put to rest for ever, he would leave and contrive never to see her again. His relationship with her company would revert to being just another business deal, which would, he knew, be as successful as all the other business deals he had made over the years.

This didn't taste of revenge, not the revenge that he had

seen as his when her brother had first entered his office on a begging mission.

This was a conclusion and it was one over which he had complete control.

He was exactly where he was meant to be and it felt good.

'I don't think marriage and I would make happy bed partners.' He propped himself up on one elbow and began undressing her. 'A successful marriage...' the shirt was off '...requires just the sort of commitment...'

Now she was wriggling out of the shorts, leaving just a pair of lacy briefs that matched her bra. Her breasts were full and firm and he could see the dark circle of her nipples through the lace.

'That I don't have...' He breathed unsteadily. 'Your breasts are driving me crazy, Sophie...' He bent to circle one nipple through the lacy bra with his mouth and she gasped and arched into his questing mouth.

They hadn't even got this far first time round. She had been as prim and as chaste as a Victorian maiden and he had held off, curbing his natural instinct to swoop and conquer. He closed his mind off to the reasons why she had been so damned prim and chaste because the only thing that mattered now was the taste of her.

He didn't unhook the bra. Instead, he pushed it over her breasts and, for a few unbelievably erotic seconds, he just stared. The big, circular discs of her nipples pouted at him. Her breasts were smooth, creamy and soft. He was a teenager again, with a teenager's crazy, wildly out-of-control hormones, trying hard not to come prematurely.

He almost wanted to laugh in disbelief at the extraordinary reaction of his normally well-behaved body.

He licked the stiffened bud of one nipple and then lost himself in something he had dreamed of, suckling and drawing her nipple into his mouth, flicking his tongue over the tip and just loving her responsive body underneath him.

Without breaking the devastating caress, he slid his hand under the small of her back so that she was arched up, writhing and squirming as he moved from nipple to the soft underside of her breast, nuzzling and tasting.

Driving himself mad.

He had to hold off for a few seconds to catch his breath; he had to grit his teeth and summon up all his willpower to withstand the urge of her hand as she reached up, blindly curving the contour of his cheek, desperate for him to resume what he had been doing.

Without his usual finesse, he clumsily ripped the remainder of her clothes off.

How long had he been waiting for this moment? It felt like for ever as he gazed down at her rosy, flushed body, his breathing laboured as if he had just completed a marathon.

She was perfect.

Her skin was silky smooth, her breasts pert, inviting all sorts of wicked thoughts, and as his eyes drifted lower…

The soft, downy hair between her legs elicited a groan that sounded decidedly helpless.

So this was what it felt like…

This heady sense of power as she watched him watching her and losing control.

By the time she had married Roger, she had known the full scale of the mistake she had made, but she had still been young and naïve enough fundamentally to trust that the lectures from her parents about the follies of youth and the transitory nature of her attraction to the wrong man were somehow rooted in truth. She hadn't, back then, been sure enough of herself to resist the wisdom of the two people she trusted and loved.

Surely time would make her see sense and make her

forget Javier and the new, wonderful feelings he had roused in her?

It wasn't as though she didn't *like* Roger, after all…

But it hadn't turned out that way. Neither of them had been able to find a way through all the muddy water under the bridge and she had discovered fast enough how easy it was for loathing to set in, forging a destructive path through affection and friendship.

She hadn't turned him on and he, certainly, had never, ever had the sort of effect on her that Javier was now having.

It was suddenly very, very important that they do this. Would he walk away if he knew that she was a virgin? Was he hoping for someone experienced, as he doubtless assumed she was, who could perform all sorts of exciting gymnastics in bed?

In her head, she balanced the scales.

Alarm and disappointment with her if he found out that he was dealing with someone who might not live up to expectation…versus her embarrassment at having to come clean and tell him the truth about the marriage into which she should never have entered…

Which in turn would lead her down all sorts of uncertain routes. Because how else could she explain away her mistake without letting him know just how much she had felt for him all those years ago, how deeply she had fallen in love with him?

And, in turn, would that lead him to start thinking that she might just go and do the same again, after he had issued his warnings and told her that this was just sex and nothing more—no romance, no courtship and certainly no repeat performance of what they had once had?

'I've never done this before.' She couldn't face the embarrassment of him pulling away, appalled that he had mistaken her for someone else, someone who might prove to be fun in bed instead of a novice waiting to be taught, guided only by instinct.

It took a few seconds for Javier to register what she had just said and he paid attention to her words only because of the tone in which they had been spoken.

He was still confused, though, as he pulled back to stare down at her.

'You mean you've never had a one-night stand with an ex-flame?'

'No.' Face flaming with embarrassment, she wriggled into a sitting position and drew the duvet cover protectively over her, suddenly shy in the face of his probing dark eyes.

'What, then?' He had never talked so much in bed with any woman. Frustrated, he raked his fingers through his hair and sighed. 'Do I need to get dressed to sit this one out?'

'What are you talking about?'

'What I'm asking is…is this going to be a long conversation involving more confidence sharing? Should I make myself a pot of tea and settle down for the long haul?'

'Why do you have to be so sarcastic?' Sophie asked, stung.

'Because,' Javier pointed out coolly, 'this should be a simple situation, Sophie. Once upon a time, there was something between us. Now there isn't—aside, that is, from the small technicality that we never actually made it past the bedroom door. Indeed, we never made it even near the bedroom door. So here we are, rectifying that oversight before going our separate ways. I'm not sure that there's anything much to talk about because it's not one of those *getting to know you* exercises.'

'I know! You've already told me that. Not that you needed to! I don't have any illusions as to why we're here…and *I know* it's not because we're *getting to know one another*!' Which didn't mean that it didn't hurt to have it laid out so flatly. 'I don't *want to get to know you*, Javier!'

Javier frowned. 'What is that supposed to mean?'

'It means that you're not the sort of guy I could ever be interested in now.'

Did that bother him? No. Why should it? 'Explain!' And if he wanted an explanation, it was simply to indulge his curiosity. Perfectly understandable.

'You're arrogant.' She ticked off on one finger. 'You're condescending. You think that, because you have stacks of money, you can say whatever you want and do whatever you please. You can't even be bothered to make a show of being polite because you don't think you ever have to be...'

Javier was outraged. 'I can't believe I'm hearing this!' He leapt out of the bed to pace the floor, glaring at the shabby wallpaper and the crumbling cornices.

Sophie watched him, shocked at what she had just said but in no way having the slightest intention of taking any of it back. She had to keep her eyes glued to his face because that glorious body of his was still doing things to her, even in the middle of the sudden squall that had blown up between them.

'That's because I bet no one has the courage to ever criticise you.'

'That's ridiculous! I *invite* openness from my staff! In fact, I welcome positive criticism from everyone!'

'Maybe you forgot to tell them.' Sophie glared. 'Because you behave just like someone who has the rack on standby for anyone who dares speak their mind!'

'Maybe...' He strolled towards the bed and then leant over, caging her in, hands on either side of her. 'You're the only one who thinks there's room for improvement in me...'

'Arrogant! Do you honestly think you're *that perfect*?'

'I haven't had complaints,' he purred, suddenly turned on and invigorated by the heat between them. 'Especially from the opposite sex. Stop arguing, Soph. And stop talking…'

There was no way he was going to allow her to dance around this any longer.

And she didn't want to.

She met his eyes steadily and took a deep breath. 'You're not going to believe this…'

'I loathe when people open a sentence with that statement.'

'I've never slept with anyone before, Javier. I'm…I'm still a virgin…'

CHAPTER EIGHT

'DON'T BE RIDICULOUS.' He shot her a look of amused disbelief. 'You can't be.'

Sophie continued to stare at him until he frowned as he continued to grapple with her bolt-from-the-blue remark.

'And there's no need to try to pique my interest by pretending,' he crooned softly. 'My interest is already piqued. In fact, my interest was piqued the second your brother walked through the door with his begging bowl and sob story...'

'What are you saying? Are you telling me that...that...?'

'I suddenly realised what had been missing for the past seven years—completion.'

'You wanted us to end up in bed?'

'I knew we would.'

'Is that why you offered to help us?' Sophie edged away from him, shaking with anger. 'Because you wanted... *completion*?'

'Why are you finding that so hard to believe?' Javier couldn't believe that the tide had turned so swiftly. One minute, he had been touching her, and now here she was, spinning him some tall story about being a virgin and staring at him as though he had suddenly transformed into the world's most wanted.

'I'm surprised...' she said bitterly, grabbing clothes

from the floor and hopping into them, beyond caring that he was watching her dress and wishing that he would follow suit and do the same '…that you didn't try to blackmail me into bed by offering me a deal in return!' Silence greeted this remark and she paused and stared up at him through narrowed eyes that were spitting fire.

'You thought about it, though, didn't you…?' she said slowly.

'This is a ridiculous conversation.' Javier slipped on his boxers and moved to stand by the window, arms folded, his expression thunderous.

'Did you pick all that stuff for the flat? I wondered about that, wondered how come everything seemed to have a personal touch when you didn't actually live there. When your taste, judging from your office, didn't run to old-fashioned… Did you think that shoving me into free accommodation where I'd be surrounded by stuff that made me feel at home was a good way to butter me up into sleeping with you, so that you could have your *completion*?'

Javier flushed darkly and glowered. 'Since when is it a criminal offence to choose what to put in your own property?'

'I'm going to add *manipulative and underhand* to *arrogant and full of yourself*!' He was all those things *and more*, yet she still couldn't tear her eyes away from his masculine perfection as he remained standing with his back to the window, which just went to show how downright *unfair* fate could be.

She should throw him out of the house, tell him what he could do with his deal and order him never to darken her doors again.

Instead, the awful truth was sinking in…

She still wanted him, still wanted to sleep with him, and for her it wasn't all about completion, even though that was what she had told herself, because that was the acceptable explanation for what she felt.

For her...

A jumble of confused, mixed-up emotions poured through her, weakening her, and she feebly pushed them aside because she didn't want to dwell on them.

Javier walked slowly towards her, half-naked, bronzed, a thing of such intense beauty that it took her breath away.

'So I weighted the scales in my favour,' he murmured. 'Where's the crime in that?' He was standing right in front of her now and he could almost *feel* the war raging inside her. Flee or stay put?

She wasn't running.

Because, like it or not, she wanted him as much as he wanted her and getting all worked up about the whys and hows didn't make a scrap of difference. The power of lust.

'I'm accustomed to getting what I want and I want you. And, yes, I did consider holding the offer of financial help over your head in exchange for that glorious body that has disturbed far too many of my nights, but I didn't.'

'Arrogant...' Sophie muttered. But she reluctantly had to concede that at least he wasn't trying to economise with the truth and the fact that he had used whatever ploys he had at hand to get what he wanted was all just part and parcel of his personality. There wasn't a scrap of shame or sheepishness in his voice.

He shrugged and smiled. 'Tell me you don't like it.'

'No one likes arrogance.' Her heart was beating madly. In the space of a heartbeat, the atmosphere had shifted right back to the sexy intimacy they had been sharing only moments earlier, before everything had gone downhill.

Before she had told him that she was a virgin.

'I've always been arrogant and you weren't complaining seven years ago. Why did you tell me that you were a virgin?'

'Because it's the truth,' she whispered stiltedly. 'I know you probably find that hard to believe.'

'Try impossible.'

'Roger…he…'

She wasn't lying or making up something to try to pique his interest. She was telling the truth. He could see it in her face and hear it in the clumsy awkwardness of her voice.

'Sit down.'

'Sorry?'

'You look as though you're about to collapse.' He guided her away from the bed with all its heated connotations of sex towards a chair that was by the window, facing into the room. Perhaps she sat there in the light evenings and read a book. It was the sort of thing he could picture her doing.

What he *couldn't* picture her doing was marrying some man only to spend her married life in a state of frustrated virginity.

Who the hell did something like that?

'You hadn't slept with the man before you…agreed to walk up the aisle with him?' This when she was sitting on the chair like a fragile wooden doll and he had dragged over the only other chair in the room, which had been in front of the oversized, dark mahogany dressing table.

'He…I…' The weight of all those nagging thoughts that she had temporarily pushed aside surged forward in a rush that made her breath hitch in her throat. She couldn't even remember what she had expected from her doomed marriage to Roger. She had half believed her parents when they had told her that her feelings for Javier were just an adolescent crush, the result of being away from home, being free for the first time in her young life. It happened to everyone, they had insisted, and it would blow over in due course. She would gravitate back towards someone on her own level, from her own social class, and the thrill of the unknown would fade away in time.

They had been very convincing, and as all those other reasons for marrying Roger had piled up, so had the tug of war going on inside her intensified.

But had she ever foreseen a satisfying sex life with the man she should never have wed?

Had she properly considered what married life was going to be like for her? Had she simply assumed that forgetting Javier would be as easy as her parents had said it would be and so all those feelings would, likewise, be easily replaced, transferred to Roger? What a complete idiot she had been! Foolish and naïve.

She now knew that what she had felt for Javier hadn't been a passing crush. She had fallen in love with him and he had been spot on when he had told her, just then, that his arrogance had never bothered her when they had been going out.

It was just something else she had adored about him. That and his utter integrity, his dry wit, his sharp intelligence and his sense of fair play.

She was still in love with him and all those traits that should have turned her off him but didn't. He had become the billionaire he had quietly always known he would end up being, and of course he had changed in the process. How could he not? But underneath the changes was the same man and she was still in love with him.

And just acknowledging that appalled and frightened her.

Because things might have stayed the same for her but they hadn't stayed the same for him.

He really did want completion. He hadn't stayed celibate over the years. He was a powerful, wealthy man now who could have any woman on the planet with a snap of his fingers. She was the one who'd got away, and he was determined to put that right, so he was having a little time out with her.

He didn't love her and whatever feelings he had had for her in the past had disappeared over the years. He'd made that perfectly clear. But she still loved him and that was a dreadful state of affairs.

Whilst one part of her realised that she must look very strange, just sitting with a blank expression on her face, another part recognised that there was nothing she could do about that because she couldn't control the racing whirlpool of her thoughts.

One thing was emerging very fast, though. She couldn't let him know how she felt. If he could be cool and controlled, then she must be as well. There was no way that she would allow him to see just how weak and vulnerable she was inside.

'There's no need to explain,' Javier said gently. He was beginning to feel all sorts of things and top of the list was intense satisfaction that he was going to be her first. He'd never thought that he was the sort of primal guy who would actually be thrilled to the core by something like that but he had clearly underestimated his own primitive side. Under the civilised veneer, he was as untamed as they came.

'What...what do you mean?' Sophie stammered. Of course, he had no insight into her murky past, but she still had a moment of wondering whether he had somehow worked everything out, including her feelings for him.

'I don't suppose you ever anticipated entering into a sexless marriage.'

Sophie went beetroot-red and didn't snatch back her hand when he reached out and idly played with her fingers.

'I...er...I...'

'No.' He stopped her mid awkward sentence. 'Like I said, there's no need to explain because I understand.'

'You do?'

'You were young. You weren't to know that it takes all sorts to make the world go round and some men find it harder than others to face their sexuality.'

'Sorry?'

For the first time in living memory, Javier wasn't seeing red when he thought about the loser she had tossed him over for. In many ways, he felt sorry for her. With financial problems surfacing on the home front, and a man with control over purse strings her family needed, she had failed to see that he had his own agenda and had tied the knot in the expectation that life would be normal.

She'd been sorely mistaken.

Javier shunted aside thorny questions about whether she had loved the guy or not. That was then and this was now and, in the interim, she sure as hell had had her wake-up call on that front.

A virgin widow and now here she was. Here they both were…

Sophie was reeling from the series of misunderstandings and misinterpretations. Red-blooded alpha male that Javier was, he had jumped to the simplest conclusion. She was good-looking, she and Roger had married… The only possible reason they might not have consummated their marriage would be because he physically hadn't been able to, and the only reason that might have been the case would be because he just wasn't attracted to women.

End of story.

Was she going to set him straight on that count? Was she going to tell him the series of events that had led to her sexless union? The depth of feeling she had carried for him, Javier? Was she going to risk him knowing how madly in love with him she had been and then finding the link and working out just how madly in love she still was with him?

'Roger, gay...' He might as well have been for the amount of notice he had paid her.

'Key thing here is this, Soph—it was nothing you did.'

'Really?' She very much doubted that but Javier nodded briskly.

'I went out with a functioning alcoholic a couple of years ago,' he confided, drawing her closer to him and liking her lack of resistance. 'You would never have guessed that she drank her daily intake of calories. She was a model with an erratic, hectic lifestyle and she was very careful.'

'Didn't you suspect anything?' Sophie stared at him, round-eyed. It was a relief to have the conversation off her for a moment.

'We were both busy, meeting in various foreign locations either where she was modelling or where I happened to be. I only twigged when she started having more ambitious plans for our...relationship.'

'What does that mean?'

'It means she decided that meeting in various foreign locations wasn't enough. She wanted something of a more permanent arrangement.'

'Poor woman,' Sophie said with heartfelt sympathy.

'Misplaced sympathies,' Javier said wryly. 'She knew the game before it started. Not my fault if somewhere along the line she forgot the rules.'

She knew the game the way I know the game, Sophie thought, *and I'd better make sure I don't forget the rules or else...*

And with a finger in the family company—frankly more than just a finger—parting company might be a little more difficult than he would want. Not just a simple case of ignoring calls and text messages after signing off with a bunch of flowers and a thanks-but-no-thanks farewell note…

'So how did you, er, find out that there was a problem?'

'She surprised me by inviting me over to her place in London for dinner.'

'And it was the first time you'd been there?'

'Like I said, the rules of the game…they don't include cosy domestic scenes.'

'You eat out all the time?'

Javier shrugged. 'It works. I'm only interested in the bedroom when it comes to any woman's house.'

Sophie thought that he'd seen more than just the bedroom of this particular house, but then, she knew, circumstances weren't exactly typical even though the ground rules would be exactly the same.

'But I went along and it didn't take me long to see just how many bottles of alcohol there were in places where food should have been stored. And it took even less time to unearth the mother lode because there had been no reason for her to hide any of it as she didn't share the flat with anyone. When I confronted her, she tried to make me believe that it was somehow my fault that she drank as much as she did, because I wouldn't commit to her. She clung and cried and said that her drinking had gone through the roof because she was depressed that our relationship wasn't going anywhere. Of course, I left her immediately and then got in touch with a private counsellor specialising in people with alcohol-related addictions. But the point I'm making is that there are just some people who won't face up to their own shortcomings and will take every opportunity to shift the blame onto other people.'

'And you think that, er, that Roger…'

'I think nothing.' Javier gestured in a way that was exotically foreign and then leant in closer to her. 'It would be a tough call for a man to find the courage to face up to his own sexual inclinations when those sexual inclinations risk putting him outside his comfort zone and alienating him from the people he has grown up with.'

'Roger was certainly a coward,' Sophie said bitterly.

'But all that is in the past.' He waved his hand elegantly. 'We find ourselves here and I'm glad you felt comfortable enough to bare all to me.'

'You would have found out anyway,' she said vaguely.

'You shouldn't have put your clothes back on. Now I'm going to have to strip them off you all over again. No, scrap that—what I'd really like is for you to take them off for me, bit by slow bit, a piece at a time, so that I can appreciate every delectable bit of your glorious body...'

'I...I can't do that.'

'You're shy...' Had she ever undressed in front of her husband? he wondered. Was all of this completely new to her? He confessed to himself that he was tickled pink and turned on like hell by the thought of that, the thought of him being the absolute first on so many counts.

Shy but unbelievably turned on...

She liked the way his dark, appreciative eyes roved over her like a physical caress. She liked the way he made her feel. She had never done any kind of striptease for a man before but now she began undressing as he had asked, very slowly, eyes never leaving his as she removed her clothing.

He made her feel safe and she knew why. It was because she loved him. She knew that he could hurt her beyond repair—knew that her love would never be returned and, after tonight, she would be left with only the memory of making love and the knowledge that what she wanted would never happen—but none of that seemed to matter. She'd thought that her heart could never again be made to beat but she'd been wrong. Her love overrode common sense and she couldn't fight it.

And what was the point of fighting anyway? She lived with enough regret on her shoulders without adding to the tally. If she had this one opportunity to grasp a bit of happiness, then why shouldn't she take it? She would deal with the aftermath later.

She unhooked her bra, stepped out of her undies and then walked slowly towards him, sashaying provocatively and seeing for herself the effect she was having on him.

Javier held his erection through his boxers, controlling the wayward effects of his surging libido. He breathed deeply and tried to think pleasant, pedestrian thoughts so that he could gather himself sufficiently to do justice to the situation.

No rushing.

'You look tense,' Sophie murmured. She was amazed at how at ease she was with her nakedness. Indeed, she was positively basking in it. She delicately stroked the side of his face with one finger and Javier grabbed it and sucked it, watching her with smouldering passion so that every bone in her body seemed to go into meltdown.

'*Tense* isn't quite the word I would use...' He drew her close to him so that their bodies were lightly pressed together and, eyes still locked to hers, he eased his hand over her hip, along her thigh and then between them.

Her wetness on his finger elicited a moan of pure satisfaction from him.

Sophie couldn't breathe. Her eyelids fluttered. There was something so erotic about them both standing, looking at one another while he rubbed his finger against the small, tight bud of her clitoris, rousing sensations like little explosions and fireworks inside her. She shifted and moaned softly.

'This is just the appetiser,' Javier murmured, kissing

her on her mouth, small, darting kisses that left her breathless. 'And there will be lots of those to enjoy before the main course.'

'I want to pleasure you too...'

'You already are. Trust me—just touching you is giving me more pleasure than you could even begin to understand.'

In one fluid movement, he swept her off her feet and carried her to the bed as easily as if she weighed nothing. He deposited her as gently as if she were a piece of priceless porcelain and then he stood back and looked at her, and Sophie looked back at him, eyes half-closed, her breathing shallow and jerky. The outline of his impressive erection made her heart skip a beat.

She realised that she had never actually considered the dynamics of sexual intercourse; how something so big would fit into her...

'Your face is as transparent as a sheet of glass,' Javier told her drily. 'There's no need to be nervous. I am going to be very gentle.'

'I know you will.' And she did. He might be ruthless on the battlefield of high finance, but here in the bedroom he was a giver and utterly unselfish. That was something she sensed.

Javier decided that he would leave the boxers on. He didn't want to scare her. He was a big boy and he had seen that flash of apprehension on her face and interpreted it without any difficulty at all. He'd said he was going to be gentle and he would be; he would ease himself into her and she would accept his largeness without anything but sheer, unadulterated pleasure.

He had forgotten that this single act was supposed to be about revenge.

He positioned her arms above her head and she shifted into the position so that her breasts were pointing at him.

Hunkering over her, he delicately circled one rosy nipple with his tongue until she was writhing in response.

'No moving,' he chastised sternly. 'Or else I might have to tie those hands of yours together above your head...'

'You wouldn't.' But now that he had put that thought in her head, she found that she rather enjoyed playing around with it in her mind.

Maybe another time, she thought with heated contentment only to realise that there wouldn't *be* another time. This was it. This was all he wanted. A night of fun so that he could get the *completion* he felt he deserved.

She felt a sharp, searing pain as she pictured him walking away from her, taking his sense of completion with him, returning to the queue of beautiful, experienced women patiently waiting for him.

She squeezed her eyes tightly shut, blocking out the intrusive, unwelcome image and succumbing to the riot of physical sensations sparked as he trailed kisses along her collarbone, down to her pouting, pink nipple.

He took his time. He drew her aching nipple into his mouth so that he could caress the tip with his tongue in firm, circular movements that had her gasping for breath. Every time she lowered her arm to clutch his hair, he pushed it back up without pausing in his devastating caress.

'Now let's try this another way,' he murmured, rising up and staring down at her flushed, drowsy face.

'I'm not pleasing you...' Sophie's voice was suddenly anxious and her eyes expressed concern that she was taking without giving anything in return.

'Shh...' Javier admonished. 'Like I said, you're doing more for me than you can ever imagine possible.' *Doing more than any woman had ever done before.*

She made him feel young again. He was no longer the boy who had grown into a man whose only focus was forging the financial stability he had grown up wanting. He was no longer the tycoon who had made it to the top, who could have anything and anyone he wanted. He was young again, without the cynicism invested in him by his upwards journey.

'Straddle me,' he commanded, flipping her so that their positions were reversed, and she was now the one over him, her full breasts dangling like ripe fruit, swinging tantalisingly close to his face. 'And move on me…move on my thigh…let me feel your wetness…'

Sophie obeyed. It was wickedly decadent. She moved against his thigh, slowly and firmly, legs parted so that she could feel the nudge of an orgasm slowly building.

She didn't care that he could see the naked, open-mouthed lust on her face or hear the heavy, laboured breathing which she could no longer get under control.

She didn't care if he watched her, in her most private moment, come against his leg.

She was so turned on, she could scarcely breathe. She gasped when he held her breasts, massaging their fullness, drawing her down towards him so that he could suckle on first one, then the other, while she continued to pleasure herself against him, hands pinned on either side of him.

As limp as a rag doll, she lay for a while on him, taking time out to quell the rise of an impending orgasm because she wanted to have it all. She didn't want to come like this. She wanted to feel him moving hard in her.

The apprehension she had earlier felt when she had seen his impressive size had faded completely.

He was in no rush. He stroked her spine and then, when she propped herself up once again, he kissed her slowly, tasting every morsel of her mouth. Her hair fell around her and he pushed his hand through its tangle and gazed at her in perfect, still silence.

'You're beautiful, Sophie.'

Sophie blushed, unused to compliments. She felt as though she had given away her carefree youth somewhere along the line and that single compliment had returned it to her for a little while.

'I bet you say that to all the women you get into bed with.' Her voice was soft and breathless and he quirked an eyebrow in amusement.

'Is that the sound of someone fishing for compliments?'

Sophie thought that actually it was the sound of someone trying to be casual when in fact she was eaten up with jealousy over lovers she had never met or seen.

'It's been a very long time since anyone paid me a compliment,' she told him truthfully and for a few moments Javier stared at her seriously.

'Weren't you tempted to get some sort of life of your own after your husband died? Or even when he was alive, given the extraordinary circumstances?'

Sophie felt a distinct twinge of guilt that she had allowed him to believe something that couldn't have been further from the truth. But then she reminded herself that she was simply avoiding opening a can of worms and where was the harm in a very small white lie? It hardly altered the fact that she was a virgin, did it?

She decided to completely skirt around the whole thorny business of life as she had known it when she had been married to Roger.

'By the time my husband died,' she said instead, snuggling against him, 'I was so snowed under with financial problems, I barely had time to eat a meal and brush my teeth, never mind launch myself into the singles scene and start trying to find a man.'

'And you must have been pretty jaded with the male sex by then,' Javier offered encouragingly.

'Um…with life in general,' she returned vaguely.

'And with your husband specifically,' Javier pressed.

'Understand one hundred percent—he lied and used you and on top of that managed to ruin what was left of your family company.'

Sophie sighed. Put like that, she marvelled that she had had the strength to go on after her mother had moved down to Cornwall. She marvelled that she just hadn't thrown in the towel and fled to the furthest corners of the earth to live on a beach somewhere.

She had been raised to be dutiful and responsible, however, and she could see now, looking back on her life, that those two traits, whilst positive, had in fact been the very things that had taken her down the wrong road. At the age of just nineteen, she had been dutiful and responsible enough to put herself last so that she could fall in line with what everyone else seemed to want from her.

'Let's not talk about all that,' she said gruffly, sensing the tears of self-pity not too far away. What a fantastic start to her one big night that would be—snotty nosed, puffy eyed and blubbing like a baby in front of him!

It enraged Javier that she still couldn't seem to find it in herself to give the man the lack of due credit and respect he so richly deserved, even with a string of unpalatable facts laid out in front of her. But, he thought with harsh satisfaction, who was she here with now? Him! And he was going to take her to such heights that by the time he walked away from her he would be the only man in her head. No one forgot their first lover.

'You're right,' he breathed huskily, expertly reversing positions so that he was the dominant one now, on top of her. 'I've always found talking superfluous between the sheets...'

Sophie sadly thanked her lucky stars that she had ended her rambling conversation before she could really begin to bore him witless. If he didn't care for women talking when they were in bed with him, then she shuddered to think what he might feel if she began weeping like a baby and clutching him like a life jacket flung into stormy seas to a drowning man.

Javier lowered himself and began to kiss her. He started with her mouth and he took his time there, until she was whimpering and squirming, then he moved to her succulent breasts, nibbling and nipping and suckling. Her skin was like satin, velvety smooth and warm. When he began to lick her stomach, her sides, the path down to her belly button, she moaned with fevered impatience.

She reached down compulsively and tangled her fingers in his hair.

'Javier!'

Sophie met his darkened gaze and blushed furiously. 'What…are you doing?'

'Trust me,' he murmured roughly. 'I'm taking you to heaven…' He gently pushed her thighs open and she fell back, then sucked in a shocked breath. The delicate darting of his tongue as he explored her was agonisingly, explosively erotic.

She moved against his mouth, rocking and undulating her hips, and groaning so loudly that it was a blessing the house was empty. She arched up, pushing herself into that slickly exploring tongue, and cried out when two fingers, gently inserted into her wetness, ratcheted up the wildly soaring sensations racing through her as fast as quicksilver.

'I'm going to…' She could scarcely get the words out before a shattering orgasm ripped through her and she clutched the sheets, driving herself upwards as his big hands supported her tightened buttocks.

It was an orgasm that went on and on, taking her to heights she had never dreamed possible, before subsiding, returning her gently back to planet Earth.

She scrambled onto her elbows, intent on apologising

for being so selfish, but Javier was already out of the bed and rooting through his trousers.

It was only when he began putting on protection that it dawned on her what he was doing.

The last thing he would want was a pregnancy.

She barely had time to register the treacherous stab of curiosity that filled her head… *What would a baby created by them look like?*

'Lie back,' he urged with a wolfish grin. 'The fun is only beginning…'

CHAPTER NINE

SOPHIE QUIVERED WITH anticipation but this time it was her decision to take things slowly. He had pleasured her in the most intimate and wonderful way possible and now it was her turn to give.

She wriggled so that she was kneeling and gently pushed him so that he was lying down. His initial expression of surprise quickly gave way to one of wicked understanding that she wanted the opportunity to take the reins instead of leaving it all to him.

'No touching,' she whispered huskily.

'That's going to be impossible.'

'You're going to have to fold your hands behind your head.' She grinned and then looked at him with haughty reprimand. 'It's only what *you* asked *me* to do.'

'Well, then,' he drawled, 'I'd better obey, hadn't I?' He lay back, arms folded behind his head. He could have watched that glorious body for ever, the shapely indent of her waist, the full heaviness of her breasts, the perfect outline of her nipples, the scattering of freckles along her collarbone, that tiny mole on the side of her left breast...

Her eyes were modestly diverted but he knew that she was aware of him with every ounce of her being and that was a real turn on for him.

He'd never felt so *alive* to the business of making love.

Somehow, he was functioning on another level, where every sensation was heightened to almost unbearable limits.

Was it because he was finally making love to the one woman who had escaped him? Was this what it felt like finally to settle old scores?

Would he be feeling this had he had her the first time round? No. That was a given. However crazy he'd been about her, he knew far more about himself now than he had back then. He knew that he wasn't cut out for permanence. If they had slept together, carried on seeing one another, if circumstances hadn't interrupted their relationship, it still wouldn't have lasted. Because, whether he liked it or not, he'd been focused on one thing and one thing only—the acquisition of the sort of wealth that would empower him, afford him the financial security he had never had growing up.

He no longer questioned his motivation, if indeed he ever had. Some things were ingrained, like scores from a branding iron, and that was one of them.

He had no burning desire for children and not once, over the years, had any of the women he had dated given him pause for thought. He expected that if he ever married—and it was a big *if*—it would be a marriage of convenience, a union years down the road with a suitable woman who would make him an acceptable companion with whom to see in his retirement. A woman of independent means, because the world was full of gold-diggers, who enjoyed the same things he enjoyed and would make no demands on him. He would look for a harmonious relationship.

Harmony in his fading years would be acceptable. Until then, he would make do with his string of women, all beautiful, all amenable, all willing to please and all so easily placated with jewellery and gifts if he ended up being unreliable.

They were all a known quantity and, in a life driven by ambition, it was soothing to have a private life where there were no surprises.

Except, right now, Sophie was the exception to the rule, and a necessary exception.

And he was enjoying every minute of her.

She straddled him and he looked down, to the slickness between her legs, and then up as she leant over him so that she could tease his hungry mouth with her dangling breasts.

He was allowed to lick, but only for a while, and allowed to suckle, but only for a while.

And he wasn't allowed to touch, which meant he had to fight off the agonising urge to pull her down so that she was on top of him and take her.

She did to him what he had done to her. She explored his torso with her mouth. She kissed the bunched muscles of his shoulders and then circled his flat, brown nipples with her mouth so that she could drizzle her tongue over them with licks as dainty as a cat's.

She could feel the demanding throb of his erection against her but it was only when she moved lower down his body that she circled its massive girth with her hand, pressing down firmly and somehow knowing what to do, how to elicit those groans from him, how to sharpen his breathing until each breath was accompanied by a shudder.

Instinct.

Or something else. Love. Love that had been born all those years ago and had forgotten that it was supposed to die. Like a weed, it had clung and survived the worst possible conditions so that now it could resume its steady growth. Against all odds and against all better judgement.

Well, worse conditions loomed round the corner, but before she encountered those she would enjoy this night to the absolute fullest.

She straightened, eyes dark with desire, and half-smiled with a sense of heady power as she registered his utter lack of control. She might be the inexperienced one here, but when it came to the power of *lust* she wasn't the only one to be in its grip. She wasn't the only one who was out of control.

And that balanced the scales a bit.

Hot and consumed with a sense of recklessness she would never have thought possible, she sat astride him so that he could breathe in the musky scent of her, positioning herself over him so that he could explore between her legs with his flicking tongue.

She breathed in sharply as he found her sensitive clitoris and probed it with the tip of his tongue.

He still wasn't touching her, still had his hands behind his head, as she had her fists clenched at her sides.

But the heat between them was indescribable all the more so because of the tantalising promise of fulfilment that lay ahead.

She let him taste her until she could stand it no longer, until her breathing was so fractured that she wanted to scream. She could move against his mouth but there was no way she was going to come again, not like this…

She worked her way down him until she was the one tasting him. The solid steel of his erection fascinated her. She took it into her mouth, sucked on the tip, played with it with her hands, tasted it and loved the way it tasted.

She explored his hard six-pack with the flat of her hand as she sucked, enjoying the hard, abrasive rub of muscle and sinew under her palm.

'Okay.' Javier rose onto his elbows to tangle his hand

in her tumbling hair. 'Enough. My blood pressure can't take any more.'

Sophie glanced at him from under her lashes.

'You're a witch,' he breathed huskily. 'Come here and kiss me.'

Their kiss was a mingling of scents and Sophie lost herself in it. She wanted to wrap her arms around him and never let him go. She wanted to be needy, clingy and demanding, and all those awful things that would have him running for the hills without a backwards glance.

She wanted to be open and honest, tell him how she felt and declare her love for him, and the fact that there was no way that she could do that felt like an impossible weight on her shoulders.

She sighed, rolling as he propelled her gently onto her back. Balancing over her, he looked at her seriously.

'Still nervous?'

'A little,' she admitted. She could have admitted a lot more. She could have admitted that what really made her nervous was the prospect of what happened when this glorious night was over and they both returned to their own little worlds. There was no way she would duck away from this but the aftermath still made her nervous.

She didn't think he would like to hear about that.

'Don't be,' he murmured. 'Trust me.'

He nudged her with the tip of his erection, felt her wetness and gently, slowly eased himself in.

She was beautifully tight. Would he have guessed that she had never made love before? Probably. She would have winced, given her inexperience away. That said, he was pleased that she had thought to confide in him and more than pleased that he was going to be her first lover.

Whatever feelings still lingered for the creep who had married her for all the wrong reasons, *he* would be the man who would be imprinted in her head for the rest of her life. Not her ex-husband. When she lay in bed, the loser she still refused to hold in contempt would no longer dominate her thoughts. No. Instead, *he* would be in her head now, and the memory of this first night spent together.

Sophie inhaled and tensed but she was already so turned on that the tension quickly evaporated. Nor did she want him treating her like a piece of china that could shatter into a thousand pieces if he happened to be just a little too rough.

She wanted him to thrust long and deep into her. She wanted his *urgency*.

'Move faster...' she moaned.

It was all the invitation Javier needed. He was unbelievably aroused. Holding on had required a superhuman feat of willpower because having her touch him had driven him wild.

He began moving with expert assurance, felt her wince as he drove deeper, then gradually relax as he picked up pace until their bodies were moving in harmony, as sweet as the coming together of the chords of a song.

Still, he refused to satisfy himself at her expense, waiting until her rhythm was inexorably building and he could feel her fingers dig into the small of his back and knew that she had raised her legs, wrapped them around his waist, all the better to receive him...

Sophie came, spinning off to a different world where nothing existed but her body and its powerful, shattering responses. She was distantly aware of Javier arching up, his whole body tensing as he reached orgasm.

Apart yet inextricably joined. She had never felt closer to anyone in her entire life. And it wasn't just because of the sex. Somewhere in the core of her she knew that it was what it was because of what she felt. She couldn't disentangle her emotions from her responses. The two were inextricably linked.

Not good. Yet so right. She couldn't imagine feeling anything like this for anyone else, ever, and that scared her because when this was over she would have no choice but to pick up the pieces and move on. She would have to put him behind her and one day find herself a partner because she couldn't envisage spending the rest of her life on her own.

She was lying in the crook of his arm, both of them staring upwards. His breathing was thick and uneven and with a little chuckle he swung her onto her side so that they were now facing one another, their bodies pressed together.

Somewhere along the line he had disposed of the condom. He was a very generously built man, however, and even with his erection temporarily subsided she was still aware of his thick length against her, stirring her, although she was aching a little and as tired as if she had run a marathon at full tilt.

She wondered what the protocol was for a one-night stand. She couldn't leap out of bed, stroll to get her clothes and head for the door, having thanked him for a good time, because it was her house. Which meant that she would have to rely on him to make the first move, and that made her feel a little awkward, because she didn't want him to imagine that she was hanging around, waiting for an encore.

She was afraid to carry on being intimate, in these most intimate of circumstances, because she didn't want him to guess the depth of her feelings for him.

She wanted to maintain her dignity. It wasn't just a case of self-preservation, but on a more realistic level: he now had a slice of the family company. He might decide to take a back seat now that they had made love and *completion* had been established, might disappear never to be seen again, but on the small chance that she bumped into him at some point in the future the last thing she needed was for him to know her feelings. If she bumped into him, she wanted him to think that she had been as detached from the whole experience, on an emotional level, as he had been. She wanted to be able to have a conversation with him, with her head held high, and preferably with a man on her arm.

'So,' Javier drawled, breaking the silence and stroking her hair away from her face.

'So…' Sophie cleared her throat and offered him a bright smile. 'That was very nice.'

Javier burst out laughing. 'That's a first,' he informed her wryly. 'I've never had a woman tell me afterwards that the sex was "very nice".'

Sophie didn't want to think about the women he had bedded or what sexy little conversations they had had post–making love.

'You don't have to tell me that.' She was going to keep it light, brace herself for when he levered himself out of bed and began getting dressed. She didn't think he'd be spending the night.

'No?'

'I already have a picture in my head of the sort of women you, er, entertain and I guess they'd be busy telling you how great you were and offering to do whatever you wanted…'

'Did you think I was great?'

Sophie blushed a vibrant red.

'Is that a *yes*…?' He nuzzled her neck and then absently rested his hand between her legs.

'What happens about the shoot?'

'I don't want to talk about the shoot. I want to talk about how great you found me between the sheets.'

Sophie didn't want to laugh but her lips twitched because there was just something so incredibly endearing and boyish about his arrogance.

'I'm glad we made love,' she told him truthfully. 'I...'

'Don't go there, Soph.' He fell onto his back and gazed upwards because this was what he didn't want. Any sort of half-hearted, limp excuses and explanations for the choices she had made seven years ago. She'd already told him enough. He knew enough. He wasn't interested in hearing any more.

'Don't go where?'

'This isn't the point where we pick up sharing our life histories.' He gathered her into him, his arm draped loosely around her. He could touch her nipple with his fingers and he liked that. He liked the way the little bud stiffened in response to the gentle pressure of his fingers rolling it. And he liked what that did to his body, the way it made him feel as though he could keep going indefinitely, his body resting between bouts of lovemaking only long enough to build back up the vigour to carry on.

After sex, no matter how good the sex had been, his instinct had always been to get out of bed as fast as he could and have a shower, his mind already racing ahead to work and business, deals that had to be done.

He'd never been one for hanging around between the sheets, chewing the fat and talking about a future that wasn't going to happen.

But he wanted to hang around between the sheets now.

Minus the chat.

He'd managed, just, to relegate her loser ex-husband to a box somewhere in his head that he could safely ignore. The last thing he wanted was for her to begin recapping her past, forcing him to confront the unpalatable truth that, whether she had come to him a virgin or not, she had still ditched him for someone else and probably still loved that someone else, even though the man in question had failed to deliver.

'No,' she agreed quickly. 'I was simply going to say

that it's probably a good idea if you head back now. Unfortunately…' she gave a derisive laugh '…the guest bedrooms aren't exactly made up for visiting crowds. No crisp white sheets and fluffy towels, I'm afraid.'

She began to slip her legs over the side of the bed and he tugged her back against him.

He wasn't ready for her to leave just yet. He hadn't quite got his fill of her. Surprising, all things considered, but nevertheless true. And he didn't want to give her time to think things over. He wanted her warm, ripe and soft like she was now; yielding.

'I'm not sure I can face the horror story of a long drive back to London,' he murmured, curving his big body against hers and pushing his thigh between her legs.

'There are hotels,' Sophie told him as her heart gave a silly little leap in her chest.

She didn't want him to go. It was exhausting pretending that she didn't care one way or another.

'This may be the back of beyond for you,' she carried on, 'compared to London, but we still have our fair share of excellent hotels. All come complete with mod cons like clean sheets, windows that open and no lingering smell of mustiness from being shut up for too long.'

Javier burst out laughing. He'd forgotten how funny she could be and that was something that hadn't been apparent over the past few weeks.

Probably over the past few years, he thought, sobering up.

'Bit of a trek going to a hotel,' he murmured. 'That would entail me getting up, getting dressed…and who's to say that they aren't all full?'

'What are you saying?'

'I could always save myself the hassle and spend the night here,' he told her.

'Some of the bedrooms… Well, I guess I could make

up the one at the end of the corridor. It's shocking to think how fast things have gone downhill here...' She sighed. 'It's as if the whole place was glued together with sticking plaster and then, one day, someone tugged some of the plaster off and everything else just came down with it. Like a house of cards being toppled. I can't imagine the stress my dad had been living under for ages. It's as well he's not alive to see the way the house has gone downhill. And it's a blessing that Mum is down in Cornwall. She honestly doesn't know the half of what's been going on here.' She pulled back and looked at him gravely. 'Sorry. I forgot you don't like conversing between the sheets.'

'That's not what I said,' Javier felt constrained to mutter. But she had hit the nail on the head. It was all tied in with his driving need to focus on the essentials—work and financial security. For the first time, he found himself projecting to places beyond those confines, the sort of places most people seemed ridiculously keen to occupy, places which he had shunned as irrelevant. 'How can your mother not know what's been happening here?' he found himself asking. 'How often do you go down to Cornwall to visit her? She surely must return here on occasion?'

'Are you really interested? Because you don't have to ask a load of questions just because you happen to be staying on here for a few more hours.'

'So you're going to put me up?'

Sophie shrugged. 'It's no bother for me.'

'Good, because I'd quite like to have a look around the house in the morning—see how bad it is in the unforgiving light of day.'

'Why?' She propped herself up on one elbow and stared down at him.

'Curiosity. You were explaining the mystery of how it is that your mother doesn't know the situation here.'

'Would you like something to eat? To drink?'

'I'm fine here.'

But, even to her, chatting like this in bed felt weirdly intimate and she could understand why he avoided doing it. It would be easy to find herself being seduced into all sorts of cosy, inappropriate feelings, into thinking this was more than it actually was.

'Well, I'm starved,' she declared briskly, disentangling herself from him and scrambling for the door so that she could head to the bathroom for a shower.

Caught on the back foot, Javier frowned as he watched her hastily departing figure.

Since when did women turn down invitations from him to stay in bed—*talking*?

Actually, since when had he made a habit of issuing invitations to women to stay in bed, talking?

He levered himself out and strolled to the bathroom which was a couple of doors along. He was surprised that the bedrooms weren't all en suite and then surmised that the house predated such luxuries and, somewhere along the line, it had become too costly to have them installed.

He pushed open the door to the succulent sight of her bending over the bath to test the water.

Her hair was swept over one shoulder, the tips almost touching the water in the bath. She had one hand on the mixer tap, the other gripping the side of the cast-iron claw-foot bath. He could see the low hang of one breast swinging as she adjusted the temperature of the water, and he moved to stand behind her, grinning as she gave a little squeak when he straddled her from behind, cupping both breasts with his hands.

'Couldn't resist,' he murmured into her hair as she straightened and leant into him so that her back was pressed against his torso.

He massaged her breasts and bent to nibble and kiss the

slender column of her neck. With a sigh of contentment, Sophie closed her eyes and covered his hands with hers.

'What are you doing?' she asked thickly.

'Is there any doubt?'

'I was just going to have a bath…then maybe get something for us to eat.'

'I have all I want to eat right here, right now…'

Sophie moaned softly at the provocative image that hoarsely spoken statement planted in her head.

They hadn't talked at all. Not really. Not about the one thing they needed to talk about. Which was *what happened next*. She knew that she shouldn't be sinking into his arms like this, should be maintaining some distance, but her body was turning to liquid as he continued to assault her senses.

She could have locked the door, of course, but somehow that would have felt silly and childish after they had just finished making love.

And maybe, she thought weakly, there was a part of her that wouldn't have wanted to stop him from coming into the bathroom anyway.

She breathed in sharply as his wicked hand drifted lower. Now he was just caressing one breast, playing with the pulsing, pink nipple while his other hand roamed over her ribcage, exploring downwards at a leisurely pace.

'Spread your legs,' he instructed softly and Sophie obeyed, as weak as a kitten.

She knew what he was going to do, yet she still gasped as he immediately found the swollen bud of her clitoris with the flat of his finger.

He knew just how to rub her there, applying just the right amount of pressure. His fingers were devastating. She could feel her wetness on his hand, and she reached behind her to hold his erection, although the angle was awkward and she couldn't begin to do half as much as she would have liked to.

And she didn't have time.

Because the rhythm of his touching grew faster, his fingers sending a million darting sensations flowing through her body until she was rocking under the impact of an orgasm, bucking against his hand, unable to contain her low groaning cries as she reached the point of utter physical fulfilment.

She spun round, blindly kissed his neck, just as he had done to her only minutes previously, and then she knelt in front of him, tossing her hair behind her, and took his rock-hard bigness into her mouth.

He tasted…like heaven.

She sucked him and he curled his fingers into her hair. She could feel his loss of self-control as she continued, sucking and licking him at the same time, her slender fingers gripping his erection, moving and massaging, working her own rhythm.

Javier had never felt so wildly out of control before. She was exciting him in ways no other woman ever had and he could no more control his own orgasm than he could have stopped the sun from rising or setting.

Spent, he pulled her back to her feet and for a few seconds their bodies were entwined into beautiful, sated pleasure, the aftermath of their physical satisfaction.

'I might have to share that oversized bath with you,' he murmured, tilting her face so that he could gently kiss her on her mouth.

Sophie smiled, as content as a cat in possession of a full tub of cream.

This was just the sort of thing he might take for granted, think nothing of, but she was so scared of taking yet another step into *him*…into losing herself in a non-relationship that wasn't going anywhere and never would.

But what was the harm in having a bath with him? What was the harm in another first experience?

'Okay.'

'And then you can cook something for me to eat.' He had never uttered those words to any woman before.

'Don't expect cordon bleu food,' Sophie warned him in alarm and he laughed.

'Beans on toast would be fine.'

Sophie lowered herself into the water a little self-consciously, drawing her knees up as he took the other end. It was an enormous bath, easily accommodating the both of them, and he made a few approving noises as he settled into the water, pulling her legs out to tangle with his, looking for the inevitable signs of deterioration in the fabric of the building as he was now accustomed to doing after only a short space of time.

'Really?' she couldn't help but ask drily. Once upon a time, perhaps, but he was no longer a 'beans on toast' kind of guy.

'And then you can tell me about your mother and how you've managed to keep this situation from her.'

He stroked her calf, which sent a frisson rippling through her body. She literally couldn't seem to get enough of him and she marvelled at her body's capacity to rouse itself at the speed of light, from satiated, pleasant torpor to wakening hunger to be touched again.

'And then we can talk about this house, which appears to be on the point of collapse. But before all that you can wriggle up and turn round so that I can begin soaping you...'

Sophie looked at the newspaper spread out on the kitchen table in front of her.

It had been *that* easy to become accustomed to having him around. It had felt so natural. Working in London, having him in and out of the office, going through paperwork with him, sitting in on interviews, being consulted on absolutely everything to do with the company…

And then, when they were on their own, those precious times when they would talk, laugh, make love…

The company had picked up in the space of just a few short months. Swept along on the coat-tails of Javier and his remarkable reputation, business that had been lost to competitors was gradually returning and returning customers were treated to reward schemes that secured their loyalty.

Little changes had been incremental and she marvelled at how simple some of the solutions were to turn the company around.

With profit came money to start working on the house. And the profits had also secured Oliver's release from the work he had never enjoyed doing.

He had returned to America to become a sports teacher at one of the prestigious private schools.

Everything had slotted into place and, of course, she had grown complacent.

Who wouldn't have?

She had actually begun secretly to see a future for them, even though he never, ever made plans; never, ever mentioned doing anything with her at some point in the future.

The one-night stand had grown into a relationship that was now almost four months old.

They hadn't talked about Christmas but she could envisage them spending at least a part of it together.

All told, hope, that dangerous emotion, had begun to take root. Loving him had taken away her objectivity, made her vulnerable to all kinds of foolish thoughts about them having a proper relationship, a relationship in which he might actually be persuaded to try to make a go of it, persuaded to think about commitment.

It was her own fault for not listening to the dictates of common sense...

No sooner had she told herself that she had to maintain some sort of emotional distance than she had hurled herself headlong into a relationship that was the equivalent of a minefield.

And this was where it had got her.

She was driven to stare at the picture occupying a large portion of the tabloid newspaper she had bought on the spur of the moment from the local newsagent. Lord knew, she wasn't much of a newspaper reader. She had an app on her mobile that kept her fully updated with what was happening in the world.

The picture had been taken at a London gallery opening. She hadn't even known that Javier had been invited. Ensconced in Yorkshire, where she had been for the past couple of weeks, getting the local offices in order and supervising decorating and refurbishment, she had seen him in fits and starts.

She looked forward to his arrivals with eager, edge-of-seat anticipation. She dressed in clothes she imagined him ripping off. She no longer felt constrained to hide how much he turned her on. Lust and the physical side of things were the only things that were out in the open between them.

She knew how much he wanted her and he knew how much she wanted him.

And he was going to be arriving any minute now. She had cooked and could smell it wafting aromatically from the kitchen, which had seen recent updates and now functioned the way it once had, with everything working and in spanking new condition.

She neatly folded the paper and then hovered until, at

seven promptly, she heard the insistent buzz of the door-bell. She closed her eyes and breathed in deeply to calm her shaky nerves.

She found that she'd even memorised the way he rang the doorbell, as if he couldn't wait to stride into the house, shedding his coat even as he reached to scoop her to-wards him.

She still hadn't become accustomed to that first sight of him. Even if she'd seen him the evening before, even if she'd seen him five minutes before, he still always blew her mind and took her breath away.

As always when he drove up north—quitting work ear-lier than he normally would because, he had confessed, those few hours behind the wheel of his car afforded him a certain amount of freedom which he deeply valued—he arrived still in his suit.

Minus jacket, which, she knew, he would have flung into the back seat of the car, oblivious to the fact that what he treated with such casual indifference had cost more than most people earned in a month.

'Have I told you that I missed you...?' Javier growled, closing the space between them in one fluid stride.

He had. It had been three days and he'd gone to sleep every evening with an erection and woken up with one. Not even those sexy phone calls late at night to her had been able to do the trick. There was only so much plea-sure to be had satisfying himself.

He kissed her thoroughly, so thoroughly that Sophie forgot that this wasn't going to be the sort of evening they had both been anticipating: an evening of chat, food and lots of very satisfying sex. No, things were going to be different this evening because of that picture.

She pushed ever so slightly against him but immedi-ately weakened as he plundered her mouth, driving her back until she was pressed against the wall.

She'd stopped wearing a bra in the house, liking the fact that he could touch her whenever he wanted without the bother of removing it, and she hadn't thought to put one on this evening. Her head fell back as he pushed up her long-sleeved tee shirt to feel her.

He'd thought of nothing but her on the drive up and now to touch her breast, feel the tautness of her nipple between his fingers, was almost indescribable.

'I want to take you right here,' he confessed unsteadily. 'I don't even think I can make it to the bedroom. Or *any* room…'

'Don't be silly,' Sophie returned breathlessly. She *needed* to talk to him. She knew that it wasn't going to be a comfortable conversation, but talking couldn't have been further from her mind as he dragged at the waistband of her jeans, fumbling to undo the button and pull down the zipper.

She rested her hands on his broad shoulders and her mind went completely blank, swamped by the powerful churn of sensation. Her tee shirt was still over her breasts and she could feel the air cooling her heated nipples. She wanted him to lick them, suckle at them, but, like him, she was frantic for them to unite, to feel him moving in her, free and unencumbered, because she was now on the pill, so there was no need for him to reach for protection.

She helped with the jeans, tugging them down and then somehow wriggling out of them, while he, likewise, dealt with his trousers and boxers.

When she opened drugged eyes, she saw that his white shirt was unbuttoned all the way down, revealing a broad slither of bronzed chest, and he had dispensed with his shoes and socks. When had that happened? Her socks were tangled up with her trousers.

They'd barely closed the front door and here they were,

practically naked in the hall, unable to keep their hands off one another.

Hands balled tightly behind her back, she literally couldn't keep still as he crouched in front of her and began tasting her, savouring her. She planted her legs apart to accommodate his questing mouth, barely able to breathe. When she glanced down to see his dark head moving between her legs, she felt unspeakably turned on.

'You need to come in me *now*!'

She heard his low laugh and then he was lifting her up and she was wrapping her legs around him, clinging to him as he began thrusting hard inside her, his hands supporting her bottom, her breasts bouncing as they moved together.

It was fast, furious, *raw* and earth-shattering. And utterly draining. For a short while, Sophie was transported to another place, another dimension, one in which difficult, awkward conversations with unpredictable outcomes didn't have to take place.

But as soon as she was back on her feet, hurriedly snatching clothes to put them on, her mind returned to what it had been chewing over before and she edged away from him, horrified at how easily she had dumped all her worries the second he had touched her.

And that was the essence of the problem, wasn't it? He did things to her, turned her to putty in his hands. He put her in a position where she couldn't seem to say *no* to him, which meant that this could go on until he got bored, and then he would chuck her aside and move on and where would her precious dignity be when that happened?

She was so cautious about never revealing the depth of her feelings for him, so fearful that he might gaze back into the past, understand how much she had meant to him then and work out how much he meant to her now. She was just so damned careful to play the adult game of keeping it cool, matching his control with control of her own.

She'd still be a mess when he decided that it was time to move on and he'd spot that in an instant.

The mere fact that she was about to tell him about that picture said it all but she didn't care because she had to find out.

'There's something I want to show you,' she told him in a rush, having put some vital distance between them. 'Well, something I want to ask you.' She sighed on a deep breath. 'Javier, we need to talk…'

CHAPTER TEN

'WHAT ABOUT?' HE TOOK his time getting dressed while she watched him from the door, arms folded, her expression revealing nothing. 'There's nothing more guaranteed to kill a good mood than *a talk*.'

'Are you speaking from personal experience?' Sophie asked coolly. She held up one interrupting hand even though he hadn't said anything. 'Of course you are. I suppose some of those women you went out with might have wanted a bit more from you than sex on tap.'

'Is that what this talk of yours is going to be about?' Javier's voice was as cool as hers, his expression suddenly wary and guarded.

Sophie spun round and began walking towards the kitchen. She could feel stinging colour washing over her because, in a way, this *was* about that. This *was* about more than just sex on tap.

'Well?' He caught up with her and held her arm, staying her, forcing her to turn to look at him. 'Is that what this *talk* of yours is going to be about? Wanting more?' He hadn't worked out the exact time scale, but it hit him that he had been seeing her now for several months, virtually on a daily basis, and he wasn't tiring of her. Immediately he felt his defences snap into position.

'I'm not an idiot,' Sophie lied valiantly. 'You'd have to be completely stupid to want *more* from a man like you!'

She yanked her arm free and glared at him. Her heart was thumping so hard and so fast in her chest that it felt as though it might explode.

She wanted to snatch the conversation back, stuff it away, take back wanting to *talk*. She wanted to pretend that she hadn't seen a picture of him at a gallery opening with some beautiful model clinging like a limpet to his arm, their body language saying all sorts of things she didn't want to hear.

'You're not capable of giving anyone anything more than sex,' she fumed, storming off towards the kitchen and the offending picture that she intended to fling in his face as proof of what she was saying.

'You weren't complaining five minutes ago,' he pointed out smoothly.

Below the belt, Sophie thought, but her face burnt when she thought about how her talk had taken a back seat the second he had touched her. He was right. She hadn't been complaining. In fact, at one point she remembered asking for more.

'I don't want more from you, Javier,' she gritted, reaching for the paper with shaking hands and flicking it open to the piece in the centre section. She tossed it to him and then stood at the opposite end of the table with her arms folded, nails biting into the soft flesh of her forearms. 'But what I *do* want is to know that you're not running around behind my back while we're an item!'

Javier stared down at the picture in front of him. He remembered the occasion distinctly. Another boring opening, this one at an art gallery. It had been full of just the sort of types he loathed—pretentious, champagne-drinking, caviar-scoffing crowds who had never given a penny to charity in their lives and had all attended top private schools courtesy of their wealthy parents. He could have given them a short lecture on the reality of being poor, but instead he had kept glancing at his watch and wondering what Sophie was doing.

As always, mixing in the jabbering, wealthy intellectual crowd was the usual assortment of beautiful hangers-on dressed in not very much and on the lookout for men with money. He had been a target from the very second he had walked through the door. He had shaken them off like flies, but by the end of the evening he had more or less given up and that was when the photographer had obviously seen fit to take a compromising snap.

In under a second, Javier could understand why Sophie had questions. He couldn't even remember the woman's name but he knew that she was a famous model and the way she was looking at him…the way she was holding on to his arm…

She didn't look like a woman on the verge of being cast aside by an indifferent stranger. Which she had been.

And snapped when, for five seconds, his attention had been caught by something the guy standing next to her had said to him and he was leaning into her, the very image of keen, while the guy to whom he had been speaking had been artfully cropped from the photo.

Not for a second was Javier tempted to launch into any kind of self-justifying speech. Why should he? He looked at her angry, hurt face and he ignored the thing inside him that twisted.

'Are you asking me to account for my actions when I'm not with you?'

'I don't think that's out of order on my part!'

'I have never felt the need to justify my behaviour to anyone. Ever.'

'Maybe you should have! Because when you're sleeping with someone, you are, actually, travelling down a two-way street whether you like it or not!'

'Meaning what?'

'Meaning it's not all about your world and what you want.'

'And maybe that will be the case one day, when I decide that I want more than a passing…situation with a woman.'

Sophie recoiled as though she had been physically struck. Suddenly all her anger seeped out of her and she was left feeling empty, hollow and utterly miserable.

Of course he would account for his behaviour one day. When he had met the right woman. In the meantime, he was having fun, and that was all that mattered. He wasn't tied to her any more than he had been tied to any of the women he had dated in the past, so if someone else came along and he was feeling energetic, then he probably thought, *why not?*

Facing up to that was like being kicked in the stomach. She literally reeled from the truth but she faced it anyway, just as she had faced the fact that she was still in love with him.

What was the point hiding from the truth? It didn't change anything. Having to deal with the mess her father had made of the company and the horror of her doomed marriage had taught her that, if nothing else.

'Did you sleep with that woman?'

'I'm not going to answer that question, Sophie.' Javier was incensed that, picture or no picture, she dared question his integrity. Did she think that he was the sort of man who couldn't control his libido and took sex wherever he found it?

He was also annoyed with himself for the way he had drifted along with this to the point where she felt okay about calling him to account. He'd been lazy. This had never been supposed to end up as anything more than an inconvenient itch that needed scratching. This had only ever been about finishing unfinished business.

'And maybe,' he said carefully, 'it's time for us to re-assess what's going on here.'

Sophie nodded curtly. The ground had just fallen away from under her feet, but she wasn't going to plead or beg or hurl herself at him, because they really *did* need to 're-assess', as he put it.

'Your company is pretty much back on its feet.' He gave an expansive gesture while she waited in hopeless resignation for the Dear John speech he would soon be delivering.

She was too miserable to think about getting in there first, being the first to initiate the break-up. It didn't matter anyway. The result was going to be the same.

'Your brother's disappeared back across the Atlantic and there's no need for you to continue taking an active part in the running of the company. The right people are all now in the right places to guide the ship. You can do whatever you want to do now, Sophie. Go back to university...get another job...disappear across the Atlantic to join your brother...'

Sophie's heart constricted because that was as good as telling her what he thought of her and she could have kicked herself for having been lulled into imagining that there was ever anything more to what they had.

'Or France.'

'Come again?'

'I've been thinking about it for a couple of weeks.'

Javier was at a loss as to what she was talking about. 'Thinking about...what, exactly?'

'Ollie's job is still up for grabs,' she said, thinking on her feet. 'And it's dealing with marketing, which is something I've found I rather like and I'm pretty good at.'

'You've been thinking about going to France?'

Sophie straightened. Did he think that she wasn't good enough for the job? Or did he think that she was always going to hang around until he got fed up with her, without giving any thought at all to life beyond Javier?

'Pretty much decided in favour of it,' she declared firmly. 'The house has found a buyer, as you know, who's happy to take it on and complete the renovations I've started, so there's literally nothing keeping me here. Aside, that is, from Mum. And I think she'd be overjoyed to come and visit Paris once a month. And, of course, I can easily get to Cornwall to see her.'

'So you're telling me that you've been concocting this scheme behind my back for weeks?'

'It's not *a scheme*, Javier.' The more she thought about it, the better it sounded. How else would she get over him if she didn't put as much distance as she possibly could between them? Affairs were in order here. Why not? Too much of her life had been taken up having other people make decisions on her behalf. 'I wasn't sure exactly when, but seeing that picture of you in the newspaper...'

'For God's sake!' He tried hard to temper his voice. 'What the hell does some half-baked picture in a sleazy tabloid have to do with anything?'

'It's made me realise that it's time for me to take the next step.'

'Next step? What next step?' Javier raked his fingers through his hair and wished she would settle on one topic and stick there. He felt as though the carpet had been yanked from under his feet and he didn't like the feeling. 'Of course you can't go to bloody France! It's a ludicrous idea!'

'You can do what you like with whoever you want to... er...do it with, Javier, but it's time for me to get back into the dating scene, meet someone I can share my life with.' She tried to visualise this mystery man and drew a blank. 'I feel like my youth has been on hold and now I have a great opportunity to reclaim it.'

'In France?' He laughed scornfully.

'That's right.'

'And what if you'd never seen that picture?' He stopped just short of doing the unthinkable and telling her that he'd never met that woman in his life before and had no intention of ever meeting her again. Because his head was too wrapped up with *her*.

Unthinkable!

'It was just a question of time,' Sophie said truthfully. 'And that time's come.'

'You're telling me, after the sex we've just had, that you want out…' He laughed in disbelief and Sophie wanted to smack him because it was just the sort of arrogant reaction she might have expected.

'I'm telling you that the time has come when it has to be more than just the sex. So I'm going to find my soulmate,' she added quickly.

'You're going to find your *soulmate*?' Javier hated himself for prolonging this conversation. As soon as she had started kicking up a fuss about that picture, he should have told her that it was over. He didn't need anyone thinking that they had claim to him. Never had, never would, whatever he had told her about a woman coming along who could tame him. Wasn't going to happen.

Except… *She hadn't been trying to claim him, had she?*

She'd just reasonably asked him if there was anything going on with the airhead who had been dripping off his arm at a forgettable gallery opening and, instead of laughing and dismissing the idea, he had returned to his comfort zone, dug his heels in and stubbornly refused to answer.

And it was too late now to do anything about that.

Not that it would have made any difference, considering she had been making all sorts of plans behind his back.

For the best, he decided. So he'd become lazy but in truth the itch had been scratched a long time ago.

'Fine.' He held up both hands and laughed indulgently. 'Good luck with that one, Sophie. Experience has taught me that there's no such thing. I'm surprised given your past that you haven't had the same learning curve.'

'Just the opposite.' She felt nauseous as she watched him start heading for the door. 'Life's taught me that there are rainbows around every corner.'

'How...kitsch.' He saluted her and she remained where she was as he strode out of the kitchen.

And out of her life for good.

From Spain to France.

When you thought about it, it was a hop and a skip and it made perfect sense. He had had no input in Sophie's company for over three months. He had delegated responsibility to his trusted CEO and withdrawn from the scene.

He'd done his bit. He'd taken over, done what taking apart had needed doing and had put back together what had needed putting back together. The company was actually beginning to pull itself out of the quagmire of debt it had been languishing in for the past decade, and it was doing so in record time.

It was a success story.

He'd moved on and was focused on another takeover, this time a chain of failing hotels in Asia.

He was adding to his portfolio and, furthermore, branching out into new terrain, which was invigorating. By definition, branching out into anything new on the business front was going to be invigorating!

He had also just had a good holiday with his parents and had persuaded them to let him buy them a little place on the beach in the south of France, where they could go whenever they wanted to relax. He had pulled the trump card of promising that he would join them at least three times a year there and he had meant it.

Somehow, he had learnt the value of relaxation.

So what if he hadn't been able to relax in the company of any woman since he had walked out of Sophie's life?

He'd been bloody busy, what with his latest takeover and various company expansions across Europe.

But he was in Spain.

France seemed ridiculously close…

And he really ought to check, first hand, on the progress being made in the Parisian arm of a company which, all told, he part-owned…

And, if he *was* going to go to Paris, it made sense to drop in and see what Sophie was up to.

He knew that she had been working there for the past six weeks. It was his duty, after all, to keep tabs on the company. Everything was easily accessible on the computer, from the salary she was pulling in to where she lived and the apartment she was renting near Montmartre.

He was surprised that she hadn't headed off to more fulfilling horizons, leaving the running of the company to the experts, as her brother had.

His decision was made in moments. Already heading away from the first-class desk, he walked briskly back, ignoring the simpering blushes of the young girl who had just seen him.

A ticket to Paris. Next flight. First class.

Sophie let herself into her apartment, slamming the door against the fierce cold outside.

She was dressed in several layers but, even so, the biting wind still managed to find all sorts of gaps in those layers, working their way past them and finding the soft warmth of her skin.

Her face tingled as she yanked off the woolly hat, the scarf and the gloves, walking through her studio apartment and luxuriating in the warmth.

She had been incredibly lucky to have found the apartment that she had. It was small but cosy, comfortable and conveniently located.

And Paris was, as she had expected, as beautiful as she remembered it from the last time she had been there nearly ten years ago.

She had wanted to leave her comfort zone behind and she had! She had climbed out of her box and was now living in one of the most strikingly beautiful cities on the planet. Her mother had already been to visit her once and was determined to come again just as soon as the weather improved.

All in all, there were loads of girls her age who would have given their right arm to be where she was now!

And if she happened to be spending a Friday night in, with plans to curl up with her tablet in her flannel pyjamas and bedroom socks, then it was simply because it was just so cold!

When spring came, she would be out there, jumping right into that dating scene, as she had promised herself she would do before she had left England.

For the moment, she was perfectly happy just chilling.

And expecting no one to come calling because, although she had been out a few times with some of the other employees in the small arm of the company in Paris, she had not thus far met anyone who might just drop by on a Friday evening to see what she was up to.

That would come in time.

Probably in spring.

So when the doorbell went, she didn't budge. She just assumed it was someone selling something and she wasn't interested.

She gritted her teeth as the buzzer kept sounding and eventually abandoned all pretence of Zen calm as she stormed to the door and pulled it open, ready to give her uninvited caller a piece of her mind.

Javier had kept his finger on the buzzer. She was in. She had a basement apartment and he could see lights on behind the drawn curtains. He wondered whether she knew that basement apartments were at the highest risk of being burgled.

Since leaving Spain, he hadn't once questioned his decision to spring this visit on her, but now that he was here, now that he could hear the soft pad of footsteps, he felt his stomach clench with an uncustomary attack of nerves.

He straightened as she opened the door and for a few seconds something bewildering seemed to happen to him: he lost the ability to think.

'You're here...' he said inanely. Her long hair was swept over one narrow shoulder and she was wearing thick flannel bottoms and a long-sleeved thermal vest. And no bra. 'Do you always just open your door to strangers?' he continued gruffly, barely knowing where this unimaginative line of conversation was coming from.

'Javier!' Temporarily deprived of speech, Sophie could just blink at him, owl-like.

She'd pretended that she'd moved on. She was in Paris, she was enjoying her job, meeting new people...

How could she *not* have moved on? Hadn't that been the whole point of Paris?

But seeing him here, lounging against the door frame in a pair of faded black jeans and a black jumper, with his coat slung over his shoulder...

She was still in the same place she'd been when she'd watched him stroll out of her flat without a backwards glance.

How dared he just show up like this and scupper all her chances of moving on?

'What are you doing here? And how the heck did you find out where I live!'

'Computers are wonderful things. You'd be shocked at the amount of information they can divulge. Especially considering you work for a company I part-own…' Javier planted himself solidly in front of her. He hadn't given much thought to what sort of welcome he was likely to receive but a hostile one hadn't really crossed his mind.

Since when were women hostile towards him?

But since when was she just *any woman*?

She never had been and she never would be and, just like that, he suddenly felt sick. Sick and vulnerable in a way he had never felt before. Every signpost that had ever guided him, every tenet he had ever held dear, disappeared and he was left groping in the dark, feeling his way towards a realisation that had always been there at the back of his mind.

'Go away. I don't want to see you.'

Javier placed his hand on the door, preventing her from shutting it in his face. 'I've come…'

'For what?' Sophie mocked.

'I…'

Sophie opened her mouth and shut it because she didn't know what was going on. He looked unsettled. Confused. *Unsure.* Since when had Javier *ever* looked unsure?

'Are you all right?' she asked waspishly, relenting just enough to let him slip inside the apartment, but then shutting the door and leaning against it with her hands behind her back.

'No,' Javier said abruptly, looking away and then staring at her.

'What are you saying?' Sophie blanched. 'Are you…?

Are you ill...?' Fear and panic gripped her in equal measure.

'Can we go sit somewhere?'

'Tell me what's wrong!' She was at his side in seconds, her small hand on his forearm, her eyes pleading for reassurance that he was okay because, whatever he was, he wasn't himself and that was scaring her half to death.

And if he saw that, she didn't care.

'I've missed you.' The words slipped out before Javier could stop them in their tracks. He had put everything on the line and he felt sick. He wondered why he hadn't thought to down a bottle of whisky before embarking on this trip.

'You've missed me?' Sophie squeaked.

'You asked what was wrong with me,' Javier threw at her accusingly.

'Is missing me wrong?' Something inside her burst and she wanted to laugh and cry at the same time. She had to tell herself that no mention had been made of love, and if he was missing her, then chances were that he was missing her body. Which was something else entirely.

She walked on wooden legs into the sitting room, where she had been watching telly on her tablet, and watched as he sat down, briefly glancing around him before settling those dark, dark eyes on her.

'Missing...' he sat down, arms loosely resting on his thighs, his body leaning towards hers '...isn't something I've ever done.'

'Then it's a good thing,'

'I couldn't focus,' he admitted heavily. Now that he had started down this road, he had no alternative but to continue, although she hadn't chucked him out and that was a good thing. 'I couldn't sleep. You got into my head and I couldn't get you out of it.'

Sophie's heart was singing. She didn't want to speak. What if she broke the spell?

'I wanted you, you know...' He looked at her gravely. 'I don't think I ever really stopped wanting you, and when your brother showed up at my office, I figured I'd been handed the perfect way of putting that want to bed for good. Literally. I was going to just...go down the simple "exchange for favours" road. Cash for a little fun between the sheets, but then I decided that I wanted more than that...I didn't want a reluctant lover motivated for the wrong reasons.'

'You're assuming I would have given you your fun between the sheets because I needed money!' But she couldn't fire herself up to anger because her heart was still singing. She itched to touch him but first she wanted to talk.

'I'm arrogant.' He shot her a crooked smile. 'As you've told me a million times. I thought that it would be a one-night stand, simple as that, and then when you told me that you were a virgin...that the ex was gay...'

'Um, about that...'

'Sleeping with you that first time was...mind-blowing.'

'Er...'

'And it wasn't just because I'd never slept with a virgin before. It was because that person was *you*...'

'I should tell you something.' Sophie took a deep breath and looked him squarely in the eyes. So what if he hadn't said anything about love? He had opened up and she could tell from the way he was groping with his words that this was a first for him. A big deal. Her turn. It would be a bigger deal, but so be it.

'He wasn't gay. Roger wasn't gay. The opposite. He was one hundred percent straight as an arrow.'

Javier stared at her, for once in his life lost for words. 'You said...'

'No, Javier, *you* said.' She sighed wearily and sifted her fingers through her hair. 'It's such a long story and I'm sorry if I just let you think that Roger...'

Javier just continued staring, his agile brain trying and failing to make connections. 'Tell me from the beginning,' he said slowly.

'And you won't interrupt?'

'I promise nothing.'

Sophie half-smiled because why would this proud, stubborn, utterly adorable man ever take orders from anyone, even if it happened to be a very simple order?

'Okay...' Javier half-smiled back and a warm feeling spread through her 'I as good as half promise.'

'I'd been sort of going out with Roger by the time I went to university,' Sophie began, staring back into the past and not flinching away from it as she always did. 'I honestly don't know why except he'd been around for ever and it was something I just drifted into. It was cosy. We mixed in the same circles, had the same friends. His mother died when he was little and he and his father spent a good deal of time at our place. When his father died, he became more or less a fixture. He was crazy about me...' she said that without a trace of vanity '...and I think both my parents just assumed that we would end up getting married. Then I left home to go to university and everything just imploded.'

'Tell me,' Javier urged, leaning forward.

'Roger didn't want me to go to university. He was three years older and hadn't gone. He'd done an apprenticeship and gone straight into work at a local company. His parents had been very well off and he'd inherited everything as an only child, so there was no need for him to do anything high-powered and, in truth, he wasn't all that bright.'

She sighed. 'He wanted to have fun and have a wife

to cater to him. But as soon as I went to university it hit me that I didn't love him. I liked him well enough but not enough to ever, ever consider marrying. I told him that but he wasn't happy and then I met you and…I stopped caring whether he was happy or not. I stopped caring about anyone or anything but you.'

'And yet you ended up marrying him. Doesn't make sense.'

'You promised you wouldn't interrupt.'

Javier raised both his hands in agreement. In truth, he was too intrigued by this tale to ask too many questions.

'My father summoned me back home,' she said. 'I went immediately. I knew it had to be important and I was worried that it was Mum. Her health hadn't been good and we were all worried for her. I never expected to be told that the family was facing bankruptcy.' She took a deep breath, eyes clouded. 'Suddenly it was like every bad thing that could happen at once had happened. Not only was the company on the verge of collapse but my father admitted that he had been ill—cancer—and it was terminal. Roger was presented to me as the only solution, given the circumstances.'

'Why didn't you come to me?'

'I wanted to but it was hard enough just fighting your corner without presenting you to my parents. They wanted nothing to do with you. They said that Roger would bring much-needed money to the table, money that would revitalise the company and drag it out of the red. Dad was worried sick that he wouldn't be around long enough to do anything about saving the company. He was broken with guilt that he had allowed things to go down the pan but I think his own personal worries, which he had kept to himself, must have been enormous.

'They told me that what I felt for you was…infatuation. That I was young and bowled over by someone who would be no good for me in the long run. You weren't in my social class and you were a foreigner. Those two things would have been enough to condemn you but, had it not been for what was happening in the company, I don't think they would have dreamt of forcing my hand.'

'But they persuaded you that marrying Roger was vital to keep the family business afloat,' Javier recapped slowly. 'And, with your father facing death, there wasn't time for long debates…'

'I still wouldn't have,' Sophie whispered. 'I was so head over heels in love with you, and I told Roger that. Pleaded with him to see it from my point of view. I knew that if he backed me up, Mum and Dad might lay off the whole convenient marriage thing, but of course he didn't back me up. He was red with anger and jealousy. He stormed off. At the time, he had a little red sports car…'

'He crashed, didn't he?'

Sophie nodded and Javier picked up the story.

'And you felt…guilty.'

'Yes. I did. Especially because it was a very bad accident. Roger was in hospital for nearly two months and, by the time he was ready to come out, I had resigned myself to doing what had to be done. I'd even come to half believe that perhaps Mum and Dad were right—perhaps what I felt for you was a flash in the pan, whereas my relationship with Roger had the weight of shared history, which would prove a lot more powerful in the long run.'

Javier was seeing what life must have been like for her. In a matter of a few disastrous weeks, her entire future and a lot of her past had been changed for ever. She hadn't used him. He had simply been a casualty of events that had been far too powerful for her to do anything about but bow her head and follow the path she had been instructed to follow.

Not old enough to know her own mind, and too attached to her parents to rebel, she had simply obeyed them.

'But it didn't go according to plan...' he encouraged.

'How did you guess? It was a disaster from the very start. We married but the accident had changed Roger. Maybe, like me, he went into it thinking that we could give it a shot, but there was too much water under the bridge. And there had been after-effects from the accident. He very quickly became addicted to painkillers. He used to play a lot of football but he no longer could. Our marriage became a battleground. He blamed me, and the more he blamed me, the guiltier I felt. He had affairs, which he proudly told me about. He wreaked havoc with the company. He gambled. There was nothing I could do because he could quickly turn violent. By the time he died, I'd... I'd grown up for ever.'

Javier looked at her long and hard. 'Why did you let me believe that he was gay?'

'Because...' She took a deep breath. 'I thought that if you knew the whole story, you would know how much you meant to me then and you would quickly work out how much you mean to me now.' She laughed sadly. 'And, besides that, I've always felt ashamed—ashamed that I let myself be persuaded into doing something I really didn't want to do.'

'When you say that I *mean something to you now*...'

'I know what this is for you, Javier. You believed that I ran out on you, and when you had the chance, you figured you would take what should have been yours all those years ago.'

Javier had the grace to flush. What else could he do?

'And, for a while, I kidded myself that that was what it was for me too. I'd dreamt about you for seven years and

I'd been given the chance to turn those dreams into reality, except for me it was much more than that. You won't want to hear this but I'll tell you anyway. I never stopped loving you. You were the real thing, Javier. You'll always be the main event in my life.'

'Sophie…' He closed the distance between them but only so that he could sit closer to her, close enough to thread his fingers through hers. His throat ached. 'I've missed you so much. I thought I could walk away, just like I thought that sleeping with you would be a simple solution to sorting out the problem of you being on my mind all the time through the years. There, at the back of my mind like a ghost that refused to go away. You'd dumped me and married someone else. It didn't matter how many times I told myself that I was well rid of someone who used me for a bit of fun until she got her head together and realised that the person she really wanted to be with wasn't me…I still couldn't forget you.'

Sophie thought that this was one of those conversations she never wanted to end. She just wanted to keep repeating it on a loop, over and over and over.

'We slept together, Sophie, and just like that my life changed. Not having you in it was unthinkable. I didn't even register that consciously until you presented me with that picture and I suddenly realised that I had succumbed to all the things I'd thought I'd ruled out of my life. You'd domesticated me to the point where I didn't want to be anywhere unless you were there, and I hadn't even realised it. I took fright, Soph. I suddenly felt the walls closing in and I reacted on instinct and scarpered.'

'And now that you're back…' She had to say this. 'I can't have a relationship with you, Javier. I can't go back to living from one day to the next, not knowing whether you'll decide that you're bored and that you have to take off.'

'How could I ever get bored with you, Sophie?' He lightly touched her cheek with his fingers and realised that he was trembling. 'And how can you not see what I need to tell you? I don't just want you, but I need you. I can't live without you, Sophie. I fell in love with you all those years ago and, yes, you're the main event in my life as well and always will be. Why do you think I came here? I came because *I had to*. I just couldn't stand not being with you any longer.'

Sophie flung herself at him and he caught her in his arms, laughing because the chair very nearly toppled over.

'So, will you marry me?' he whispered into her hair and she pulled back, smiling, wanting to laugh and shout all at the same time.

'You mean it?'

'With every drop of blood that flows through my veins. Let me show you how great marriage can be.' He laughed. 'I never thought I'd hear myself say that.'

'Nor did I.' She kissed him softly and drew back. 'And now that you have, I won't allow you to take it back, so, yes, my darling. I'll marry you…'

* * * * *

A MARRIAGE FIT
FOR A SINNER

MAYA BLAKE

CHAPTER ONE

'ONE PLATINUM CHRONOGRAPH WATCH. A pair of diamond-studded cufflinks. Gold signet ring. Six hundred and twenty-five pounds cash, and…Obsidian Privilege Card. Right, I think that's everything, sir. Sign here to confirm return of your property.'

Zaccheo Giordano didn't react to the warden's sneer as he scrawled on the barely legible form. Nor did he react to the resentful envy in the man's eyes when his gaze drifted to where the sleek silver limousine waited beyond three sets of barbed wire.

Romeo Brunetti, Zaccheo's second-in-command and the only person he would consider draping the term *friend* upon, stood beside the car, brooding and unsmiling, totally unruffled by the armed guard at the gate or the bleak South East England surroundings.

Had Zaccheo been in an accommodating mood, he'd have cracked a smile.

But he wasn't in an accommodating mood. He hadn't been for a very long time. Fourteen months, two weeks, four days and nine hours to be exact. Zaccheo was positive he could count down to the last second if required.

No one would require it of him, of course. He'd served his time. With three and a half months knocked off his eighteen-month sentence *for good behaviour.*

The rage fused into his DNA bubbled beneath his skin. He showed no outward sign of it as he pocketed his belongings. The three-piece Savile Row suit he'd entered prison in stank of decay and misery, but Zaccheo didn't care.

He'd never been a slave to material comforts. His need for validation went far deeper. The need to elevate himself into a better place had been a soul-deep pursuit from the moment he was old enough to recognise the reality of the life he'd been born into. A life that had been a never-ending whirlpool of humiliation, violence and greed. A life that had seen his father debased and dead at thirty-five.

Memories tumbled like dominoes as he walked down the harshly lit corridor to freedom. He willed the overwhelming sense of injustice that had festered for long, harrowing months not to explode from his pores.

The doors clanged shut behind him.

Zaccheo froze, then took his first lungful of free air with fists clenched and eyes shut. He absorbed the sound of birds chirping in the late-winter morning sun, listened to the distant rumble of the motorway as he'd done many nights from his prison cell.

Opening his eyes, he headed towards the fifteen-foot gate. A minute later, he was outside.

'Zaccheo, it's good to see you again,' Romeo said gravely, his eyes narrowing as he took him in.

Zaccheo knew he looked a sight. He hadn't bothered with a razor blade or a barber's clippers in the last three months and he'd barely eaten once he'd unearthed the truth behind his incarceration. But he'd spent a lot of time in the prison gym. It'd been that or go mad with the clawing hunger for retribution.

He shrugged off his friend's concern and moved to the open door.

'Did you bring what I asked for?' he asked.

Romeo nodded. '*Sì*. All three files are on the laptop.'

Zaccheo slid onto the plush leather seat. Romeo slid in next to him and poured them two glasses of Italian-made cognac.

'*Salute,*' Romeo muttered.

Zaccheo took the drink without responding, threw back the amber liquid and allowed the scent of power and affluence—the tools he'd need for his plan to succeed—to wash over him.

As the low hum of the luxury engine whisked him away from the place he'd been forced to call home for over a year, Zaccheo reached for the laptop.

Icy rage trembled through his fingers as the Giordano Worldwide Inc. logo flickered to life. His life's work, almost decimated through another's greed and lust for power. It was only with Romeo's help that GWI hadn't gone under in the months after Zaccheo had been sent to prison for a crime he didn't commit. He drew quiet satisfaction that not only had GWI survived—thanks to Romeo—it had thrived.

But his personal reputation had not.

He was out now. Free to bring those culpable to justice. He didn't plan on resting until every last person responsible for attempting to destroy his life paid with the destruction of theirs.

Shaking out his hand to rid it of its tremble, he hit the Open key.

The information was thorough although Zaccheo knew most of its contents. For three months he'd checked and double-checked his sources, made sure every detail was nailed down tight.

He exhaled at the first picture that filled his screen.

Oscar Pennington III. Distant relative to the royal family. Etonian. Old, if spent, money. Very much part of the establishment. Greedy. Indiscriminate. His waning property portfolio had received a much-needed injection of capital exactly fourteen months and two weeks ago when he'd become sole owner of London's most talked about building—The Spire.

Zaccheo swallowed the savage growl that rumbled from his soul. Icily calm, he flicked through pages of Pennington celebrating his revived success with galas, lavish dinner parties and polo tournaments thrown about like confetti. One picture showed him laughing with one of his two children.

Sophie Pennington. Private education all the way to finishing school. Classically beautiful. Ball-breaker. She'd proven beyond a doubt that she had every intention of becoming Oscar's carbon copy.

Grimly, he closed her file and moved to the last one.

Eva Pennington.

This time the growl couldn't be contained. Nor could he stem the renewed shaking in his hand as he clicked her file.

Caramel-blonde hair tumbled down her shoulders in thick, wild waves. Dark eyebrows and lashes framed moss-green eyes, accentuated dramatically with black eyeliner. Those eyes had gripped his attention with more force than he'd been comfortable with the first time he'd looked into them. As had the full, bow-shaped lips currently curved in a smouldering smile. His screen displayed a head-and-shoulders shot, but the rest of Eva Pennington's body was imprinted indelibly on Zaccheo's mind. He didn't struggle to recall the petite, curvy shape, or that she forced herself to wear heels even though she hated them, in order to make herself taller.

He certainly didn't struggle to recall her individual atrocity. He'd lain in his prison bed condemning himself for being astounded by her singular betrayal, when the failings of both his parents and his dealings with the *establishment* should've taught him better. He'd prided himself on reading between the lines to spot schemers and gold-diggers ten miles away. Yet he'd been fooled.

The time he'd wasted on useless bitterness was the most excruciating of all; time he would gladly claw back if he could.

Firming his lips, he clicked through the pages, running through her life for the past year and a half. At the final page, he froze.

'How new is this last information?'

'I added that to the file yesterday. I thought you'd want to know,' Romeo replied.

Zaccheo stared at the newspaper clipping, shock waves rolling through him. *'Sì, grazie...'*

'Do you wish to return to the Esher estate or the penthouse?' Romeo asked.

Zaccheo read the announcement again, taking in pertinent details. Pennington Manor. Eight o'clock. Three hundred guests. Followed by an intimate family dinner on Sunday at The Spire.

The Spire...the building that should've been Zaccheo's greatest achievement.

'The estate,' he replied. It was closer.

He closed the file as Romeo instructed the driver.

Relaxing against the headrest, Zaccheo tried to let the hum of the engine soothe him. But it was no use. He was far from calm.

He'd have to alter his plan. Not that it mattered too much in the long run.

A chain is only as strong as its weakest link. While all three Penningtons had colluded in his incarceration, this new information demanded he use a different tactic, one he'd first contemplated and abandoned. Either way, Zaccheo didn't plan to rest until all of them were stripped of what they cherished most—their wealth and affluence.

He'd intended to wait a day or two to ensure he had Oscar Pennington where he wanted him before he struck. That plan was no longer viable.

Bringing down the family who'd framed him for criminal negligence couldn't wait till Monday.

His first order of business would be tackled *tonight*.

Starting with the youngest member of the family—Eva Pennington.

His ex-fiancée.

Eva Pennington stared at the dress in her sister's hand. 'Seriously? There's no way I'm wearing that. Why didn't you tell me the clothes I left behind had been given away?'

'Because you said you didn't want them when you moved out. Besides, they were old and out of fashion. I had *this* couriered from New York this morning. It's the latest couture and on loan to us for twenty-four hours,' Sophie replied.

Eva pursed her lips. 'I don't care if it was woven by ten thousand silk worms. I'm not wearing a dress that makes me look like a gold-digger *and* a slut. And considering the state of our finances, I'd have thought you'd be more careful what you splashed money on.' She couldn't stem her bewilderment as to why Sophie and her father blithely ignored the fact that money was extremely tight.

Sophie huffed. 'This is a one-of-a-kind dress, and, unless I'm mistaken, it's the kind of dress your future husband likes his women to wear. Anyway, you'll be out of it in less than four hours, once the right photographs have been taken, and the party's over.'

Eva gritted her teeth. 'Stop trying to manage me, Sophie. You're forgetting who pulled this bailout together. If I hadn't come to an agreement with Harry, we'd have been sunk come next week. As to what he likes his women to wear, if you'd bothered to speak to me first I'd have saved you the trouble of going to unnecessary expense. I dress for myself and no one else.'

'Speak to you first? When you and Father neglected to afford me the same courtesy before you hatched this plan behind my back?' Sophie griped.

Eva's heart twisted at the blatant jealousy in her sister's voice.

As if it weren't enough that the decision she'd spent the past two weeks agonising over still made her insides clench in horror. It didn't matter that the man she'd agreed to marry was her friend and she was helping him as much as he was helping her. Marriage was a step she'd rather not have taken.

It was clear, however, her sister didn't see it that way. Sophie's escalating discontentment at any relationship Eva tried to forge with their father was part of the reason Eva had moved out of Pennington Manor. Not that their father was an easy man to live with.

For as long as she could remember, Sophie had been possessive of their father's attention. While their mother had been alive, it'd been bearable and easier to accept that Sophie was their father's preferred child, while Eva was her mother's, despite wanting to be loved equally by both parents.

After their mother's death, every interaction Eva had tried to have with their father had been met with bristling confrontation from Sophie, and indifference from their father.

But, irrational as it was, it didn't stop Eva from trying to reason with the sister she'd once looked up to.

'We didn't go behind your back. You were away on a business trip—'

'Trying to use the business degree that doesn't seem to mean anything any more. Not when *you* can swoop in after three years of performing tired ballads in seedy pubs to save the day,' Sophie interjected harshly.

Eva hung on to her temper by a thread, but pain stung deep at the blithe dismissal of her passion. 'You know I resigned from Penningtons because Father only hired me so I could attract a suitable husband. And just because my dreams don't coincide with yours—'

'That's just it. You're twenty-four and still *dreaming*. The rest of us don't have that luxury. And we certainly don't land on our feet by clicking our fingers and having a millionaire solve all our problems.'

'Harry is saving *all of us*. And you really think I've *landed on my feet* by getting engaged for the second time in two years?' Eva asked.

Sophie dropped the offensive dress on Eva's bed. 'To everyone who matters, this is your first engagement. The other one barely lasted five minutes. Hardly anyone knows it happened.'

Hurt-laced anger swirled through her veins. '*I* know it happened.'

'If my opinion matters around here any more, then I suggest you don't broadcast it. It's a subject best left in the past, just like the man it involved.'

Pain stung deeper. 'I can't pretend it didn't happen because of what occurred afterwards.'

'The last thing we need right now is any hint of scandal. And I don't know why you're blaming Father for what happened when you should be thanking him for extricating you from that man before it was too late,' Sophie defended heatedly.

That man.

Zaccheo Giordano.

Eva wasn't sure whether the ache lodged beneath her ribs came from thinking about him or from the reminder of how gullible she'd been to think he was any different from every other man who'd crossed her path.

She relaxed her fists when they balled again.

This was why she preferred her life away from their family home deep in the heart of Surrey.

It was why her waitress colleagues knew her as Eva Penn, a hostess at Siren, the London nightclub where she also sang part-time, instead of Lady Eva Pennington, daughter of Lord Pennington.

Her relationship with her father had always been difficult, but she'd never thought she'd lose her sister so completely, too.

She cleared her throat. 'Sophie, this agreement with Harry wasn't supposed to undermine anything you were doing with Father to save Penningtons. There's no need to be upset or jealous. I'm not trying to take your place—'

'Jealous! Don't be ridiculous,' Sophie sneered, although the trace of panic in her voice made Eva's heart break. 'And you could never take my place. I'm Father's right hand, whereas you...you're nothing but—' She stopped herself and, after a few seconds, stuck her nose in the air. 'Our guests are arriving shortly. Please don't be late to your own engagement party.'

Eva swallowed down her sorrow. 'I've no intention of being late. But neither do I have any intention of wearing a dress that has less material than thread holding it together.'

She strode to the giant George III armoire opposite the bed, even though her earlier inspection had shown less than a fraction of the items she'd left behind when she'd moved out on her twenty-first birthday.

These days she was content with her hostess's uniform when she was working or lounging in jeans and sweaters while she wrote her music on her days off. Haute couture, spa days and primping herself beautiful in order to please anyone were part of a past she'd happily left behind.

Unfortunately this time there'd been no escaping. Not when she alone had been able to find the solution to saving her family.

She tried in vain to squash the rising memories being back at Pennington Manor threatened to resurrect.

Zaccheo was in her past, a mistake that should never have happened. A reminder that ignoring a lesson learned only led to further heartache.

She sighed in relief when her hand closed on a silk wrap. The red dress would be far too revealing, a true spectacle for the three hundred guests her father had invited to gawp at. But at least the wrap would provide a little much-needed cover.

Glancing at the dress again, she shuddered.

She'd rather be anywhere but here, participating in this sham. But then hadn't her whole life been a sham? From parents who'd been publicly hailed as the couple to envy, but who'd fought bitterly in private until tragedy had struck in the form of her mother's cancer, to the lavish parties and expensive holidays that her father had secretly been borrowing money for, the Penningtons had been one giant sham for as long as Eva could remember.

Zaccheo's entry into their lives had only escalated her father's behaviour.

No, she refused to think about Zaccheo. He belonged to a chapter of her life that was firmly sealed. Tonight was about Harry Fairfield, her family's saviour, and her soon-to-be fiancé.

It was also about her father's health.

For that reason alone, she tried again with Sophie.

'For Father's sake, I want tonight to go smoothly, so can we try to get along?'

Sophie stiffened. 'If you're talking about Father's hospitalisation two weeks ago, I haven't forgotten.'

Watching her father struggle to breathe with what the doctors had termed a cardiac event had terrified Eva. It'd been the catalyst that had forced her to accept Harry's proposition.

'He's okay today, isn't he?' Despite her bitterness at her family's treatment of her, she couldn't help her concern for her remaining parent. Nor could she erase the secret yearning that the different version of the father she'd connected with very briefly after her mother's death, the one who wasn't an excess-loving megalomaniac who treated her as if she was an irritating inconvenience, hadn't been a figment of her imagination.

'He will be, once we get rid of the creditors threatening us with bankruptcy.'

Eva exhaled. There was no backing out; no secretly hoping that some other solution would present itself and save her from the sacrifice she was making.

All avenues had been thoroughly explored—Eva had demanded to see the Pennington books herself and spent a day with the company's accountants to verify that they were indeed in dire straits. Her father's rash acquisition of The Spire had stretched the company to breaking point. Harry Fairfield was their last hope.

She unzipped the red dress, resisting the urge to crush it into a wrinkled pulp.

'Do you need help?' Sophie asked, although Eva sensed the offer wasn't altruistic.

'No, I can manage.'

The same way she'd managed after her mother's death; through her father's rejection and Sophie's increasingly unreasonable behaviour; through the heartbreak of finding out about Zaccheo's betrayal.

Sophie nodded briskly. 'I'll see you downstairs, then.'

Eva slipped on the dress, avoiding another look in the mirror when the first glimpse showed what she'd feared most. Her every curve was accentuated, with large swathes of flesh exposed. With shaky fingers she applied her lipstick and slipped her feet into matching platform heels.

Slipping the gold and red wrap around her shoulders, she finally glanced at her image.

Chin up, girl. It's show time.

Eva wished the manageress of Siren were uttering the words, as she did every time before Eva stepped onto the stage.

Unfortunately, she wasn't at Siren. She'd promised to marry a man she didn't love, for the sake of saving her precious family name.

No amount of pep talk could stem the roaring agitation flooding her veins.

CHAPTER TWO

THE EVENT PLANNERS had outdone themselves. Potted palms, decorative screens and subdued lighting had been strategically placed around the main halls of Pennington Manor to hide the peeling plaster, chipped wood panelling and torn Aubusson rugs that funds could no longer stretch to rectify.

Eva sipped the champagne she'd been nursing for the last two hours and willed time to move faster. Technically she couldn't throw any guest out, but *Eight to Midnight* was the time the costly invitations had stated the party would last. She needed something to focus on or risk sliding into madness.

Gritting her teeth, she smiled as yet another guest demanded to see her engagement ring. The monstrous pink diamond's sole purpose was to demonstrate the Fairfields' wealth. Its alien weight dragged her hand down, hammering home the irrefutable point that she'd sold herself for her pedigree.

Her father's booming voice interrupted her maudlin thoughts. Surrounded by a group of influential politicians who hung onto his every word, Oscar Pennington was in his element.

Thickset but tall enough to hide the excess weight he carried, her father cut a commanding figure despite his recent spell in hospital. His stint in the army three decades ago had lent him a ruthless edge, cleverly counteracted by his natural charm. The combination made him enigmatic enough to attract attention when he walked into a room.

But not even that charisma had saved him from economic devastation four years ago.

With that coming close on the heels of her mother's illness, their social and economic circles had dwindled to nothing almost overnight, with her father desperately scrambling to hold things together.

End result—his association with Zaccheo Giordano.

Eva frowned, bewildered that her thoughts had circled back to the man she'd pushed to the dark recesses of her mind. A man she'd last seen being led away in handcuffs—

'There you are. I've been looking for you everywhere.'

Eva started, then berated herself for feeling guilty. Guilt belonged to those who'd committed crimes, who lied about their true motives.

Enough!

She smiled at Harry.

Her old university friend—a brilliant tech genius—had gone off the rails when he'd achieved fame and wealth straight out of university. Now a multimillionaire with enough money to bail out Penningtons, he represented her family's last hope.

'Well, you found me,' she said.

He was a few inches taller than her five feet four; she didn't have to look up too far to meet his twinkling soft brown eyes.

'Indeed. Are you okay?' he asked, his gaze reflecting concern.

'I'm fine,' she responded breezily.

He looked unconvinced. Harry was one of the few people who knew about her broken engagement to Zaccheo. He'd seen beneath her false smiles and assurances that she could handle a marriage of convenience and asked her point-blank if her past with Zaccheo Giordano would be a problem. Her swift *no* seemed to have satisfied him.

Now he looked unsure.

'Harry, don't fret. I can do this,' she insisted, despite the hollowness in her stomach.

He studied her solemnly, then called over a waiter and exchanged his empty champagne glass for a full one. 'If you say so, but I need advanced warning if this gets too weird for you, okay? My parents will have a fit if they read about me in the papers this side of Christmas.'

She nodded gratefully, then frowned. 'I thought you were going to take it easy tonight?' She indicated his glass.

'Gosh, you already sound like a wife.' He sniggered. 'Leave off, sweetness, the parents have already given me an earful.'

Having met his parents a week ago, Eva could imagine the exchange.

'Remember why *you're* doing this. Do you want to derail the PR campaign to clean up your image before it's even begun?'

While Harry couldn't care less about his social standing, his parents were voracious in their hunger for prestige and a pedigree to hang their name on. Only the threat to Harry's business dealings had finally forced him to address his reckless playboy image.

He took her arm and tilted his sand-coloured head affably towards hers. 'I promise to be on my best behaviour. Now that the tedious toasts have been made and we're officially engaged, it's time for the best part of the evening. The fireworks!'

Eva set her champagne glass down and stepped out of the dining-room alcove that had been her sanctuary throughout her childhood. 'Isn't that supposed to be a surprise?'

Harry winked. 'It is, but, since we've fooled everyone into thinking we're *madly* in love, faking our surprise should be easy.'

She smiled. 'I won't tell if you don't.'

Harry laid a hand across his heart. 'Thank you, my fair Lady Pennington.'

The reminder of why this whole sham engagement was happening slid like a knife between her ribs. Numbing herself to the pain, she walked out onto the terrace that overlooked the manor's multi-acre garden.

The gardens had once held large koi ponds, a giant summer house and an elaborate maze, but the prohibitive cost of the grounds' upkeep had led to the landscape being levelled and replaced with rolling carpet grass.

A smattering of applause greeted their arrival and Eva's gaze drifted over the guests to where Sophie, her father and Harry's parents stood watching them.

She caught her father's eye, and her stomach knotted.

While part of her was pleased that she'd found a solution to their family problems, she couldn't help but feel that nothing she did would ever bring her closer to her sister or father.

Her father might have accepted her help with the bailout from Harry, but his displeasure at her chosen profession was yet another bone of contention between them. One she'd made clear she wouldn't back down on.

Turning away, she fixed her smile in place and exclaimed appropriately when the first elaborate firework display burst into the sky.

'So…my parents want us to live together,' Harry whispered in her ear.

'What?'

He laughed. 'Don't worry, I convinced them you hate my bachelor pad so we need to find a place that's *ours* rather than mine.'

Relief poured through her. 'Thank you.'

He brushed a hand down her cheek. 'You're welcome. But I deserve a reward for my sacrifice,' he said with a smile. 'How about dinner on Monday?'

'As long as it's not a paparazzi-stalked spectacle of a restaurant, you're on.'

'Great. It's a date.' He kissed her knuckles, much to the delight of the guests, who thought they were witnessing a true love match.

Eva allowed herself to relax. She might find what they were doing distasteful, but she was grateful that Harry's visit to Siren three weeks ago had ended up with him bailing her out, and not a calculating stranger.

'That dress is a knockout on you, by the way.'

She grimaced. 'It wasn't my first choice, but thank you.'

The next series of firework displays should've quieted the guests, yet murmurs around her grew.

'*Omigod*, whoever it is must have a death wish!' someone exclaimed.

Harry's eyes narrowed. 'I think we may have a last-minute guest.'

Eva looked around and saw puzzled gazes fixed at a point in the sky as the faint *thwopping* sound grew louder. Another set of fireworks went off, illuminating the looming object.

She frowned. 'Is that...?'

'A helicopter heading straight for the middle of the fireworks display? Yep. I guess the organisers decided to add another surprise to the party.'

'I don't think that's part of the entertainment,' Eva shouted to be heard over the descending aircraft.

Her heart slammed into her throat as a particularly elaborate firework erupted precariously close to the black-and-red chopper.

'Hell, if this is a stunt, I take my hat off to the pilot. It takes iron balls to fly into danger like that.' Harry chuckled.

The helicopter drew closer. Mesmerised, Eva watched it settle in the middle of the garden, her attention riveted to its single occupant.

The garden lights had been turned off to showcase the fireworks to maximum effect so she couldn't see who their unexpected guest was. Nevertheless, an ominous shiver chased up her spine.

She heard urgent shouts for the pyrotechnician to halt the display, but another rocket fizzed past the rotating blades.

A hush fell over the crowd as the helicopter door opened. A figure stepped out, clad from head to toe in black. As another blaze of colour filled the sky his body was thrown into relief.

Eva tensed as if she'd been shot with a stun gun.

It couldn't be...

He was behind bars, atoning for his ruthless greed. Eva squashed the sting of guilt that accompanied the thought.

Zaccheo Giordano and men of his ilk arrogantly believed they were above the law. They didn't deserve her sympathy, or the disloyal thought that he alone had paid the price when, by association, her father should've borne some of the blame. Justice ensured they went to jail and stayed there for the duration of their term. They weren't released early.

They certainly didn't land in the middle of a firework display at a private party as if they owned the land they walked on.

The spectacle unfolding before her stated differently.

Lights flickered on. Eva tracked the figure striding imperiously across the grass and up the wide steps.

Reaching the terrace, he paused and buttoned his single-breasted tuxedo.

'Oh, God,' she whispered.

'Wait...you know this bloke?' Harry asked, his tone for once serious.

Eva wanted to deny the man who now stood, easily head and shoulders above the nearest guests, his fierce, unwavering gaze pinned on her.

She didn't know whether to attribute the crackling electricity to his appearance or the look in his eyes. Both were viscerally menacing to the point of brutality.

The Zaccheo Giordano she'd had the misfortune of briefly tangling with before his incarceration had kept his hair trimmed short and his face clean-shaven.

This man had a full beard and his hair flowed over his shoulders in an unruly sea of thick jet waves. Eva swallowed at the pronounced difference in him. The sleek, almost gaunt man she'd known was gone. In his place breathed a Neanderthal with broader shoulders, thicker arms and a denser chest moulded by his black silk shirt. Equally dark trousers hugged lean hips and sturdy thighs to fall in a precise inch above expensive handmade shoes. But nothing of his attire disguised the aura he emanated.

Uncivilised. Explosively masculine. Lethal.

Danger vibrated from him like striations on baking asphalt. It flowed over the guests, who jostled each other for a better look at the impromptu visitor.

'Eva?' Harry's puzzled query echoed through her dazed consciousness.

Zaccheo released her from his deadly stare. His eyes flicked to the arm tucked into Harry's before he turned away. The breath exploded from her lungs. Sensing Harry about to ask another question, she nodded.

'Yes. That's Zaccheo.'

Her eyes followed Zaccheo as he turned towards her family.

Oscar's look of anger was laced with a heavy dose of apprehension. Sophie looked plain stunned.

Eva watched the man she'd hoped to never see again cup his hands behind his back and stroll towards her father. Anyone would've been foolish to think that stance indicated supplication. If anything, its severe mockery made Eva want to do the unthinkable and burst out laughing.

She would've, had she not been mired in deep dread at what Zaccheo's presence meant.

'Your ex?' Harry pressed.

She nodded numbly.

'Then we should say hello.'

Harry tugged on her arm and she realised too late what he meant.

'No. Wait!' she whispered fiercely.

But he was either too drunk or genuinely oblivious to the vortex of danger he was headed for to pay attention. The tension surrounding the group swallowed Eva as they approached. Heart pounding, she watched her father's and Zaccheo's gazes lock.

'I don't know what the hell you think you're doing here, Giordano, but I suggest you get back in that monstrosity and leave before I have you arrested for trespass.'

A shock wave went through the crowd.

Zaccheo didn't bat an eyelid.

'By all means do that if you wish, but you know exactly why I'm here, Pennington. We can play coy if you prefer. You'll be made painfully aware when I tire of it.' The words were barely above a murmur, but their venom raised the hairs on Eva's arms, triggering a gasp when she saw Sophie's face.

Her usually unflappable sister was severely agitated, her face distressingly pale.

'*Ciao*, Eva,' Zaccheo drawled without turning around. That deep, resonant voice, reminiscent of a tenor in a soulful opera, washed over her, its powerfully mesmerising quality reminding her how she'd once longed to hear him speak just for the hell of it. 'It's good of you to join us.'

'This is my engagement party. It's my duty to interact with my guests, even unwelcome ones who will be asked to leave immediately.'

'Don't worry, *cara*, I won't be staying long.'

The relief that surged up her spine disappeared when his gaze finally swung her way, then dropped to her left hand. With almost cavalier laziness, he caught her wrist and raised it to the light. He examined the ring for exactly three seconds. 'How predictable.'

He released her with the same carelessness he'd captured her.

Eva clenched her fist to stop the sizzling electricity firing up her arm at the brief contact.

'What's that supposed to mean?' Harry demanded.

Zaccheo levelled steely grey eyes on him, then his parents. 'This is a private discussion. Leave us.'

Peter Fairfield's laugh held incredulity, the last inch of

champagne in his glass sloshing wildly as he raised his arm. 'I think you've got the wrong end of the stick there, mate. You're the one who needs to take a walk.'

Eva caught Harry's pained look at his father's response, but could do nothing but watch, heart in her throat, as Zaccheo faced Peter Fairfield.

Again she was struck by how much his body had changed; how the sleek, layered muscle lent a deeper sense of danger. Whereas before it'd been like walking close to the edge of a cliff, looking into his eyes now was like staring into a deep, bottomless abyss.

'Would you care to repeat that, *il mio amico*?' The almost conversational tone belied the savage tension beneath the words.

'Oscar, who *is* this?' Peter Fairfield demanded of her father, who seemed to have lost the ability to speak after Zaccheo's succinct taunt.

Eva inserted herself between the two men before the situation got out of hand. Behind her, heat from Zaccheo's body burned every exposed inch of skin. Ignoring the sensation, she cleared her throat.

'Mr and Mrs Fairfield, Harry, we'll only be a few minutes. We're just catching up with Mr Giordano.' She glanced at her father. A vein throbbed in his temple and he'd gone a worrying shade of puce. Fear climbed into her heart. 'Father?'

He roused himself and glanced around. A charming smile slid into place, but it was off by a light year. The trickle of ice that had drifted down her spine at Zaccheo's unexpected arrival turned into a steady drip.

'We'll take this in my study. Don't hesitate to let the staff know if you need anything.' He strode away, followed by a disturbingly quiet Sophie.

Zaccheo's gaze swung to Harry, who defiantly withstood the laser gaze for a few seconds before he glanced at her.

'Are you sure?' Harry asked, that touching concern again in his eyes.

Her instinct screamed a terrible foreboding, but she nodded. 'Yes.'

'Okay. Hurry back, sweetness.' Before she could move, he dropped a kiss on her mouth.

A barely audible lethal growl charged through the air.

Eva flinched.

She wanted to face Zaccheo. Demand that he crawl back behind the bars that should've been holding him. But that glimpse of fear in her father's eyes stopped her. She tugged the wrap closer around her.

Something wasn't right here. She was willing to bet the dilapidated ancestral pile beneath her feet that something was seriously, *dangerously* wrong—

'Move, Eva.'

The cool command spoken against her ear sent shivers coursing through her.

She moved, only because the quicker she got to the bottom of why he was here, the quicker he would leave. But with each step his dark gaze probed her back, making the walk to her father's study on the other side of the manor the longest in her life.

Zaccheo shut the door behind him. Her father turned from where he'd been gazing into the unlit fireplace. Again Eva spotted apprehension in his eyes before he masked it.

'Whatever grievance you think you have the right to air, I suggest you rethink it, son. Even if this were the right time or place—'

'I am *not* your son, Pennington.' Zaccheo's response held lethal bite, the first sign of his fury breaking through. 'As for why I'm here, I have five thousand three hundred and twenty-two pieces of documentation that proves you colluded with various other individuals to pin a crime on me that I didn't commit.'

'What?' Eva gasped, then the absurdity of the statement made her shake her head. 'We don't believe you.'

Zaccheo's eyes remained on her father. 'You may not, but your father does.'

Oscar Pennington laughed, but the sound lacked its usual boom and zest. When sweat broke out over his forehead, fear gripped Eva's insides.

She steeled her spine. 'Our lawyers will rip whatever evidence you think you have to shreds, I'm sure. If you're here to seek some sort of closure, you picked the wrong time to do it. Perhaps we can arrange to meet you at some other time?'

Zaccheo didn't move. Didn't blink. Hands once again tucked behind his back, he simply watched her father, his body a coiled predator waiting to strike a fatal blow.

Silence stretched, throbbed with unbearable menace. Eva looked from her father to Sophie and back again, her dread escalating. 'What's going on?' she demanded.

Her father gripped the mantel until his knuckles shone white. 'You chose the wrong enemy. You're sorely mistaken if you think I'll let you blackmail me in my own home.'

Sophie stepped forward. 'Father, don't—'

'Good, you haven't lost your hubris.' Zaccheo's voice slashed across her sister's. 'I was counting on that. Here's what I'm going to do. In ten minutes I'm going to leave here with Eva, right in front of all your guests. You won't lift a finger to stop me. You'll tell them exactly who I am. Then you'll make a formal announcement that I'm the man your daughter will marry two weeks from today and that I have your blessing. I don't want to trust something so important to phone cameras and social media, although your guests will probably do a pretty good job. I noticed a few members of the press out there, so that part of your task should be easy. If the articles are written to my satisfaction, I'll be in touch on Monday to lay out how you can begin to make reparations to me. However, if by the time Eva and I wake up tomorrow morning the news of our engagement isn't in the press, then all bets are off.'

Oscar Pennington's breathing altered alarmingly. His

mouth opened but no words emerged. In the arctic silence that greeted Zaccheo's deadly words, Eva gaped at him.

'You're clearly not in touch with all of your faculties if you think those ridiculous demands are going to be met.' When silence greeted her response, she turned sharply to her father. 'Father? Why aren't you saying something?' she demanded, although the trepidation beating in her chest spelled its own doom.

'Because he can't, Eva. Because he's about to do exactly as I say.'

She rounded on him, and was once again rocked to the core by Zaccheo's visually powerful, utterly captivating transformation. So much so, she couldn't speak for several seconds. 'You're out of your mind!' she finally blurted.

Zaccheo's gaze didn't stray from its laser focus on her father. 'Believe me, *cara mia*, I haven't been saner than I am in this moment.'

CHAPTER THREE

ZACCHEO WATCHED EVA'S head swivel to her father, confusion warring with anger.

'Go on, Oscar. She's waiting for you to tell me to go to hell. Why don't you?'

Pennington staggered towards his desk, his face ashen and his breathing growing increasingly laboured.

'Father!' Eva rushed to his side—ignoring the poisonous look her sister sent her—as he collapsed into his leather armchair.

Zaccheo wanted to rip her away, let her watch her father suffer as his sins came home to roost. Instead he allowed the drama to play out. The outcome would be inevitable and would only go one way.

His way.

He wanted to look into Pennington's eyes and see the defeat and helplessness the other man had expected to see in his eyes the day Zaccheo had been sentenced.

Both sisters now fussed over their father and a swell of satisfaction rose at the fear in their eyes. Eva glanced his way and he experienced a different punch altogether. One he'd thought himself immune to, but had realised otherwise the moment he'd stepped off his helicopter and singled her out in the crowd.

That unsettling feeling, as if he were suffering from vertigo despite standing on terra firma, had intrigued and annoyed him in equal measures from the very first time he'd seen her, her voice silkily hypnotic as she crooned into a mic on a golden-lit stage, her fingers caressing the black microphone stand as if she were touching a lover.

Even knowing exactly who she was, what she represented,

he hadn't been able to walk away. In the weeks after their first meeting, he'd fooled himself into believing she was different, that she wasn't tainted with the same greed to further her pedigree by whatever means necessary; that she wasn't willing to do whatever it took to secure her family's standing, even while secretly scorning his upbringing.

Her very public denouncement of any association between them on the day of his sentencing had been the final blow. Not that Zaccheo hadn't had the scales viciously ripped from his eyes by then.

No, by that fateful day fourteen months ago, he'd known just how thoroughly he'd been suckered.

'What the hell do you think you're doing?' she muttered fiercely, her moss-green eyes firing lasers at him.

Zaccheo forced himself not to smile. The time for gloating would come later. 'Exacting the wages of sin, *dolcezza*. What else?'

'I don't know what you're talking about, but I don't think my father is in a position to have a discussion with you right now, Mr Giordano.'

Her prim and proper tones bit savagely into Zaccheo, wiping away any trace of twisted mirth. That tone said he ought to *know his place*, that he ought to stand there like a good little servant and wait to be addressed instead of upsetting the lord of the manor with his petty concerns.

Rage bubbled beneath his skin, threatening to erupt. Blunt nails bit into his wrist, but the pain wasn't enough to calm his fury. He clenched his jaw for a long moment before he trusted himself to speak.

'I gave you ten minutes, Pennington. You now have five. I suggest you practise whatever sly words you'll be using to address your guests.' Zaccheo shrugged. 'Or not. Either way, things *will* go my way.'

Eva rushed at him, her striking face and flawless skin flushed with a burst of angry colour as she stopped a few feet away.

Out on the terrace, he'd compelled himself not to stare too long at her in case he betrayed his feelings. In case his gaze devoured her as he'd wanted to do since her presence snaked like a live wire inside him.

Now, he took in that wild gypsy-like caramel-blonde hair so out of place in this polished stratosphere her family chose to inhabit. The striking contrast between her bright hair, black eyebrows and dark-rimmed eyes had always fascinated him. But no more than her cupid-bow lips, soft, dark red and sinfully sensual. Or the rest of her body.

'You assume I have no say in whatever despicable spectacle you're planning. That I intend to meekly stand by while you humiliate my family? Well, think again!'

'Eva…' her father started.

'No! I don't know what exactly is going on here, but I intend to play no part in it.'

'You'll play your part, and you'll play it well,' Zaccheo interjected, finally driving his gaze up from the mouth he wanted to feast on more than he wanted his next breath. *That'll come soon enough*, he promised himself.

'Or what? You'll carry through with your empty threats?'

His fury eased a touch and twisted amusement slid back into place. It never ceased to amaze him how the titled rich felt they were above the tenets that governed ordinary human beings. His own stepfather had been the same. He'd believed, foolishly, that his pedigree and connections would insulate him from his reckless business practices, that the Old Boys' Club would provide a safety net despite his poor judgement.

Zaccheo had taken great pleasure in watching his mother's husband squirm before him, cap in hand, when Zaccheo had bought his family business right from underneath his pompous nose. But even then, the older man had continued to treat him like a third-class citizen…

Just as Oscar Pennington had done. Just as Eva Pennington was doing now.

'You think my threats empty?' he enquired softly. 'Then do nothing. It's after all your privilege and your right.'

Something of the lethal edge that rode him must have transmitted itself to her. Apprehension chased across her face before she firmed those impossibly sumptuous lips.

'Do nothing, and watch me bury your family in the deepest, darkest, most demeaning pit you can dream of. Do nothing and watch me unleash a scandal the scale of which you can only imagine on your precious family name.' He bared his teeth in a mirthless smile and her eyes widened in stunned disbelief. 'It would be *my* privilege and pleasure to do so.'

Oscar Pennington inhaled sharply and Zaccheo's gaze zeroed in on his enemy. The older man rose from the chair. Though he looked frail, his eyes reflected icy disdain. But Zaccheo also glimpsed the fear of a cornered man weighing all the options to see how to escape the noose dangling ever closer.

Zaccheo smiled inwardly. He had no intention of letting Pennington escape. Not now, not ever.

The flames of retribution intensifying within him, he unclasped his hands. It was time to bring this meeting to an end.

'Your time's up, Pennington.'

Eva answered instead of her father. 'How do we know you're not bluffing? You say you have something over us, prove it,' she said defiantly.

He could've walked out and let them twist in the wind of uncertainty. Pennington would find out soon enough the length of Zaccheo's ruthless reach. But the thought of leaving Eva here when he departed was suddenly unthinkable. So far he'd allowed himself a brief glimpse of her body wrapped in that obscenely revealing red dress. But that one glimpse had been enough. Quite apart from the rage boiling his blood, the steady hammer of his pulse proved that he still wanted her with a fever that spiked higher with each passing second.

He would take what he'd foolishly and piously denied

himself two years ago. He would *take* and *use*, just as they'd done to him. Only when he'd achieved every goal he'd set himself would he feel avenged.

'You can't, can you?' Oscar taunted with a sly smile, bringing Zaccheo back to the room and the three aristocratic faces staring at him with varying degrees of disdain and fear.

He smiled, almost amused by the older man's growing confidence. 'Harry Fairfield is providing you with a bridging loan of fifteen million pounds because the combined running costs of the Pennington Hotels and The Spire have you stretched so thin the banks won't touch you. While you desperately drum up an adequate advertising budget to rent out all those overpriced but empty floors in The Spire, the interest owed to the Chinese consortium who own seventy-five per cent of the building is escalating. You have a meeting with them on Monday to request more time to pay the interest. In return for Fairfield's investment, you're handing him your daughter.'

Eva glared at him. 'So you've asked a few questions about Penningtons' business practices. That doesn't empower you to make demands of any of us.'

Zaccheo took a moment to admire her newfound grit. During their initial association, she'd been a little more timid, and in her father's shadow, but it looked as if the kitten had grown a few claws. He curbed the thrill at what was to come and answered.

'Yes, it does. Would you be interested to know the Chinese consortium sold their seventy-five per cent of The Spire to me three days ago? So by my calculation you're in excess of three months late on interest payments, correct?'

A rough sound, a cross between a cough and a wheeze, escaped Pennington's throat. There was no class or grace in the way he gaped at Zaccheo. He dropped back into his chair, his face a mask of hatred.

'I knew you were a worthless bet the moment I set eyes on you. I should've listened to my instincts.'

The red haze he'd been trying to hold back surged higher. 'No, what you wanted was a spineless scapegoat, a *capro espiatorio*, who would make you rich and fat and content and even give up his life without question!'

'Mr Giordano, surely we can discuss this like sensible business-minded individuals,' Sophie Pennington advanced, her hands outstretched in benign sensibility. Zaccheo looked from the hands she willed not to tremble to the veiled disdain in her eyes. Then he looked past her to Eva, who'd returned to her father's side, her face pale but her eyes shooting her displeasure at him.

Unexpectedly and very much unwelcome, a tiny hint of compassion tugged at him.

Basta!

He turned abruptly and reached for the door handle. 'You have until I ready my chopper for take-off to come to me, Eva.' He didn't need to expand on that edict. The *or else* hung in the air like the deadly poison he intended it to be.

He walked out and headed for the terrace, despite every nerve in his body straining to return to the room and forcibly drag Eva out.

True, he hadn't bargained for the visceral reaction to seeing her again. And yes, he hadn't quite been able to control his reaction to seeing another man's ring on her finger, that vulgar symbol of ownership hollowing out his stomach. The knowledge that she'd most likely shared that hapless drunk's bed, given the body he'd once believed to be his to another, ate through his blood like acid on metal. But he couldn't afford to let his emotions show.

Every strategic move in this game of deadly retribution hinged on him maintaining his control; on not letting them see how affected he was by all this.

He stepped onto the terrace and all conversation ceased. Curious faces gaped and one or two bolder guests even tried to intercept him. Zaccheo cut through the crowd, his gaze on the chopper a few dozen yards away.

She would come to him. As an outcome of his first salvo, nothing else would be acceptable.

His pulse thudded loud and insistent in his ears as he strolled down the steps towards the aircraft. The fireworks amid which he'd landed had long since gone quiet, but the scent of sulphur lingered in the air, reminding him of the volatility that lingered beneath his own skin, ready to erupt at the smallest trigger.

He wouldn't let it erupt. Not yet.

A murmur rose behind him, the fevered excitement that came with the anticipation of a spectacle. A *scandal*.

Zaccheo compelled himself to keep walking.

He ducked beneath the powerful rotors of his aircraft and reached for the door.

'Wait!'

He stopped. Turned.

Three hundred pairs of eyes watched with unabashed interest as Eva paused several feet from him.

Behind her, her father and sister stood on the steps, wearing similar expressions of dread. Zaccheo wanted them to stew for a while longer, but he found his attention drawn to the woman striding towards him. Her face reflected more defiance than dread. It also held pride and not a small measure of bruised disdain. Zaccheo vowed in that moment to make her regret that latter look, make her take back every single moment she'd thought herself above him.

Swallowing, he looked down at her body.

She held the flimsy wrap around her like armour. As if that would protect her from him. With one ruthless tug, he pulled it away. It fluttered to the ground, revealing her luscious, heart-stopping figure to his gaze. Unable to stem the frantic need crashing through him, he stepped forward and speared his fingers into the wild tumble of her hair.

Another step and she was in his arms.

Where she belonged.

* * *

The small pocket of air Eva had been able to retain in her lungs during her desperate flight after Zaccheo evaporated when he yanked her against him. Her body went from shivering in the crisp January air to furnace-hot within seconds. The fingers in her hair tightened, his other arm sliding around her waist.

Eva wanted to remain unaffected, slam her hands against his chest and remove herself from that dangerous wall of masculinity. But she couldn't move. So she fought with her words.

'You may think you've won, that you own me, but you don't,' she snapped. 'You never will!'

His eyes gleamed. 'Such fire. Such determination. You've changed, *cara mia*, I'll give you that. And yet here you are, barely one minute after I walked out of your father's study. Mere hours after you promised yourself to another man, here you are, Eva Pennington, ready to promise yourself to me. Ready to become whatever I want you to be.'

Her snigger made his eyes narrow, but she didn't care. 'Keep telling yourself that. I look forward to your shock when I prove you wrong.'

That deadly smile she'd first seen in her father's study reappeared, curling fear through her. It reeked with far too much gratification to kill that unshakeable sensation that she was standing on the edge of a precipice, and that, should she fall, there would be no saving her.

She realised the reason for the smile when he lifted her now bare fingers to his eye level. 'You've proved me right already.'

'Are you completely sure about that?' The question was a bold but empty taunt.

The lack of fuss with which Harry had taken back his ring a few minutes ago had been a relief.

She might not have an immediate solution to her family's

problems, but Eva was glad she no longer had to pretend she was half of a sham couple.

Zaccheo brought her fingers to his mouth and kissed her ring finger, stunning her back to reality. Flashes erupted as his actions were recorded, no doubt to be streamed across the fastest mediums available.

Recalling the conversation she'd just had with her father, she tried to pull away. 'This pound-of-flesh taking isn't going to last very long, so I suggest you enjoy it while it lasts. I intend to return to my life before midnight—'

Her words dried up when his face closed in a mask of icy fury, and his hands sealed her body even closer to his.

'Your first lesson is to stop speaking to me as if I'm the hired help. Refraining from doing so will put me in a much calmer frame of mind to deal with you than otherwise,' he said with unmistakeable warning.

Eva doubted that anyone had dared to speak to Zaccheo Giordano in the way she referred, but she wasn't about to debate that point with him with three hundred pairs of eyes watching. She was struggling enough to keep upright what with all the turbulent sensations firing through her at his touch. 'Why, Zaccheo, you sound as if you've a great many lessons you intend to dole out…' She tried to sound bored, but her voice emerged a little too breathless for her liking.

'Patience, *cara mia*. You'll be instructed as and when necessary.' His gaze dropped to her mouth and her breath lodged in her sternum. 'For now, I wish the talking to cease.'

He closed the final inch between them and slanted his mouth over hers. The world tilted and shook beneath her feet. Expertly sensual and demanding, he kissed her as if he owned her mouth, as if he owned her whole body. In all her adult years, Eva had never imagined the brush of a beard would infuse her with such spine-tingling sensations. Yet she shivered with fiery delight as Zaccheo's silky facial hair caressed the corners of her mouth.

She groaned at the forceful breach of his tongue. Her arms drifted over his taut biceps as she became lost in the potent magic of his kiss. At the first touch of his tongue against hers, she shuddered. He made a rough sound and his sharp inhalation vibrated against her. His fingers convulsed in her hair and his other hand drifted to her bottom, moulding her as he stepped back against the aircraft and widened his stance to bring her closer.

Eva wasn't sure how long she stood there, adrift in a swirl of sensation as he ravaged her mouth. It wasn't until her lungs screamed and her heart jackhammered against her ribs did she recall where she was…what was happening.

And still she wanted to continue.

So much so she almost moaned in protest when firm hands set her back and she found herself staring into molten eyes dark with savage hunger.

'I think we've given our audience enough to feed on. Get in.'

The calm words, spoken in direct counteraction to the frenzied look in his eyes, doused Eva with cold reality. That she'd made even more of a spectacle of herself hit home as wolf whistles ripped through the air.

'This was all for *show*?' she whispered numbly, shivering in the frigid air.

One sleek eyebrow lifted. 'Of course. Did you think I wanted to kiss you because I was so desperate for you I just couldn't help myself? You'll find that I have more self-restraint than that. Get in,' he repeated, holding the steel and glass door to the aircraft open.

Eva brushed cold hands over her arms, unable to move. She stared at him, perhaps hoping to find some humanity in the suddenly grim-faced block of stone in front of her. Or did she want a hint of the man who'd once framed her face in his hands and called her the most beautiful thing in his life?

Of course, that had been a lie. Everything about Zaccheo

had been a lie. Still she probed for some softness beneath that formidable exterior.

His implacable stare told her she was grasping at straws, as she had from the very beginning, when she'd woven stupid dreams around him.

A gust of icy wind blew across the grass, straight into her exposed back. A flash of red caught her eye and she blindly stumbled towards the terrace. She'd barely taken two steps when he seized her arm.

'What the hell do you think you're doing?' Zaccheo enquired frostily.

'I'm cold,' she replied through chattering teeth. 'My wrap…' She pointed to where the material had drifted.

'Leave it. This will keep you warm.' With one smooth move, he unbuttoned, shrugged off his tuxedo and draped it around her shoulders. The sudden infusion of warmth was overwhelming. Eva didn't want to drown in the distinctively heady scent of the man who was wrecking her world, didn't welcome her body's traitorous urge to burrow into the warm silk lining. And most of all, she didn't want to be beholden to him in any way, or accept any hint of kindness from him.

Zaccheo Giordano had demonstrated a ruthless thirst to annihilate those he deemed enemies in her father's study.

But she was no longer the naive and trusting girl she'd been a year and a half ago. Zaccheo's betrayal and her continued fraught relationship with her father and sister had hardened her heart. The pain was still there—would probably always be there—but so were the new fortifications against further hurt. She had no intention of laying her heart and soul bare to further damage from the people she'd once blithely believed would return the same love and devotion she offered freely.

She started to shrug off the jacket. 'No, thanks. I'd prefer not to be stamped as your possession.'

He stopped her by placing both hands on her arms.

Dark grey eyes pinned her to the spot, the sharper, icier

burst of wind whipping around them casting him in a deadlier, more dangerous light.

'You're already my possession. You became mine the moment you made the choice to follow me out here, Eva. You can kid yourself all you want, but this is your reality from here on in.'

CHAPTER FOUR

@Ladystclare OMG! Bragging rights=mine! Beheld fireworks w/in fireworks @P/Manor last night when LadyP eloped w/convict lover! #amazeballs

@Aristokitten Bet it was all a publicity stunt, but boy that kiss? Sign me up! #Ineedlatinlovelikethat

@Countrypile That wasn't love. That was an obscene and shameless money-grabbing gambit at its worst! #Donotencouragerancidbehaviour

EVA FLINCHED, her stomach churning at each new message that flooded her social-media stream.

The hours had passed in a haze after Zaccheo flew them from Pennington Manor. In solid command of the helicopter, he'd soared over the City of London and landed on the vertiginous rooftop of The Spire.

The stunning split-level penthouse's interior had barely registered in the early hours when Zaccheo's enigmatic aide, Romeo, had directed the butler to show her to her room.

Zaccheo had stalked away without a word, leaving her in the middle of his marble-tiled hallway, clutching his jacket.

Sleep had been non-existent in the bleak hours that had followed. At five a.m., she'd given up and taken a quick shower before putting on that skin-baring dress again.

Wishing she'd asked for a blanket to cover the acres of flesh on display, she cringed as another salacious offering popped into her inbox displayed on Zaccheo's tablet.

Like a spectator frozen on the fringes of an unfolding train wreck, she read the latest post.

@Uberwoman Hey ConvictLover, that flighty poor little rich girl is wasted on you. Real women exist. Let ME rock your world!

Eva curled her fist, refusing to entertain the image of any woman rocking Zaccheo's world. She didn't care one way or the other. If she had a choice, she would be ten thousand miles away from this place.

'If you're thinking of responding to any of that, consider yourself warned against doing so.'

She jumped at the deep voice a whisper from her ear. She'd thought she would be alone in the living room for at least another couple of hours before dealing with Zaccheo. Now she wished she'd stayed in her room.

She stood and faced him, the long black suede sofa between them no barrier to Zaccheo's towering presence.

'I've no intention of responding. And you really shouldn't sneak up on people like that,' she tagged on when the leisurely drift of those incisive eyes over her body made her feel like a specimen under a microscope.

'I don't sneak. Had you been less self-absorbed in your notoriety, you would've heard me enter the room.'

Anger welled up. 'You accuse *me* of being notorious? All this is happening because *you* insisted on gatecrashing a private event and turning it into a public spectacle.'

'And, of course, you were so eager to find out whether you're trending that you woke up at dawn to follow the news.'

She wanted to ask how he'd known what time she'd left her room, but Eva suspected she wouldn't like the answer. 'You assume I slept at all when sleep was the last thing on my mind, having been blackmailed into coming here. And, FYI, I don't read the gutter press. Not unless I want the worst kind of indigestion.'

He rounded the sofa and stopped within arm's length. She stood her ground, but she couldn't help herself ogling the breathtaking body filling her vision.

It was barely six o'clock and yet he looked as vitally masculine as if he'd been up and ready for hours. A film of sweat covered the hair-dusted arms beneath the pulled-up sleeves, and his damp white T-shirt moulded his chiselled torso. His black drawstring sweatpants did nothing to hide thick thighs and Eva struggled to avert her gaze from the virile outline of his manhood against the soft material. Dragging her gaze up, she stared in fascination at the hands and fingers wrapped in stained boxing gauze.

'Do you intend to spend the rest of the morning ogling me, Eva?' he asked mockingly.

She looked into his eyes and that potent, electric tug yanked hard at her. Reminding herself that she was immune from whatever spell he'd once cast on her, she raised her chin.

'I intend to attempt a reasonable conversation with you in the cold light of day regarding last night's events.'

'That suggests you believe our previous interactions have been unreasonable?'

'I did a quick search online. You were released yesterday morning. It stands to reason that you're still a little affected by your incarceration—'

His harsh, embittered laugh bounced like bullets around the room. Eva folded her arms, refusing to cower at the sound.

He stepped towards her, the tension in his body barely leashed. 'You think I'm a *"little affected"* by my incarceration? Tell me, *bella*,' he invited softly, 'do you know what it feels like to be locked in a six-by-ten, damp and rancid cage for over a year?'

A brief wave of torment overcame his features, and a different tug, one of sympathy, pulled at her. Then she reminded herself just who she was dealing with. 'Of course not. I just don't want you to do anything that you'll regret.'

'Your touching concern for my welfare is duly noted. But I suggest you save it for yourself. Last night was merely you and your family being herded into the eye of the storm. The real devastation is just getting started.'

As nightmarish promises went, Zaccheo's chilled her to the bone. Before she could reply, several pings blared from the tablet. She glanced down and saw more lurid posts about what *real women* wanted to do to Zaccheo.

She shut the tablet and straightened to find him slowly unwinding the gauze from his right hand, his gaze pinned on her. Silence stretched as he freed both hands and tossed the balled cloth onto the glass-topped coffee table.

'So, do I get any sort of itinerary for this impending apocalypse?' she asked when it became clear he was content to let the silence linger.

One corner of his mouth lifted. 'We'll have breakfast in half an hour. After that, we'll see whether your father has done what I demanded of him. If he has, we'll take it from there.'

Recalling her father's overly belligerent denial once Zaccheo had left the study last night, anxiety skewered her. 'And if he hasn't?'

'Then his annihilation will come sooner rather than later.'

Half an hour later, Eva struggled to swallow a mouthful of buttered toast and quickly chased it down with a sip of tea before she choked.

A few minutes ago, a brooding Romeo had entered with the butler who'd delivered a stack of broadsheets. The other man had conversed in Italian with a freshly showered and even more visually devastating Zaccheo.

Zaccheo's smile after the short exchange had incited her first panic-induced emotion. He'd said nothing after Romeo left. Instead he'd devoured a hearty plate of scrambled eggs, grilled mushrooms and smoked pancetta served on Italian bread with unsettling gusto.

But as the silence spread thick and cloying across the room she finally set her cup down and glanced to where he stood now at the end of the cherrywood dining table, his hands braced on his hips, an inscrutable expression on his face.

Again, Eva was struck by the change in him. Even now he was dressed more formally in dark grey trousers and a navy shirt with the sleeves rolled up, her eyes were drawn to the gladiator-like ruggedness of his physique.

'Eva.' Her name was a deep command. One she desperately wanted to ignore. It held a quiet triumph she didn't want to acknowledge. The implications were more than she could stomach. She wasn't one for burying her head in the sand, but if her father had done what Zaccheo had demanded, then—

'Eva,' he repeated. Sharper. Controlled but demanding.

Heart hammering, she glanced at him. 'What?'

He stared back without blinking, his body deathly still. 'Come here.'

Refusing to show how rattled she was, she stood, teetered on the heels she'd had no choice but to wear again, and strode towards him.

He tracked her with chilling precision, his eyes dropping to her hips for a charged second before he looked back up. Eva hated her body for reacting to that look, even as her breasts tingled and a blaze lit between her thighs.

Silently she cursed herself. She had no business reacting to that look, or to any man on any plane of emotion whatsoever. She had proof that path only ended in eviscerating heartache.

She stopped a few feet from him, made sure to place a dining chair between them. But the solid wood couldn't stop her senses from reacting to his scent, or her nipples from furling into tight, needy buds when her gaze fell on the golden gleam of his throat revealed by the gap in his shirt. Quickly crossing her arms, she looked down at the newspapers.

That they'd made headlines was unmistakeable. Bold black letters and exclamation marks proclaimed Zaccheo's antics. And as for *that* picture of them locked together...

'I can't believe you landed a helicopter in the middle of a fireworks display,' she threw out, simply because it was easier than acknowledging the other words written on the page binding her to Zaccheo, insinuating they were something they would never be.

He looked from her face to the front-page picture showing him landing his helicopter during a particularly violent explosion. 'Were you concerned for me?' he mocked.

'Of course not. You obviously don't care about your own safety so why should I?'

A simmering silence followed, then he stalked closer. 'I hope you intend to act a little more concerned towards my well-being once we're married.'

Any intention of avoiding looking at him fled her mind. '*Married*? Don't you think you've taken this far enough?' she snapped.

'Excuse me?'

'You wanted to humiliate my father. Congratulations, you've made headlines in every single newspaper. Don't you think it's time to drop this?'

His eyes turned into pools of ice. 'You think this is some sort of game?' he enquired silkily.

'What else can it be? If you really had the evidence you claim to have, why haven't you handed it over to the police?'

'You believe I'm bluffing?' His voice was a sharp blade slicing through the air.

'I believe you feel aggrieved.'

'Really? And what else did you *believe*?'

Eva refused to quail beneath the look that threatened to cut her into pieces. 'It's clear you want to make some sort of statement about how you were treated by my father. You've done that now. Let it go.'

'So your father did all this—' he indicated the papers '—just to stop me throwing a childish tantrum? And what about you? Did you throw yourself at my feet to buy your family time to see how long my bluff would last?'

She flung her arms out in exasperation. 'Come on, Zaccheo—'

They both stilled at her use of his name. Eva had no time to recover from the unwitting slip. Merciless fingers speared into her hair, much as they had last night, holding her captive as his thumb tilted her chin.

'How far are you willing to go to get me to be *reasonable*? Or perhaps I should guess? After all, just last night you'd dropped to an all-time low of whoring yourself to a drunken boy in order to save your family.' The thick condemnation feathered across her skin.

Rage flared in her belly, gave her the strength to remain upright. He stood close. Far too close. She stepped back, but only managed to wedge herself between the table and Zaccheo's towering body. 'As opposed to what? Whoring myself to a middle-aged criminal?'

He leaned down, crowding her further against the polished wood. 'You know exactly how old I am. In fact, I recall precisely where we both were when the clock struck midnight on my thirtieth birthday. Or perhaps you need me to refresh your memory?' His smooth, faintly accented voice trailed amused contempt.

'Don't bother—'

'I'll do it anyway, it's no hardship,' he offered, as if her sharp denial hadn't been uttered. 'We were newly engaged, and you were on your knees in front of my penthouse window, uncaring that anyone with a pair of decent binoculars would see us. All you cared about was getting your busy, greedy little hands on my belt, eager to rid me of my trousers so you could wish me a happy birthday in a way most men fantasise about.'

Her skin flushed with a wave of heat so strong, she feared spontaneous combustion. 'That wasn't my idea.'

One brow quirked. 'Was it not?'

'No, you dared me to do it.'

His mouth twitched. 'Are you saying I forced you?'

Those clever fingers were drifting along her scalp, lazily caressing, lulling her into showing her vulnerability.

Eva sucked in a deep breath. 'I'm saying I don't want to talk about the past. I prefer to stick to the present.'

She didn't want to remember how gullible she'd been back then, how stupidly eager to please, how excited she'd been that this god of a man, who could have any woman he wanted with a lazy crook of his finger, had pursued *her*, chosen *her*.

Even after learning the hard way that men in positions of power would do anything to stay in that power, that her two previous relationships had only been a means to an end for the men involved, she'd still allowed herself to believe Zaccheo wanted her for herself. Finding out that he was no better, that he only wanted her to secure a *business deal*, had delivered a blow she'd spent the better part of a year burying in a deep hole.

At first his demands had been subtle: a business dinner here, a charity event there—occasions she'd been proud and honoured to accompany him on. Until that fateful night when she'd overheard a handful of words that had had the power to sting like nothing else.

She's the means to an end. Nothing more...

The conversation that had followed remained seared into her brain. Zaccheo, impatiently shutting her down, then brazenly admitting he'd said those words. That he'd used her.

Most especially, she recalled the savage pain in knowing she had got him so wrong, had almost given herself to a man who held such careless regard for her, and only cared about her pedigree.

And yet his shock when she'd returned his ring had made her wonder whether she'd done the right thing.

His arrest days later for criminal negligence had confirmed what sort of man she'd foolishly woven her dreams around.

She met his gaze now. 'You got what you wanted—your name next to mine on the front page. The whole world knows I left with you last night, that I'm no longer engaged to Harry.'

His hand slipped to her nape, worked over tense muscles. 'And how did Fairfield take being so unceremoniously dumped?' he asked.

'Harry cares about me, so he was a complete gentleman about it. Shame I can't say the same about you.'

Dark grey eyes gleamed dangerously. 'You mean he wasn't torn up at the thought of never having access to this body again?' he mocked.

She lifted a brow. 'Never say never.'

Tension coiled his body. 'If you think I'll tolerate any further interaction between you and Fairfield, you're severely mistaken,' he warned with a dark rumble.

'Why, Zaccheo, you sound almost jealous.'

Heat scoured his cheekbones and a tiny part of her quailed at her daring. 'You'd be wise to stop testing me, *dolcezza*.'

'If you want this to stop, tell me why you're doing this.'

'I'm only going to say it one more time, so let it sink in. I don't intend to stop until your father's reputation is in the gutter and everything he took from me is returned, plus interest.'

'Can I see the proof of what you accuse my father of?'

'Would you believe even if you saw it? Or will you cling to the belief that I'm the big, bad ogre who's just throwing his weight about?' he taunted.

Eva looked down at the papers on the table, every last one containing everything Zaccheo had demanded. Would her father have done it if Zaccheo's threats were empty?

'Last night, when you said you and I…' She stopped, unable to process the reality.

'Would be married in two weeks? *Sì*, I meant that, too. And to get that ball rolling, we're going shopping for an engagement ring in exactly ten minutes, after which we have a full day ahead, so if you require further sustenance I suggest you finish your breakfast.'

He dropped his fingers from her nape and stepped back. With a last look filled with steely determination, he picked up the closest paper and walked out of the room.

CHAPTER FIVE

THEIR FIRST STOP was an exclusive coat boutique in Bond Street. Zaccheo told himself it was because he didn't want to waste time. The truth mocked him in the form of needing to cover Eva Pennington's body before he lost any more brain cells to the lust blazing through his bloodstream.

In the dark cover of her family terrace and the subsequent helicopter journey home, he'd found relief from the blatant temptation of her body.

In the clear light of day, the red dress seemed to cling tighter, caress her body so much more intimately that he'd had to fight the urge to lunge for her each time she took a breath.

He watched her now, seated across from him in his limo as they drove the short twenty-minute distance to Threadneedle Street where his bankers had flown in the diamond collection he'd requested from Switzerland.

Her fingers plucked at the lapel of the new white cashmere coat, then dropped to cinch the belt tighter at her tiny waist.

'You didn't need to buy me a coat,' she grumbled. 'I have a perfectly good one back at my flat.'

He reined in his fascination with her fingers. 'Your flat is on the other side of town. I have more important things to do than waste an hour and a half sitting in traffic.'

Her plump lips pursed. 'Of course, extracting your pound of flesh is an all-consuming business, isn't it?'

'I don't intend to stop at a mere pound, Eva. I intend to take the whole body.'

One eyebrow spiked. 'You seem so confident I'm going to hand myself to you on a silver platter. Isn't that a tad foolish?'

There was that tone again, the one that said she didn't believe him.

'I guess we'll find out one way or the other when the sordid details are laid out for you on Monday. All you need to concern yourself about today is picking out an engagement ring that makes the right statement.'

Her striking green eyes clashed with his and that lightning bolt struck again. 'And what statement would that be?' she challenged.

He let loose a chilling half-smile that made his enemies quake. 'Why, that you belong to me, of course.'

'I told you, I've no intention of being your possession. A ring won't change that.'

'How glibly you lie to yourself.'

She gasped and he was once again drawn to her mouth. A mouth whose sweet taste he recalled vividly, much to his annoyance. 'Excuse me?'

'We both know you'll be exactly who and what I want you to be when I demand it. Your family has too much at stake for you to risk doing otherwise.'

'Don't mistake my inclination to go along with this farce to be anything but my need to get to the bottom of why you're doing this. It's what families *do* for each other. Of course, since you don't even speak about yours, I assume you don't know what I'm talking about.'

Zaccheo called himself ten kinds of fool for letting the taunt bite deep. He'd lost respect for his father long before he'd died in shame and humiliation. And watching his mother whore herself for prestige had left a bitter taste in his mouth. As families went, he'd been dealt a bad hand, but he'd learned long ago that to wish for anything you couldn't create with your own hard-working hands was utter folly. He'd stopped making wishes by the time he hit puberty. Recalling the very last wish he'd prayed night and day for as a child, he clenched his fists. Even then he'd known fate would laugh at his wish for a brother or sister. He'd known that wish, despite his mother being pregnant, would not come true. He'd *known*.

He'd programmed himself not to care after that harrowing time in his life.

So why the hell did it grate so much for him to be reminded that he was the last Giordano?

'I don't talk about my family because I have none. But that's a situation I intend to rectify soon.'

She glanced at him warily. 'What's that supposed to mean?'

'It means I had a lot of time in prison to re-examine my life, thanks to your family.' He heard the naked emotion in his voice and hardened his tone. 'I intend to make some changes.'

'What sort of changes?'

'The type that means you'll no longer have to whore out your integrity for the sake of the great Pennington legacy. You should thank me, since you seem to be the one doing most of the heavy lifting for your family.'

Zaccheo watched her face pale.

'I'm not a whore!'

He lunged forward before he could stop himself. 'Then what the hell were you doing dressed like a tart, agreeing to marry a drunken playboy, if not for cold, hard cash for your family?' The reminder of what she wore beneath the coat blazed across his mind. His temperature hiked, along with the increased throbbing in his groin.

'I didn't do it for money!' She flushed, and bit down on her lower lip again. 'Okay, yes, that was part of the reason, but I also did it because—'

'Please spare me any declarations of *true love*.' He wasn't sure why he abhorred the idea of her mentioning the word love. Or why the idea of her mentioning Fairfield's name filled him with rage.

Zaccheo knew about her friendship with Fairfield. And while he knew their engagement had been a farce, he hadn't missed the camaraderie between them, or the pathetic infatuation in the other man's eyes.

Sì, he was jealous—Eva would be his and no one else's. But he also pitied Fairfield.

Because love, in all forms, was a false emotion. Nothing but a manipulative tool. Mothers declared their love for their children, then happily abandoned them the moment they ceased to be a convenient accessory. Fathers professed to have their children's interest at heart because of *love*, but when it came right down to it they put themselves above all else. And sometimes even forgot that their children *existed*.

As for Eva Pennington, she'd shown how faithless she was when she'd dropped him and distanced herself mere days before his arrest.

'I wasn't going to say that. Trust me, I've learned not to toss the word *love* about freely—'

'Did you know?' he sliced at her before he could stop himself.

Fine brows knitted together. 'Did I know what?'

'Did you know of your father's plans?' The question had been eating at him far more than he wanted to admit.

'His plans to do what?' she asked innocently. And yet he could see the caginess on her face. As if she didn't want him to probe deeper.

Acrid disappointment bit through him. He was a fool for thinking, perhaps *wishing*, despite all the signs saying otherwise, that she'd been oblivious to Oscar Pennington's plans to make him the ultimate scapegoat.

'We're here, sir.' His driver's voice came through the intercom.

Zaccheo watched her dive for the door. He would've laughed at her eagerness to get away from the conversation that brought back too many volatile memories, had he not felt disconcerting relief that his question had gone unanswered.

He'd been a fool to pursue it in the first place. He didn't need more lies. He had cold, hard facts proving the Penningtons' guilt. Dwelling on the whys and wherefores of Eva's actions was a fool's errand.

He stepped out into the winter sunshine and nodded at the bank director.

'Mr Giordano, welcome.' The older man's expression vacillated between obsequiousness and condescension.

'You received my further instructions?' Zaccheo took Eva's arm, ignoring her slight stiffening as he walked her through the doors of the bank.

'Yes, sir. We've adhered to your wishes.' Again he caught the man's assessing gaze.

'I'm pleased to hear it. Otherwise I'm sure there would be other banks who would welcome GWI's business.'

The banker paled. 'That won't be necessary, Mr Giordano. If you'll come with me, the jewellers have everything laid out for you.'

It should've given him great satisfaction that he'd breached the hallowed walls of the centuries-old establishment, that he'd finally succeeded where his own father had tried so hard and failed, giving his life in pursuit of recognition.

But all Zaccheo could hear, could *feel*, was Eva's presence, a reminder of why his satisfaction felt hollow. She was proof that, despite all he'd achieved, he was still regarded as the lowest of the low. A nobody. An expendable patsy who would take any treatment his betters doled out without protest.

We shall see.

They walked down several hallways. After a few minutes, Eva cleared her throat. 'What instructions did you give him?' she asked.

He stared down at her. 'I told him to remove all pink diamonds from the collection and instruct my jewellers that I do not wish to deal with diamonds of that colour in the future.'

'Really? I thought pink diamonds were all the rage these days?'

He shrugged. 'Not for me. Let's call it a personal preference.'

The penny dropped and she tried to pull away from his hold. He refused to let go. 'Are you really that petty?' she

asked as they approached a heavy set of oak doors. 'Just because Harry gave me a pink diamond…' Her eyes widened
when he caught her shoulders and pinned her against the
wall. When she started to struggle, he stepped closer, caging her in with his body.

'You'll refrain from mentioning his name in my presence
ever again. Is that understood?' Zaccheo felt his control slipping as her scent tangled with his senses and her curvy figure moved against him.

'Let me go and you'll need never hear his name again,'
she snapped back.

'Not going to happen.' He released her. 'After you.'

She huffed a breath and entered the room. He followed
and crossed to the window, struggling to get himself under
control as the director walked in with three assistants bearing large velvet trays. They set them on the polished conference table and stepped back.

'We'll give you some privacy,' the director said before
exiting with his minions.

Zaccheo walked to the first tray and pulled away the protective cloth. He stared at the display of diamonds in all cuts
and sizes, wondering for a moment how his father would've
reacted to this display of obscene wealth. Paolo Giordano had
never managed to achieve even a fraction of his goals despite
sacrificing everything, including the people he should've held
dear. Would he have been proud, or would he have bowed and
scraped as the bank director had a few moments ago, eager
to be deemed worthy of merely touching them?

'Perhaps we should get on with choosing a stone. Or are
we going to stare at them all day?' Eva asked.

Eva watched his face harden and bit her tongue. She wasn't
sure why she couldn't stop goading him. Did part of her want
to get under his skin as he so effortlessly got under hers?

Annoyed with herself for letting the whole absurd situation get to her, she stepped forward and stared down at the

dazzling array of gems. Large. Sparkling. Flawless. Each worth more than she would earn in half her lifetime.

None of them appealed to her.

She didn't want to pick out another cold stone to replace the one she'd handed back to Harry before running after Zaccheo last night.

She didn't want to be trapped into yet another consequence of being a Pennington. She wanted to be free of the guilty resentment lurking in her heart at the thought that nothing she did would ever be enough for her family. Or the sadness that came with the insurmountable knowledge that her sister would continue to block any attempt to forge a relationship with her father.

She especially didn't want to be trapped in any way with Zaccheo Giordano. That display of his displeasure a few moments ago had reminded her she wanted nothing to do with him. And it was not about his temper but what she'd felt when her body had been thrust against his. She'd wanted to be held there…indefinitely.

Touching him.

Soothing his angry brow and those brief flashes of pain she saw in his eyes when he thought she wasn't looking.

God, even a part of her wanted to coax out that heart-stopping smile she'd glimpsed so very rarely when he was pursuing her!

What was wrong with her?

'Is that the one you wish for?'

She jumped and stared down at the stone that had somehow found its way into her palm. She blinked in shock.

The diamond was the largest on the tray and twice as obscene as the one that had graced her finger last night. No wonder Zaccheo sounded so disparaging.

'No!' She hastily dropped it back into its slot. 'I'd never wear anything so gratuitous.'

His coldly mocking gaze made her cringe. 'Really?'

Irritation skated over her skin. 'For your information, I didn't choose that ring.'

'But you accepted it in the spirit it was given—as the cost of buying your body in exchange for shares in Penningtons?'

Icy rage replaced her irritation. 'Your continuous insults make me wonder why you want to put up with my presence. Surely revenge can't be as sweet as you wish it if the object of your punishment enrages you this much?'

'Perhaps I enjoy tormenting you.'

'So I'm to be your punching bag for the foreseeable future?'

'Is this your way of trying to find out how long your sentence is to be?'

'A sentence implies I've done something wrong. I *know* I'm innocent in whatever you believe I've done.'

His smile could've turned a volcano into a polar ice cap. 'I've found that proclamations of innocence don't count for a thing, not when the right palm is greased.'

She inhaled at the fury and bitterness behind his words. 'Zaccheo…'

Whatever feeble reply she'd wanted to make died when his eyes hardened.

'Choose the diamond you prefer or I'll choose it for you.'

Eva turned blindly towards the table and pointed to the smallest stone. 'That one.'

'No.'

She gritted her teeth. 'Why not?'

'Because it's pink.'

'No, it's not…' She leaned closer, caught the faint pink glow, and frowned. 'Oh. I thought—'

A mirthless smile touched his lips. 'So did I. Perhaps I'll change bankers after all.' He lifted the cover of the second tray and Eva stared dispassionately at the endless rows of sparkling jewels. None of them spoke to her. Her heart hammered as it finally dawned on her why.

'Is there any reason why you want to buy me a new ring?'

He frowned. *'Scusi?'*

'When you proposed the first time, you gave me a different ring. I'm wondering why you're buying me a different one. Did you lose it?' Despite the circumstances surrounding his proposal and her subsequent rejection of him, she'd loved that simple but exquisite diamond and sapphire ring.

'No, I didn't lose it.' His tone was clipped to the point of brusqueness.

'Then why?'

'Because I do not wish you to have it.'

Her heart did an achy little dance as she waited for further elaboration. When she realised none would be forthcoming, she pulled her gaze from his merciless regard and back to the display.

He didn't want her to have it. Why? Because the ring held special meaning? Or because she was no longer worthy of it?

Berating herself for feeling hurt, she plucked a stone from the middle of the tray. According to the size chart it sat in mid-range, a flawless two carat, square-cut that felt light in her palm. 'This one.' She turned and found him staring at her, his gaze intense yet inscrutable.

Wordlessly, he held out his hand.

Her fingers brushed his palm as she dropped the stone and she bit back a gasp as that infernal electricity zinged up her arm.

His eyes held hers for a long moment before he turned and headed for the door. The next few minutes passed in a blur as Zaccheo issued clipped instructions about mountings, scrolls and settings to the jeweller.

Before she could catch her breath, Eva was back outside. Flashes went off as a group of paparazzi lunged towards them. Zaccheo handed her into the car before joining her. With a curt instruction to the driver, the car lurched into traffic.

'If I've achieved my publicity quota for the day, I'd like to be dropped at my flat, please.'

Zaccheo focused those incisive eyes on her. 'Why would I do that?'

'Aren't we done? I'd catch a bus home, but I left my handbag and phone at Pennington Manor—'

'Your belongings have been brought to my penthouse,' he replied.

'Okay, thanks. As soon as I collect them, I'll be out of your hair.' She needed to get out of this dress, shower and practise the six songs she would be performing at the club tonight. Saturday nights were the busiest of the week, and she couldn't be late. The music producer who'd been frequenting the club for the last few weeks might make another appearance tonight.

A little bubble of excitement built and she squashed it down as that half-smile that chilled her to the bone appeared on Zaccheo's face.

'You misunderstand. When I mentioned your belongings, I didn't mean your handbag and your phone. I meant everything you own in your bedsit has been removed. While we were picking your engagement ring, your belongings were relocated. Your rent has been paid off with interest and your landlady is busy renting the property to someone else.'

'What on earth are you talking about?' she finally asked when she'd picked up her jaw from the floor and sifted through his words. 'Of course I still live there. Mrs Hammond wouldn't just let you into my flat. And she certainly wouldn't arbitrarily end my lease without speaking to me first.'

Zaccheo just stared back at her.

'How dare you? Did you threaten her?'

'No, Eva. I used a much more effective tool.'

Her mouth twisted. 'You mean you threw so much money at her she buckled under your wishes?'

He shrugged rugged, broad shoulders. 'You of all people

should know how money sways even the most veracious hearts. Mrs Hammond was thrilled at the prospect of receiving her new hip replacement next week instead of at the end of the year. But it also helps that she's a hopeless romantic. The picture of us in the paper swayed any lingering doubts she had.'

Eva's breath shuddered out. Her landlady had lamented the long waiting list over shared cups of tea and Eva had offered a sympathetic ear. While she was happy that Mrs Hammond would receive her treatment earlier than anticipated and finally be out of pain, a huge part of her couldn't see beyond the fact that Zaccheo had ripped her safe harbour away without so much as a by your leave.

'You had absolutely no right to do that,' she blazed at him.

'Did I not?' he asked laconically.

'No, you didn't. This is nothing but a crude demonstration of your power. Well, guess what, I'm unimpressed. Go ahead and do your worst! Whatever crimes you think we've committed, maybe going to prison is a better option than this…this kidnapping!'

'Believe me, prison isn't an option you want to joke with.'

His lacerated tone made her heart lurch. She looked into his face and saw the agony. Her eyes widened, stunned that he was letting her witness that naked emotion.

'You think you know what it feels like to be robbed of your freedom for months on end? Pray you never get to find out, Eva. Because you may not survive it.'

'Zaccheo… I…' She stuttered to a halt, unsure of what to make of that raw statement.

His hand slashed through the air and his mask slid back into place. 'I wanted you relocated as swiftly as possible with a minimum of fuss,' he said.

A new wave of apprehension washed over her. 'Why? What's the rush?'

'I thought that would be obvious, Eva. I have deep-seated trust issues.'

Sadly, she'd reaped the rewards of betrayed trust, but the fierce loyalty to her family that continued to burn within her made her challenge him. 'How is that my family's fault?'

His nostrils flared. 'I trusted your father. He repaid that trust with a betrayal that sent me to prison! And you were right there next to him.'

Again she heard the ragged anguish in his voice. A hysterical part of her mind wondered whether this was the equivalent of a captor revealing his face to his prisoner. Was she doomed now that she'd caught a glimpse of what Zaccheo's imprisonment had done to him?

'So you keeping me against my will is meant to be part of *my* punishment?'

He smiled. 'You don't have to stay. You have many options available to you. You can call the police, tell them I'm holding you against your will, although that would be hard to prove since three hundred people saw you chase after me last night. Or you can insist I return your things and reinstate your lease. If you choose to walk away, no one will lift a finger to stop you.'

'But that's not quite true, is it? What real choice do I have when you're holding a threat over my father's head?'

'Leave him to flounder on his own if you truly believe you're guilt-free in all of this. You want to make a run for it? Here's your chance.'

His pointed gaze went to the door and Eva realised they'd completed the short journey from the bank to the iconic building that had brought Zaccheo into her life and turned it upside down.

She glanced up at the building *Architectural Digest* had called 'innovative beyond its years' and 'a heartbreakingly beautiful masterpiece'.

Where most modern buildings boasted elaborate glass edifices, The Spire was a study in polished, tensile steel. Thin sheets of steel had been twisted and manipulated around the towering spear-like structure, making the tallest building in

London a testament to its architect's skill and innovation. Its crowning glory was its diamond-shaped, vertiginous platform, within which was housed a Michelin-starred restaurant surrounded by a clear twenty-foot waterfall.

One floor beneath the restaurant was Zaccheo's penthouse. Her new home. Her prison.

The sound of him exiting the car drew her attention. When he held out his hand to her, she hesitated, unable to accept that this was her fate.

A muscle ticced in his jaw as he waited.

'You'd love that, wouldn't you? Me helping you bury my father?'

'He's going down either way. It's up to you whether he gets back up or not.'

Eva wanted to call his bluff. To shut the door and return everything to the way it was this time yesterday.

The memory of her father in that hospital bed, strung up to a beeping machine, stopped her. She'd already lost one parent. No matter how difficult things were between them, she couldn't bear to lose another. She would certainly have no hope of saving her relationship with her sister if she walked away.

Because one thing was certain. Zaccheo meant to have his way.

With or without her co-operation.

CHAPTER SIX

EVA BLEW HER fringe out of her eyes and glanced around her. The guest suite, a different one from the one she'd slept in last night, was almost three times the size of her former bedsit. And every surface was covered with designer gowns and accessories. Countless bottles of exclusive perfumes and luxury grooming products were spread on the dresser, and a team of six stylists each held an item of clothing, ready to pounce on her the moment she took off the dress she was currently trying on.

She tried hard to see the bright side of finally being out of the red dress. Unfortunately, any hint of brightness had vanished the moment she'd stepped out of the car and re-entered Zaccheo's penthouse.

'How many more before we're done?' She tried to keep her voice even, but she knew she'd missed amiability by a mile when two assistants exchanged wary glances.

'We've done your home and evening-wear package. We just need to do your vacation package and we'll be done with wardrobe. Then we can move on to hair and make-up,' Vivian, the chief stylist, said with a megawatt smile.

Eva tried not to groan. She needed to be done so she could find her phone and call her father. There was no way she was twiddling her thumbs until Monday to get a proper answer.

Being made into Zaccheo's revenge punchbag…his *married* revenge punchbag…wasn't a role she intended to be placed in. When she'd thought there was a glimmer of doubt as to Zaccheo's threat being real, she'd gone along with this farce. But with each hour that passed with silence from her father, Eva was forced to believe Zaccheo's threats weren't empty.

Would he go to such lengths to have her choose precious gems, remove her from her flat, and hire a team of stylists to turn her into the sort of woman he preferred to date, if this was just some sort of twisted game?

Her hand clenched as her thoughts took a different path. What exactly was Zaccheo trying to turn her into? Obviously he wasn't just satisfied with attaining her pedigree for whatever his nefarious purposes were. He wanted her to look like a well-dressed mannequin while he was at it.

'Careful with that, Mrs Giordano. That lace is delicate.'

She dropped the dress, her heart hammering far too fast for her liking. 'Don't call me that. I'm not Mrs Giordano—'

'Not yet, at least, right, *bellissima*?'

Eva heard the collective breaths of the women in the room catch. She turned as Zaccheo strode in. His eyes were fixed on her, flashing a warning that made her nape tingle. Before she could respond, he lifted her hands to kiss her knuckles, one after the other. Her breathing altered precariously as the silky hairs of his beard and the warm caress of his mouth threw her thoughts into chaos.

'It's only a few short days until we're husband and wife, *sì*?' he murmured intimately, but loud enough so every ear in the room caught the unmistakeable statement of possession.

She struggled to think, to *speak*, as sharp grey eyes locked with hers.

'No…I mean, yes…but let's not tempt fate. Who knows what could happen in a *few short days*?' She fully intended to have placed this nightmare far behind her.

His thumbs caressed the backs of her hands in false intimacy. 'I've moved mountains to make you mine, *il mio prezioso*. Nothing will stand in my way.' His accent was slightly more pronounced, his tone deep and captivating.

Envious sighs echoed around the room, but Eva shivered at the icy intent behind his words. She snatched her hands from his. Or she attempted to.

'In that case, I think you ought to stop distracting me so I can get on with making myself beautiful for you.' She hoped her smile looked as brittle as it felt. That her intention to end this was clear for him to see. 'Or was there something in particular you wanted?'

His eyes held hers for another electrifying second before he released her. 'I came to inform you that your belongings have been unpacked.' He surveyed the room, his gaze taking in the organised chaos. 'And to enquire whether you wish to have lunch with me or whether you want lunch brought to you so you can push through?' He turned back to her, his gaze mockingly stating that he knew her choice before she responded.

She lifted her chin. 'Seeing as this makeover was a complete *surprise* that I'd have to *make* time for, we'll take lunch in here, please.'

He ignored her censorious tone and nodded. 'Your wish is my command, *dolcezza*. But I insist you be done by dinnertime. I detest eating alone.'

She bit her tongue against a sharp retort. The cheek of him, making demands on her time when *he'd* been the one to call in the stylists in the first place! She satisfied herself with glaring at his back as he walked out, his tall, imposing figure owning every square inch of space he prowled.

The women left three excruciating hours later. The weak sun was setting in grey skies by the time Eva dragged her weary body across the vast hallway towards the suite she'd occupied last night. Her newly washed and styled hair bounced in silky waves down her back and her face tingled pleasantly from the facial she'd received before the barely there makeup had been applied.

The cashmere-soft, scooped-neck grey dress caressed her hips and thighs as she approached her door. She'd worn it only because Vivian had insisted. Eva hadn't had the heart to tell her she intended to leave every single item untouched. But Eva couldn't deny that the off-shoulder, floor-length dress felt elegant and wonderful and exactly what she'd have chosen to wear for dinner. Even if it was a dinner she wasn't looking forward to.

Her new four-inch heels clicked on the marble floor as she opened the double doors and stopped. Her hands flew to cover her mouth as she surveyed the room. Surprise was followed a few seconds later by a tingle of awareness that told her she was no longer alone.

Even then, she couldn't look away from the sight before her.

'Is something wrong?' Zaccheo's enquiry made her finally turn.

He was leaning against the door frame, his hands tucked into the pockets of his black tailored trousers. The white V-necked sweater caressed his muscular arms and shoulders and made his grey eyes appear lighter, almost eerily silver. His slightly damp hair gleamed a polished black against his shoulders and his beard lent him a rakish look that was absolutely riveting.

His gaze caught and held hers for several seconds before conducting a detailed appraisal over her face, hair and down her body that made the tingling increase. When his eyes returned to hers, she glimpsed a dark hunger that made her insides quake.

Swallowing against the pulse of undeniable attraction, she turned back to survey the room.

'I can't believe everything's been arranged so precisely,' she murmured.

'You would've preferred that they fling your things around without thought or care?'

'That's not what I mean and you know it. You've reproduced my room almost exactly how it was before.'

He frowned. 'I fail to see how that causes you distress.'

She strolled to the white oak antique dresser that had belonged to her mother. It'd been her mother's favourite piece of furniture and one of the few things Eva had taken when she'd left Pennington Manor.

Her fingers drifted over the hairbrush she'd used only yesterday morning. It had been placed in the little stand just as she normally did. 'I'm not distressed. I'm a little disconcerted that my things are almost exactly as I left them at my flat yesterday morning.' When he continued to stare, she pursed her lips. 'To reproduce this the movers would've needed photographic memories.'

'Or a few cameras shots as per my instructions.'

She sucked in a startled breath. 'Why would you do that?'

His lashes swept down for a moment. Then he shrugged. 'It was the most efficient course of action.'

'Oh.' Eva wasn't sure why she experienced that bolt of disappointment. Was she stupid enough to believe he'd done that because he *cared*? That he'd wanted her to be comfortable?

She silently scoffed at herself.

Lending silly daydreams to Zaccheo's actions had led to bitter disappointment once before. She wasn't about to make the same mistake again.

She spotted her handbag on the bed and dug out her phone. The battery was almost depleted, but she could make a quick call to her father before it died. She started to press dial and realised Zaccheo hadn't moved.

'Did you need something?'

The corner of his mouth quirked, but the bleakness in his eyes didn't dissipate. 'I've been in jail for over a year, *dolcezza*. I have innumerable needs.' The soft words held a note of deadly intent as his gaze moved from her to the bed. Her heart jumped to her throat and the air seemed to evaporate from the room. 'But my most immediate need is sustenance. I've ordered dinner to be brought from upstairs. It'll be here in fifteen minutes.'

She managed to reply despite the light-headedness that assailed her. 'Okay. I'll be there.'

With a curt nod, he left.

Eva sagged sideways onto the bed, her grip on the phone tightening until her bones protested. In the brief weeks she'd dated Zaccheo a year and half ago, she'd seen the way women responded to his unmistakeable animal magnetism. He only needed to walk into the room for every female eye to zero in on him. She'd also witnessed his reaction. Sometimes he responded with charm, other times with arrogant aloofness. But always with an innate sexuality that spoke of a deep appreciation for women. She'd confirmed that appreciation by a quick internet search in a weak moment, which had unearthed the long list of gorgeous women he'd had shockingly brief liaisons with in the past. A young, virile, wealthy bachelor, he'd been at the top of every woman's 'want to bed' list. And he'd had no qualms about helping himself to their amorous attentions.

To be deprived of that for almost a year and a half…

Eva shivered despite the room's ambient temperature. No, she was the last woman Zaccheo would *choose* to bed.

But then, he'd kissed her last night as if he'd wanted to devour her. And the way he'd looked at her just now?

She shook her head.

She was here purely as an instrument of his vengeance. The quicker she got to the bottom of *that*, the better.

Her call went straight to voicemail. Gritting her teeth, she left a message for her father to call her back. Sophie's phone rang for almost a minute before Eva hung up. Whether her sister was deliberately avoiding her calls or not, Eva intended to get some answers before Monday.

Resolving to try again after dinner, Eva plugged in her phone to charge and left her room. She met two waiters wheeling out a trolley as she entered the dining room. A few seconds later, the front door shut and Eva fought the momentary panic at being alone with Zaccheo.

She avoided looking at his imposing body as he lifted the silver domes from several serving platters.

'You always were impeccably punctual,' he said without turning around.

'I suppose that's a plus in my favour.'

'Hmm…' came his non-committal reply.

She reached her seat and froze at the romantic setting of the table. Expensive silverware and crystal-cut glasses gleamed beneath soft lighting. And already set out in a bed of ice was a small silver tub of caviar. A bottle of champagne chilled in an ice stand next to Zaccheo's chair.

'Do you intend to eat standing up?'

She jumped when his warm breath brushed her ear. When had he moved so close?

'Of course not. I just wasn't expecting such an elaborate meal.' She urged her feet to move to where he held out her chair, and sat down. 'One would almost be forgiven for thinking you were celebrating something.'

'Being released from prison isn't reason enough to enjoy something better than grey slop?'

Mortified, she cursed her tactlessness. 'I…of course. I'm sorry, that was… I'd forgotten…' *Oh, God, just shut up, Eva.*

'Of course you had.'

She tensed. 'What's that supposed to mean?'

'You're very good at putting things behind you, aren't you? Or have you forgotten how quickly you walked away from me the last time, too?'

She glanced down at her plate, resolutely picked up her spoon and helped herself to a bite of caviar. The unique taste exploded on her tongue, but it wasn't enough to quell the anxiety churning her stomach. 'You know why I walked away last time.'

'Do I?'

'Yes, you do!' She struggled to keep her composure. 'Can we talk about something else, please?'

'Why, because your actions make you uncomfortable? Or does it make your skin crawl to be sharing a meal with an ex-convict?'

Telling herself not to rise to the bait, she took another bite of food. 'No, because you snarl and your voice turns arctic, and also because I think we have different definitions of what really happened.'

He helped himself to a portion of his caviar before he responded. 'Really? Enlighten me, *per favore*.'

She pressed her lips together. 'We've already been through this, remember? You admitted that you proposed to me simply to get yourself into the Old Boys' Club. Are you going to bother denying it now?'

He froze for several heartbeats. Then he ate another mouthful. 'Of course not. But I believed we had an agreement. That you knew the part you had to play.'

'I'm sorry, I must have misplaced my copy of the Zaccheo Giordano Relationship Guide.' She couldn't stem the sarcasm or the bitterness that laced her voice.

'You surprise me.'

'How so?' she snapped, her poise shredding by the second.

'You're determined to deny that you know exactly how this game is played. That you aristocrats haven't practised the *something-for-something-more* tenet for generations.'

'You seem to be morbidly fascinated with the inner workings of the peer class. If we disgust you so much, why do you insist on soiling your life with our presence? Isn't it a bit convenient to hold us all responsible for every ill in your life?'

A muscle ticced in his jaw and Eva was certain she'd struck a nerve. 'You think having my freedom taken away is a subject I should treat lightly?'

The trembling in her belly spread out to engulf her whole body. 'The *evidence* led to your imprisonment, Zaccheo. Now we can change the subject or we can continue to fight to see who gives whom indigestion first.'

He remained silent for several moments, his eyes boring into hers. Eva stared back boldly, because backing down would see her swallowed whole by the deadly volcanic fury lurking in his eyes. She breathed a tiny sigh of relief when that mocking half-smile made an appearance.

'As you wish.' He resumed eating and didn't speak again until their first course was done. 'Let's play a game. We'll call it *What If*,' he said into the silence.

Tension knotted her nape, the certainty that she was toying with danger rising higher. 'I thought you didn't like games?'

'I'll make an exception this time.'

She took a deep breath. 'Okay. If you insist.'

'What if I wasn't the man you think I am? What if I happened to be a stranger who was innocent of everything he's been accused of? What if that stranger told you that every day he'd spent in prison felt like a little bit of himself was being chipped away for ever? What would you say to him?' His voice held that pain-laced edge she'd first heard in the car.

She looked at his face but his eyes were downcast, his white-knuckled hand wrapped around his wine glass.

This was no game.

The tension that gripped her vibrated from him, engulfing them in a volatile little bubble.

'I'd tell you how sorry I was that justice wasn't served properly on your behalf.' Her voice shook but she held firm. 'Then I'd ask you if there was anything I could do to help you put the past behind you.'

Arctic grey eyes met hers. 'What if I didn't want to put it behind me? What if everything I believe in tells me the only way to achieve satisfaction is to make those responsible pay?'

'I'd tell you it may seem like a good course of action, but doing that won't get back what you've lost. I'd also ask why you thought that was the only way.'

His eyes darkened, partly in anger, partly with anguish. She half expected him to snarl at her for daring to dissuade him from his path of retribution.

Instead, he rose and went to dish out their second course. 'Perhaps I don't know another recourse besides crime and punishment?' he intoned, disturbingly calm.

Sorrow seared her chest. 'How can that be?'

He returned with their plates and set down her second course—a lobster thermidor—before taking his seat. His movements were jerky, lacking his usual innate grace.

'Let's say hypothetically that I've never been exposed to much else.'

'But you know better or you wouldn't be so devastated at the hand you've been dealt. You're angry, yes, but you're also wounded by your ordeal. Believe me, yours isn't a unique story, Zaccheo.'

He frowned at the naked bitterness that leaked through her voice. 'Isn't it? Enlighten me. How have *you* been wounded?'

She cursed herself for leaving the door open, but, while she couldn't backtrack, she didn't want to provide him with more ammunition against her. 'My family…we're united where it counts, but I've always had to earn whatever regard I receive, especially from my father. And it hasn't always been easy, especially when walls are thrown up and alliances built where there should be none.'

He saw through her vagueness immediately. 'Your father and your sister against your mother and you? There's no need to deny it. It's easy to see your sister is fashioning herself in the image of her father,' he said less than gently.

Eva affected an easy shrug. 'Father started grooming her when we were young, and I didn't mind. I just didn't understand why that meant being left out in the cold, especially…' She stopped, realising just how much she was divulging.

'Especially…?' he pressed.

She gripped her fork tighter. 'After my mother died. I thought things would be different. I was wrong.'

His mouth twisted. 'Death is supposed to be a profound leveller. But it rarely changes people.'

She looked at him. 'Your parents—'

'Were the individuals who brought me into the world. They weren't good for much else. Take from that what you will. We're also straying away from the subject. *What if* this stranger can't see his way to forgive and forget?' That ruthless edge was back in his voice.

Eva's hand shook as she picked up her glass of Chianti. 'Then he needs to ask himself if he's prepared to live with the consequences of his actions.'

His eyebrows locked together in a dark frown, before his lashes swept down and he gave a brisk nod. 'Asked and answered.'

'Then there's no further point to this game, is there?'

One corner of his mouth lifted. 'On the contrary, you've shown a soft-heartedness that some would see as a flaw.'

Eva released a slow, unsteady breath. Had he always been like this? She was ashamed to admit she'd been so dazzled with Zaccheo from the moment he'd walked into Siren two years ago, right until the day he'd shown her his true colours, that she hadn't bothered to look any deeper. He'd kissed her on their third date, after which, fearing she'd disappoint him, she'd stumblingly informed him she was a virgin.

His reaction had been something of a fairy tale for her. She'd made him out as her Prince Charming, had adored the way he'd treated her like a treasured princess, showering her with small, thoughtful gifts, but, most of all, his undivided time whenever they were together. He'd made her feel precious, adored. He'd proposed on their sixth date, which had coincided with his thirtieth birthday, and told her he wanted to spend the rest of his life with her.

And it had all been a lie. The man sitting in front of her had no softness, only that ruthless edge and deadly charm.

'Don't be so sure, Zaccheo. I've learnt a few lessons since our unfortunate association.'

'Like what?'

'I'm no longer gullible. And my family may not be perfect, but I'm still fiercely protective of those I care about. Don't forget that.'

He helped himself to his wine. 'Duly noted.' His almost

bored tone didn't fool her into thinking this subject had stopped being anything but volatile.

They finished their meal in tense silence.

Eva almost wilted in relief when the doorbell rang and Zaccheo walked away to answer it.

Catching sight of the time, she jumped up from the dining table and was crossing the living room when Zaccheo's hand closed over her wrist.

'Where do you think you're going?' he demanded.

'Dinner's over. Can you let me go, please? I need to get going or I'll be late.'

His brows furrowed, giving him a look of a dark predator. 'Late for what?'

'Late for work. I've already taken two days off without pay. I don't want to be late on top of everything else.'

'You still work at Siren?' His tone held a note of disbelief.

'I have to make a living, Zaccheo.'

'You still sing?' His voice had grown deeper, his eyes darkening to a molten grey as he stared down at her. Although Zaccheo's expression could be hard to decipher most of the time, the mercurial changes in his eyes often spelled his altered mood.

This molten grey was one she was familiar with. And even though she didn't want to be reminded of it, a pulse of decadent sensation licked through her belly as she recalled the first night she'd seen him.

He'd walked into Siren an hour before closing, when she'd been halfway through a sultry, soulful ballad—a song about forbidden love, stolen nights and throwing caution to the wind. He'd paused to order a drink at the bar, then made his way to the table directly in front of the stage. He'd sipped his whisky, not once taking his eyes off her. Every lyric in the three songs that had followed had felt as if it had been written for the man in front of her and the woman she'd wanted to be for him.

She'd been beyond mesmerised when he'd helped her off

the stage after her session. She'd said yes immediately when he'd asked her out the next night.

But she'd been wrong, so very wrong to believe fate had brought Zaccheo to the club. He'd hunted her down with single-minded intent for his own selfish ends.

God, how he must have laughed when she'd fallen so easily into his arms!

She yanked her arm free. 'Yes, I still sing. And I'd be careful before you start making any threats on my professional life, too. I've indulged you with the engagement-ring picking and the makeover and the homecoming dinner. Now I intend to get back to *my* reality.'

She hurried away, determined not to look over her shoulder to see whether he was following. She made it to her room and quickly changed into her going-to-work attire of jeans, sweater, coat and a thick scarf to ward off the winter chill. Scooping up her bag, she checked her phone.

No calls.

The unease in her belly ballooned as she left her suite.

Zaccheo was seated on the sofa in the living room, examining a small black velvet box. His eyes tracked her, inducing that feeling of being helpless prey before a ruthless marauder. She opened her mouth to say something to dispel the sensation, but no words emerged. She watched, almost paralysingly daunted as he shut the box and placed it on the coffee table next to him.

'Would it be too *indulgent* to demand a kiss before you leave for work, *dolcezza*?' he enquired mockingly.

'Indulgent, no. Completely out of the question, most definitely,' she retorted. Then silently cursed her mouth's sudden tingling.

He shook his head, his magnificent mane gleaming under the chandelier. 'You wound me, Eva, but I'm willing to wait until the time when you will kiss me freely without me needing to ask.'

'Then you'll be waiting an eternity.'

CHAPTER SEVEN

ZACCHEO PACED THE living room and contemplated leaving another voicemail message.

He'd already left five, none of which Eva had bothered to answer. It was nearly two a.m. and she hadn't returned. In his gloomy mood, he'd indulged in one too many nightcaps to consider driving to the club where she worked.

His temperament had been darkening steadily for the last four hours, once he'd found out what Eva's father was up to. Pennington was scrambling—futilely of course, because Zaccheo had closed every possible avenue—to find financial backing. That was enough to anger Zaccheo, but what fuelled his rage was that Pennington, getting more desperate by the hour, was offering more and more pieces of The Spire, the building that he would no longer own come Monday, as collateral. The blatant fraud Pennington was willing to perpetrate to fund his lifestyle made Zaccheo's fists clench as he stalked to the window.

The view from The Spire captured the string of bridges from east to west London. The moment he'd brought his vision of the building to life with the help of his experienced architects had been one of the proudest moments of his life. More than the properties he owned across the world and the empire he'd built from the first run-down warehouse he'd bought and converted to luxury accommodation at the age of twenty, this had been the one he'd treasured most. The building that should've been his crowning glory.

Instead it'd become the symbol of his downfall.

Ironically, the court where he'd been sentenced was right across the street. He looked down at the courthouse, jaw clenched.

He intended it to be the same place where his name was cleared. He would not be broken and humiliated as his father had been by the time he'd died. He would not be whispered about behind his back and mocked to his face and called a parasite. Earlier this evening, Eva had demanded to know why he'd been so fascinated with her kind.

For a moment, he'd wondered whether his burning desire to prove they were not better than him was a weakness. One he should *put behind him*, as Eva had suggested, before he lost a lot more of himself than he already had.

As much as he'd tried he hadn't been able to dismiss her words. Because he'd lied. He knew how to forgive. He'd forgiven his father each time he'd remembered that Zaccheo existed and bothered to take an interest in him. He'd forgiven his mother the first few times she'd let his stepfather treat him like a piece of garbage.

What Zaccheo hadn't told Eva was that he'd eventually learned that forgiveness wasn't effective when the recipient didn't have any use for it.

A weakening emotion like forgiveness would be wasted on Oscar Pennington.

A keycard clicked and he turned as the entry code released the front door.

Sensation very close to relief gut-punched him.

'Where the hell have you been?' He didn't bother to obviate his snarl. Nor could he stop checking her over from head to toe, to ascertain for himself that she wasn't hurt or hadn't been a victim of an accident or a mugging. When he was sure she was unharmed, he snapped his gaze to her face, to be confronted with a quizzical look.

Dio, was she *smirking* at him?

He watched her slide her fingers through her heavy, silky hair and ignored the weariness in the gesture.

'Is it Groundhog Day or something? Because I could've sworn we had a conversation about where I was going earlier this evening.'

He seethed. 'You finished work an hour and a half ago. Where have you been since then?'

She tossed a glare his way before she shrugged off her coat. The sight of the jeans and sweater she'd chosen to wear instead of the roomful of clothes he'd provided further stoked his dark mood.

'How do you know when I finished work?'

'Answer the question, Eva.'

She tugged her handbag from her shoulder and dropped it on the coffee table. Then she kicked off her shoes and pushed up on the balls of her feet in a smooth, practised stretch reminiscent of a ballet dancer.

'I took the night bus. It's cheaper than a cab, but it took forty-five minutes to arrive.'

'*Mi scusi?* You took the *night bus*?' His brain crawled with scenarios that made his blood curdle. He didn't need a spell in prison to be aware of what dangerous elements lurked at night. The thought that Eva had exposed herself, *willingly*, to—

'Careful there, Zaccheo, you almost sound like one of those snobs you detest so much.'

She pushed up again, her feet arching and flattening in a graceful rise and fall.

Despite his blood boiling, he stared, mesmerised, as she completed the stretches. Then he let his gaze drift up her body, knowing he shouldn't, yet unable to stop himself. The sweater, decorated with a D-minor scale motif, hugged her slim torso, emphasising her full, heavy breasts and tiny waist before ending a half-inch above her jeans.

That half-inch of flesh taunted him, calling to mind the smooth warmth of her skin. The simmering awareness that had always existed between them, like a fuse just waiting to be lit, throbbed deep inside. He'd tried to deny it earlier this evening in the hallway, when he'd discovered she still sang at Siren.

He'd tried to erase the sound of her sultry voice, the evocative way Eva Pennington performed on stage. He'd cursed himself when his body had reacted the way it had the very first time he'd heard her sing. That part of his black mood also stemmed from being viscerally opposed to any other man experiencing the same reaction he did from hearing her captivating voice, the way he had been two years ago, was a subject he wasn't willing to acknowledge, never mind tackle.

He pulled his gaze from the alluringly feminine curve of her hips and shapely legs and focused on the question that had been burning through him all night.

'Explain to me how you have two million pounds in your bank account, but take the bus to and from work.'

Her mouth gaped for several seconds before she regained herself. 'How the hell do you know how much money I have in my bank account?' she demanded.

'With the right people with the right skills, very easily. I'm waiting for an answer.'

'You're not going to get one. What I do with my money and how I choose to travel is *my* business.'

'You're wrong, *cara*. As of last night, your welfare is very much my business. And if you think I'm willing to allow you to risk your safety at times when drunken yobs and muggers crawl out of the woodwork, you're very much mistaken.'

'*Allow* me? Next you'll be telling me I need your permission to breathe!'

He spiked his fingers through his hair, wondering if she'd ever been this difficult and he'd somehow missed it. The Eva he remembered, before his eyes had been truly opened to her character, had possessed a quiet passion, not this defiant, wild child before him.

But no, there'd never been anything *child*like about Eva.

She was all woman. His libido had thrilled to it right from the first.

Understandably this acute reaction was because he'd been without a woman for over a year. Now was not the time to let it out of control. The time would arrive soon enough.

She tossed her head in irritation, and the hardening in his groin threatened to prove him wrong.

'Since I need you alive for the foreseeable future, no, you don't require my permission to breathe.'

She had the nerve to roll her eyes. 'Thank you very much!'

'From now on you'll be driven to and from work.'

'No, thanks.'

He gritted his teeth. 'You prefer to spend hours freezing at a bus stop than accept my offer?'

'Yes, because the *offer* comes at a price. I may not know what it is yet, but I've no intention of paying it.'

'Why do you insist on fighting me when we both know you don't have a choice? I'm willing to bet your father didn't return a single one of your phone calls last night.'

Wide, startled eyes met his for a second before she looked away. 'I'm sure he has his reasons.'

It spoke volumes that she didn't deny trying to reach Oscar. 'Reasons more important than answering the phone to his daughter? Do you want to know what he's been up to?'

'I'm sure you're about to apprise me whether I want to hear it or not.'

'He's been calling in every single favour he thinks he's owed. Unfortunately, a man as greedy as your father cashed in most of his favours a long time ago. He's also pleading and begging his way across the country in a bid to save himself from the hole he knows I'm about to bury him in. He didn't take your calls, but he took mine. I recorded it if you wish me to play it back to you?'

Her fists clenched. 'Go to hell, Zaccheo,' she threw at him, but he glimpsed the pain in her eyes.

He almost felt sorry for her. Then he remembered her part in all this.

'Come here, Eva,' he murmured.

She eyed him suspiciously. 'Why?'

'Because I have something for you.'

Her gaze dropped to his empty hands before snapping

back to his face. 'There's nothing you have that I could possibly want.'

'If you make me come over there, I'll take that kiss you owe me from last night.' *Dio*, why had he said that? Now it was all he could think about.

Heat flushed her cheeks. 'I don't owe you a thing. And I certainly don't owe you any kisses.'

The women he'd dated in the past would've fallen over themselves to receive any gift he chose to bestow on them, especially the one he'd tucked into his back pocket.

Slowly, he walked towards her. He made sure his intent was clear. The moment she realised, her hands shot out. 'Stop! Didn't your mother teach you about the honey versus vinegar technique?'

Bitterness drenched him. 'No. My mother was too busy climbing the social ladder after my father died to bother with me. When he was alive, she wasn't much use either.'

She sucked in a shocked breath and concern furrowed her brow. 'I'm sorry.'

Zaccheo rejected the concern and let the sound of her husky voice, scratchy from the vocal strain that came with singing, wash over him instead. He didn't want her concern. But the sex he could deal with.

The need he'd been trying to keep under tight control threatened to snap. He took another step.

'Okay! I'm coming.' She walked barefooted to him. 'I've done as you asked. Give me whatever it is you want to give me.'

'It's in my back pocket.'

She inhaled sharply. 'Is this another of your games, Zaccheo?'

'It'll only take a minute to find out. Are you brave enough, *dolcezza*?' he asked.

Her gaze dropped and he immediately tilted her chin up with one finger. 'Look at me. I want to see your face.'

She blinked, then gathered herself in that way he'd always found fascinating. Slowly, she reached an arm around him. Her fingers probed until she found the pocket opening.

They slipped inside and he suppressed a groan as her fingers caressed him through his trousers. His blood rushed faster south as she searched futilely.

'It's empty,' she stated with a suspicious glare.

'Try the other one.'

She muttered a dirty word that rumbled right through him. Her colour deepened when he lifted his eyebrow.

'Let's get this over with.' She searched his right pocket and stilled when she encountered the box.

'Take it out,' he commanded, then stifled another groan when her fingers dug into his flesh to remove the velvet box. It took all the control he could muster not to kiss her when her lips parted and he glimpsed the tip of her tongue.

During his endless months in prison, he'd wondered whether he'd overrated the chemistry that existed between Eva and him. The proof that it was as potent as ever triggered an incandescent hunger that flooded his loins.

Sì, this part of his revenge that involved Eva in his bed, being inside her and implanting her with his seed, would be easy enough and pleasurable enough to achieve.

'I cannot wait to take you on our wedding night. Despite you no longer being a virgin, I'll thoroughly enjoy making you mine in every imaginable way possible. By the time I'm done with you, you'll forget every other man that you dared to replace me with.'

Her eyelids fluttered and she shivered. But the new, assertive Eva came back with fire. 'A bold assertion. But one, sadly, we'll both see unproven since there'll be no wedding *or* wedding night. And in case I haven't mentioned it, you're the last man I'd ever welcome in my bed.'

Zaccheo chose not to point out that she still had her hand in his pocket, or that her fingers were digging more firmly into his buttock.

Instead, he slid his phone from his front pocket, activated the recording app and hit the replay button.

Despite her earlier assertion that she'd grown a thicker skin, shadows of disbelief and hurt criss-crossed her face as she listened to the short conversation summoning her father to a meeting first thing on Monday. Unlike the night before where Pennington had blustered his way through Zaccheo's accusations, he'd listened in tense silence as Zaccheo had told him he knew what he was up to.

Zaccheo had given him a taster of the contents of the documents proving his innocence and the older man had finally agreed to the meeting. Zaccheo had known he'd won when Pennington had declined to bring his lawyers to verify the documents.

Thick silence filled the room after the recording ended.

'Do you believe me now, Eva? Do you believe that your family has wronged me in the most heinous way and that I intend to exact equal retribution?'

Her nostrils flared and her mouth trembled before she wrenched back control. But despite her composure, a sheen of tears appeared in her eyes, announcing her tumultuous emotion. 'Yes.'

'Take the box out of my pocket.'

She withdrew it. His instructions on the mount and setting had been followed to the letter.

'I intended to give it to you after dinner last night. Not on bended knee, of course. I'm sure you'll agree that once was enough?'

Her eyes darkened, as if he'd hurt her somehow. But of course, that was nonsense. She'd returned his first ring and walked away from him after a brief argument he barely recalled, stating that she didn't wish to be married to *a man like him*.

At the time, Zaccheo had been reeling at his lawyers' news that he was about to be charged with criminal negligence. He hadn't been able to absorb the full impact of Eva's betrayal until weeks later, when he'd already been in prison. His trial had been swift, the result of a young, overeager judge desperate to make a name for himself.

But he'd had over a year to replay the last time he'd seen Eva. In court, sitting next to her father, her face devoid of emotion until Zaccheo's sentence had been read out.

In that moment, he'd fooled himself into thinking she'd experienced a moment of agony on his behalf. He'd murmured her name. She'd looked at him. It was then that he'd seen the contempt.

That single memory cleared his mind of any extraneous feelings. 'Open the box and put on the ring,' he said tersely.

His tone must have conveyed his capricious emotional state. She cracked open the small case and slid on the ring without complaint.

He caught her hand in his and raised it, much as he had on Friday night. But this time, the acute need to rip off the evidence of another man's ownership was replaced by a well of satisfaction. 'You're mine, Eva. Until I decide another fate for you, you'll remain mine. Be sure not to forget that.'

Turning on his heel, he walked away.

Eva woke on Monday morning with a heavy heart and a stone in her gut that announced that her life was about to change for ever. It had started to change the moment she'd heard Zaccheo's recorded conversation with her father, but she'd been too shocked afterwards to decipher what her father's guilt meant for her.

Tired and wrung out, she'd stumbled to bed and fallen into a dreamless sleep, then woken and stumbled her way back to work.

Reality had arrived when she'd exited Siren after her shift to find Zaccheo's driver waiting to bring her back to the penthouse. She'd felt it when Zaccheo had told her to be ready to attend his offices in the morning. She'd felt it when she'd walked into her suite and found every item of clothing she'd tried on Saturday neatly stacked in the floor-to-ceiling shelves in her dressing room.

She felt it now when she lifted her hand to adjust her collar and caught the flash of the diamond ring on her finger. The flawless gem she'd chosen so carelessly had been mounted on a bezel setting, with further diamonds in decreasing sizes set in a platinum ring that fitted her perfectly.

You're mine, Eva. Until I decide another fate for you, you'll remain mine.

She was marrying Zaccheo in less than a week. He'd brought forward the initial two-week deadline by a whole week. She would marry him or her father would be reported to the authorities. He'd delivered that little bombshell last night after dinner. No amount of tossing and turning had altered that reality.

When she'd agreed to marry Harry, she'd known it would be purely a business deal, with zero risk to her emotions.

The idea of attaching herself to Zaccheo, knowing the depth of his contempt for her and his hunger for revenge, was bad enough. That undeniably dangerous chemistry that hovered on the point of exploding in her face when she so much as looked at him…*that* terrified her on an unspeakable level. And not because she was afraid he'd use that against her.

What she'd spent the early hours agonising over was her own helplessness against that inescapable pull.

The only way round it was to keep reminding herself why Zaccheo was doing this. Ultimate retribution and humiliation was his goal. He didn't want anything more from her.

An hour later, she sat across from her father and sister and watched in growing horror as Zaccheo's lawyers listed her father's sins.

Oscar Pennington sat hunched over, his pallor grey and his forehead covered in light sweat. Despite having heard Zaccheo's recording last night, she couldn't believe her father would sink so low.

'How could you do this?' she finally blurted when it got

too much to bear. 'And how the hell did you think you'd get away with it?'

Her father glared at her. 'This isn't the time for histrionics, Eva.'

'And you, Sophie? Did you know about this?' Eva asked her sister.

Sophie glanced at the lawyers before she replied, 'Let's not lose focus on why we're here.'

Anger shot through Eva. 'You mean let's pretend that this isn't really happening? That we're not here because Father *bribed* the builders to take shortcuts and blamed someone else for it? And you accuse me of not living in the real world?'

Sophie's lips pursed, but not before a guilty flush rushed into her face. 'Can we not do this now, please?' Her agitated gaze darted to where Zaccheo sat in lethal silence.

Eva stared at her sister, a mixture of anger and sadness seething within her. She was beginning to think they would never get past whatever was broken between them. And maybe she needed to be more like Zaccheo, and divorce herself from her feelings.

Eva glanced at him and the oxygen leached from her lungs.

God!

On Friday night, his all-black attire had lent him an air of suave but icy deadliness reminiscent of a lead in a mafia movie. Since then his casual attires, although equally formidable in announcing his breathtaking physique, had lulled her into a lesser sense of danger.

This morning, in a dark grey pinstripe suit, teamed with a navy shirt, and precisely knotted silver and blue tie, and his hair and beard newly trimmed, Zaccheo was a magnificent vision to behold.

The bespoke clothes flowed over his sleekly honed muscles and olive skin, each movement drawing attention to his powerfully arresting figure.

It was why more than one female employee had stared in

blatant interest as they'd walked into GWI's headquarters in the City this morning. It was why she'd avoided looking at him since they'd sat down.

But she'd made the mistake of looking now. And as he started to turn his head she *knew* she wouldn't be able to look away.

His gaze locked on her and she read the ruthless, possessive statement of ownership in his eyes even before he opened his mouth to speak. 'Eva has already given me what I want—her word that she's willing to do whatever it takes to make reparations.' His gaze dropped to the ring on her finger before he faced her father. 'Now it's your turn.'

CHAPTER EIGHT

'HERE'S A LIST of businesses who withdrew their contracts because of my incarceration.' Zaccheo nodded to one of his lawyers, who passed a sheet across the desk to her father.

Eva caught a glimpse of the names on the list and flinched. While the list was only half a page, she noticed more than one global conglomerate on there.

'You'll contact the CEO of each of those companies and tell them your side of the story.'

Fear flashed across her father's face. 'What's to stop them from spilling the beans?'

Zaccheo gave that chilling half-smile. 'I have a team of lawyers who'll ensure their silence if they ever want to do business with me again.'

'You're sure they'll still want your business?' Her father's voice held a newly subdued note.

'I have it on good authority their withdrawal was merely a stance. Some to gain better leverage on certain transactions and others for appearances' sake. Once they know the truth, they'll be back on board. But even if they don't come back to GWI, the purpose of your phone call would've been achieved.'

'Is this really necessary? Your company has thrived, probably beyond your wildest dreams, even while you were locked up. And this morning's stock-market reports show your stock at an all-time high.' Eva could hear the panic in her father's voice. 'Do I really need to genuflect in front of these people to make you happy?' he added bitterly.

'Yes. You do.'

Her father's face reddened. 'Look here. Judging by that rock I see on Eva's finger, you're about to marry my daughter. We're about to be *family*. Is this really how you wish to start our familial relationship?'

Bitterness pushed aside her compassion when she realised her father was once again using her as leverage for his own ends.

'You don't think this is the least you can do, Father?' she asked.

'You're taking his side?' her father demanded.

Eva sighed. 'I'm taking the side of doing the right thing. Surely you can see that?'

Her father huffed, and Zaccheo's lips thinned into a formidable line. 'I have no interest in building a relationship with you personally. You can drop dead for all I care. Right after you carry out my instructions, of course.'

'Young man, be reasonable,' her father pleaded, realising that for once he'd come up against an immoveable object that neither his charm nor his blustering would shift.

Zaccheo stared back dispassionately. No one in the room could harbour the misguided idea that he would soften in any way.

'I don't think you have a choice in the matter, Father,' Sophie muttered into the tense silence.

Eva glanced at her sister, searching for that warmth they'd once shared. But Sophie kept her face firmly turned away.

Eva jumped as her father pushed back his chair. 'Fine, you win.'

Zaccheo brushed off imaginary lint from his sleeve. 'Excellent. And please be sure to give a convincing performance. My people will contact each CEO on that list by Friday. Make sure you get it done by then.'

Her father's barrel chest rose and fell as he tried to control his temper. 'It'll be done. Sophie, we're leaving.'

Eva started to rise, too, only to find a hand clamped on her hip. The electricity that shot through her body at the bold contact had her swaying on her feet.

'What are you doing?' she demanded.

Zaccheo ignored her, but his thumb moved lazily over her hip bone as he addressed her father. 'You and Sophie may leave. I still have things to discuss with my fiancée. My secretary will contact you with details of the wedding in the next day or two.'

Her father looked from her face to Zaccheo's. Then he stormed out of the door.

Eva turned to Zaccheo. 'What more could we possibly have to discuss? You've made everything crystal clear.'

'Not quite everything. Sit down.' He waited until she complied before he removed his hand.

Eva wasn't sure whether it was relief that burst through her chest or outrage. Relief, most definitely, she decided. Lacing her fingers, she waited as he dismissed all except one lawyer.

At Zaccheo's nod, the man produced a thick binder and placed it in front of Zaccheo, after which he also left.

She could feel Zaccheo's powerful gaze on her, but she'd already unsettled herself by looking at him once. And she was reeling from everything that had taken place here in the last hour.

When the minutes continued to tick by in silence, she raised her head. 'You want my father to help rebuild the damage he caused to your reputation, but what about your criminal record? I would've thought that would be more important to you.'

'You may marry a man with a criminal record come Saturday, but I won't remain that way for long. My lawyers are working on it.'

Her heart lurched at the reminder that in a few short days she would be his wife, but she forced herself to ask the question on her mind. 'How can they do that without implicating my father? Isn't withholding evidence a crime?'

'Nothing will be withheld. How the authorities choose to apply the rule of law is up to them.'

Recalling the state of her father's health, she tightened

her fists in anxiety. 'So you're saying Father can still go to prison? Despite letting him believe he won't?'

The kick in his stare struck deep in her soul. 'I'm the one who was wronged. I have some leeway in speaking on his behalf, should I choose to.'

The implied threat didn't escape her notice. They would either toe his line or suffer the consequences.

She swallowed. 'What did you want to discuss with me?'

He placed a single sheet of paper in front of her.

'These are the engagements we'll be attending this week. Make sure you put them in your diary.'

She pursed her lips, denying that the deep pang in her chest was hurt. 'At least you're laying your cards on the table this time round.'

'What cards would those be?'

She shrugged. 'The ones that state your desire to conquer the upper class, of course. Wasn't that your aim all along? To walk in the hallowed halls of the Old Boys' Club and show them all your contempt for them?'

His eyes narrowed, but she caught a shadow in the grey depths. 'How well you think you know me.'

She cautioned herself against probing the sleeping lion, but found herself asking anyway, 'Why, Zaccheo? Why is it so important that you bring us all down a peg or two?'

He shifted in his seat. If she hadn't known that he didn't possess an ounce of humility, she'd have thought he was uneasy. 'I don't detest the whole echelon. Just those who think they have a right to lord it over others simply because of their pedigree. And, of course, those who think they can get around the laws that ordinary people have to live by.'

'What about me? Surely you can't hate me simply because our relationship didn't work out?'

'Was that what we had—a *relationship*?' he sneered. 'I thought it was a means for you to facilitate your father's plans.'

'*What?* You think I had something to do with my father scapegoating you?'

'Perhaps you weren't privy to his whole plan like your sister was. But the timing of it all was a little too convenient, don't you think? You walked away *three days* before I was charged, with a flimsy excuse after an even flimsier row. What was it? Oh, yes, you didn't want to marry *a man like me*?'

She surged to her feet, her insides going cold. 'You think I staged the whole thing? Need I remind you that you were the one who initiated our first meeting? That you were the one to ask me out?'

'An event carefully orchestrated by your father, of course. Do you know why I was at Siren that night?'

'Will you believe me if I said no?'

'I was supposed to meet your father and two of his investors there. Except none of them showed.'

She frowned. 'That's not possible. My father hates that I sing. He hates it even more that I work in a nightclub. I don't think he even knows where Siren is.'

'And yet he suggested it. Highly recommended it, in fact.'

The idea that her father had engineered their first meeting coated her mouth with bitterness. He'd used her strong loyalty to their family to manipulate her long before she'd taken a stand and moved out of Pennington Manor. But this further evidence showed a meticulousness that made her blood run cold.

'Were you even a virgin back then?' Zaccheo sliced at her.

The question brought her back to earth. 'Excuse me?'

'Or was it a ploy to sweeten the deal?'

'I didn't know you existed until you parked yourself in front of the stage that night!'

'Maybe not. But you must've known who I was soon after. Isn't that what women do these days? A quick internet search while they're putting on their make-up to go on the first date?'

Eva couldn't stop her guilty flush because it was exactly what she'd done. But not with the reprehensible intentions he'd implied. Zaccheo's all-consuming interest in her had seemed too good to be true. She'd wanted to know more about the compelling man who'd zeroed in on her with such unnerving interest.

What she'd found was a long list of conquests ranging from supermodels to famous sports stars. She'd been so intimidated, she'd carefully kept her inexperience under wraps. It was that desperately embarrassing need to prove her sophistication that had led to her boldly accepting his dare to perform oral sex on him on his thirtieth birthday. She'd been so anxious, she'd bungled it even before she'd unfastened his belt. In the face of his wry amusement, she'd blurted her inexperience.

The inexperience he was now denouncing as a ploy.

'I don't care what you think. All I care about is that I know what I'm letting myself in for now. I know exactly the type of man you are.' One whose ruthless ambition was all he cared about.

He regarded her for several tense seconds. 'Then this won't surprise you too much.' He slid a thick burgundy folder across to her. 'It's a prenuptial agreement. On the first page you'll find a list of independent lawyers who can guide you through the legalese should you require it. The terms are non-negotiable. You have twenty-four hours to read and sign it.'

She glanced from him to the folder, her mouth dropping open in shock. 'Why would I need a prenup? I've agreed to your demands. Isn't this overkill?'

'My lawyers go spare if I don't get everything in writing. Besides, there are a few items in there we haven't discussed yet.'

Something in his voice made her skin prickle. Her belly quaked as she turned the first page of the thick document. The first few clauses were about general schedules and routines, making herself available for his engagements within reason, how many homes he owned and her duty to oversee the running of them, and his expectation of her availability to travel with him on his business trips should he require it.

'If you think I'm going to turn myself into a pet you can pick up and hop on a plane with whenever it suits you, you're in for a shock.'

He merely quirked an eyebrow at her. She bristled but carried on reading.

She paused at the sixth clause. 'We can't be apart for more than five days in the first year of marriage?'

The half-smile twitched. 'We don't want tongues wagging too soon, do we?'

'You mean after the first year I can lock myself in a nunnery for a year if I choose to?'

For the first time since Zaccheo had exploded back into her life, she glimpsed a genuine smile. It was gone before it registered fully, but the effect was no less earth-shattering. 'No nunnery would accept you once you've spent a year in my bed.'

Her face flamed and the look in his eyes made her hurriedly turn the page.

The ninth made her almost swallow her tongue. 'I don't want your money! And I certainly don't need that much money *every* month.' The sum stated was more than she earned in a year.

He shrugged. 'Then donate it to your favourite charity.'

Since she wasn't going to win that one, she moved on to the tenth and last clause.

Eva jerked to her feet, her heart pounding as she reread the words, hoping against hope that she'd got it wrong the first time. But the words remained clear and stark and *frightening*. 'You want…*children*?' she rasped through a throat gone bone dry with dread.

'*Sì,*' he replied softly. 'Two. An heir and a spare, I believe you disparagingly refer to that number in your circles. More if we're lucky—stop shaking your head, Eva.'

Eva realised that was exactly what she was doing as he rose and stalked her. She took a step back, then another, until her backside bumped the sleek black cabinet running the length of the central wall.

He stopped in front of her, leaned his tall, imposing frame over hers. 'Of all the clauses in the agreement, this is non-negotiable.'

'You said they were all non-negotiable.'

'They are, but some are more non-negotiable than others.'

A silent scream built inside her. 'If this one is the most important why did you put it last?'

'Because you would be signing directly below it. I wanted you to feel its import so there would be no doubt in your mind what you were agreeing to.'

She started to shake her head again but froze when he angled himself even closer, until their lips were an inch apart. Their breaths mingling, he stared her down. Eva's heart climbed into her throat as she struggled to sift through the emotions those words on the page had evoked.

Zaccheo was asking the impossible.

Children were the reasons why her last two relationships before him had failed before they'd even begun.

Children were the reason she'd painfully resigned herself to remaining single. To spurning any interest that came her way because she hadn't been able to bear the thought of baring her soul again only to have her emotions trampled on.

She wouldn't cry. She wouldn't break down in front of Zaccheo. Not today. *Not ever.* He'd caused her enough turmoil to last a lifetime.

But he was asking the impossible. 'I can't.'

His face hardened but he didn't move a muscle. 'You can. You *will*. Three days ago you were agreeing to marry another man. You expect me to believe the possibility of children weren't on the cards with Fairfield?'

She shook her head. 'My agreement with Harry was different. Besides, he…' She stopped, unwilling to add to the flammable tension.

'He what?' Zaccheo enquired silkily.

'He didn't *hate* me!'

He seemed almost surprised at her accusation. Surprise slowly gave way to a frown. 'I don't hate you, Eva. In fact, given time and a little work, we might even find common ground.'

She cursed her heart for leaping at his words. 'I can't—'

'You have twenty-four hours. I suggest you take the time and review your answer before saying another word.'

Her stomach clenched. 'And if my answer remains the same?'

His expression was one of pure, insufferable arrogance. 'It won't. You make feeble attempts to kick at the demands of your ancestry and title, but inevitably you choose blood over freedom. You'll do anything to save your precious family name—'

'You really think so? After the meeting we just had? Are you really that blind, or did you not see the way my sister and my father treat me? We are not a close family, Zaccheo. No matter how much I wish it…' Her voice shook, but she firmed it. 'Have you stopped to think that you pushing me this way may be the catalyst I need to completely break away from a family that's already broken?'

Her terse words made his eyes narrow. But his expression cleared almost immediately. 'No, you're loyal. You'll give me what I want.'

'No—'

'Yes,' he breathed.

He closed the gap between them slowly, as if taunting her with the knowledge that she couldn't escape the inevitability of his possession.

His mouth claimed hers—hot, demanding, powerfully erotic. Eva moaned as her emotions went into free fall. He feasted on her as if he had all the time in the world, taking turns licking his way into her mouth before sliding his tongue against hers in an expert dance that had her desperately clutching his waist.

Wild, decadent heat swirled through her body as he lifted her onto the cabinet, tugged up the hem of her dress and planted himself between her thighs. Her shoulders met the wall and she gasped as one hand gripped her thigh.

Push him away. You need to push him away!

Her hands climbed from his waist to his chest, albeit far slower and in a far more exploratory fashion than her screeching brain was comfortable with. But she made an effort once she reached his broad shoulders.

She pushed.

And found her hands captured in a firm one-handed hold above her head. His other hand found her breast and palmed it, squeezing before flicking his thumb over her hardened nipple.

Sensation pounded through her blood. Her legs curled around his thickly muscled thighs and she found herself pulled closer to the edge of the cabinet, until the powerful evidence of his erection pushed at her core.

Zaccheo gave a deep groan and freed her hands to bury his in her hair. Angling her head for a deeper invasion, he devoured her until the need for air drove them apart.

Chests heaving, they stared at each other for several seconds before Eva scrambled to untangle her legs from around him. Every skin cell on fire, she struggled to stand up. He stopped her with a hand on her belly, his eyes compelling hers so effortlessly, she couldn't look away.

The other hand moved to her cheek, then his fingers drifted over her throbbing mouth.

'As much as I'd like to take you right here on my boardroom cabinet, I have a dozen meetings to chair. It seems everyone wants a powwow with the newly emancipated CEO. We'll pick this up again at dinner. I'll be home by seven.'

She diverted enough brainpower from the erotic images it was creating to reply. 'I won't be there. I'm working tonight.'

A tic throbbed at his temple as he straightened his tie. 'I see that I need to put aligning our schedules at the top of my agenda.'

She pushed him away and stood. 'Don't strain yourself too much on my account,' she responded waspishly. She was projecting her anger at her weakness onto him, but she couldn't help herself. She tugged her dress down, painfully aware of the sensitivity between her unsteady legs as she moved away from him and picked up her handbag and the folder containing the prenup. 'I'll see you when I see you.'

He took her hand and walked her to the door. 'I guarantee you it'll be much sooner than that.' He rode the lift down with her to the ground floor, barely acknowledging the keen interest his presence provoked.

Romeo was entering the building as they exited. The two men exchanged a short conversation in Italian before Zaccheo opened the door to the limo.

When she went to slide in, he stopped her. 'Wait.'

'What is it?' she demanded.

His lips firmed and he seemed in two minds as to his response. 'For a moment during the meeting, you took my side against your father. I'll factor that favourably into our dealings from now on.'

Eva's heart lifted for a moment, then plunged back to her toes. 'You don't get it, do you?'

He frowned. 'Get what?'

'Zaccheo, for as long as I can remember, all I've wished was for there to be *no sides*. For there not to be a *them* against *us*. Maybe that makes me a fool. Or maybe I'll need to give up that dream.'

His eyes turned a shade darker with puzzlement, then he shrugged. '*Sì, bellissima*, perhaps you might have to.'

And right in front of the early lunch crowd, Zaccheo announced his ownership of her with a long, deep kiss.

* * *

Eva could barely hear herself think above the excited buzz in Siren's VIP lounge as she cued the next song.

She was sure the unusually large Monday night crowd had nothing to with Ziggy Preston, the famous record producer who'd been coming to watch her perform on and off for the past month, and everything to do with the pictures that had appeared in the early-evening paper of her kissing Zaccheo outside his office this afternoon. Avoiding the news had been difficult, seeing as that kiss and a large-scale picture of her engagement ring had made front-page news.

One picture had held the caption *'Three Ring Circus'*— with photos of her three engagement rings and a pointed question as to her motives.

It'd been a relief to leave Zaccheo's penthouse, switch off her phone and immerse herself in work. Not least because blanking her mind stopped her from thinking about the last clause in the prenup, and the reawakened agony she'd kept buried since her doctor had delivered the harrowing news six years ago. News she'd only revealed twice, with devastating consequences.

She almost wished she could blurt it out to Zaccheo and let the revelation achieve what it had in the past—a swift about-face from keen interest to cold dismissal, with one recipient informing her, in the most callous terms, that he could never accept her as a full woman.

Pain flared wider, threatening the foundations she'd built to protect herself from that stark truth. Foundations Zaccheo threatened.

She clutched the mic and forced back the black chasm that swirled with desolation. Her accompanying pianist nodded and she cleared her throat, ready to sing the ballad that ironically exhorted her to be brave.

She was halfway through the song when he walked in. As usual, the sight of him sent a tidal wave of awareness through her body and she managed to stop herself from stumbling by the skin of her teeth. Heads turned and the buzz in the room grew louder.

Zaccheo's eyes raked her from head to toe before settling on her face. A table miraculously emptied in front of the stage. Someone took his overcoat and Eva watched him release the single button to his dinner jacket before pulling out a chair and seating himself at the roped-off table before her.

The sense of déjà vu was so overwhelming, she wanted to abandon the song and flee from the stage. She finished, she smiled and accepted the applause, then made her way to where he pointedly held out a chair for her.

'What are you doing here?' she whispered fiercely.

He took his time to answer, choosing instead to pull her close and place a kiss on each cheek before drawing back to stare at her.

'You couldn't make dinner, so I brought dinner to you.'

'You really shouldn't have,' she replied, fighting the urge to rub her cheeks where his lips had been. 'Besides, I can't. My break is only twenty minutes.'

'Tonight your break is an hour, as it will be every night I choose to dine with you here instead of at our home. Now sit down and smile, *mio piccolo uccello che canta*, and pretend to our avid audience that you're ecstatically happy to see your fiancé,' he said with a tone edged in steel.

CHAPTER NINE

ZACCHEO WATCHED MYRIAD expressions chase across her face. Rebellion. Irritation. Sexual awareness. A touch of embarrassment when someone shouted their appreciation of her singing from across the room. One glance from Zaccheo silenced that inebriated guest.

But it was the shadows that lurked in her eyes that made his jaw clench. All day, through the heady challenge of getting back into the swing of business life, that look in her eyes when she'd seen his last clause in the prenuptial agreement had played on his mind. Not enough to disrupt his day, but enough for him to keep replaying the scene. Her reaction had been extreme and almost...distressed.

Yes, it bothered him that she saw making a family with him abhorrent, even though he'd known going in that, had she been given a choice, Eva would've chosen someone else, someone more *worthy* to father her children. Nevertheless, her reaction had struck hard in a place he'd thought was no longer capable of feeling hurt.

The feeling had festered, like a burr under his skin, eating away at him as the day had progressed. Until he'd abruptly ended a videoconference and walked out of his office.

He'd intended to return home and help himself to fine whisky in a toast to striking the first blow in ending Oscar Pennington's existence. Instead he'd found himself swapping his business suit for a dinner jacket and striding back out of his penthouse.

The woman who'd occupied far too much of his thoughts today swayed to her seat and sat down. The pounding in his blood that had never quite subsided after that kiss in his boardroom, and increased the moment he'd entered the

VIP room and heard her singing, accelerated when his gaze dropped to her scarlet-painted lips.

Before he'd met Eva Pennington, Zaccheo had never labelled himself a possessive guy. Although he enjoyed the thrill of the chase and inevitable capture, he'd been equally thrilled to see the back of the women he'd dated, especially when the clinginess had begun.

With Eva, he'd experienced an unprecedented and very caveman-like urge to claim her, to make sure every man within striking distance knew she belonged to him. And only him. That feeling was as unsettling as it was hard to eradicate. It wasn't helped when she toyed with her champagne glass and avoided eye contact.

'I don't appreciate you messing with my schedule behind my back, Zaccheo,' she said.

He wasn't sure why the sound of his name on her lips further spiked his libido, but he wanted to hear it again. He wanted to hear it fall from her lips in the throes of passion, as he took her to the heights of ecstasy.

Dio, he was losing it. Losing sight of his objective. Which was to make sure she understood that he intended to give no quarter in making her his.

He took a bracing sip of champagne and nodded to the hovering waiters ready to serve the meal he'd ordered.

'It was dinner here or summoning you back to the penthouse. You should be thanking me for bending like this.'

She glared. 'You really are a great loss to the Dark Ages, you know that?'

'In time you'll learn that I always get my way, Eva. *Always*.'

Her eyes met his and that intense, inexplicable connection that had throbbed between them right from the very start pulled, tightened.

'Did it even occur to you that I may have said yes if you'd asked me to have dinner with you?'

Surprise flared through him, and he found himself asking, 'Would you?'

She shrugged. 'I guess you'll never know. We need to discuss the prenup,' she said.

He knew instinctively that she was about to refuse him again. A different sort of heat bloomed in his chest. 'This isn't the time or place.'

'I don't...' She paused when the waiters arrived at the table with their first course. As if recalling where they were, she glanced round, took a deep breath, and leaned forward. 'I won't sign it.'

Won't, not *can't*, as she'd said before.

Bitterness surged through his veins. 'Because the thought of my seed growing inside you fills you with horror?'

Her fingers convulsed around her knife, but, true to her breeding, she directed it to her plate with understated elegance to cut her steak.

'Why would you want me as the mother of your children, anyway? I would've thought you'd want to spare yourself such a vivid reminder of what you've been through.'

'Perhaps I'm the one to give the Pennington name the integrity it's been so sorely lacking thus far.'

She paled, and he cursed himself for pursuing a subject that was better off discussed in private. Although he'd made sure their table was roped off and their conversation couldn't be overheard, there was still more than enough interest in them for each expression flitting across Eva's face to be captured and assessed.

'So we're your personal crusade?' she asked, a brittle smile appearing on her face as she acknowledged someone over his shoulder.

'Let's call it more of an experiment.'

Her colour rose with the passionate fury that intrigued him. 'You'd father children based on an *experiment*? After what you've been through...what we've both been through, you think that's fair to the children you intend to have to be used solely as a means for you to prove a point?' Her voice was ragged and he tensed.

'Eva—'

'No, I won't be a part of it!' Her whisper was fierce. 'My mother may have loved me in her own way, but I was still the tool she used against my father when it suited her. If my grades happened to be better than Sophie's, she would imply my father was lacking in some way. And believe me, my father didn't pull his punches when the situation was reversed.' She swallowed and raised bruised eyes to his. 'Even if I cou—wanted to why would I knowingly subject another child to what I went through? Why would I give you a child simply to use to *prove a point*?'

'You mistake my meaning. I don't intend to fail my children or use them as pawns. I intend to be there for them through thick and thin, unlike my parents were for me.' He stopped when her eyes widened. 'Does that surprise you?'

'I… Yes.'

He shrugged, even though it occurred to him that he'd let his guard down more with her than he ever had with anyone. But she had no power to hurt him. She'd already rejected him once. This time he knew the lay of the land going in. So it didn't matter if she knew his parental ambitions for the children they'd have.

'My children will be my priority, although I'll be interested to see how your family fares with being shown that things can be done differently. The *right* way.'

He watched her digest his response, watched the shadows he was beginning to detest mount in her eyes. He decided against probing further. There'd been enough turbulent emotions today. He suspected there would be further fireworks when she found out the new business negotiations he'd commenced this afternoon.

That a part of him was looking forward to it made him shift in his seat.

Since when had he craved verbal conflict with a woman?

Never. And yet he couldn't seem to help himself when it came to Eva.

He was debating this turn of events as their plates were removed when a throat cleared next to them.

The man was around his age, with floppy brown hair and a cocky smile that immediately rubbed Zaccheo the wrong way.

'Can I join you for a few minutes?' he asked.

The *no* that growled up Zaccheo's chest never made it. Eva was smiling—her first genuine smile since he'd walked in—and nodding. 'Mr Preston, of course!'

'Thanks. And call me Ziggy, please. Mr Preston is my headmaster grandfather.'

'What can we do for you, *Ziggy*?' Zaccheo raised an eyebrow at the furious look Eva shot him.

The other man, who was staring at Eva with an avidness that made Zaccheo's fist clench, finally looked in his direction. 'I came to pay my compliments to your girlfriend. She has an amazing voice.'

Eva blushed at his words.

Zaccheo's eyes narrowed when he noticed she wasn't wearing her engagement ring. 'Eva's my fiancée, not my girlfriend. And I'm very much aware of her exceptional talent,' he said, the harsh edge to his voice getting through to the man, who looked from him to Eva before his smile dimmed.

'Ah, congratulations are in order, then?'

'*Grazie,*' Zaccheo replied. 'Was there something else you wanted?'

'Zaccheo!' Eva glared harder, and turned to Ziggy. 'Pardon my *fiancé*. He's feeling a little testy because—'

'I want her all to myself but find other *things* standing in my way. And because you're not wearing your engagement ring, *dolcezza*.'

She covered her bare fingers with her hand, as if that would remove the evidence of the absence of his ring. 'Oh,

I didn't want to risk losing it. I'm still getting used to it.' The glance she sent him held a mixture of defiance and entreaty.

Ziggy cleared his throat again. 'I don't want to play the *Do-you-know-who-I-am?* card, but—'

'Of course I know who you are,' Eva replied with a charming laugh.

Ziggy smiled and produced a business card. 'In that case, would you like to come to my studio next week? See if we can make music together?'

Eva's pleased gasp further darkened Zaccheo's mood. 'Of course I can—'

'Aren't you forgetting something, *luce mio*?' he asked in a quietly lethal tone.

'What?' she asked, so innocently he wanted to grab her from the chair, spread her across the table and make her see nothing, no one, but him. Make her recall that she had given her word to be his and only his.

'You won't be available next week.' He didn't care that he hadn't yet apprised her of the details. He cared that she was smiling at another man as if *he* didn't exist. 'We'll be on our honeymoon on my private island off the coast of Brazil where we'll be staying for the next two weeks.'

Her eyes rounded, but she recovered quickly and took the business card. 'I'll *make* time to see you before I go. Surely you don't want to deny me this opportunity, *darling*?' Her gaze swung to him, daring him to respond in the negative.

Despite his irritation, Zaccheo curbed a smile. 'Of course. Anything for you, *dolcezza*.'

Ziggy beamed. 'Great! I look forward to it.'

The moment he was out of earshot, she turned to Zaccheo. 'How dare you try and sabotage me like that?'

'Watching you smile at another man like that fills me with insane jealousy. It also brings out the jerk in me. My apologies,' he growled. Her mouth dropped open. 'Close your mouth, Eva.'

She shook her head as if reeling from a body blow.

Welcome to my world.

'Where's your ring?' He stared at her, his control on a knife-edge.

Perhaps sensing the dangerously shifting currents, she pulled up the gold chain that hung between her pert, full breasts. His ring dangled from it.

'Put it on. Now,' he said, struggling to keep his voice even.

Undoing the clasp, she took the ring off the chain and slid it back on her finger. 'There. Can I return to work now or are you going to harangue me about something else?'

He told himself he did it because he needed to put his rampaging emotions *somewhere*. That it was her fault for pushing him to his limit. But when he plucked her from her seat, placed her in his lap and kissed her insanely tempting mouth, Zaccheo knew it was because he couldn't help himself. She *got* to him in a way no one else did.

By the time he pulled away, they were both breathing hard. Her high colour filled him with immense satisfaction, helping him ignore his own hopeless loss of control.

'Don't take the ring off again, Eva. You underestimate the lengths I'm prepared to go to in making sure you stick to your word, but for your sake I hope you start taking me seriously.'

In contrast to the vividness of Zaccheo's presence, the rest of the night passed in a dull blur after he left. By the time Eva collapsed into bed in the early hours, her head throbbed with the need to do something severely uncharacteristic. Like scream. Beat her fists against the nearest wall. Shout her anger and confusion to the black skies above.

She did nothing of the sort. More than anything, she craved a little peace and quiet.

After that kiss in the club, even more eyes had followed her wherever she went. Hushed whispers had trailed her to the bathroom. By the time her shift had ended three hours later, she'd been ready to walk out and never return.

She wouldn't, of course. Working at Siren gave her the free time to write her songs while earning enough to live on. Despite Zaccheo's heavy-handedness, she could never see a time when she'd be dependent on anyone other than herself.

'You underestimate the lengths I'm prepared to go to...'

The forceful statement had lingered long after he'd left, anchored by the heavy presence of the prenuptial agreement in her handbag.

He'd said he wouldn't negotiate. Eva didn't see that he had a choice in this matter. Refusing to marry him might well spell the end for her father, but withholding the truth and marrying him knowing she could never fulfil her part of the bargain would be much worse.

Turning in bed, she punched her pillow, dreading the long, restless night ahead. Only to wake with sunshine streaming through the window and her clock announcing it was ten o'clock.

Rushing out of bed, she showered quickly and entered the dining room just as Romeo was exiting, having finished his own breakfast. The table was set for one and Eva cursed herself for the strange dip in her belly that felt very much like disappointment.

'Good morning. Shall I get the chef to make you a cooked breakfast?' The man whose role she was beginning to suspect went deeper than a simple second-in-command asked.

'Just some toast and tea, please, thank you.'

He nodded and started to leave.

'Is Zaccheo around or has he left for the office?'

'Neither. He left this morning for Oman. An unexpected hiccup in the construction of his building there.'

Eva was unprepared for the bereft feeling that swept through her. She should be celebrating her temporary reprieve. Finding a way to see if she could work around that impossible clause. 'When will he be back?'

'In a day or two. Latest by the end of the week to be ready in time for the wedding,' Romeo said in that deep, modu-

lated voice of his. 'This is for you.' He handed her a folded
note and left.

The bold scrawl was unmistakeably Zaccheo's.

Eva,
  Treat my absence as you wish, but never as an ex-
cuse to be complacent.
  My PA will be in touch with details of your wedding
dress fitting this morning and your amended sched-
ule for the week.
  You have my permission to miss me.
Z

Ugh! She grimaced at the arrogance oozing from the
paper. Balling the note, she flung it across the table. Then
quickly jumped up and retrieved it before Romeo returned.
The last thing she wanted was for him to report her loss of
temper to Zaccheo.

Her traitorous body had a hard enough time controlling itself when Zaccheo was around. She didn't want him to know
he affected her just as badly when he was absent.

By the time breakfast was delivered, she'd regained her
composure. Which was just as well, because close on the
chef's heel was a tall, striking brunette dressed in a grey
pencil skirt and matching jacket.

'Good morning, my name is Anyetta, Mr Giordano's PA.
He said you were expecting me?'

'I was expecting a phone call, not a personal visit.'

Anyetta delivered a cool smile. 'Mr Giordano wanted his
wishes attended to personally.'

Eva's appetite fled. 'I bet he did,' she muttered.

She poured herself a cup of tea as Anyetta proceeded
to fill up her every spare hour between now and Saturday
morning.

Eva listened until her temper began to flare, then tuned

out until she heard the word *makeover*. 'I've already had one makeover. I don't need another one.'

Anyetta's eyes drifted over Eva's hair, which she admitted was a little wild since she hadn't brushed it properly before she'd rushed out to speak to Zaccheo. 'Not even for your wedding day?'

Since there wasn't likely to be a wedding day once she told Zaccheo she had no intention of signing the agreement, she replied, 'It'll be taken care of.'

Anyetta ticked off a few more items, verified that Eva's passport was up to date, then stood as the doorbell rang. 'That'll be Margaret with your wedding dress.'

The feeling of being on a runaway train intensified as Eva trailed Anyetta out of the dining room. She drew to a stunned halt when she saw the middle-aged woman coming towards her with a single garment bag and a round veil and shoebox.

'Please tell me you don't have a team of assistants lurking outside ready to jump on me?' she asked after Anyetta left.

Margaret laughed. 'It's just me, Lady Pennington. Your fiancé was very specific about his wishes, and, meeting you now, I see why he chose this dress. He did say I was to work with you, of course. So if you don't like it, we can explore other options.'

Eva reminded herself that this situation hadn't arisen out of a normal courtship, that Zaccheo choosing her wedding dress for her shouldn't upset her so much. Besides, the likelihood of this farce ever seeing the light of day was very low so she was better off just going along with it.

But despite telling herself not to care, Eva couldn't suppress her anxiety and excitement.

She gasped as the dress was revealed.

The design itself was simple and clean, but utterly breathtaking. Eva stared at the fitted white satin gown overlaid with lace and beaded with countless tiny crystals. Delicate capped sleeves extended from the sweetheart neckline and the tiniest train flared out in a beautiful arc. At the back, more crystals had been embedded in mother-of-pearl buttons that went from nape to waist. Unable to resist, Eva reached out to touch the dress, then pulled herself back.

There was no point falling in love with a dress she'd never wear. No point getting butterflies about a marriage that would never happen once she confessed her flaw to Zaccheo. Her hands fisted and she fought the desolation threatening to break free inside her.

For six years, she'd successfully not dwelt on what she could never have—a husband who cared for her and a family of her own. She'd made music her life and had found fulfilment in it. She wasn't about to let a heartbreakingly gorgeous dress dredge up agonies she'd sealed in a box marked *strictly out of bounds*.

'Are you ready to try it on?' Margaret asked.

Eva swallowed. 'Might as well.'

If the other woman found her response curious, she didn't let on. Eva avoided her gaze in the mirror as the dress was slipped over her shoulders and the delicate chiffon and lace veil was fitted into place. She mumbled her thanks as Margaret helped her into matching-coloured heels.

'Oh, I'm pleased to see we don't need to alter it in any way, Lady Pennington. It fits perfectly. Looks like your fiancé was very accurate with your measurements. You'd be surprised how many men get it wrong...'

She kept her gaze down, frightened to look at herself, as Margaret tweaked and tugged until she was happy.

Eva dared not look up in case she began to *hope* and *wish*. She murmured appropriate responses and turned this way and that when asked and breathed a sigh of relief when the ordeal was over. The moment Margaret zipped up the bag and left, Eva escaped to her suite. Putting her headphones on, she activated the music app on her tablet and proceeded to drown out her thoughts the best way she knew how.

But this time no amount of doing what she loved best could obliterate the thoughts tumbling through her head.

At seventeen when her periods had got heavier and more painful with each passing month, she'd attributed it to life's natural cycle. But when stronger painkillers had barely alleviated the pain, she'd begun to suspect something major was wrong.

Collapsing during a university lecture had finally prompted her to seek medical intervention.

The doctor's diagnosis had left her reeling.

Even then, she'd convinced herself it wasn't the end of the world, that compared to her mother's fight against cancer, a fight she'd eventually lost a year later, Eva's problem was inconsequential. Women dealt with challenging problems like hers every day. When the time came, the man she chose to spend the rest of her life with would understand and support her.

Eva scoffed at her naiveté. Scott, the first man she'd dated in the last year of university, had visibly recoiled from her when she'd mentioned her condition. She'd been so shocked by his reaction, she'd avoided him for the rest of her time at uni.

Burnt, she'd sworn off dating until she'd met George Tremayne, her fellow business intern during her brief stint at Penningtons. Flattered by his attentiveness, she'd let down her guard and gone on a few dates before he'd begun to pressure her to take things further. Her gentle rejection and confession of her condition had resulted in a scathing volley of insults, during which she'd found out exactly why her father had been pressing her to work at Penningtons after graduation.

Oscar Pennington, already secure in his conscript of Sophie as his heir, was eager to offload his remaining daughter and had lined up a list of suitable men, George Tremayne, the son of a viscount, being on the top of that list. George's near-identical reaction to Scott's had hurt twice as much, and convinced Eva once and for all that her secret was best kept to herself.

Finding out she was yet another means to an end for Zaccheo had rocked her to the core, but she'd taken consolation in the fact the secret she'd planned on revealing to him shortly after their engagement was safe.

That secret was about to be ripped open.

As she turned up the volume of her music Eva knew disclosing it to Zaccheo would be the most difficult thing she would ever do.

CHAPTER TEN

ZACCHEO SCROLLED THROUGH the missed calls from Eva on his phone as he was driven away from the private hangar. Romeo had relayed her increasingly frantic requests to reach him. Zaccheo had deliberately forbidden his number from being given to her until this morning, once he'd confirmed his return to London.

His jaw flexed as he rolled tight shoulders. The number of fires he'd put out in Oman would've wiped out a lesser man. But Zaccheo's name and ruthless nature weren't renowned for nothing, and although it'd taken three days to get the construction schedule back on track, his business partners were in no doubt that he would bring them to their knees if they strayed so much as one millimetre from the outcome he desired.

It was the same warning he'd given Oscar Pennington when he'd called yesterday and attempted an ego-stroking exercise to get Zaccheo to relent on his threats. Zaccheo had coldly reminded him of the days he'd spent in prison and invited Pennington to ask for clemency when hell froze over.

No doubt Eva's eagerness to contact him was born of the same desire as her father's. But unlike her father, the thought of speaking to Eva sent a pleasurable kick of anticipation through his blood, despite the fact that with time and distance he'd looked back on their conversations since his release with something close to dismay.

Had he really revealed all those things about his time in prison and his childhood to her?

What was even more puzzling was her reaction. She hadn't looked down her nose at him in those moments. Had in fact exhibited nothing but empathy and compassion. Pushing the bewildering thought away, he dialled her number, gratified when she picked up on the first ring.

'*Ciao*, Eva. I understand you're experiencing pre-wedding jitters.'

'You understand wrong. This wedding isn't going to happen. Not once you hear what I have to say.'

His tension increased until the knots in his shoulders felt like immoveable rocks. He breathed through the red haze blurring his vision. 'I take it you didn't miss me, then?' he taunted.

She made a sound, a cross between a huff and a sigh. 'We really need to talk, Zaccheo.'

'Nothing you say will alter my intention to make you mine tomorrow,' he warned.

She hesitated. Then, 'Zaccheo, it's important. I won't take up too much of your time. But I need to speak to you.'

He rested his head against the seat. 'You have less than twenty-four hours left as a single woman. I won't permit anything like male strippers anywhere near you, of course, but I won't be a total bore and deny you a hen party if you wish—'

'I don't want a damn hen party! What I want is five minutes of your time.'

'Are you dying of some life-threatening disease?'

'*What?* Of course not!'

'Are you afraid I won't be a good husband?' he asked, noting the raw edge to his voice, but realising how much her answer meant to him.

'Zaccheo, this is about me, not you.'

He let her non-answer slide. 'You'll be a good wife. And despite your less than auspicious upbringing, you'll be a good mother.'

He heard her soft gasp. 'How do you know that?'

'Because you're passionate when you care. You just need to channel that passion from your undeserving family to the one we will create.'

'I can't just switch my feelings towards my family off.

Everyone deserves someone who cares about them, no matter what.'

His heart kicked hard and his grip tightened around the phone as bitterness washed through him. 'Not everyone gets it, though.'

Silence thrummed. 'I'm sorry about your parents. Is... your mother still alive?' Her voice bled the compassion he'd begun to associate with her.

It warmed a place inside him even as he answered. 'That depends on who you ask. Since she relocated to the other side of the world to get away from me, I presume she won't mind if I think her dead to me.'

'But she's alive, Zaccheo. Which means there's hope. Do you really want to waste that?' Her pain-filled voice drew him up short, reminding him that she'd lost her mother.

When had this conversation turned messy and emotional?

'You were close to your mother?' he asked.

'When she wasn't busy playing up to being a Pennington, or using me to get back at my father, she was a brilliant mother. I wish... I wish she'd been a mother to both Sophie *and* me.' She laughed without humour. 'Hell, I used to wish I'd been born into another family, that my last name wasn't Pennington—' She stopped and a tense silence reigned.

Zaccheo frowned. Things weren't adding up with Eva. He'd believed her surname was one she would do just about anything for, including help cover up fraud. But in his boardroom on Monday, she'd seemed genuinely shocked and hurt by the extent of her father's duplicity. And there was also the matter of her chosen profession and the untouched money in her bank account.

A less cynical man would believe she was the exception to the abhorrent aristocratic rule...

'At least you had one parent who cared for you. You were lucky,' he said, his mind whirling with the possibility that he could be wrong.

'But that parent is gone, and I feel as if I have no one now,' she replied quietly.

The need to tell her she had him flared through his mind. He barely managed to stay silent. After a few seconds, she cleared her throat. Her next words made him wish he'd hung up.

'I haven't signed the prenup,' she blurted out. 'I'm not going to.'

Because of the last clause.

For a brief moment, Zaccheo wanted to tell her why he wanted children. That the bleak loneliness that had dogged him through his childhood and almost drowned him in prison had nearly broken him. That he'd fallen into a pit of despair when he'd realised no one would miss him should the worst happen.

His mother had emigrated to Australia with her husband rather than stay in the same city as him once Zaccheo had fully established himself in London. That had cut deeper than any rejection he'd suffered from her in the past. And although the news of his trial and sentencing had been world-wide news, Zaccheo had never once heard from the woman who'd given him life.

He could've died in prison for all his mother cared. That thought had haunted him day and night until he'd decided to do something about it.

Until he'd vowed to alter his reality, ensure he had someone who would be proud to bear his name. Someone to whom he could pass on his legacy.

He hadn't planned for that person to be Eva Pennington until he'd read about her engagement in the file. But once he had, the decision had become iron cast.

Although this course was very much a sweeter, more lasting experience, Zaccheo couldn't help but wonder if it was all worth the ground shifting so much beneath his feet.

Eva was getting beneath his skin. And badly.

Dio mio. Why were the feelings he'd bottled up for over two decades choosing *now* to bubble up? He exhaled harshly.

Rough and ruthless was his motto. It was what had made him the man he was today. 'You'll be in your wedding dress at noon tomorrow, ready to walk down the aisle where our six hundred guests will be—'

'*Six hundred?* You've invited six *hundred* people to the wedding?' Her husky disbelief made his teeth grind.

'You thought I intended to have a hole-in-the-wall ceremony?' A fresh wave of bitterness rolled over him. 'Or did you think my PA was spouting gibberish when she informed you of all this on Tuesday?'

'Sorry, I must've tuned out because, contrary to what you think, I don't like my life arranged for me,' she retorted. 'That doesn't change anything. I *can't* do this…'

Zaccheo frowned at the naked distress in her voice.

Eva was genuinely torn up about the prospect of giving herself to him, a common man only worthy of a few kisses but nothing as substantial as the permanent state of matrimony.

Something very much like pain gripped his chest. 'Is that your final decision? Are you backing out of our agreement?'

She remained silent for so long, he thought the line was dead. 'Unless you're willing to change the last clause, yes.'

Zaccheo detested the sudden clenching of his stomach, as if the blow he'd convinced himself would never come had been landed. The voice taunting him for feeling more than a little stunned was ruthlessly smashed away.

He assured himself he had another way to claim the justice he sought. 'Very well. *Ciao.*'

He ended the phone call. And fought the urge to hurl his phone out of the window.

Eva dropped the phone onto the coffee-shop table. She'd arrived at work only to discover she'd been taken off the roster due to her impending wedding. Since she had holiday due to her anyway, Eva hadn't fought too hard at suddenly finding herself with free time.

Her session with Ziggy yesterday had gone well, despite her head being all over the place. If nothing else came of it, she could add that to her CV.

Curbing a hysterical snort, she stared at her phone.

She'd done the right thing and ended this farce before it went too far. Before the longings she'd harboured in the last three days got any more out of control.

Deep in her heart, she knew Zaccheo would react the same way to her secret as Scott and George had. He wouldn't want to marry half a woman, especially when he'd stated his expectations in black and white in a formal agreement drafted by a team of lawyers, and then confounded her with his genuine desire to become a father.

So why hadn't she just told him over the phone?

Because she was a glutton for punishment?

Because some part of her had hoped telling him face-to-face would help her gauge whether there was a chance he would accept her the way she was?

Fat chance.

It was better this way. Clean. Painless.

She jumped as her phone pinged. Heart lurching, she accessed the message, but it was only the manageress from Siren, wishing her a lovely wedding and sinfully blissful honeymoon.

Eva curled her hand around her fast-cooling mug. Once the news got out that she'd broken her third engagement in two years, her chances of marrying anyone, let alone a man who would accept her just as she was, would shrink from nil to no chance in hell.

Pain spiked again at the reminder of her condition. Exhaling, she wrenched her mind to more tangible things.

Like finding a place to live.

She weighed her options, despair clutching her insides

when, two hours later, she faced the only avenue open to her. Going back home to Pennington Manor.

Reluctantly, she picked up her phone, then nearly dropped it when it blared to life. The name of the caller made her frown.

'Sophie?'

'Eva, what's going on?' The fear in her voice shredded Eva's heart.

'What do you mean?'

'I've just had to call the doctor because Father's had another episode!'

Eva jerked to her feet, sending her coffee cup bouncing across the table. 'What?'

'We got a call from Zaccheo Giordano an hour ago to say the wedding was off. Father's been frantic. He was about to call you when he collapsed. The doctor says if he's subjected to any more stress he could have a heart attack or a stroke. Is it true? Did you call off the wedding?' The strain in her sister's voice was unmistakeable.

'Yes,' Eva replied. She grabbed her bag and hurried out of the coffee shop when she began to attract peculiar looks. Outside, she shrugged into her coat and pulled up her hoodie to avoid the light drizzle.

'Oh, God. Why?' her sister demanded.

'Zaccheo wanted me to sign a prenuptial agreement.'

'So? Everyone does that these days.'

'One of the terms…he wants *children*.'

Her sister sighed. 'So he backed out when you told him?'

'No, he doesn't know.'

'But… I'm confused,' Sophie replied.

'I tried to tell him but he wouldn't listen.'

'You tried. Isn't that enough?'

Eva ducked into a quiet alley and leaned against a wall. 'No, it's *not* enough. We've caused enough harm where he's concerned. I won't go into this based on a lie.'

'Father's terrified, Eva.'

'Can I talk to him?'

'He's sleeping now. I'll let him know you called when he wakes up.' Sophie paused. 'Eva, I've been thinking...what you said on Saturday, about you not being out to replace me... I shouldn't have bitten your head off. It's just... Father isn't an easy man to please. He was relying on me to see us through this rough patch...'

'I didn't mean to step on your toes, Sophie.'

Her sister inhaled deeply. 'I know. But everything seems so effortless for you, Eva. It always has. I envied you because Mother chose you—'

'Parents shouldn't choose which child to love and which to keep at arm's length!'

'But that was our reality. He wanted a son. And I was determined to be that son. After Mother died, I was scared Father would think I wasn't worth his attention.'

'You were. You still are.'

'Only because I've gone along with whatever he's asked of me without complaint, even when I knew I shouldn't. This thing with Zaccheo... Father's not proud of it. Nor am I. I don't know where we go from here, but once we're through this, can we get together?' Sophie asked, her voice husky with the plea.

Eva didn't realise her legs had given way until her bottom touched the cold, hard ground.

'Yes, if you want,' she murmured. Her hands shook as she hung up.

The last time she'd seen Sophie's rigid composure crumble had been in the few weeks after they'd buried their mother. For a while she'd had her sister back. They'd been united in their grief, supporting each other when their loss overwhelmed them.

As much as Eva missed *that* Sophie, she couldn't stomach having her back under similar circumstances. Nor could she bear the danger that her father faced.

She wasn't sure how long she sat there.

Cold seeped into her clothes. Into her bones. Into her heart.

Feeling numb, she dug into her bag and extracted the pre-nup and read through it one more time.

She couldn't honour Zaccheo's last clause, but that didn't mean she couldn't use it to buy herself, and her father, time until they met and she explained. Despite his own past, he wanted a family. Maybe he would understand why she was trying to salvage hers.

Slowly, she dialled. After endless rings, the line clicked through.

'Eva.' His voice was pure cold steel.

'I...' She attempted to say the words but her teeth still chattered. Squeezing her eyes shut, she tried again. 'I'll sign the agreement. I'll marry you tomorrow.'

Silence.

'Zaccheo? Are you there?'

'Where are you?'

She shivered at his impersonal tone. 'I'm...' She looked up at the street sign in the alley and told him.

'Romeo will be there in fifteen minutes. He'll witness the agreement and bring it to me. You'll return to the penthouse and resume preparations for the wedding.' He paused, as if waiting for her to disagree.

'Will I see you today?' She hated how weak her voice sounded.

'No.'

Eva exhaled. 'Okay, I'll wait for Romeo.'

'Bene.' The line went dead.

The grey mizzle outside aptly reflected Eva's mood as she sat, hands clasped in her lap, as the hairdresser finished putting up her hair. Behind her, Sophie smiled nervously.

Eva smiled back, knowing her sister's nervousness stemmed from the fear that Eva would change her mind again.

But this time there was no going back. She meant to come clean to Zaccheo at the first opportunity and open herself up to whatever consequences he sought.

Just how she would manage that was a puzzle she hadn't untangled yet, but since Zaccheo was hell-bent on this marriage, and she was giving him what he wanted, technically she was fulfilling her side of the bargain.

God, when had she resorted to seeing things in shades of grey instead of black and white, truth and lie? Was Zaccheo right? Did her Pennington blood mean she was destined to do whatever it took, even if it meant compromising her integrity, for the sake of her family and pedigree?

No. She wouldn't care if she woke up tomorrow as ordinary Eva Penn instead of Lady Pennington. And she *would* come clean to Zaccheo, no matter what.

Except that was looking less likely to happen *before* the wedding. Zaccheo hadn't returned to the penthouse last night. She hadn't deluded herself that he was observing the quaint marriage custom. If anything, he was probably making another billion, or actively sowing his last wild oats. She jerked at the jagged pain that shot through her.

Sophie stood up. 'What's wrong?'

'Nothing. How's Father?'

Sophie's face clouded. 'He insists he's well enough to walk you down the aisle.' Her sister's eyes darted to the hairdresser who had finished and was walking out to get Margaret. 'He's desperate that everything goes according to plan today.'

Eva managed to stop her smile from slipping. 'It will.'

Sophie met her gaze in the mirror. 'Do you think I should talk to Zaccheo…explain?'

Eva thought about the conversation she'd had with Zaccheo yesterday, the merciless tone, the ruthless man on a mission who'd been released from prison a mere week ago. 'Maybe not just yet.'

Sophie nodded, then flashed a smile that didn't quite make it before she left Eva alone as Margaret entered.

Any hopes of talking to Zaccheo evaporated when she found herself at the doors of the chapel an hour later.

Catching sight of him for the first time since Monday, she felt her heart slam around her chest.

Romeo stood in the best-man position and Eva wondered again at the connection between the two men. Did Zaccheo have any friends? Or had he lost all of them when her family's actions had altered his fate?

The thought flitted out of her head as her gaze returned almost magnetically to Zaccheo.

He'd eschewed a morning coat in favour of a bespoke three-piece suit in the softest dove-grey silk. Against the snowy white shirt and white tie completing the ensemble, his long hair was at once dangerously primitive and yet so utterly captivating, her mouth dried as her pulse danced with a dark, decadent delight. His beard had been trimmed considerably and a part of her mourned its loss. Perhaps it was that altered look that made his eyes so overwhelmingly electrifying, or it was the fact that his face was set in almost brutal lines, but the effect was like lightning to her system the moment her eyes connected with his.

The music in the great hall of the cathedral he'd astonishingly managed to secure on such short notice disappeared, along with the chatter of the goggle-eyed guests who did nothing to hide their avid curiosity.

All she could see was him, the man who would be her husband in less than fifteen minutes.

She stumbled, then stopped. A murmur rose in the crowd. Eva felt her father's concerned stare, but she couldn't look away from Zaccheo.

His nostrils flared, his eyes narrowing in warning as fear clutched her, freezing her feet.

'Eva?' Her father's ragged whisper caught her consciousness.

'Why did you insist on walking me down the aisle?' she asked him, wanting in some way to know that she wasn't doing all of this to save a man who had very little regard for her.

'What? Because you're my daughter,' her father replied with a puzzled frown.

'So you're not doing it just to keep up appearances?'

His face creased with a trace of the vulnerability she'd glimpsed only once before, when her mother died, and her heart lurched. 'Eva, I haven't handled things well. I know that. I was brought up to put the family name above all else, and I took that responsibility a little too far. Despite our less than perfect marriage, your mother was the one who would pull me back to my senses when I went a little too far. Without her…' His voice roughened and his hand gripped hers. 'We might lose Penningtons, but I don't want to lose you and Sophie.'

Eva's throat clogged. 'Maybe you should tell her that? She needs to know you're proud of her, Father.'

Her father looked to where her sister stood, and he nodded. 'I will. And I'm proud of you, too. You're as beautiful as your mother was on our wedding day.'

Eva blinked back her tears as murmurs rose in the crowd.

She turned to find Zaccheo staring at her. Something dark, sinister, curled through his eyes and she swallowed as his mouth flattened.

I can't marry him without him knowing! He deserves to know that I can't give him the family he wants.

'My dear, you need to move now. It's time,' her father pleaded.

Torn by the need for Zaccheo to know the truth and the need to protect her father, she shook her head, her insides churning.

Churning turned into full-blown liquefying as Zaccheo stepped from the dais, his imposing body threatening to block out the light as he headed down the aisle.

She desperately sucked in a breath, the knowledge that Zaccheo would march her up the aisle himself if need be finally scraping her feet from the floor. He stopped halfway, his gaze unswerving, until she reached him.

He grasped her hand, his hold unbreakable as he turned and walked her to the altar.

Trembling at the hard, pitiless look in his eyes, she swallowed and tried to speak. 'Zaccheo—'

'No, Eva. No more excuses,' he growled.

The priest glanced between them, his expression benign but enquiring.

Zaccheo nodded.

The organ swelled. And sealed her fate.

CHAPTER ELEVEN

'GLARING AT IT won't make it disappear, unless you have superhero laser vision.'

Eva jumped at the mocking voice and curled her fingers into her lap, hiding the exquisite diamond-studded platinum ring that had joined her engagement ring three hours ago.

'I wasn't willing it away.' On the contrary, she'd been wondering how long it would stay on her finger once Zaccheo knew the truth.

The reception following the ceremony had been brief but intense. Six hundred people clamouring for attention and the chance to gawp at the intriguing couple could take a lot out of a girl. With Zaccheo's fingers laced through hers the whole time, tightening commandingly each time she so much as moved an inch away from him, Eva had been near-blubbering-wreck status by the time their limo had left the hall.

Once she'd stopped reeling from the shock of being married to Zaccheo Giordano, she'd taken a moment to take in her surroundings. The Great Hall in the Guildhall was usually booked for years in advance. That Zaccheo had managed to secure it in a week and thrown together a stunning reception was again testament that she'd married a man with enough power and clout to smash through any resistance.

Zaccheo, despite his spell in prison, remained a formidable man, one, she suspected, who didn't need her father's intervention to restore his damaged reputation. So why was he pursuing it so relentlessly? Throughout the reception, she'd watched him charm their guests with the sheer force of his charisma. By the time her father had got round to giving the edifying toast welcoming Zaccheo to the Pennington family, the effort had seemed redundant.

She watched Zaccheo now as the car raced them to the airport, and wondered if it was a good time to broach the subject burning a hole in her chest.

'Something on your mind?' he queried without raising his gaze from his tablet.

Her heart leapt into her throat. She started to speak but noticed the partition between them and Romeo, who sat in the front passenger seat, was open. Although she was sure Romeo knew the ins and outs of the document he'd been asked to witness yesterday, Eva wasn't prepared to discuss her devastating shortcomings in his presence.

So she opted for something else plaguing her. She smoothed her hands on her wedding dress. 'Do I have your assurance that you'll speak on my father's behalf once you hand over the documents to the authorities?'

He speared her with incisive grey eyes. 'You're so eager to see him let off the hook, aren't you?'

'Wouldn't you be, if it was your father?' she asked.

Eva was unprepared for the strange look that crossed his face. The mixture of anger, sadness, and bitterness hollowed out her stomach.

'My father wasn't interested in being let off the hook for his sins. He was happy to keep himself indebted to his betters because he thought that was his destiny.'

Her breath caught. 'What? That doesn't make sense.'

'Very little of my father's actions made sense to me, not when I was a child, and not as an adult.'

The unexpected insight into his life made her probe deeper. 'When did he die?'

'When I was thirteen years old.'

'I'm sorry.' When he inclined his head and continued to stare at her, she pressed her luck. 'How did he—?'

'Zaccheo,' Romeo's deep voice interrupted them. 'Perhaps this is not a subject for your wedding day?'

A look passed between the friends.

When Zaccheo looked at her again, that cool impassivity he'd worn since they'd left the reception to thunderous applause had returned.

'Your father has done his part adequately for now. Our lawyers will meet in a few days to discuss the best way forward. When my input is needed, I'll provide it. *Your* role, on the other hand, is just beginning.'

Before she could reply, the door opened. Eva gaped at the large private jet standing mere feet away. Beside the steps, two pilots and two stewardesses waited.

Zaccheo exited and took her hand. The shocking electricity of his touch and the awareness in his eyes had her scrambling to release her fingers, but he held on, and walked her to his crew, who extended their congratulations.

Eva was grappling with their conversation when she stepped into the unspeakable luxury of the plane. To the right, a sunken entertainment area held a semicircular cream sofa and a separate set of club chairs with enough gadgets to keep even the most attention-deficient passenger happy. In a separate area a short flight of stairs away, there was a conference table with four chairs and a bar area off a top-line galley.

Zaccheo stepped behind her and her body zapped to life, thrilling to his proximity. She suppressed a shiver when he let go of her fingers and cupped her shoulders in his warm hands.

'I have several conference calls to make once we take off. And you…' He paused, traced a thumb across her cheek. The contact stunned her, as did the gentle look in his eyes. 'You look worn out.'

'Is that a kind way of saying I look like hell?' She strove for a light tone and got a husky one instead.

That half-smile appeared, and Eva experienced something close to elation that the icy look had melted from his face. 'You could never look like hell, *cara*. A prickly and challenging puzzle that I look forward to unravelling, most definitely. But never like hell.'

The unexpected response startled her into gaping for several seconds before she recovered. 'Should I be wary that you're being nice to me?'

'I can be less…monstrous when I get my way.'

The reminder that he wouldn't be getting his way and the thought of his reaction once he found out brought a spike of anxiety, rendering her silent as he led her to a seat and handed her a flute of champagne from the stewardess's tray.

'Zaccheo…' She stopped when his thumb moved over her lips. Sensation sizzled along her nerve endings, setting her pulse racing as he brushed it back and forth. The heat erupting between her thighs had her pressing her legs together to soothe the desperate ache.

She hardly felt the plane take off. All she was aware of was the mesmerising look in Zaccheo's eyes.

'I haven't told you how stunning you look.' He leaned closer and replaced his thumb with his lips at the corner of her mouth.

Delicious flames warmed her blood. 'Thank you.' Her voice shook with the desire moving through her. More than anything, she was filled with the blind need to turn her head and meet his mouth with hers.

When his lips trailed to her jaw, then to the curve between her shoulder and neck, Eva let out a helpless moan, her heart racing with sudden, debilitating hunger.

His fingers linked hers and she found herself being led to the back of the plane. Eva couldn't summon a protest. Nor could she remind herself that she needed to come clean, sooner rather than later.

The master bedroom was equally stunning. Gold leaf threaded a thick cream coverlet on a king-sized bed and plush carpeting absorbed their footsteps as he shut the door.

'I intend us to have two uninterrupted weeks on the island. In order for that to happen, I need to work with Romeo to clear my plate work-wise. Rest now. Whatever's on your mind can wait for a few more hours.' Again there was no bite to his words, leaving her lost as to this new side of the man she'd married.

She stood, almost overpowered by the strength of her emotions, as he positioned himself behind her and slowly undid her buttons. The heavy dress pooled at her feet and she stood in only her white strapless bra, panties, and the garter and sheer stocking set that had accompanied her dress.

A rough, tortured sound echoed around the room. *'Stai mozzafiato,'* Zaccheo muttered thickly. 'You're breathtaking,' he translated when she glanced at him.

A fierce blush flared up. Eyes darkening, he circled her, tracing her high colour with a barest tip of his forefinger. Her gaze dropped to the sensual line of his mouth and she bit her own lip as need drowned her.

She gasped, completely enthralled, as he dropped to his knees and reached for her garter belt, eyes locked on hers. He pulled it off and tucked it deep in his inner pocket. When he stood, the hunger on his face stopped her breath, anticipation sparking like fireworks through her veins.

He lightly brushed her lips with his.

'Our first time won't be on a plane within listening distance of my staff.' He walked to the bed and pulled back the covers. He waited until she got in and tucked her in. About to walk away, he suddenly stopped. 'We will make this marriage work, Eva.'

Her mouth parted but, with no words to counter that unexpected vow, she slowly pressed her lips together as pain ripped through her.

'Sleep well, *dolcezza*,' he murmured, then left.

Despite her turmoil, she slept through the whole flight, rousing refreshed if unsettled as to what the future held.

Dressing in a light cotton sundress and open sandals, she left her hair loose, applied a touch of lip gloss and sunscreen and exited the plane.

They transferred from jet to high-speed boat with Romeo at the wheel. The noise from the engine made conversation impossible but, for the first time, the silence between Zaccheo and Eva felt less fraught. The strange but intense feeling that had engulfed them both as he'd undressed her on the plane continued to grip them as they raced towards their final destination. When she caught her hair for the umpteenth time to keep it from flying in the wind, he captured the strands in a tight grip at the base of her neck, then used the hold to pull her closer until she curved into his side. With his other arm sprawled along the back of their seat, he appeared the most at ease Eva had ever seen him.

Perhaps being forced to wait for a while to tell him hadn't been a bad thing.

She let the tension ooze out of her.

Despite the shades covering his eyes, he must have sensed her scrutiny, because he turned and stared down at her for endless minutes. She felt the power of that look to the tips of her toes and almost fell into him when he took her mouth in a voracious kiss.

He let her up for air when her lungs threatened to burst. Burying his face in her throat, he rasped for her ears only, 'I cannot wait to make you mine.'

By the time the boat slowed and pulled into a quiet inlet, Eva was a nervous wreck.

'Welcome to Casa do Paraíso,' he said once the engine died.

Enthralled, Eva looked around. Tropical trees and lush vegetation surrounded a spectacular hacienda made of timber and glass, the mid-morning sun casting vibrant shades of green, orange and blue on the breathtaking surroundings. Wide glass windows dominated the structure and, through them, Eva saw white walls and white furniture with splashes of colourful paintings on the walls perpetuated in an endless flow of rooms.

'It's huge,' she blurted.

Zaccheo jumped onto the sugary sand and grabbed her hand.

'The previous owner built it for his first wife and their eight children. She got it in the divorce, but hated the tropical heat so never visited. It was run-down by the time I bought the island from her, so I made substantial alterations.'

The mention of children ramped up the tension crawling through her belly and, despite her trying to shrug the feeling away, it lingered as she followed him up the wide front porch into the stunning living room.

A staff of four greeted them, then hurried out to where Romeo was securing the vessel. She gazed around in stunned awe, accepting that Zaccheo commanded the best when it came to the structures he put his stamp on, whether commercial or private.

'Come here, Eva.' The order was impatient.

She turned from admiring the structure to admire the man who'd created it. Tall, proud and intensely captivating, he stood at the base of a suspended staircase, his white-hot gaze gleaming dangerously, promising complete sexual oblivion.

Desire pulsed between them, a living thing that writhed, consumed with a hunger that demanded to be met, fulfilled.

Eva knew she should make time now they were here to tell him. Lay down the truth ticking away inside her like a bomb.

After years of struggling to forge a relationship with her father and sister, she'd finally laid the foundations of one today.

How could she live with herself if she continued to keep Zaccheo in the dark about the family he hoped for himself?

Her feet slapped against the large square tiles as she hurried across the room. His mouth lifted in a half-smile of satisfaction. She'd barely reached him when he swung her into his arms and stormed up the stairs.

And then the need to disclose her secret was suddenly no longer urgent. It'd been superseded by another, more pressing demand. One that every atom in her body urged her to assuage. *Now.* Before the opportunity was taken from her. Before her confession once again found her in the brutal wasteland of rejection.

His heat singed where they touched. Unable to resist, she sank her fingers into his hair and buried her face in his neck, eager to be closer to his rough primitiveness.

Feeling bold, she nipped at his skin.

His responding growl was intoxicating. As was the feeling of being pressed against the hard, masculine planes of his body when he slowly lowered her to her feet.

'I've waited so long to be inside you. I won't wait any longer,' he vowed, the words fierce, stamped with decadent intent.

Arms clamped around her waist, he walked her backwards to the vast white-sheeted bed. In one clean move, he pulled her dress over her head and dropped it. Her bra and panties swiftly followed.

Zaccheo stopped breathing as he stared down at her exposed curves.

As he'd done on the plane, he circled her body, this time trailing more fingers over her heated skin, creating a fiery path that arrowed straight between her thighs. She was swaying under the dizzying force of her arousal by the time he faced her again.

'Beautiful. So beautiful,' he murmured against her skin, then pulled her nipple into his mouth, surrounding the aching bud with heat and want.

Eva cried out and clutched his shoulders, her whole body gripped with a fever that shook her from head to toe. He moved his attention to her twin breast while his fingers teased the other, doubling the pleasure, doubling her agony.

'Zaccheo,' she groaned.

He straightened abruptly and reefed his black T-shirt over his head, exposing hard, smooth pecs and a muscle-ridged stomach. But as intensely delectable as his torso was, it wasn't what made her belly quiver. It was the intriguing tattooed band of Celtic knots linked by three slim lines that circled his upper arm. The artwork was flawless and beautiful, flowing gracefully when he moved. Reaching out, she touched the first knot. He paused and stared down at her.

It struck her hard in that moment just how much she didn't know about the man she'd married.

'You seem almost nervous, *dolcezza*.'

Eva struggled to think of a response that wouldn't make her sound gauche. 'Don't you feel nervous, even a little, your first time with a new lover?' she replied.

He froze and his lips compressed for a fraction of a second, as if she'd said something to displease him. Then his fingers went to his belt. 'Nerves, no. Anticipation that a long-held desire is about to be fulfilled? Most definitely.' He removed his remaining clothes in one swift move.

Perfection. It was the only word she could think of.

'Even when you've experienced it more than a few dozen times?'

She gasped when his fingers gripped hers in a tight hold. When he spoke, his voice held a bite that jarred. 'Perhaps we should refrain from the subject of past lovers.'

Hard, demanding lips slanted over hers, his tongue sliding into her mouth, fracturing the last of her senses. She clung to him, her body once again aflame from the ferocious power of his.

Cool sheets met her back and Zaccheo sprawled beside her. After an eternity of kissing, he raised his head.

'There are so many ways I wish to take you I don't know where to begin.'

Heat burst beneath her skin and he laughed softly.

'You blush with the ease of an innocent.' He trailed his hand down her throat, lingering at her racing pulse, before it curved around one breast. 'It's almost enough to make me forget that you're not.' Again that bite, but less ferocious this time, his accent growing thicker as he bent his head and tongued her pulse.

She jerked against him, her fingers gliding over his warm skin of their own accord. 'On what basis do you form the opinion that I'm not?' she blurted before she lost her nerve.

He stilled, grey eyes turning that rare gunmetal shade that announced a dangerously heightened emotional state. His hand abandoned her breast and curled around her nape in an iron grip. 'What are you saying, Eva?' His voice was a hoarse rumble.

She licked nervous lips. 'That I don't want to be treated like I'm fragile…but I don't wish my first time to be without mercy either.'

He sucked in a stunned breath. 'Your *first… Madre di Dio.*' His gaze searched hers, his breathing growing increasingly erratic.

Slowly, he drew back from her, scouring her body from head to toe as if seeing her for the first time. He parted her thighs and she moved restlessly, helplessly, as his eyes lingered at her centre. Stilling her with one hand, he lowered his head and kissed her eyes, her mouth, her throat. Then lower until he reached her belly. He licked at her navel, then rained kisses on her quivering skin. Firm hands held her open, then his shoulders took over the job. Reading his intention, she raised her head from the pillow.

'Zaccheo.' She wasn't sure whether she was pleading for or rejecting what was coming.

He reared up for a second, his hands going to his hair to twist the long strands into an expert knot at the back of his head. The act was so unbelievably hot, her body threatened to melt into a useless puddle. Then he was back, broad shoulders easily holding her legs apart as he kissed his way down her inner thighs.

'I know what I crave most,' he muttered thickly. 'A taste of you.'

The first touch of his mouth at her core elicited a long, helpless groan from her. Her spine arched off the bed, her thighs shaking as fire roared through her body. He held her

down and feasted on her, the varying friction from his mouth
and beard adding an almost unholy pleasure that sent her
soaring until a scream ripped from her throat and she fell
off the edge of the universe.

She surfaced to feel his mouth on her belly, his hands
trailing up her sides. That gunmetal shade of grey reflected
deep possession as he rose above her and kissed her long
and deep.

'Now, *il mio angelo*. Now I make you mine.'

He captured her hands above her head with one hand. The
other reached between her thighs, gently massaging her core
before he slid one finger inside her tight sheath. His groan
echoed hers. Removing his finger, he probed her sex with
his thick shaft, murmuring soft, soothing words as he pushed
himself inside her.

'Easy, *dolcezza*.'

Another inch increased the burn, but the hunger rushing
through her wouldn't be denied. Her fingers dug into his
back, making him growl. 'Zaccheo, please.'

'*Sì*, let me please you.' He uttered a word that sounded
like an apology, a plea.

Then he pushed inside her. The dart of pain engulfed her,
lingered for a moment. Tears filled her eyes. Zaccheo cursed,
then kissed them away, murmuring softly in Italian.

He thrust deeper, slowly filling her. Eva saw the strain
etched on his face.

'Zaccheo?'

'I want this to be perfect for you.'

'It won't be unless you move, I suspect.'

That half-smile twitched, then stretched into a full, heart-
stopping smile. Eva's eyes widened at the giddy dance her
heart performed on seeing the wave of pleasure transform
his face. Her own mouth curved in response and a feeling
unfurled inside her, stealing her breath with its awesome
power. Shakily, she raised her hand and touched his face,
slid her fingers over his sensual mouth.

He moved. Withdrew and thrust again.

She gasped, her body caught in a maelstrom of sensation so turbulent, she feared she wouldn't emerge whole.

Slowly his smile disappeared, replaced by a wild, predatory hunger. He quickened the pace and her hands moved to his hair, slipping the knot free and burying her fingers in the thick, luxurious tresses. When her hips moved of their own accord, meeting him in an instinctive dance, he groaned deep and sucked one nipple into his mouth. Drowning in sensation, she felt her world begin to crumble. The moment he captured her twin nipple, a deep tremor started inside her. It built and built, then exploded in a shower of lights.

'Perfetto.'

Zaccheo sank his fingers into Eva's wild, silky hair, curbing the desire to let loose the primitive roar bubbling within him.

Mine. Finally, completely mine.

Instead he held her close until her breathing started to return to normal, then he flipped their positions and arranged her on top of him.

He was hard to the point of bursting, but he was determined to make this experience unforgettable for her. Seeing his ring on her finger, that primitive response rose again, stunning him with the strength of his desire to claim her.

His words on the plane slashed through his mind.

Sì, he *did* want this to work. Perhaps Eva had been right. Perhaps there was still time to salvage a piece of his soul…

Her eyes met his and a sensual smile curled her luscious mouth. Before he could instruct her, she moved, taking him deeper inside her before she rose. Knowing he was fast losing the ability to think, he met her second thrust. Her eyes widened, her skin flushing that alluring shade of pink as she chased the heady sensation. Within minutes, they were both panting.

Reaching down, he teased her with his thumb and watched

her erupt in bliss. Zaccheo followed her, his shout announcing the most ferocious release he'd experienced in his life.

Long after Eva had collapsed on top of him, and slipped into an exhausted sleep, he lay awake.

Wondering why his world hadn't righted itself.

Wondering what the hell this meant for him.

CHAPTER TWELVE

EVA CAME AWAKE to find herself splayed on top of Zaccheo's body.

The sun remained high in the sky so she knew she hadn't slept for more than an hour or two. Nevertheless, the thought that she'd dropped into a coma straight after sex made her cringe.

She risked a glance and found grey eyes examining her with that half-smile she was growing to like a little more than she deemed wise.

He brushed a curl from her cheek and tucked it behind her ear. The gentleness in the act fractured her breathing.

'*Ciao, dolcezza.*'

'I didn't mean to fall asleep on you,' she said, then immediately felt gauche for not knowing the right after-sex etiquette.

He quirked a brow. 'Oh? Who did you mean to fall asleep on?' he asked.

She jerked up. 'No, that's not what I meant…' she started to protest, then stopped when she saw the teasing light in his eyes.

She started to settle back down, caught a glimpse of his chiselled pecs and immediately heat built inside her. A little wary of how quickly she was growing addicted to his body, she attempted to slide off him.

He stopped her with one hand at her nape, the other on her hip. The action flexed his arm and Eva's gaze was drawn to the tattoo banding his upper arm.

'Does this have a special meaning?'

His smile grew a little stiffer. 'It's a reminder not to accept less than I'm worth or compromise on what's important to me. And a reminder that, contrary to what the privileged would have us believe, all men are born equal. It's power that is wielded unequally.'

Eva thought of the circumstances that had brought her to this place, of the failings of her own family and the sadness she'd carried for so long, but now hoped to let go of.

'You wield more than enough share of power. Men cower before you.'

A frown twitched his forehead. 'If they do, it is their weakness, not mine.'

She gave an incredulous laugh. 'Are you saying you don't know you intimidate people with just a glance?'

His frown cleared. 'You're immune to this intimidation you speak of. To my memory, you've been disagreeable more often than not.'

She traced the outline of the tattoo, revelling in the smooth warmth of his skin. 'I've never been good at heeding bellowed commands.'

The hand on her hip tightened. 'I do not bellow.'

'Maybe not. But sometimes the effect is the same.'

She found herself flipped over onto her back, Zaccheo crouched over her like a lethal bird of prey. 'Is that why you hesitated as you walked down the aisle?' he asked in a harsh whisper. The look in his eyes was one of almost…hurt.

Quickly she shook her head. 'No, it wasn't.'

'Then what was it? You thought that I wasn't good enough, perhaps?' he pressed. And again she glimpsed a hint of vulnerability in his eyes that caught at a weak place in her heart.

She opened her mouth to *finally* tell him. To lay herself bare to the scathing rejection that would surely follow her confession.

The words stuck in her throat.

What she'd experienced in Zaccheo's bed had given her a taste that was unlike anything she'd ever felt before. The need to hold on to that for just a little while longer slammed into her, knocking aside her good intentions.

Eva knew she was playing with volcanic fire, that the eventual eruption would be devastating. But for once in her life, she wanted to be selfish, to experience a few moments of unfettered abandon. She could have that.

She'd sacrificed herself for this marriage, but in doing so she'd also been handed a say in when it ended.

And it would be sooner rather than later, because she couldn't stand in the way of what he wanted…what he'd been deprived of his whole life…a proper family of his own.

She also knew Zaccheo would want nothing to do with her once he knew the truth. Sure, he wasn't as monstrous as he would have others believe, but that didn't mean he would shackle himself to a wife who couldn't give him what he wanted.

She squashed the voice that cautioned she was naively burying her head in the sand.

Was it really so wrong if she chose to do it just for a little while?

Could she not live in bliss for a few days? Gather whatever memories she could and hang on to them for when the going got tough?

'Eva?'

'I had a father-daughter moment, plus bridal nerves,' she blurted. He raised a sceptical eyebrow and she smiled. 'Every woman is entitled to have a moment. Mine was thirty seconds of hesitation.'

'You remained frozen for five *minutes*,' he countered.

'Just time enough for anyone who'd been dozing off to wake up,' she responded, wide-eyed.

The tension slowly eased out of his body and his crooked smile returned. Relief poured through her and she fell into the punishing kiss he delivered to assert his displeasure at her hesitation.

She was clinging to him by the time he pulled away, and Eva was ready to protest when he swung out of bed. Her protest died when she got her first glimpse of his impressive manhood, and the full effect of the man attached to it.

Dry-mouthed and heart racing, she stared. And curled her fingers into the sheets to keep from reaching for him.

'If you keep looking at me like that, our shower will have to be postponed. And our lunch will go cold.'

A blush stormed up her face.

He laughed and scooped her up. 'But I'm glad that my body is not displeasing to you.'

She rolled her eyes. *As if.* 'False humility isn't an attractive trait, Zaccheo,' she chided as he walked them through a wide door and onto an outdoor bamboo-floored shower. Despite the rustic effects, the amenities were of the highest quality, an extra-wide marble bath sitting opposite a multi-jet shower, with a shelf holding rows upon rows of luxury bath oils and gels.

Above their heads, a group of macaws warbled throatily, then flew from one tree to the next, their stunning colours streaking through the branches.

As tropical paradises went, Eva was already sure this couldn't be topped, and she had yet to see the rest of it.

Zaccheo set her down and grabbed a soft washcloth. 'Complete compatibility in bed isn't a common thing, despite what magazines would have you believe,' he said.

'I wouldn't know.' There was no point pretending otherwise. He had first-hand knowledge of her innocence.

His eyes flared with possession as he turned on the jets and pulled her close.

'No, you wouldn't. And if that knowledge pleases me to the point of being labelled a caveman, then so be it.'

They ate a sumptuous lunch of locally caught fish served with pine-nut sauce and avocado salad followed by a serving of fruit and cheeses.

After lunch, Zaccheo showed her the rest of the house and the three-square-kilometre island. They finished the trek on the white sandy beach where a picnic had been laid out with champagne chilling in a silver bucket.

Eva popped a piece of papaya in her mouth and sighed at the beauty of the setting sun casting orange and purple streaks across the aquamarine water. 'I don't know how you can ever bear to leave this place.'

'I learned not to grow attached to things at an early age.'

The crisp reply had her glancing over at him. His shades were back in place so she couldn't read his eyes, but his body showed no signs of the usual forbidding *do not disturb* signs so she braved the question. 'Why?'

'Because it was better that way.'

She toyed with the stem of her champagne flute. 'But it's also a lonely existence.'

Broad shoulders lifted in an easy shrug. 'I had a choice of being lonely or just…solitary. I chose the latter.'

Her heart lurched at the deliberate absence of emotion from his voice. 'Zaccheo—'

He reared up from where he'd been lounging on his elbows, his mouth set in a grim line. 'Don't waste your time feeling sorry for me, *dolcezza*,' he said, his voice a hard snap that would've intimidated her, had she allowed it.

'I wasn't,' she replied. 'I'm not naive enough to imagine everyone has a rosy childhood. I know I didn't.'

'You mean the exclusive country-club memberships, the top boarding schools, the winters in Verbier weren't enough?' Despite the lack of contempt in his voice this time round, Eva felt sad that they were back in this place again.

'Don't twist my words. Those were just *things*, Zaccheo. And before you accuse me of being privileged, yes, I was. My childhood was hard, too, but I couldn't help the family I was born into any more than you could.'

'Was that why you moved out of Pennington Manor?'

'After my mother died, yes. Two against one became unbearable.'

'And the father-daughter moment you spoke of? Did that help?' he asked, watching her with a probing look.

A tiny bit of hope blossomed. 'Time will tell, I guess. Will you try the same with your mother and stepfather?'

'No. My mother didn't think I was worth anything. My stepfather agreed.'

Her heart twisted. 'Yet you've achieved success beyond most people's wildest dreams. Surely the lessons of your childhood should make you proud of who you are now, despite hating some aspects of your upbringing?'

'I detested all of mine,' he said with harsh finality. 'I wouldn't wish it on my worst enemy.'

The savage edge of pain in his voice made her shiver. She opened her mouth to ask him, but he surged to his feet.

'I don't wish to dwell in the past.' That half-smile flashed on and off. 'Not when I have a sunset as stunning as this and a wife to rival its beauty.' He plucked the glass from her hand and pulled her up.

Tucking her head beneath his chin, he enfolded her in his arms, one around her waist and the other across her shoulders. Eva knew it was a signal to drop the subject, but she couldn't let it go. Not just yet.

She removed his shades and stared into his slate-coloured eyes. 'For what it's worth, I gave away my country-club membership to my best friend, I hated boarding school, and I couldn't ski to save my life so I didn't even try after I turned ten. I didn't care about my pedigree, or who I was seen with. Singing and a family who cared for me were the only things that mattered. One helped me get through the other. So, you see, sometimes the grass *may* look greener on the other side, but most of the time it's just a trick of the light.'

Several emotions shifted within his eyes. Surprise. Shock. A hint of confusion. Then the deep arrogance of Zaccheo Giordano slid back into place.

'The sunset, *dolcezza*,' he said gruffly. 'You're missing it.'

* * *

The feeling of his world tilting out of control was escalating. And it spun harder out of sync the more he fought it.

Zaccheo had been certain he knew what drove Eva and her family. He'd been sure it was the same greed for power and prestige that had sent his father to a vicious and premature death. It was what had made his mother abandon her homeland to seek a rich husband, turn herself inside out for a man who looked down his nose at her son and ultimately made Clara Giordano pack her bags and move to the other side of the world.

But right from the start Eva had challenged him, forced him to confront his long-held beliefs. He hadn't needed to, of course. Oscar Pennington's actions had proven him right. Eva's own willingness to marry Fairfield for the sake of her family had cemented Zaccheo's belief.

And didn't you do the same thing?

He stared unseeing at the vivid orange horizon, his thoughts in turmoil.

He couldn't deny that the discovery of her innocence in bed had thrown him for a loop. Unsettled him in a way he hadn't been for a long time.

For as long as he could remember, his goal had been a fixed, tangible certainty. To place himself in a position where he erased any hint of neediness from his life, while delivering an abject lesson to those who thought themselves entitled and therefore could treat him as if he were common. A spineless fool who would prostrate himself for scraps from the high table.

He'd proven conclusively yesterday at his wedding reception that he'd succeeded beyond his wildest dreams. He'd watched blue-blooded aristocrats fall over themselves to win his favour.

And yet he'd found himself unsatisfied. Left with a hollow, bewildering feeling inside, as if he'd finally grasped the brass ring, only to find it was made of plastic.

It had left Zaccheo with the bitter introspection of whether a different, deeper goal lay behind the burning need to prove himself above the petty grasp for power and prestige.

The loneliness he'd so offhandedly dismissed had in fact eaten away at him far more effectively than his mother's rejection and the callous disregard his father had afforded him when he was alive.

Impatiently, he dismissed his jumbled feelings. He didn't do *feelings*. He *achieved*. He *bested*. And he *triumphed*.

One miscalculation didn't mean a setback. Finding out Eva had had no previous lovers had granted him an almost primitive satisfaction he wasn't going to bother to deny.

And if something came of this union sooner rather than later… His heart kicked hard.

Sliding a hand through her silky hair, he angled her face to his. Her beauty was undeniable. But he wouldn't be risking any more heart-to-hearts. She was getting too close, sliding under his skin to a place he preferred to keep out of bounds. A place he'd only examined when the cold damp of his prison cell had eroded his guard.

He was free, both physically and in guilt. He wouldn't return to that place. And he wouldn't allow her to probe further. Satisfied with his resolution, he kissed her sexy, tempting mouth until the need to breathe forced him to stop.

The sun had disappeared. Lights strung through the trees flickered on and he nodded to the member of staff who hovered nearby, ready to pack up their picnic.

He caught the glazed, flushed look on his wife's face and came to a sudden, extremely pleasing decision.

'Tonight, *il mio angelo*, we'll have an early night.'

The first week flew by in a dizzy haze of sun, sea, exquisite food, and making love. Lots and lots of making love.

Zaccheo was a fierce and demanding lover, but he gave so much more in return. And Eva was so greedy for everything he had to give, she wondered whether she was turning into a sex addict. She'd certainly acted like one this morning, when she'd initiated sex while Zaccheo had been barely awake. That her initiative had seemed to please him had been beside the point.

She'd examined her behaviour afterwards when Zaccheo had been summoned to an urgent phone call by Romeo.

This was supposed to be a moment out of time, a brief dalliance, which would end the moment she spilled her secret to him. And yet with each surrender of her body, she slid down a steeper slope, one she suspected would be difficult to climb back up. Because it turned out that, for her, sex wasn't a simple exchange of physical pleasure. With each act, she handed over a piece of herself to him that she feared she'd never reclaim.

And that more than anything made her fear for herself when this was over.

A breeze blew through an open window and Eva clutched the thin sarong she'd thrown over her bikini. Dark clouds were forming ominously over the island. Shivering, she watched the storm gather, wondering if it was a premonition for her own situation.

Lightning flashed, and she jumped.

'Don't worry, Mrs Eva.' Zaccheo's housekeeper smiled as she entered and turned on table lamps around the living room. 'The storm passes very quickly. The sun will be back out in no time.'

Eva smiled and nodded, but she couldn't shake the feeling that *her* storm wouldn't pass so quickly.

As intense rain pounded the roof she went in search of Zaccheo. Not finding him in his study, she climbed the stairs, her pulse already racing in anticipation as she went down the hallway.

She entered their dressing room and froze.

'What are you doing?' she blurted.

'I would've thought it was obvious, *dolcezza*.' He held clippers inches from his face.

'I can see what you're doing but...*why*?' she snapped. 'You already got rid of most of it for the wedding.' Her voice was clipped, a feeling she couldn't decipher moving through her.

Zaccheo raised an eyebrow, amusement mingled with something else as he watched her. 'I take it this look works for you?'

She swallowed twice before she could speak. When she finally deciphered the feeling coursing through her, she was so shocked and so afraid he would read her feelings, she glanced over his head.

'Yes. I prefer it,' she replied.

For several seconds he didn't speak. Her skin burned at his compelling stare. Schooling her features, she glanced into his eyes.

'Then it will remain untouched.' He set the clippers down and faced her.

Neither of them moved for several minutes. The storm raged outside, beating against the windows and causing the timber to creak.

'Come here, Eva.' Softly spoken, but a command nonetheless.

'I'm beginning to think those are your three favourite words.'

'They are only when you comply.'

She rolled her eyes, but moved towards him. He swivelled in his chair and pulled her closer, parting his thighs to situate her between them.

'Was that very hard to admit?' he rasped.

Her skin grew tight, awareness that she stood on a precipice whose depths she couldn't quite fathom shivering over her. 'No.'

He laughed. 'You're a pathetic liar. But I appreciate you finding the courage to ask for what you want.'

'An insult and a compliment?' she said lightly.

'I wouldn't want you to think me soft.' He caught her hands and placed them on his shoulders. 'You realise that

I'll require a reward for keeping myself this way for your pleasure?'

The way he mouthed *pleasure* made hot need sting between her thighs. Several weeks ago, she would've fought it. But Eva was fast learning it was no use. Her body was his slave to command as and when he wished. 'You got your stylists to prod and primp me into the image you wanted. I've earned the right to do the same to you.' Her fingers curled into the hair she would've wept to see shorn.

He smiled and relaxed in the chair. 'I thought being primped and plucked to perfection was every woman's wish?'

'You thought wrong. I was happy with the way I looked before.'

That wasn't exactly true. Although she'd loved her thick and wild hair, she had to admit it was much easier to tend now the wildness had been tamed a little. And she loved that she could brush the tresses without giving herself a headache. As for the luxurious body creams she'd been provided with, she marvelled at how soft and silky her skin felt now compared to before.

But she kept all of it to herself as he untied the knot in her sarong and let it fall away. 'You were perfect before. You're perfect now. And mine,' he breathed.

Within seconds, Eva was naked and craving what only he could give her, her eventual screams as loud as the storm raging outside.

CHAPTER THIRTEEN

'COME ON, we're taking the boat out today. As much as I'd like to keep you to myself, I think we need to see something of Rio before we leave tomorrow.'

Eva stopped tweaking the chorus of the melody she'd been composing and looked up as Zaccheo entered the living room.

The perverse hope that he would grow less breathtaking with each day was hopelessly thwarted. Dressed in khaki linen trousers and a tight white T-shirt with his hair loose around his shoulders, Zaccheo was so visually captivating, she felt the punch to her system each time she stared at him.

He noticed her staring and raised an eyebrow. Blushing, she averted her gaze to her tablet.

'Where are we going?' She tried for a light tone and breathed an inward sigh of relief when she succeeded.

'To Ilha São Gabriel, three islands away. It's a tourist hotspot, but there are some interesting sights to see there.' He crouched before her, his gaze going to the tablet. Reaching out, he scrolled through her compositions, his eyes widening at the three dozen songs contained in the file.

'You wrote all these?' he asked.

She nodded, feeling self-conscious as he paused at a particularly soul-baring ballad about unrequited love and rejection. She'd written that one a week after Zaccheo had gone to prison. 'I've been composing since I was sixteen.'

His eyes narrowed on her face. 'You've had two million pounds in your bank account for over a year and a half, which I'm guessing is your shareholder dividend from your father's deal on my building?'

Warily, she nodded.

'That would've been more than enough money to pursue your music career without needing to work. So why didn't you use it?' he queried.

She tried to shrug the question away, but he caught her chin in his hand. 'Tell me,' he said.

'I suspected deep down that the deal was tainted. I hated doubting my father's integrity, but I could never bring myself to use the money. It didn't feel right.' Being proved right had brought nothing but hurt.

He watched her for a long time, a puzzled look on his face before he finally nodded. 'How was your session with Ziggy Preston?' he asked.

She saw nothing of the sour expression he'd sported that night in the club. 'Surprisingly good, considering I'd thought he'd have me on the blacklist of every music producer after your behaviour.'

An arrogant smile stretched his lips. 'They'd have had to answer to me had they chosen that unfortunate path. You're seeing him again?'

She nodded. 'When we get back.'

'Bene.' He rose and held out his hand.

She slipped her feet into one of the many stylish sandals now gracing her wardrobe and he led her outside to the jetty.

Climbing on board, he placed her in front of the wheel and stood behind her. She looked around, expecting Zaccheo's right-hand man to be travelling with them. 'Isn't Romeo coming?'

'He had business to take care of in Rio. He'll meet us there.'

The trip took twenty-five minutes, and Eva understood why the Ilha São Gabriel was so popular when she saw it. The island held a mountain, on top of which a smaller version of the Cristo Redentor in Rio had been erected. Beneath the statue, bars, restaurants, parks and churches flowed right down to the edge of a mile-long beach.

Zaccheo directed her to motor past the busy beach and round the island to a quieter quay where they moored the boat. 'We're starting our tour up there.' He pointed to a quaint little building set into the side of a hill about a quarter of a mile up a steep path.

She nodded and started to walk up when she noticed Romeo a short distance away. He nodded a greeting but didn't join them as they headed up. The other man's watchfulness made Eva frown.

'Something on your mind?' Zaccheo asked.

'I was just wondering…what's the deal with Romeo?'

'He's many things.'

'That's not really an answer.'

Zaccheo shrugged. 'We work together, but I guess he's a confidant.'

'How long have you known him?'

When Zaccheo pulled his shades from the V of his T-shirt and placed them on, she wondered whether she'd strayed into forbidden territory. But he answered, 'We met when I was thirteen years old.'

Her eyes rounded in surprise. 'In London?'

'In Palermo.'

'So he's your oldest friend?'

Zaccheo hesitated for a second. 'Our relationship is complicated. Romeo sees himself as my protector. A role I've tried to dissuade him from to no avail.'

Her heart caught. 'Protector from what?'

His mouth twitched. 'He seems to think you're a handful that he needs to keep an eye on.'

She looked over her shoulder at the quiet, brooding man.

'My father worked for his father,' he finally answered.

'In what capacity?'

'As whatever he wanted him to be. My father didn't discriminate as long as he was recognised for doing the job. He would do anything from carrying out the trash to kneecapping a rival gang's members to claiming another man's bastard child so his boss didn't have to. No job was too small or large,' he said with dry bitterness.

The blood drained from her face. 'Your father worked for the *Mafia*?'

His jaw clenched before he jerked out a nod. 'Romeo's father was a *don* and my father one of his minions. His role was little more than drudge work, but he acted as if he was serving the Pope himself.'

She glanced over her shoulder at Romeo, her stomach dredging with intense emotions she recognised as anguish— even without knowing what Zaccheo was about to divulge.

'That bastard child you mentioned…'

He nodded. 'Romeo. His father had an affair with one of his many mistresses. His mother kept him until he became too much of a burden. When he was thirteen, she dumped him on his father. He didn't want the child, so he asked my father to *dispose* of him. My father, eager to attain recognition at all costs, brought the child home to my mother. She refused but my father wouldn't budge. They fought every day for a month until she ended up in hospital. It turned out she was pregnant. After that she became even more adamant about having another woman's child under her roof. When she lost her baby, she blamed my father and threatened to leave. My father, probably for the only time in his life, decided to place someone else's needs above his ambition. He tried to return Romeo to his father, who took grave offence. He had my father beaten to death. And I…' his face tightened '…I went from having a friend, a mother and father, and a brother or sister on the way, to having nothing.'

Eva frowned. 'But your mother—'

'Had hated being the wife of a mere gofer. My father's death bought her the fresh start she craved, but she had to contend with a child who reminded her of a past she detested. She moved to England a month after he died and married a man who hated the sight of me, who judged me because of who my father was and believed my common blood was an affront to his distinguished name.' The words were snapped out in a staccato narrative, but she felt the anguished intensity behind them.

Eva swallowed hard. Stepping close, she laid her head on his chest. 'I'm so sorry, Zaccheo.'

His arms tightened around her for a heartbeat before he pulled away and carried on up the steps. 'I thought Romeo had died that night, too, until he found me six years ago.'

She glanced at Romeo and her heart twisted for the pain the unfortunate friends had gone through.

They continued up the hill in silence until they reached the building.

They entered the cool but dim interior and as her eyes adjusted to the dark she was confronted by a stunning collection of statues. Most were made of marble, but one or two were sculpted in white stone.

'Wow, these are magnificent.'

'A local artist sculpted all the patron saints and donated them to the island over fifty years ago.'

They drifted from statue to statue, each work more striking than the last. When they walked through an arch, he laced his fingers with hers. 'Come, I'll show you the most impressive one. According to the history, the artist sculpted them in one day.'

Smiling, she let him tug her forward. She gasped at the double-figured display of St Anne and St Gerard. 'Patron saints of motherhood and fertility…' She stopped reading as her heart dropped to her stomach.

Zaccheo traced a forefinger down her cheek. 'I can't wait to feel our child kick in your belly,' he murmured.

A vice gripped her heart, squeezed until it threatened to stop beating. 'Zaccheo—'

His finger stopped her. 'I meant what I said, Eva. We can make this work. And we may not have had the best of role models in parents, but we know which mistakes to avoid. That's a good basis for our children, *si*?' he asked, his tone gentle, almost hopeful.

She opened her mouth, but no words formed. Because the truth she'd been hiding from suddenly reared up and slapped her in the face.

Zaccheo wanted children, not as a tool for revenge, but for himself. The man who'd known no love growing up wanted a family of his own.

And she'd led him on, letting him believe he could have it with her. The enormity of her actions rocked her to the core, robbing her of breath.

'Eva? What's wrong?' he asked with a frown.

She shook her head, her eyes darting frantically around the room.

'You're as pale as a ghost, *dolcezza*. Talk to me!'

Eva struggled to speak around the misery clogging her throat. 'I…I'm okay.'

His frown intensified. 'You don't look okay. Do you want to leave?'

She grasped the lifeline. 'Yes.'

'Okay, let's go.'

They emerged into bright sunlight. Eva took a deep breath, which did absolutely nothing to restore the chaos fracturing her mind.

The urge to confess *now*, spill her secret right then and there, powered through her. But it was neither the time nor the place. A group of tourist students had entered the room and the place was getting busier by the second.

Zaccheo led her down the steps. He didn't speak, but his concerned gaze probed her.

The island seemed twice as crowded by the time they descended the hill. The midday sun blazed high and sweat trickled down her neck as they navigated human traffic on the main promenade. When Zaccheo steered her to a restaurant advertising fresh seafood, Eva didn't complain.

Samba music blared from the speakers, thankfully negating the need for conversation. Sadly it didn't free her from her thoughts, not even when, after ordering their food, Zaccheo moved his chair closer, tugged her into his side and trailed his hand soothingly through her hair.

It was their last day in Rio. Possibly their last as husband and wife. Her soul mourned what she shouldn't have craved.

Unbearable agony ripped through her. She'd been living in a fool's paradise. Especially since she'd told herself it wouldn't matter how much time passed without her telling Zaccheo.

It mattered very much. She'd heard his pain when he'd recounted his bleak childhood. With each day that had passed without her telling him she couldn't help him realise his dream, she'd eroded any hope that he would understand why she'd kept her secret from him.

A moan ripped from her throat and she swayed in her seat. Zaccheo tilted her face to his and she read the worry in his eyes.

'Do you feel better?'

'Yes, much better.'

'*Bene*, then perhaps you'd like to tell me what's going on?' he asked.

She jerked away, her heart hammering. 'I got a little lightheaded, that's all.'

His frown returned and Eva held her breath. She was saved when Romeo entered. 'Everything all right?' he asked.

Romeo's glance darted to her. The knowledge in his eyes froze her insides, but he said nothing, directing his gaze back to his friend.

Zaccheo nodded. '*Sì*. We'll see you back at Paraíso.'

The moment he left, Zaccheo lowered his head and kissed her, not the hungry devouring that tended to overtake them whenever they were this close, but a gentle, reverent kiss.

In that moment, Eva knew she'd fallen in love with him.

And that she would lose the will to live the moment she walked away from him.

Their food arrived and they ate. She refused coffee and the slice of *chocotorta* the waiter temptingly offered. Zaccheo ordered an espresso, shooting her another concerned glance. Praying he wouldn't press her to reveal what was wrong just yet, she laid her head on his shoulder and buried her face in his throat, selfishly relishing the moment. She would never get a moment like this once they returned to Casa do Paraíso. He placed a gentle kiss on her forehead and agony moved through her like a living entity.

You brought this on yourself. No use crying now.

She started as the group they'd met on their exit from the museum entered the restaurant. Within minutes, someone had started the karaoke machine. The first attempt, sung atrociously to loud jeers, finished as the waiter returned with Zaccheo's espresso.

Eva straightened in her seat, watching the group absently as each member refused to take the mic. The leader cast his eyes around the room, met Eva's gaze and made a beeline for her.

'No.' She shook her head when he reached her and offered the mic.

He clasped his hands together. *'Por favor,'* he pleaded.

She opened her mouth to refuse, then found herself swallowing her rebuttal. She glanced at Zaccheo. He regarded her steadily, his face impassive. And yet she sensed something behind his eyes, as if he didn't know what to make of her mood.

She searched his face harder, wanting him to say something, *anything*, that would give her even the tiniest hope that what she had to tell him wouldn't break the magic they'd found on his island. Wouldn't break *her*.

In a way it was worse when he offered her that half-smile. Recently his half-smiles had grown genuine, were often a precursor to the blinding smiles that stole her breath...made her heart swell to bursting.

The thought that they would soon become a thing of the past had her surging to her feet, blindly striding for the stage to a round of applause she didn't want.

All Eva wanted in that moment was to drown in the oblivion of music.

She searched through the selection until she found a song she knew by heart, one that had spoken to her the moment she'd heard it on the radio.

She sang the first verse with her eyes shut, yearning for the impossible. She opened her eyes for the second verse. She could never tell Zaccheo how she felt about him, but she could sing it to him. Her eyes found his as she sang the last line.

His gaze grew hot. Intense. Her pulse hammered as she sang the third verse, offering her heart, her life to him, all the while knowing he would reject it once he knew.

She stifled a sob as the machine clicked to an end. She started to step off the stage, but the group begged for another song.

Zaccheo rose and moved towards her. They stared at each other as the clamouring grew louder. Her breath caught when the emotion in his eyes altered, morphing into that darker hue that held a deeper meaning.

He wasn't angry. Or ruthlessly commanding her to bend to his will. Or even bitter and hurt, as he'd been on the hill.

There was none of that in his expression. This ferocity was different, one that made her world stop.

Until she shook herself back to reality. She was grasping at straws, stalling with excuses and foolish, reckless hope. She might have fallen in love with Zaccheo, but nothing he'd said or done had indicated he returned even an iota of what she felt. Their relationship had changed from what it'd been in the beginning, but she couldn't lose sight of *why* it'd begun in the first place. Or why she couldn't let it continue.

Heavy-hearted, she turned back to the machine. She'd seen the song earlier and bypassed it, because she hadn't been ready to say goodbye.

But it was time to end this. Time to accept that there was no hope.

Something was wrong. It'd been since they'd walked down the hill.

But for once in his life, he was afraid to confront a problem head-on because he was terrified the results would be unwelcome. So he played worst-case scenarios in his head.

Had he said or done something to incite this troubled look on Eva's face? Had his confession on the hill reminded her that he wasn't the man she would've chosen for herself? A wave of something close to desolation rushed over him. He clenched his jaw against the feeling. Would it really be the end of the world if Eva decided she didn't want him? The affirmative answer echoing through him made him swallow hard.

He discarded that line of thought and chose another, dissecting each moment he'd spent with her this afternoon.

He'd laid himself bare, something he'd never done until recently. She hadn't shown pity or disgust for the debasing crimes his father had committed, or for the desperately lonely child he'd been. Yet again she'd only showed compassion. Pain for the toll his jagged upbringing had taken on him.

And the songs…what had they meant, especially the second one, the one about saying *goodbye*? He'd witnessed the agony in her eyes while she'd sung that one. As if her heart was broken—

A knock came at his study door, where he'd retreated to pace after they'd returned and Eva had expressed the need for a shower. Alone.

'Zaccheo?'

He steeled himself to turn around, hoping against hope that the look on her face would be different. That she would smile and everything would return to how it was before they'd gone on that blasted trip.

But it wasn't. And her next words ripped through him with the lethal effect of a vicious blade.

'Zaccheo, we need to talk.'

CHAPTER FOURTEEN

EVERY WORD SHE'D practised in the shower fled her head as Eva faced him. Of course, her muffled sobs had taken up a greater part of the shower so maybe she hadn't got as much practice in as she'd thought.

'I...' Her heart sank into her stomach when a forbidding look tightened his face. 'I can't stay married to you.'

For a moment he looked as if she'd punched him hard in the solar plexus, then ripped his heart out while he struggled to breathe. Gradually his face lost every trace of pain and distress. Hands shoved deep in his pockets, he strolled to where she stood, frozen inside the doorway.

'Was this your plan all along?' he bit out, his eyes arctic. 'To wait until I'd spoken on your father's behalf and he was safe from prosecution before you asked for a divorce?'

She gasped. 'You did that? When?' she asked, but his eyes poured scorn on her question.

'Is being married to me that abhorrent to you, Eva? So much so you couldn't even wait until we were back in London?'

'No! Believe me, Zaccheo, that's not it.'

'*Believe* you? Why should I? When you're not even prepared to give us a chance?' He veered sharply away from her and strode across the room, his fingers spiking through his hair before he reversed course and stopped in front of her once more. 'What I don't understand is why. Did I do something? Say something to make you think I wouldn't want this relationship to work?'

The confirmation that this marriage meant more to him was almost too hard to bear.

'Zaccheo, please listen to me. It's not you, it's—'

His harsh laughter echoed around the room. 'Are you *seriously* giving me that line?'

Her fists balled. 'For once in your life, just shut up and listen! I can't have children,' she blurted.

'You've already used that one, *dolcezza*, but you signed along the dotted line agreeing to my clause, remember? So try again.'

Misery quivered through her stomach. 'It's true I signed the agreement, but I lied to you. I *can't* have children, Zaccheo. I'm infertile.'

He sucked in a hoarse breath and reeled backwards on his heels. 'Excuse me?'

'I tried to tell you when I first saw the clause, but you wouldn't listen. You'd made up your mind that I'd use any excuse not to marry you because I didn't want you.'

The stunned look morphed into censure. 'Then you should've put me straight.'

'How? Would you have believed me if I'd told you about my condition? Without evidence to back it up? Or perhaps I should've told Romeo or your PA since they had more access to you than I did in the week before the wedding?'

He looked at her coldly. 'If your conscience stung you so deeply the first time round, why did you change your mind?'

Her emotions were raw enough for her to instinctively want to protect herself. But what did she have to lose? Zaccheo would condemn her actions regardless of whether she kept her innermost feelings to herself or not. And really, how much worse could this situation get? Her heart was already in shreds.

She met his gaze head on. 'You know I lost my mother to cancer when I was eighteen. She was diagnosed when I was sixteen. For two years we waited, hoping for the best, fearing the worst through each round of chemo. With each treatment that didn't work we knew her time was growing shorter. Knowing it was coming didn't make it any easier. Her death ripped me apart.' She stopped and gathered her courage. 'My father has been suffering stress attacks in the last couple of months.' She risked a glance and saw his brows clamped in a forbidding frown. 'He collapsed on Friday after you called to tell him the wedding was off.'

Zaccheo's mouth compressed, but a trace of compassion flashed through his eyes. 'And you blame me? Is that what this is all about?'

'No, I don't. We both know that the blame for our current circumstances lies firmly with my father.' She stopped and licked her lips. 'He may have brought this on himself, but the stress was killing him, Zaccheo. I've watched one parent die, helpless to do anything but watch them fade away. Condemn me all you want, but I wasn't going to stand by and let my father worry himself to death over what he'd done. And I didn't do it for my family name or my blasted *pedigree*. I did it because that's what you do for the people you love.'

'Even when they don't love you back?' he sneered, his voice indicating hers was a foolish feeling. 'Even when they treat you like an afterthought for most of your life?'

Sadness engulfed her. 'You can't help who you love. Or choose who will love you back.'

His eyes met hers for a charged second, before his nostrils flared. 'But you can choose to tell the truth no matter how tough the telling of it is. You can choose *not* to start a marriage based on lies.'

Regret crawled across her skin. 'Yes. And I'm sorry—'

His hand slashed through air, killing off her apology. Walking around her, he slammed the door shut and jerked his chin towards the sofa. He waited until she'd sat down, then prowled in front of her.

'Tell me of this condition you have.'

Eva stared at her clasped hands because watching his face had grown unbearable. 'It's called endometriosis.' She gave him the bare facts, unwilling to linger on the subject and prolong her heartache. 'It started just before I went to university, but, with everything going on with my mother, I didn't pay enough attention to it. I thought it was just something that would right itself eventually. But the pain got worse. One day I collapsed and was rushed to hospital. The diagnosis was made.' She stopped, then made herself go on. 'The doctor said the…scarring was too extensive…that I would never conceive naturally.'

She raised her head and saw that he'd stopped prowling and taken a seat opposite her with his elbows on his knees. 'Go on,' he bit out.

Eva shrugged. 'What else is there to add?' She gave a hollow laugh. 'I never thought I'd be in a position where the one thing I couldn't give would be the difference between having the future I want and the one I'd have to settle for. You accused me of starting this marriage based on lies, but I didn't know you wanted a real marriage. You did all this to get back at my father, remember?'

'So you never sought a second opinion?' he asked stonily, as if she hadn't mentioned the shifted parameters of their marriage.

'Why would I? I'd known something was wrong. Having the doctor confirm it merely affirmed what I already suspected. What was the point of putting myself through further grief?'

Zaccheo jerked to his feet and began prowling again. The set of his shoulders told her he was holding himself on a tight leash.

Minutes ticked by and he said nothing. The tension increased until she couldn't stand it any more. 'You can do whatever you want with me, but I want your word that you won't go after my family because of what I've done.'

He froze, his eyes narrowing to thin shards of ice. 'You think I want you to martyr yourself on some noble pyre for my sick satisfaction?'

She jumped to her feet. 'I don't know! You're normally so quick to lay down your demands. Or throw out orders and expect them to be followed. So tell me what you want.'

That chilling half-smile returned with a vengeance. 'What I want is to leave this place. There's really no point staying, is there, since the honeymoon is well and truly over?'

The flight back was markedly different from the outbound journey. The moment Zaccheo immersed himself in his work, she grabbed her tablet and locked herself in the bedroom.

She threw herself on the bed and sobbed long and hard into the pillow. By the time the plane landed in London, she was completely wrung out. Exhaustion seeped into her very bones and all she wanted was to curl into a foetal position and wish the world away.

She sank further into grey gloom when she descended the steps of the aircraft to find Zaccheo's limo waiting on the tarmac, along with a black SUV.

Zaccheo, wearing a black and navy pinstriped suit, stopped next to her, his expression remote and unfriendly.

'I'm heading to the office. Romeo will drive you to the penthouse.'

He strode to the SUV and drove off.

Eva realised then that throughout their conversation on the island, she'd made the same mistake as when she'd foolishly disclosed her condition before. She'd allowed herself to *hope* that the condition fate had bestowed on her wouldn't matter to that one *special person*. That somehow *love* would find a way.

A sob bubbled up her chest and she angrily swallowed it down.

Grow up, Eva. You're letting the lyrics of your songs cloud your judgement.

'Eva?' Romeo waited with the car door open.

She hastily averted her gaze from the censure in his eyes and slid in.

The penthouse hadn't changed, and yet Eva felt as if she'd lived a lifetime since she was last here.

After unpacking and showering, she trailed from room to room, feeling as if some tether she hadn't known she was tied to had been severed. When she rushed to the door for the third time, imagining she'd heard the keycard activate, she grabbed her tablet and forced herself to work on her compositions.

But her heart wasn't in it. Her mood grew bleaker when Romeo found her curled on the sofa and announced that Zaccheo wouldn't be home for dinner either tonight or the next two weeks, because he'd returned to Oman.

The days bled together in a dull grey jumble. Determined not to mope—because after all she'd been here before—Eva returned to work.

She took every spare shift available and offered herself for overtime without pay.

But she refused to sing.

Music had ceased to be the balm she'd come to rely on. Her heart only yearned for one thing. Or *one man*. And he'd made it abundantly clear that he didn't want her.

Because two weeks stretched to four, then six with no word from Zaccheo, and no answer to her phone calls.

At her lowest times, Eva hated herself for her lethargy, for not moving out of the penthouse. For sitting around, wishing for a miracle that would never materialise.

But the thought of flat-hunting, or, worse, moving back to Pennington Manor, filled her with a desperate heartache that nothing seemed to ease.

Romeo had brought her coffee this morning at the breakfast table. The pitying look he'd cast her had been the final straw.

'If you have something to say, just say it, Romeo.'

'You're not a weak woman. One of you has to take the situation in hand sooner or later,' he'd replied.

'Fine, but he won't return my calls so give him a message from me, will you?'

He'd nodded in that solemn way of his. 'Of course.'

'Tell him I'm fast reaching my tolerance level for his stupid silence. He can stay in Oman for the rest of his life for all I care. But he shouldn't expect to find me here when he deigns to return.'

That outburst had been strangely cathartic. She'd called her ex-landlady and discovered her flat was still unlet. After receiving a hefty payday from Zaccheo, the old woman hadn't been in a hurry to interview new tenants. She'd invited Eva to move back whenever she wanted.

Curiously, that announcement hadn't made her feel better—

'You've been cleaning that same spot for the last five minutes.'

Eva started and glanced down. 'Oh.'

Sybil, Siren's unflappable manageress, eyed her. 'Time for a break.'

'I don't need a—'

'Sorry, love,' Sybil said firmly. 'Orders from above. The new owner was very insistent. You take a break now or I get docked a week's wages.'

Eva frowned. 'Are you serious? Do we know who this new owner is?'

Sybil's eyes widened. 'You don't know?' When she shook her head, the manageress shrugged. 'Well, I'm not one to spread gossip. Shoo! Go put your feet up for a bit. I'll finish up here.'

Eva reluctantly handed over the cleaning supplies. She turned and stopped as the doors swung open and Ziggy Preston walked in.

The smile she tried for failed miserably. 'Ziggy, hello.'

He smiled. 'I heard you were back in town.'

She couldn't summon the curiosity to ask how he knew. 'Oh?'

'You were supposed to call when you got back. I hope that doesn't mean you've signed up with someone else? Because that'd devastate me,' he joked.

Eva tried for another smile. Failed again. 'I didn't sign with anyone, and I don't think I will.'

His face fell. 'Why not?'

She had a thousand and one reasons. But only one that mattered. And she wasn't about to divulge it to another soul. 'I've decided to give the music thing a break for a while.' Or for ever, depending on whether she felt anything but numb again.

Ziggy shoved his hands into his coat pocket, his features pensive.

'Listen, I was supposed to do a session with one of my artists tomorrow afternoon, but they cancelled. Come to the studio, hang out for a while. You don't have to sing if you don't want to. But come anyway.'

She started to shake her head, then stopped. It was her day off tomorrow. The extra shift she'd hoped to cover had suddenly been filled. She could either occupy herself at Ziggy's studio or wander Zaccheo's penthouse like a lost wraith, pining for what she could never have. 'Okay.'

'Great!' He handed her another business card, this one with his private number scribbled on the back, and left.

A couple of months ago, being pursued by a top music producer would've been a dream come true. And yet, Eva could barely summon the enthusiasm to dress the next day, especially when Romeo confirmed he'd given Zaccheo her message but had no reply for her.

Jaw clenched, she pulled on her jeans and sweater, determined not to succumb to the unending bouts of anguish that had made her throw up this morning after her conversation with Romeo.

She wasn't a pearl-clutching Victorian maiden, for heaven's sake!

Her life might *feel* as if it were over, but she'd been through the wringer more than once in her life. She'd survived her diagnosis. She'd survived her mother's death. Despite the odds, she'd mended fences with her father and sister.

Surely she could survive decimating her heart on a love that had been doomed from the start?

Deliberately putting a spring in her step, she arrived at Ziggy's studio in a different frame of mind. Looking around, she repeated to herself that *this* was a tangible dream. Something she could hang on to once Zaccheo returned and she permanently severed the ties that had so very briefly bound them.

Eva was sure she was failing in her pep talk to herself when Ziggy gave up after a third attempt to get her to sample an upbeat pop tune.

'Okay, shall we try one of yours?' he suggested with a wry smile.

Half-heartedly, she sifted through her list, then paused, her heart picking up its sluggish beat as she stared at the lyrics to the song she'd composed that last morning on the island.

'This one,' she murmured.

At Ziggy's nod, she sang the first line.

His eyes widened. 'Wow.' Nodding to the sound booth, he said, 'I'd love to hear the whole thing if you're up to it?'

Eva thought of the raw lyrics, how they offered love, pleaded for for ever and accepted any risks necessary, and breathed deeply.

If this was what it took to start healing herself, then so be it. 'Sure.'

She was singing the final notes when an electrifying wave of awareness swept over her. Her gaze snapped up to the viewing gallery above the booth, where she knew music moguls sometimes listened in on artists. Although the mirrored glass prevented her from seeing who occupied it, she swore she could smell Zaccheo's unique scent.

'Are you okay?' Ziggy asked.

She nodded absently, her gaze still on the gallery window.

'Can you sing the last two lines again?'

'Umm…yes,' she mumbled.

She really was losing it. If she couldn't sing a song she'd
written with Zaccheo in mind without imagining she could
feel him, smell him, she was in deep trouble. Because as she
worked through the other songs Ziggy encouraged her to record, Eva realised all her songs were somehow to do with
the man who'd taken her heart prisoner.

She left the studio in a daze and got into the waiting limo.
Physically and emotionally drained, she couldn't connect
two thoughts together. When she finally accepted what she
needed to do, she turned to Romeo.

'Can you take me to Zaccheo's office, please?'

He looked up from the laptop he'd been working on. After
a few probing seconds, he nodded.

A wave of dizziness hit her as they waited for the lift at
GWI. She ignored the curious glances, and concentrated on
staying upright, putting one foot in front of the other as she
made her way down the plushly decorated corridor to Zaccheo's office.

Anyetta's coolly professional demeanour visibly altered
when she saw Eva, then turned to shock as her gaze travelled
from her head to her toes.

Eva wanted to laugh, but she couldn't be sure she wouldn't
dissolve into hysteria. When Anyetta stood, Eva waved her
away.

'I know he's not in. I was hoping *you* would email him
for me.'

'But—'

'It won't take long, I promise.'

The tall brunette looked briefly bewildered, but her features settled back into serene composure and she sat down.

'Mark it *urgent*. Presumably, you can tell when he opens
emails from you?' Eva asked.

Warily, Zaccheo's PA nodded.

'Good.' Eva approached, pushing back the errant curls
obscuring her vision. She folded her arms around her middle
and prayed for just a few more minutes of strength.

Anyetta's elegant fingers settled on the keyboard.

Eva cleared her throat.

Zaccheo.

Since you refuse to engage with me, I can only conclude that I'm free of my obligations to you. To that end, I'd be grateful if you would take the appropriate steps to end this marriage forthwith. My family lawyers will be on standby when you're ready, but I'd be obliged if you didn't leave it too late. I refuse to put my life on hold for you, so take action or I will. For the record, I won't be accepting any of the monetary compensation offered, nor will I be seeking anything from you, except my freedom. If you choose to pursue my family, then you'll do so without my involvement, because I've done my duty to my family and I'm moving on. I won't let you use me as a pawn in your vendetta against my father. You're aware of the state of my father's health, so I hope you'll choose mercy over retribution.

Regardless of your decision, I'll be moving out of the penthouse tomorrow.

Please don't contact me.

Eva.

'Send it, please,' she said.

Anyetta clicked the button, then looked up. 'He just opened it.'

Eva nodded jerkily. 'Thank you.'

She walked out with scalding tears filling her eyes. A solid presence registered beside her and when Romeo took her arm, Eva didn't protest.

At the penthouse, she dropped her bag in the hallway, tugged off her boots and coat as her vision greyed. She made it into bed as her legs gave way and she curled, fully clothed, into a tight ball. Her last thought before blessed oblivion claimed her was that she'd done it.

She'd survived her first hour with a heart broken into a million tiny pieces. If there was any justice, she might just make it through the rest of her life with a shredded heart.

CHAPTER FIFTEEN

IN THE SPLIT SECOND before wakefulness hit, Eva buried her nose in the pillow that smelled so much like Zaccheo she groaned with pure, incandescent happiness.

Reality arrived with searing pain so acute, she cried out.

'Eva.'

She jolted upright at the sound of her name. Jagged thoughts pierced her foggy brain like shards of bright light through glass.

She was no longer in her own suite, but in Zaccheo's.

Her clothes were gone, and she was stripped down to her bra and panties.

Zaccheo was sitting in an armchair next to the bed, his eyes trained on her.

And he was clean-shaven.

His thick stubble was gone, his hair trimmed into a short, neat style that left his nape bare.

Despite his altered appearance, his living, breathing presence was far too much to bear. She jerked her head away, stared down at the covers she clutched like a lifeline.

'What are you doing here?' she asked.

'You summoned me. So here I am,' he stated.

She shook her head. 'Please. Don't make it sound as if I have any power over your actions. If I did you would've answered my numerous phone calls like a normal person. And that email wasn't a summons. It was a statement of intent, hardly demanding your presence.'

'Nevertheless, since you went to so much trouble to make sure it reached me, I thought it only polite to answer it in person.'

'Well, you needn't have bothered,' she threw back hotly,

'especially since we both know you don't have a polite bone in your body. Things like *consideration* and *courtesy* are alien concepts to you.'

He looked perturbed by her outburst. Which made her want to laugh. And cry. And scream. 'Are you going to sit there with that insulting look that implies I'm out of my mind?'

'You must forgive me if that's what my expression implies. I meant to wear a look that says I was hoping for a civilised conversation.'

She threw out her hands. 'You have a damned nerve, do you know that? I…' She stopped, her eyes widening in alarm as an unpleasant scent hit her nostrils. Swivelling, she saw the breakfast tray containing scrambled eggs, smoked pancetta, coffee, and the buttered brioche she loved.

Correction. She'd *once* loved.

Shoving the covers aside, she lunged for the bathroom, uncaring that she was half-naked and looked like a bedraggled freak. All she cared about was making it to the porcelain bowl in time.

She vomited until she collapsed against the shower stall, desperately catching her breath. When Zaccheo crouched at her side, she shut her eyes. 'Please, Zaccheo. Go away.'

He pressed a cool towel to her forehead, her eyelids, her cheeks. 'A lesser man might be decimated at the thought that his presence makes you physically ill,' he murmured gravely.

Her snort grated her throat. 'But you're not a lesser man, of course.'

He shrugged. 'I'm saved by Romeo's report that you've been feeling under the weather recently.'

Eva opened her eyes, looked at him, then immediately wished she hadn't. She'd thought his beard and long mane made him gloriously beautiful, but the sight of his chiselled jaw, the cut of his cheekbones, and the fully displayed sensual lips was almost blinding.

'I can't do this.' She tried to stand and collapsed back against the stall.

With a muttered oath, he scooped her up in his arms and strode to the vanity. Setting her down, he handed her a toothbrush and watched as she cleaned her teeth.

Eva told herself the peculiar look turning his eyes that gunmetal shade meant nothing. Zaccheo had probably come to ensure she vacated his penthouse before succumbing to whatever was ailing her.

Steeling her spine, she rinsed her mouth. He reached for her as she moved away from the vanity, but she sidestepped him, her heart banging against her ribs. 'I can walk on my own two feet.'

Zaccheo watched her go, her hips swaying in that impertinent, yet utterly sexy way that struck pure fire to his libido.

He slowly followed, paused in the doorway and watched her pace the bedroom.

Although he'd primed himself for her appearance, he hadn't been quite prepared for when he'd finally returned to the penthouse last night and found her asleep in her suite. All the excuses he'd given himself for staying away had crumbled to dust.

As he'd stood over her, his racing heart had only been able to acknowledge one thing—that he'd missed her more than his brain could accurately fathom. He'd thought the daily reports on her movements would be enough. He'd thought buying Siren and ensuring she didn't overwork herself, or silently watching her from the gallery at Preston's studio yesterday, listening to her incredible voice, would be enough.

It wasn't until he'd received her email that his world had stopped, and he'd forced himself to face the truth.

He was nothing without her.

For the last six weeks he'd woken to a tormenting existence each morning. Each time, something had broken inside him. Something that would probably slot neatly under

the banner of heartache. It had nothing to do with the loneliness that had plagued his childhood and led him to believe
he needed a family to soothe the ache. It had nothing to do
with the retribution he was no longer interested in exacting
from Oscar Pennington.

It had everything to do with Eva. Flashes of her had struck
him at the most inappropriate times—like the brightness of
her smile when he was involved in tense negotiation. The
feeling of being deep inside her when he was teetering on the
edge of a platform three hundred metres above ground, with
no net to catch him should he fall. And everywhere he'd gone,
he'd imagined the faintest trace of her perfume in the air.

Nothing had stopped him from reaching out for her in
the dead of the night, when his guard was at its lowest and
all he could feel was *need*. Ferocious, all-consuming need.

Even the air of sadness that hung around her now wasn't
enough to make him *not* yearn for her.

His heart kicked into his stomach, knowing it was his
fault she wore that look.

Her throat worked to find the words she needed. He forced
himself to remain still, to erect a force field against anything
she might say.

'Let's end this now, Zaccheo. Divorce me. Surely you'd
prefer that to this mockery of a marriage?'

He'd expected it. Hell, her email had left him in no doubt
as to her state of mind.

Yet the words punched him in the gut…*hard*. Zaccheo
uttered an imprecation that wasn't fit for polite company.

*Give her what she wants. Stop this endless misery and
be done with it.*

It was the selfless thing to do. And if he needed to have
learned anything from the stunning, brave woman in front of
him, it was selflessness. She'd sacrificed herself for her family and turned over her innermost secrets when she could've
just kept quiet and reaped untold wealth. She'd continued to

stay under his roof, continued to seek him out, when fear had sent *him* running.

He *needed* to be selfless for her.

But he couldn't. He walked stiffly to the side table and poured a coffee he didn't want.

'There will be no divorce.'

She glared at him. 'You do realise that I don't need your permission?'

He knew that. He'd lived with that fear ever since she'd announced back in Rio that she didn't want to be married to him any more.

'*Sì,*' he replied gruffly. 'You can do whatever you want. The same way I can choose to tie you up in endless red tape for the next twenty years.'

Her mouth dropped open, then she shut her beautiful, pain-filled eyes. 'Why would you do that, Zaccheo?'

'Why indeed?'

She shook her head, and her hair fluttered over her shoulders. 'Surely you can't want this? You deserve a family.'

There it was again. That selflessness that cut him to the core, that forced him to let go, to be a better man. *Dio mio*, but he wanted her to be selfish for once. To claim what she wanted. To claim him!

'How very noble of you to think of me. But I don't need a family.'

Shock widened her eyes. 'What did you say?'

'I don't need a family, *il mio cuore*. I don't need anything, or anyone, if I have you.' *She* was all he wanted. He'd prostrate himself at her feet if that was what it took.

She stared at him for so long, Zaccheo felt as if he'd turned to stone. He knew that any movement would see him shatter into useless pieces.

But he had to take the leap. The same leap she'd taken on the island, when she'd shared something deeply private and heartbreaking with him.

'If you have *me*?'

He risked taking a breath. 'Yes. I love you, Eva. I've been racking my brain for weeks, trying to find a way to make you stay, convince you to stay my wife—'

'You didn't think to just *ask* me?'

'After walking away from you like a coward?' He shook his head. 'You've no idea how many times I picked up the phone, how many times I summoned my pilot to bring me back to you. But I couldn't face the possibility of you saying no.' He gave a hollow laugh. 'Believe it or not, I convinced myself I'd rather spend the rest of my life living in another country but still married to you, than face the prospect of never having even the tiniest piece of you.'

Her face crumbled and he nearly roared in pain. 'That's no life at all, Zaccheo.'

'It was a reason for me to *breathe*. A selfish but *necessary* reason for me to keep functioning, knowing I had a piece of you even if it was your name next to mine on a marriage certificate.'

'Oh, God!' Tears filled her eyes and he cursed. He wanted to take her in his arms. But he had no right. He'd lost all rights when he'd forced her into marriage and then condemned her for trying to protect herself from his monstrous actions.

He clenched his fists against the agony ripping through him. 'But that's no life for you. If you wish for a divorce, then I'll grant you one.'

'What?' Her face lost all colour. She started to reach for him, but faltered. 'Zaccheo...'

A different sort of fear scythed through him as she started to crumple.

'Eva!'

By the time he caught her she was unconscious.

Muted voices pulled her back to consciousness. The blinds in the strange room were drawn but there was enough light to work out that she was no longer in Zaccheo's penthouse. The drip in her right arm confirmed her worst fears.

'What…happened?' she croaked.

Shadowy figures turned, and Sophie rushed to her side.

'You fainted. Zaccheo brought you to the hospital,' Sophie said.

'Zaccheo…' Memory rushed back. Zaccheo telling her he loved her. Then telling her he would divorce her…

No!

She tried to sit up.

The nurse stopped her. 'The doctors are running tests. We should have the results back shortly. In the meantime, you're on a rehydrating drip.'

Eva touched her throbbing head, wishing she'd stop talking for a moment so she could—

She stared at her bare fingers in horror. 'Where are my rings?' she cried.

The nurse frowned. 'I don't know.'

'No…please. I need…' She couldn't catch her breath. Or take her eyes off her bare fingers. Had Zaccheo done it so quickly? While she'd been unconscious?

But he'd said he loved her. Did he not love her enough? Tears brimmed her eyes and fell down her cheeks.

'It's okay, I'll go and find out.' The nurse hurried out.

Sophie approached. Eva forced her pain back and looked at her.

'I hope you don't mind me being here? You didn't call when you got back so I assume you don't want to speak to me, but when Zaccheo called—'

Eva shook her head, her thoughts racing, her insides shredding all over again. 'You're my family, Sophie. It may take a while to get back to where we were before, but I don't hate you. I've just been a little…preoccupied.' Her gaze went to the empty doorway. 'Is…Zaccheo still here?'

Sophie smiled wryly. 'He was enraged that you didn't have a team of doctors monitoring your every breath. He went to find the head of the trauma unit.'

Zaccheo walked into the room at that moment, and Sophie

hastily excused herself. The gunmetal shade of his eyes and the self-loathing on his face made Eva's heart thud slowly as she waited for the death blow.

He walked forward like a man facing his worst nightmare.

Just before she'd fainted, she'd told herself she would fight for him, as she'd fought for her sister and father. Seeing the look on his face, she accepted that nothing she did would change things. Her bare fingers spoke their own truth.

'Zaccheo, I know you said...you loved me, but if it's not enough for you—'

Astonishment transformed his face. 'Not enough for *me*?'

'You agreed to divorce me...'

Anguish twisted his face. 'Only because it was what *you* wanted.'

She sucked in a breath when he perched on the edge of the bed. His fingers lightly brushed the back of her hand, over and over, as if he couldn't help himself.

'You know what I did last night before I came home?'

She shook her head.

'I went to see your father. I had no idea where I was headed until I landed on the lawn at Pennington Manor. Somewhere along the line, I entertained the idea that I would sway your feelings if I smoothed my relationship with your father. Instead I asked him for your hand in marriage.'

'You did what?'

He grimaced. 'Our wedding was a pompous exhibition from start to finish. I wanted to show everyone who'd dared to look down on me how high I'd risen.'

Her heart lurched. 'Because of what your mother and stepfather did?'

He sighed. 'I hated my mother for choosing her aristocrat husband over me. Like you, I didn't understand why it had to be an either-or choice. Why couldn't she love me *and* her husband? Then I began to hate everything he stood for. The need to understand why consumed me. My stepfather was easy to break. Your father was a little more cunning.

He used you. From the moment we met, I couldn't see beyond you. He saw that. I don't know if I'll ever be able to forgive that, but he brought us together.' He breathed deep and shoved a hand through his short hair. 'Possessing you blinded me to what he was doing. And I blamed you for it, right along with him when the blame lay with me and my obsession to get back at you when I should've directed my anger elsewhere.'

'You were trying to understand why you'd been rejected. I tried for years to understand why my father couldn't be satisfied with what he had. Why he pushed his family obsession onto his children. He fought with my mother over it, and it ripped us apart. Everything stopped when she got sick. Perversely, I hoped her illness would change things for the better. For a while it did. But after she died, he reverted to type, and I couldn't take it any more.' She glanced at him. 'Hearing you tell that newspaper tycoon that I was merely a means to an end brought everything back to me.'

Zaccheo shut his eyes in regret. He lifted her hand and pressed it against his cheek. 'He was drunk, prying into my feelings towards you. I was grappling with them myself and said the first idiotic thing that popped into my head. I don't deny that it was probably what I'd been telling myself.'

'But afterwards, when I asked you…'

'I'd just found out about the charges. I knew your father was behind it. You were right there, his flesh and blood, a target for my wrath. I regretted it the moment I said it, but you were gone before I got the chance to take it back.' He brought her hand to his mouth and kissed it, then her palm before laying it over his heart. *'Mi dispiace molto, il mio cuore.'*

His heart beat steady beneath her hand. But her fingers were bare.

'Zaccheo, what you said before I fainted…'

Pain ravaged his face before he nodded solemnly. 'I meant it. I'll let you go if that's what you want. Your happiness means everything to me. Even if it's without me.'

She shook her head. 'No, not that. What you said before.'

He looked deep into her eyes, his gaze steady and true. 'I love you, Eva. More than my life, more than everything I've ever dared to dream of. You helped me redeem my soul when I thought it was lost.'

'You touched mine, made me love deeper, purer. You taught me to take a risk again instead of living in fear of rejection.'

He took a sharp breath. 'Eva, what are you saying?'

'That I love you too. And it tears me apart that I won't be able to give you children—'

His kiss stopped her words. 'Prison was hell, I won't deny it. In my lowest times, I thought having children would be the answer. But you're the only family I need, *amore mio.*'

Zaccheo was rocking her, crooning softly to comfort her when the doctor walked in.

'Right, Mrs Giordano. You'll be happy to hear we've got to the bottom of your fainting spell. There's nothing to worry about besides—'

'Dehydration and the need to eat better?' she asked with a sniff.

'Well, yes, there's that.'

'Okay, I promise I will.'

'I'll make sure she keeps to it,' Zaccheo added with a mock frown. He settled her back in the bed and stood. 'I'll go get the car.'

The doctor shook his head. 'No, I'm afraid you can't leave yet. You need to rest for at least twenty-four hours while we monitor you and make sure everything's fine.'

Zaccheo tensed and caught her hand in his. 'What do you mean? Didn't you say you'd got to the bottom of what ails her?' His eyes met hers, and Eva read the anxiety there.

'Zaccheo…'

'Mr Giordano, no need to panic. The only thing that should ail your wife is a short bout of morning sickness and perhaps a little bed rest towards the end.'

Zaccheo paled and visibly trembled. 'The *end*?'

Eva's heart stopped. 'Doctor, what are you saying?' she whispered.

'I'm saying you're pregnant. With twins.'

EPILOGUE

ZACCHEO EMERGED FROM the bedroom where he'd gone to change his shirt—the second of the day due to his eldest son throwing up on him—to find Eva cross-legged on the floor before the coffee table, their children cradled in her arms as she crooned Italian nursery rhymes she'd insisted he teach her.

On the screen via a video channel, Romeo leaned in closer to get a better look at the babies.

Zaccheo skirted the sofa and sat behind his wife, cradling her and their children in his arms.

'Do you think you'll make it for Christmas?' she asked Romeo. Zaccheo didn't need to lean over to see that his wife was giving his friend her best puppy-dog look.

'*Sì*, I'll do my best to be there tomorrow.'

Eva shook her head. 'That's not good enough, Romeo. I know Brunetti International is a huge company, and you're a super busy tycoon, but it's your godsons' first Christmas. They picked out your present all by themselves. The least you can do is turn up and open it.'

Zaccheo laughed silently and watched his friend squirm until he realised denying his wife anything her heart desired was a futile exercise.

'If that's what you wish, *principessa*, then I'll be there.'

Eva beamed. Zaccheo spread his fingers through her hair, resisting the urge to smother her cheek and mouth in kisses because she thought it made Romeo uncomfortable.

The moment Romeo signed off, Zaccheo claimed his kiss, not lifting his head until he was marginally satisfied.

'What was that for?' she murmured in that dazed voice that was like a drug to his blood.

'Because you're my heart, *dolcezza*. I cannot go long without it. Without you.'

Eva's heart melted as Zaccheo relieved her of their youngest son, Rafa, and tucked his tiny body against his shoulder. Then he held out his hand and helped her up with Carlo, their eldest by four minutes.

Zaccheo pulled them close until they stood in a loose circle, his arms around her. Then, as he'd taken to doing, he started swaying to the soft Christmas carols playing in the background.

Eva closed her eyes to stem the happy tears forming. She'd said a prayer every day of her pregnancy as they'd faced hurdles because of her endometriosis. When the doctors had prescribed bed rest at five months, Zaccheo had immediately stepped back from GWI and handed over the day-to-day running of the company to his new second-in-command.

Their sons had still arrived two weeks early but had both been completely healthy, much to the joy and relief of their parents. Relations were still a little strained with her father and sister, but Oscar doted on his grandsons, and Sophie had fallen in love with her nephews at first sight. But no one loved their gorgeous boys more than Zaccheo. The love and adoration in his eyes when he cradled his sons often made her cry.

And knowing that love ran just as deep for her filled her heart with so much happiness, she feared she would burst from it.

'You've stopped dancing,' he murmured.

She began to sway again, her free hand rising to his chest. She caught sight of her new rings—the engagement ring belonging to his grandmother, which he'd kept but not given her because the circumstances hadn't been right, and the new wedding band he'd let her pick out for their second, family-only wedding—and her thoughts turned pensive. 'I was thinking about your mother.'

Zaccheo tensed slightly. She caressed her hand over his heart until the tension eased out of him. 'What were you thinking?' he asked grudgingly.

'I sent her pictures of the boys yesterday.'

A noise rumbled from Zaccheo's chest. 'She's been asking for one since the day they were born.'

She leaned back and looked into her husband's eyes. 'I know. I also know you've agreed to see her at Easter after my first album comes out.'

Tension remained between mother and son, but when his mother had reached out, Zaccheo hadn't turned her away.

Standing on tiptoe, Eva caressed the stubble she insisted he grow again, and kissed him. 'I'm very proud of you.'

'No, Eva. Everything good in my life is because of *you*.' He sealed her lips with another kiss. A deeper, more demanding kiss.

By mutual agreement, they pulled away and headed for the nursery. After bestowing kisses on their sleeping sons, Zaccheo took her hand and led her to the bedroom.

Their lovemaking was slow, worshipful, with loving words blanketing them as they reached fulfilment and fell asleep in each other's arms.

When midnight and Christmas rolled around, Zaccheo woke her and made love to her all over again. Afterwards, sated and happy, he spread his fingers through her hair and brought her face to his.

'*Buon Natale, amore mio,*' he said. 'You're the only thing I want under my Christmas tree, from now until eternity.'

'Merry Christmas, Zaccheo. You make my heart sing every day and my soul soar every night. You're everything I ever wished for.'

He touched his forehead to hers and breathed deep. '*Ti amero per sempre, dolcezza mia.*'

* * * * *

MISTRESS OF
HIS REVENGE

CHANTELLE SHAW

CHAPTER ONE

THE HONOURABLE HUGO FFAULKS—with two Fs—was drunk and being sick into a vase. Not just any vase, Sabrina noted, her lips tightening with annoyance. The vase was a fine example of early eighteenth-century English porcelain and had been valued at fifteen hundred pounds by an auction house that had recently catalogued the antiques at Eversleigh Hall.

Compared to the value of the hall's art collection, which included two Gainsboroughs and a portrait by Joshua Reynolds, fifteen hundred pounds was not a vast sum, but in Sabrina's current financial crisis she needed every penny she could lay her hands on and selling the vase would at least allow her to pay the staff's wages and the farrier's bill.

A frown crossed her smooth brow. If only horses did not need shoeing every six weeks. The cost of the farrier, plus vet's bills, feed and hay meant that Monty was becoming an expense she simply could not justify. She had spoken to a reputable horse dealer who had assured her that she should get a good price for a seven-year-old thoroughbred, but the thought of selling Monty was unbearable.

She turned her attention to Hugo, who was now leaning on one of the other party guests and trying to stagger in the direction of the bar.

'Take him to the kitchen and get some black coffee into him,' Sabrina instructed Hugo's friend. She wished she could phone Brigadier Ffaulks and ask him to come and collect his son, but Hugo's parents had paid her a sizeable fee to organise a twenty-first birthday party at Eversleigh Hall. Hugo and fifty of his friends had arrived the previous evening and would be staying at the hall for the weekend. Tomorrow after breakfast—if any of them could face a full English breakfast—they would be able to enjoy clay-pigeon shooting on the estate and fishing in the private lake.

Opening up Eversleigh Hall for weddings and parties was the only way that Sabrina could afford the huge running costs of the estate until her father returned. *If he ever returned.* She quickly pushed her fears about the earl to the back of her mind with the rest of her worries and smiled at the elderly butler who was walking stiffly across the drawing room.

'I'd better fetch a mop and clear up the mess, Miss Sabrina.'

'I'll do it, John. I don't expect you to clear up after *my* guests.' She could not disguise the rueful note in her voice. The butler was well aware that she hated seeing Eversleigh Hall being treated carelessly by the likes of Hugo and his friends, who seemed to think that having money, and in some cases aristocratic titles, gave them the right to behave like animals. And that was an insult to animals, Sabrina thought when she caught sight of a female guest lighting up a cigarette.

'How many times must I repeat the "no smoking in the house" rule?' she muttered.

'I'll escort the young lady out to the garden,' John murmured. 'You have a visitor, Miss Sabrina. A Mr Delgado arrived a few minutes ago.'

She stiffened. 'Delgado—are you sure that was the name he gave?'

The butler looked affronted. 'Quite sure. I would hazard that he is a foreign gentleman. He said he wishes to discuss Earl Bancroft.'

My father!' Sabrina's heart missed another beat. She took a deep breath and groped for her common sense. Just because the unexpected visitor's name was Delgado did not automatically mean that it was Cruz. In fact the likelihood was zero, she reassured herself. It was ten years since she had last seen him. The date their relationship had ended and the date a week earlier when she had suffered a miscarriage and lost their baby were ingrained on her memory. Every year, she found April a poignant month, with lambs in the fields and birds busy building nests, the countryside bursting with new life while she quietly mourned her child who had never lived in the world.

'I asked Mr Delgado to wait in the library.'

'Thank you, John.' Sabrina forced her mind away from painful memories. As she walked across the entrance hall, past the portraits of her illustrious ancestors, she tried to mentally compose herself. It was likely that the mystery visitor was a journalist sniffing around for information about Earl Bancroft. Or perhaps Delgado was one of her father's creditors—heaven knew there were enough of them. But in either case she was unable to help.

She had no idea where her father was, and since he had been officially declared a missing person his bank accounts had been frozen. Sabrina thought of the mounting pile of bills that arrived at Eversleigh Hall daily. Since the earl's disappearance she had used all of her savings to pay for the upkeep of the house, but if her father did not return soon there was a strong possibility that she would be forced to sell her family's ancestral home.

A week earlier in Brazil

'We have to face the facts, Cruz. Old Betsy is finished. She's given us the last of her diamonds and there's no point wasting any more of our time and money on her.'

Cruz Delgado fixed his olive-green eyes on his friend and business partner, Diego Cazorra. 'I'm convinced that Old Betsy hasn't revealed all her secrets,' he said with amusement in his voice. He could not remember now if it had been him or Diego who had christened the diamond mine they had bought as a joint venture six years ago Old Betsy, but the name had stuck.

'Your belief that there could be deposits of diamonds deeper underground is founded purely on speculation fuelled by rumour and the drunken ramblings of an old miner.' Diego lifted a hand to shield his eyes from the blazing Brazilian sun and glanced around the two-thousand-acre mine site.

The ochre-coloured earth was baked as hard as clay and lorry tyre marks criss-crossed the dusty ground. Directly above the mineshaft stood the tall metal structure of the head frame, looking like a bizarre piece of modern art, and next to it were the huge winding drums used to operate the hoist that transported men and machinery down into the mine. In the distance, the glint of silver denoted the river, and beyond it was the dense green rainforest. An alluvial processing plant stretched along one river bank, its purpose to recover diamonds found in sediment sifted from the river bed. But the best diamonds, those of gem quality and high carat weight, were hidden beneath the earth's surface and could only be retrieved by men and machinery tunnelling deep underground.

'I believe Jose's story of the existence of another mine, or at least an extension of the original mine,' Cruz said. 'It confirms what my father told me before he died, that Earl Bancroft had discovered some historic drawings of tunnels that run far deeper than we currently operate.'

Cruz removed his hat and swept his sweat-damp hair back from his brow. Like Diego, he was over six feet tall and his muscular physique was the result of years of hard physical labour working in the mining industry. Both men were deeply tanned, but Cruz's hair was black while Diego's was dirty blond—evidence that his father had been a European, although that was all Diego knew about the man who had seduced his mother and abandoned her when she had fallen pregnant.

Cruz and Diego had been friends since they were boys growing up in a notorious *favela*—a slum in Belo Horizonte, the largest city in the state of Minas Gerais. When Cruz's father had moved his family north to the town of Montes Claros to find work in a diamond mine, Cruz had persuaded Diego to join them at a mine owned by an English earl. They had been excited by the idea of making their fortunes but it had been many years before they had struck lucky and too late for Cruz's father.

'The geological sampling and magnetotelluric sur-

veys we commissioned showed up nothing of interest,'
Diego pointed out. 'Do you really believe a story about
an abandoned mine over modern scientific surveying
techniques?'

'I believe what my father told me with his dying
breath.' Cruz's jaw hardened. 'When Papai discovered
the Estrela Vermelha, Earl Bancroft persuaded him that
there could be other rare red diamonds. My father said
the earl showed him and the old miner Jose a map of a
forgotten section of the mine, which had tunnels running deeper than a thousand metres.'

'But Earl Bancroft sold the mine soon after your
father died following the accident. If there *had* been a
map, Bancroft should have given it to the prospector
who bought the mine from him. When we raised the
money to buy Old Betsy from the prospector six years
ago, you asked him about an old map but he denied any
knowledge of one.'

Cruz shrugged. 'So maybe the earl kept the map a
secret from the prospector. It wouldn't surprise me. I
remember Henry Bancroft was a wily fox who looked
after his own interests at the expense of the men he employed. The roof fall was a direct result of Bancroft's
cost cutting and failure to adhere to safety procedures.
When he sent my father into an area of the mine that
he knew to be dangerous he effectively signed Papai's
death warrant.'

Bitterness swept through Cruz as he thought of the
mining accident that had claimed his father's life. Ten
years ago Vitor Delgado had been buried beneath tons
of rock, but Cruz remembered it as if it had happened
yesterday. Clawing at the rubble of the collapsed mine
roof with his barc hands, choking on the thick dust as

he had desperately tried to reach his father. It had been two days before they had brought Vitor to the surface—alive, but so severely injured that he had died from internal bleeding a few hours later.

Cruz closed his eyes and the years fell away. He was back in a hospital room, with the smell of disinfectant and the beep of the machine that was monitoring his father's failing heartbeat. His mother and sisters were sobbing.

'Don't try to speak, Papai. You need all your strength to get better.'

He had refused to believe Vitor would not recover even though the doctor had murmured that there was no hope. Cruz had put his face close to his father's and struggled to understand the injured man's incoherent mutterings.

'Earl Bancroft showed me a map of tunnels dug many years ago. He believes there are red diamonds as big as the one I found deeper underground. Ask him, Cruz...ask him about the map...'

Even as he was dying Vitor had been obsessed with diamonds. Amongst miners it was known as diamond fever—the desperate lengths men would go to in their quest for the glittering gemstones that could make them rich.

For Cruz and Diego the dream had come true.

After his father died Cruz had become responsible for his mother and young sisters. Mining was the only job he knew and he worked in a coal mine where the filth and sweat and danger were at least repaid with good wages, which allowed him to pay for college evening classes.

Three years later, armed with a business degree, he

got a job with a private bank and quickly proved his brilliance in the boardroom. Other people were surprised by his ruthless determination to succeed but they hadn't seen the things Cruz had witnessed in the *favela*: the violence of the drug gangs, the drive-by shootings. They had never felt hunger in their bellies, or fear, and they had no idea that Cruz sought success and money because he knew what it was like to have nothing.

He was offered a position on the bank's board of directors and bought his mother and sisters a house in an affluent part of the city. Cruz was on his way up and his family would never be hungry again. But he wanted more. He didn't want to work for the bank—he wanted to be one of its millionaire clients.

He remembered the Estrela Vermelha—the Red Star diamond his father had found in the Montes Claros mine. The diamond had an estimated value of several million dollars, but it had belonged to Earl Bancroft, not to Vitor. It was mine owners who got rich, not the men who crawled through tunnels and risked their lives laying explosives to break through solid rock. So Cruz took the biggest gamble of his life and he and Diego bought the mine that had once belonged to Earl Bancroft. The prospector who sold it to them thought they were crazy—he hadn't found diamonds of any significant value in the mine—but he understood that diamond fever could turn sane men mad.

Six months later, kimberlite rock containing diamonds estimated to be worth something in the region of four hundred million dollars was discovered in Old Betsy. Cruz became the most valued client of the bank where he had once worked, and he established a prestigious jewellery company, Delgado Diamonds. Diego invested in a gold mine as well as various other business ventures, but both men remembered what it was like to be poor and hungry and they gave financial support to a charity set up to help Brazil's street children.

'If Earl Bancroft had really believed there was a deeper mine, why would he have sold up? Why didn't he open up the tunnels shown on the map?' Diego demanded.

'Perhaps he kept the map as a form of insurance policy in case he needed money in the future. He knew that whoever owned the mine would be likely to pay a fortune for a map of a second mine with the potential of containing more diamonds.'

Diego frowned. 'Are you suggesting we should offer to buy the map from the earl?'

'The hell I am,' Cruz growled. 'Legally the map, if it exists—and I believe it does—belongs to us. Any documents pertaining to the mine are the property of whoever owns it. Bancroft should have given the map to the prospector, and in turn it should have come to us when we became the new owners of the mine.

'For the past five and a half years we have mined good quality diamonds, but now the supply is virtually exhausted. You're right—to continue mining Old Betsy makes no economic sense. But if there *is* a second mine then I want what is rightfully ours, and I intend to go to Eversleigh Hall in England and demand that Earl Bancroft hands over the map.'

Diego gave Cruz a speculative look. 'It's possible you'll meet Sabrina at Eversleigh Hall. How would you feel about seeing her again?'

Cruz gave a short laugh. 'After ten years I might not even recognise her. She was eighteen when she came to

Brazil. I imagine she is married by now—no doubt to a duke or lord, or some other peer of the realm with an aristocratic pedigree as long as her own. The honourable Lady Sabrina made it clear that she didn't want a commoner for a husband,' he said sardonically.

Sabrina had definitely not wanted to marry a lowly miner who scraped a living crawling through tunnels beneath the ground like a worm, Cruz brooded. She had not even wanted their child—her lack of emotion after she had suffered a miscarriage proved that she had regarded their affair and her subsequent pregnancy as a mistake.

He recalled the first time he had set eyes on Sabrina Bancroft. She had arrived from England to visit her father, and Cruz, walking out of the mining office next to the earl's ranch house, had been arrested by the sight of her alighting from a taxi.

He had never seen a woman like her before, certainly not in the *favela*. With her pale, almost translucent skin and light blonde hair, she had looked ethereal, untouchable. Cruz had stared down at his blackened hands and felt conscious of the sweat stains on his shirt. But Lady Sabrina had barely glanced at him before she had turned her elegant head away. It had been as if he did not exist, as if he was so far beneath her that he simply did not register on her radar. As he'd watched her poised figure walk into the house, a hot flood of desire had swept through Cruz and he had vowed he would make the English rose notice him.

Cruz's mouth tightened into a hard line. He had made a fool of himself over Sabrina, but in his defence he had been far less cynical at twenty-four than he was a decade later. In the intervening years when he had rapidly ascended the world's rich list he had learned the games people played and it amused him that he could take his pick of any of the women who would once have dismissed him as worthless.

Sabrina had rejected him when he'd had nothing to offer her but his heart. It would be interesting to see her reaction to him now that he could afford to buy her precious Eversleigh Hall. Although Cruz knew it was highly unlikely that the Bancrofts' ancestral home would ever come onto the market. Sabrina had once explained that the stately house and surrounding estate in Surrey had been owned by her family for more than five hundred years, passed down through the generations from father to son. Her brother would one day inherit the house and the earldom.

The implication was that there were some things money could not buy, but Cruz did not believe that. In his experience everything had a price. He fully expected that Earl Bancroft would be willing to sell him the map of the secret mine if he offered enough money.

As for the possibility that he would meet Sabrina again, Cruz shrugged. He had not thought about her for years and he wasn't interested in the past. All he cared about was the future and claiming the map of the diamond mine that legally and morally belonged to him.

CHAPTER TWO

THROUGH THE LIBRARY window at Eversleigh Hall Cruz could see a half-naked woman dancing in the fish pond. Her gyrating body was illuminated by the lights blazing from every window in the house. Shouts of encouragement came from the group of young men standing on the lawn, swigging champagne from a bottle, before one of them jumped into the water and grabbed hold of the woman while his friends called out obscene suggestions.

Classy, Cruz thought sardonically. He had seen similar behaviour in the *favela* where he had spent most of his childhood, although the *putas*—the hookers— had been drunk on beer rather than Bollinger. For all the English aristocracy's wealth and privilege and their education at the finest schools, some of them were no more refined than the slum-dwellers from the poorest areas of Brazil.

His lip curled as he remembered an incident that had occurred at a high-society party he had attended in London a few days ago. The hosts, Lord and Lady Porchester, were 'old money' but in recent years crippling death duties and some diabolical business decisions had left the family fortune dwindling and they were desperately seeking investors to save their manu-facturing company.

Cruz had been under no illusions about why he was an honoured guest. Porchester had sucked up to him all evening, but when Cruz had stepped outside onto the terrace for some fresh air he had been hidden in the shadows and had overheard his host discussing him with another guest.

'Delgado's a self-made millionaire from South America. Apparently he bought a diamond mine and struck lucky. Of course you can always pick out the nouveau riche by their lack of breeding.'

The two men had laughed and Cruz had gritted his teeth and reminded himself that he would have the last laugh because money was money at the end of the day, and Porchester needed a loan. But Lord Porchester's meaning had been clear. It did not matter how many millions Cruz had in the bank, he would never be accepted by the social elite. Not that he gave a damn about other people's opinion of him, Cruz brooded. But he was determined to establish Delgado Diamonds as one of Europe's most exclusive jewellers and being regarded as an outsider by the aristocracy was a disadvantage.

Perhaps he should have accepted Porchester's daughter's unsubtle hints that she hoped he would take her to bed, he mused. If he was seen to be dating a lord's daughter it could open doors for him. Business relied on networking and making useful contacts. Unfortunately, the half an hour he had spent listening to Lisette Porchester gossiping about her 'Chelsea Set' friends had bored him rigid.

But there were plenty of other upper-class women he could choose from. Cruz knew it was not just his millionaire status that the opposite sex found attractive. Women were drawn to the sensual promise in his eyes and the athleticism of his muscular body. They called him a stud and he was happy to prove it. Since he was a youth, women had thrown themselves at him. Maybe that was why he found the cut and thrust of business so exciting—there was an element of risk and the possibility of failure that was never present in his numerous sex-without-strings affairs.

He turned away from the window, bored by the scene of drunken debauchery taking place on the lawn, and glanced around the library. Eversleigh Hall deserved its reputation as one of England's finest stately homes. From the outside the house was a gracious manor house, predominantly Georgian in style, although some of the original sixteenth-century building still remained. Inside, the impressive entrance hall and the library had a rather faded elegance about them—as if the house had been trapped in a time warp when grand country houses were run by dozens of staff.

The only member of staff Cruz had seen was the elderly butler who had admitted him into the house. He frowned. Had he imagined an odd expression had crossed the butler's face when he'd asked to see Earl Bancroft?

He wondered why the earl was hosting a party for guests who seemed to be barely out of high school. Perhaps the party was for Sabrina's younger brother, he mused. Tristan Bancroft must be in his early twenties now. Ten years ago Sabrina had used the excuse that she wanted to return to Eversleigh Hall because her kid brother needed her. The real reason, Cruz knew, was because she'd felt trapped in Brazil when she had been expecting his child. After she'd lost the baby she had rushed back to England and the privileged lifestyle she was used to.

His mind snapped back to the present as he noticed the door handle turn, and his jaw hardened at the prospect of meeting Earl Bancroft—the man he held responsible for his father's death.

The door opened and Cruz stiffened.

'It *is* you.' Shock stole Sabrina's breath and her voice emerged as a thread of sound. Cruz was instantly recognisable and yet he looked different from the man she had known ten years ago. Of course he was older, and the boyishly handsome features she remembered were harder, his face leaner, with slashing cheekbones and a chiselled jaw that gave him an uncompromising air of power and authority combined with devastating sensuality.

The curve of his lips was achingly familiar and memories of the feel of his mouth on hers flooded back. How could she remember his kiss so vividly after all this time? she wondered, dismayed by her reaction to him. She unconsciously flicked her tongue across her lower lip and saw his eyes narrow on the betraying gesture.

Cruz had always been able to decimate her equilibrium with one glittering glance from his olive-green eyes, Sabrina thought ruefully. She recalled the first time she had seen him in Brazil. Even as a young man, his body had been honed and muscular from working in the diamond mine. His jeans and shirt had been filthy, and when he'd taken his hat off, she had noticed that his black hair curling onto his brow was damp with sweat.

She had never met a man so overwhelmingly male

before. The sheltered life she had led at Eversleigh Hall and at an all-girls boarding school had not prepared her for Cruz's smouldering sensuality. She'd taken one look at him and scorching heat had swept through her body. Disconcerted by her reaction, she had behaved with an uncharacteristic lack of manners and ignored him. But a few days later she had met him while she was out walking and he had told her that his name was Cruz Delgado before he'd pulled her into his arms and kissed her with a blazing passion that had set the pattern of their relationship.

For a moment Sabrina felt like a shy, unworldly eighteen-year-old again and she was tempted to run out of the library away from Cruz's brooding stare. She was twenty-eight, had a PhD and was highly regarded in her field of expertise in antique furniture restoration, she reminded herself. His unexpected appearance at Eversleigh Hall was undeniably a shock, but she assured herself that she was immune to his simmering sexual chemistry.

'Why are you here?'

She was thankful her voice sounded normal. But seeing him again brought back memories of her miscarriage just four and a half months into her pregnancy. She wondered if Cruz ever imagined what their son would be like if her pregnancy had gone to term. Did he sometimes picture, as she did, a strong-jawed, dark-haired boy with his father's green eyes, or perhaps his mother's grey ones? The raw pain that had torn her apart in the weeks and months after the miscarriage had faded with time, but there would always be a lingering ache in her heart for the child she had lost.

'I need to speak to your father.'

Fool, Sabrina berated herself, remembering that the butler had said Cruz had asked to see Earl Bancroft. The reason for his visit had nothing to do with her. He hadn't cared about her ten years ago. The only reason he had asked her to marry him was because he had wanted his child. But having witnessed her parents' disastrous marriage, Sabrina had been wary of making such a commitment. She had been sure Cruz did not love her and so she had turned him down.

Cruz did not look as though he was besieged by memories of the past. He was dressed in an impeccably tailored grey suit that moulded the lean lines of his body, and a white shirt that contrasted with his darkly tanned face. He looked the phenomenally successful multimillionaire businessman that she had read about in both the financial pages and the gossip columns of the newspapers. Yet beneath his air of suave sophistication she sensed there was still a wild, untameable quality about Cruz Delgado that had so intrigued her when they had been lovers.

Once again she felt the urge to flee from the library but she forced herself to walk into the room, closing the door behind her with a decisive click.

Cruz was standing behind the desk, his hawk-like features set in an arrogant expression as if he owned Eversleigh Hall, damn him. A memory slid into her mind of when she had been a little girl called into her father's study to explain some misdemeanour. Earl Bancroft had not been a particularly strict parent, more an uninterested one. He'd spent most of his time abroad and when Sabrina was a child her father had been a stranger who upset her mother and created a fraught tension in the house that disappeared when he went away again.

Lifting her chin, Sabrina walked around the desk to where Cruz was standing by the window, but she regretted her actions when she realised how close she was to him. She was sure it was not by accident that he'd moved his position slightly so that she was trapped between his powerful body and the desk. The musk of his sandalwood cologne was instantly familiar and she recognised the brand of aftershave she had given him as a present soon after she had given him her virginity. Had he deliberately worn that particular brand tonight to torment her?

Unwilling to meet his gaze, she glanced towards the window and made a choked sound when she saw what appeared to be a group orgy taking place on the lawn. 'For heaven's sake!' she muttered as she quickly twitched the curtains shut.

'Your friends are clearly enjoying themselves,' Cruz drawled.

'They're not my friends.' Sabrina could feel her face burning. She wasn't a prude but the behaviour going on—not to mention the amount of clothes coming off—in the garden was unacceptable.

'Are they your brother's friends?' Cruz was curious. 'Is it Tristan's party?'

'Tristan is away at university.' Thankfully her brother was nothing like Hugo Ffaulk and his ilk, Sabrina thought to herself. Tris knew that to fulfil his ambition of being an airline pilot he had to gain a first-class degree. Of course there was also the little matter of the one hundred thousand pounds required for the pilot training. The merry-go-round of worries inside her head did another circuit. Somehow, she vowed, she would find the money for her brother to train for the career that he had dreamed of since he was a small boy.

'So, are those people your father's guests?'

Sabrina had no intention of telling Cruz that giving parties at Eversleigh Hall was a business venture. No one apart from her and the bank manager knew of the financial catastrophe that was looming over Eversleigh, and so far she had managed to keep the news that Earl Bancroft was missing out of the media.

'They are my guests, who I invited to my party,' she said stiffly. 'Some of them are just a little over-exuberant, that's all.'

Cruz gave her a sardonic look. 'I've heard gossip on the London social scene about the wild parties you throw at Eversleigh Hall. What does Earl Bancroft think about his stately home being overrun by upper-class yobs?'

'My father isn't here. He's away on a trip and I don't know when he'll be back. I'm sorry I can't be of more help.' She tried to step past him and gave a startled cry when he caught hold of her arm.

'That's it?' Cruz growled. 'I see you haven't changed in the past ten years, *gatinha*. You still think you can dismiss me as if I am dirt beneath your shoe.'

'Don't be ridiculous.' She tried to jerk her arm out of his grip. 'And don't call me that. I'm not your kitten.' Hearing him use the affectionate name he had called her when they had been lovers, in a sarcastic tone, hurt more than it had any right to.

His gravelly, sexy accent brought her skin out in goose bumps. She wanted to stop staring at him but she could not tear her eyes from the sculpted planes of his face and his sensual mouth. 'I never treated you like dirt,' she muttered, startled by the accusation. Surely she had made it embarrassingly obvious ten years ago that she'd worshipped the ground he walked on?

'The first time we saw each other you put your nose in the air and ignored me.'

She gave a shaky laugh. 'I was eighteen and painfully naïve. The nuns who taught at St Ursula's College for Ladies never explained about handsome men who could make a girl feel…' She broke off, flushing as Cruz's gaze narrowed on her face.

'Feel…what?' he demanded. Sabrina recognised the predatory gleam in his eyes and she instinctively backed away from him until her spine was jammed against the desk.

'You know how you made me feel.' She silently cursed the huskiness in her voice. 'And I didn't ignore you for long. You made sure of that.'

He'd had her in his bed within a week of her arrival in Brazil. Memories assailed her of blistering hot days when they'd had blisteringly exciting sex in the shade of the rubber trees, and sultry, steamy nights when Cruz had climbed up to her balcony at the ranch house and they'd made love beneath the stars.

The rasp of Cruz's breath warned her that he was also remembering their scorching passion. But sex was all they had shared, Sabrina thought. Their response to each other ten years ago had simply been a chemical reaction. Disturbingly, the mysterious alchemy of sexual attraction was at work again now. She could see it in the way his olive-green eyes had darkened so that they were almost black.

Her spine would be bruised from where she was

pressing against the desk. She searched her mind for something to say to break the simmering tension in the room. 'Why do you want to see my father?'

'I believe he has something that belongs to me, and I want what is mine.'

Cruz stared at the stunning diamond pendant Sabrina was wearing around her neck. The Estrela Vermelha—the Red Star—was one of the largest red diamonds ever to have been found in Brazil. Cruz knew that diamonds could occur in a variety of colours, with red being the rarest. When his father had found the gem, the uncut, unpolished stone had not looked as though it was worth a fortune.

Earl Bancroft had had the stone triangular-cut, or trilliant-cut as it was known to gemologists. The red diamond had been set in a border of white diamonds and the contrast between the red and white sparkling gems was truly breathtaking. The pendant had never been for sale, but conservative estimates suggested it was worth well over a million pounds.

When Sabrina had entered the library Cruz had been so fixated on her that he had barely noticed the Estrela Vermelha, he acknowledged grimly. Her ruby-red dress was a perfect match for the red diamond nestling between her breasts. The silk jersey dress clung to every dip and curve of her slender figure and when she walked, the side split in the skirt parted to reveal one long, lissom leg.

The dress was overtly sexy, and with her pale blonde hair tumbling in silky, glossy waves around her shoulders Sabrina looked like every red-blooded male's fantasy, yet she still retained an air of elegance and re-finement that spoke of her aristocratic bloodline.

A haze of jealousy clouded Cruz's mind as he won-dered who Sabrina had dressed like a vamp for. He glanced down at her left hand and saw that it was ring-less. So, it was likely that she was unmarried. Not that he gave a damn, he assured himself. Had she chosen to wear the scarlet dress to impress a lover? A vision sprang into his mind of Sabrina in the arms of another man. Why the hell did that make his blood boil? he asked himself impatiently.

He had been her first lover but he was damned sure he hadn't been her last—not when she had the body of Venus and a luscious mouth that simply begged to be kissed. Her lips were coated in a scarlet gloss that em-phasised their sensual shape and her grey eyes were enhanced by a smoky shadow on her eyelids.

Cruz visualised the innocent girl he had known a de-cade ago. Sabrina had been an exceptionally pretty teen-ager, but now she was a stunningly beautiful woman, entirely aware of her sensuality and with the self-confidence to wear clothes that showed off her exqui-site figure.

It was still there. He had not seen her for ten years, but one look was all it had taken to make him realise that he had never desired any woman as much as Sa-brina Bancroft. Thinking of her family name reminded him of why he had come to Eversleigh and the hatred he felt for Earl Bancroft.

He reached out his hand and touched the Estrela Ver-melha. The jewel was as cold and hard as his anger as he remembered his father's excitement when Vitor had discovered the rare diamond.

'It's likely that there are more red diamonds in the part of the mine where I found the first one. If I find more, Earl Bancroft has promised I will receive a share of their value.'

'Don't go back there, Papai,' Cruz had pleaded with his father. 'That part of the mine is dangerous. Some of the miners say that the roof supports aren't strong enough.'

But Vitor had ignored him. 'I have to go back.'

The earl had sent Vitor to search for more diamonds and had sent him to his death. Cruz still had nightmares about when he'd heard the incredible roaring noise of the mine roof collapsing as tons of rock had crashed down on his father and buried him alive.

He snatched his hand away from the Estrela Vermelha. 'Red is a fitting colour for a diamond which is stained with my father's blood.'

A shiver ran through Sabrina. She couldn't explain why she had never liked the Red Star diamond even though she admired its flawless beauty. The only reason she had worn it tonight was because she had wanted to impress the party guests. People booked parties at Eversleigh Hall because they liked the grandeur and history of the stately home, and they had no idea that, short of a miracle, the hall might soon have to be sold and would no longer be the ancestral home of the Bancroft family.

The dark red diamond was the colour of blood, but Cruz's words did not make any sense to Sabrina. 'What do you mean? What does your father have to do with the Red Star?'

'He found it, and it was his right to claim part of the value of the diamond. But he died before he received his percentage share. My father was killed doing your

father's dirty work,' Cruz said harshly. 'Earl Bancroft
sent him into the mine to search for more red diamonds.
Your father has Vitor's blood on his hands and I have
come to Eversleigh to demand compensation for my
father's life.'

CHAPTER THREE

'I WANT YOU to leave.'

Sabrina whirled away from Cruz and faced him across the desk, breathing hard as she struggled to control her temper. 'How dare you turn up at Eversleigh uninvited and make a ridiculous accusation against my father, who isn't even here to defend himself?'

'He couldn't defend himself against the truth.' Cruz welcomed his anger as a distraction from the infuriating knowledge that when Sabrina had squeezed past him, her breasts had brushed against his chest and his body had reacted with humiliating predictability. His eyes were drawn to the low-cut neckline of her dress and the jerky rise and fall of her breasts. He pictured her naked beneath him, the erotic contrast of her milky pale body against his dark bronze skin, and he remembered her soft, kitten-like cries in the throes of orgasm.

Inferno! It was two months since he had dumped his last mistress and clearly he had gone too long without sex, he thought with savage self-derision. The purpose of his visit was to persuade Earl Bancroft to hand over the map of the abandoned mine, but all he could think of was how much he wanted to bend Sabrina over the desk and push her dress up to her waist, baring her silken thighs so that he could…

Ruthlessly he controlled his imagination but he could not control the painful throb of desire in his groin as he tried to focus on what she was saying.

'I didn't know your father had died.' She hesitated. 'I'm sorry… I know how close you were to him. But I don't believe my father was responsible. How could he have had anything to do with Vitor's death?'

'When my father found the Estrela Vermelha, the earl sent him back to an area of the mine that he knew was unsafe to look for more diamonds.' Cruz's jaw hardened. 'Don't pretend you didn't know. Bancroft must have told you about the accident at the mine even if he failed to admit his culpability for what happened.'

'My father didn't confide in me,' Sabrina admitted. 'We've never been close. I grew up at Eversleigh, but my father had inherited land and the diamond mine in Brazil from an uncle and he spent months at a time abroad. I visited him when I was eighteen, which is when I met you, but when I came back to England I had little contact with him.'

She fell silent, remembering the bleakest period of her life when she had hidden away at Eversleigh like a wounded animal. There had been no one she could talk to about the miscarriage. Four years earlier, when she had been fourteen, her mother had walked out of her marriage to Earl Bancroft and abandoned her children for her lover, and Sabrina had learned a valuable lesson—that she could not trust anyone and she had to rely on herself.

When she'd fallen pregnant by Cruz in Brazil she had told her father about her pregnancy. Typically he had said little then, or later, when she'd informed him that she had lost the baby. His only comment had been that he thought she had made the right decision to return to England and take up the university place she had deferred.

The earl had paid an unexpected visit to Eversleigh Hall during the summer ten years ago, Sabrina suddenly recalled. Her father had been in a strange mood and even more uncommunicative than usual, but he had made the surprising announcement that he intended to sell his diamond mine. He'd made no mention of Vitor Delgado's fatal accident, or of Cruz, and Sabrina's pride had refused to allow her to ask about him.

She had spent her first weeks back at Eversleigh hoping that Cruz would come after her, but as time went by she had been forced to accept that he wasn't coming and he did not care about her. Now she'd learned that he had suffered a terrible tragedy soon after she had returned home. Following his father's death his focus would understandably have been on taking care of his mother and much younger twin sisters.

She studied his face and noticed the fine lines around his eyes and deep grooves on either side of his mouth that had not been there ten years ago. He had idolised his father and would have felt Vitor's loss deeply. She felt a faint tug on her heart. 'When did the accident at the mine happen?'

'Three weeks after you had left me and returned to England. It was the worst time of my life. First you lost our baby and then I lost my father.'

Sabrina stiffened. 'An estimated one in seven pregnancies ends in miscarriage,' she said huskily, repeating what numerous medical experts had told her when she had sought an answer as to why she had lost her baby. 'We were unlucky.'

'Perhaps it was simply bad luck.' Cruz's tone was devoid of any emotion, but Sabrina was convinced she had heard criticism in his voice. She curled her hands into tight balls until her fingernails cut into her palms.

'Riding my horse did not cause me to miscarry,' she said in a low tone. 'I was seventeen weeks into my pregnancy and beyond the risk period of the first three months. The doctor said I was not to blame.' But she had always blamed herself, she acknowledged bleakly, and she had suspected that Cruz thought she'd been irresponsible to have gone riding.

'If you'd had your way, you would have wrapped me in cotton wool for nine months,' she burst out.

His over-the-top concern had been for the baby, not for her. Every day, when Cruz had gone to work at the mine he had left her under the watchful and disapproving eyes of his mother. Sabrina had felt lonely and bored in Brazil. She'd been delighted at her three-month scan when the doctor had said that her pregnancy was progressing well and there was no reason why she should not do the things she normally did. She had thought it would be safe to take her horse for a gentle ride, aware that her mother had ridden during both of her pregnancies.

Cruz's chiselled features were impassive. 'There is no point in dragging up the past.'

His harsh voice jerked Sabrina from her painful memories. Her long lashes swept down, but not before Cruz glimpsed raw emotion in her grey eyes that shocked him. Ten years ago her lack of emotion after the miscarriage had made him realise that she had not wanted their child, and her hurried departure from Brazil had proved that she did not have any feelings for him.

His jaw hardened and he told himself he must have imagined the pained expression in her eyes. 'You said that the earl is away, but I need to speak to him urgently. I assume you keep in contact with him by phone or email?'

She shook her head. 'All I know is that he is probably in Africa. He has investments in a couple of mines there, and he often takes trips into remote areas to investigate new mining opportunities.'

Everything she had said was true, Sabrina assured herself. Her father often went abroad on what he called his adventures. But he had never stayed out of contact for this long. She had last spoken to Earl Bancroft when he had called her from a town somewhere in Guinea, but, after eighteen months when nothing had been seen or heard of him, Sabrina was seriously concerned for her father's safety.

'I'm afraid my father is incommunicado at the moment,' she murmured.

There was something odd about the situation, Cruz mused. Something Sabrina wasn't telling him. With difficulty he restrained his impatience.

'Well, if I can't talk to Earl Bancroft perhaps you will be able to help me. I believe your father has some information about the Montes Claros diamond mine. Before my father died, the earl showed Vitor a map of an abandoned section of the mine. The map is the legal property of the mine owner. You might be aware that I bought the mine six years ago, which means that the map belongs to me.'

Sabrina shrugged. 'I don't know anything about a

map. I told you my father rarely confides in me about his business dealings.'

A vague memory pushed into her mind. At the time she hadn't paid much attention to the incident, but Cruz's words made her wonder about her father's curious behaviour when she had walked into his study and found him looking at a document spread out on his desk. Earl Bancroft had snatched up the piece of paper before Sabrina had got a clear glimpse of it and thrust it into an envelope.

'This is my pension fund for when I retire,' he'd said, laughing. *'It's much safer to keep it hidden here at Eversleigh than in a bank.'*

'Why is the map important?' she asked Cruz curiously.

'I believe it shows a section of the mine that was dug many years ago.' He shrugged. 'There may be nothing down there, but the Estrela Vermelha was found in the deepest section of where we currently operate and it's possible that there are other diamonds in the abandoned mine.' Cruz's eyes raked Sabrina's face and she quickly dropped her gaze.

'Did your father ever show you a map?'

'No,' she said truthfully.

'Do you know where he might have put a map? Does he have a safe where he keeps important documents?'

She shook her head. 'He wouldn't need to lock things in a safe. Eversleigh Hall had dozens of secret places to hide valuables—and people, come to that. Many old English houses have secret chambers and priest holes, which were built hundreds of years ago when Catholic priests were persecuted,' she explained. 'For instance, one of the wooden panels in this room conceals a secret cupboard. My father knows the location of all the hiding places at the hall.'

'And do you also know where the secret chambers are?'

'I know where some are, but not all of them. Even if I knew every hiding place I wouldn't show you their location without my father's permission.'

Sabrina felt a sense of loyalty towards Earl Bancroft despite the fact that they had never shared a close emotional bond. Since her father's mysterious disappearance she had realised that she loved him. She looked at Cruz steadily. 'If you are really the rightful owner of the map then I'm sure my father would have given it to you when you took over the mine.'

'Don't pretend to be naïve,' Cruz growled. 'I won't go so far as to say that Earl Bancroft is a crook, but some of his business dealings are decidedly shady.'

'How dare you—?'

'I worked for him,' Cruz cut her off impatiently. 'I saw how your father ignored safety regulations in the mine to save money.'

Sabrina's eyes flashed with anger. 'My father isn't here to defend himself and I only have your word on what happened.'

'And of course you, with your aristocratic title and privileged lifestyle, would not believe the word of someone who grew up in dire poverty in a slum,' Cruz said sardonically. 'You always thought I was beneath you, didn't you, *princesa*?'

'That's not true.' During their affair she'd hated it when he had mockingly called her princess to emphasise that they came from different ends of the social spectrum. 'I never cared about where you came from, or that you didn't have much money.'

He gave a harsh laugh. 'You made it obvious that you were desperate to return to Eversleigh Hall.' He glanced around the comfortable library with its shelves of books from floor to ceiling and plush velvet curtains hanging at the windows. 'I can understand why you hated living in a cramped miner's cottage with a corrugated-iron roof, when you were used to living in a grand mansion.'

'I didn't hate the cottage, but we lived there with your parents and your mother never made me feel welcome.' Sabrina saw disbelief in Cruz's eyes and knew it would be pointless trying to convince him that she hadn't minded the basic living accommodation in Brazil. But his mother's unfriendliness had been hard to cope with. Ana-Maria Delgado had patently adored her son, and perhaps in Cruz's mother's eyes no woman would be good enough for him, Sabrina mused.

As Cruz had said, there was no point in dragging up the past. It had all happened a long time ago and their lives had moved on. Ironically their fortunes had reversed for Cruz was now a millionaire, while since her father's disappearance she had spent every last penny she had paying for the upkeep of Eversleigh Hall, and she and the house were practically bankrupt.

'Some things about you haven't changed. Your eyes still darken to the colour of storm clouds when you lie.'

Cruz's deep voice jolted Sabrina from her thoughts and she tensed as he walked around the desk and stood unsettlingly close to her.

'Ten years ago when I asked you if you were happy to live in Brazil with me and have my child, you assured me that you were, but your eyes were as dark as

pewter and revealed the truth—that you wanted to return to Eversleigh Hall.'

She flushed guiltily and looked away from his intent gaze that seemed to bore into her skull and read
her thoughts. 'I missed my brother,' she said quietly.
'Tristan was just a kid of eleven. After my mother left
we had become very close and I was worried about
him living here with just a nanny to take care of him.'

'I don't believe that concern for your brother was
the only reason for your eagerness to leave Brazil, any
more than I believe you are unable to contact Earl Bancroft if you wish to,' he said sardonically. 'I also think
you know more about the map than you have admitted.'

She had forgotten how tall he was, Sabrina thought,
feeling a frisson of panic when she realised that he had
moved imperceptibly closer to her. She could see the
shadow of black chest hairs beneath his crisp white shirt
and the faint delineation of his powerful abdominal
muscles. Seductive images taunted her subconscious:
Cruz's naked, bronzed body pressed against hers, hard
against soft, dark against her whiteness. She visualised
him pulling her down on top of him, his strong arms
holding her as he guided her onto his erect shaft while
she slowly took him inside her.

Heat coursed through her veins. The few lovers she'd
had in the past ten years had never evoked more than
her mild interest, and sex had been disappointing. But
to her shame she was bombarded by memories of Cruz's
magnificent virility and she was aware of a betraying
dampness between her legs.

Anger was her only defence against the insidious
ache of longing in the pit of her stomach. 'I've told you

I know nothing about a map and it's not my problem if you refuse to believe me.'

Even though she was wearing four-inch heels she had to tilt her head to look at his face. Ten years ago she hadn't stood a chance against him, she thought bitterly, feeling an ache in her heart for the innocent girl she had once been who had looked forward to going to university. Cruz had taken one look at her and decided he wanted her, but within months of the start of their affair she had been pregnant and facing a very different life in Brazil from the one she had been used to in England.

If he had loved her she would have coped with her new lifestyle, she thought sadly. But when her pregnancy had been confirmed Cruz's desire for her had died and it had quickly become clear that they had nothing between them to sustain a relationship.

She felt the ache of tears at the back of her throat. It was silly to cry for a lost love that in truth had only ever been an illusion, she reminded herself.

'I want you to leave,' she said tautly. She frowned when he made no response, merely raised his dark eyebrows and surveyed her with an arrogance that made her seethe.

'I suppose you think I should be intimidated by your air of menace. Perhaps you think you can force the whereabouts of the map out of me, but I have plenty of staff in the house.' She mentally crossed her fingers behind her back as she thought of John and his wife, Mary. The butler and housekeeper were the only remaining staff living at Eversleigh and were past retirement age. 'If you lay a finger on me I'll scream.'

She spun on her heels, intending to march over to

the door, but his hand shot out and he caught hold of her arm and jerked her round to face him.

'I don't think force will be necessary to persuade you to give me what I want,' he murmured.

Sabrina's stomach muscles clenched as his sensuous, molten-syrup voice tugged on her senses. Time seemed to be suspended and her breath was trapped in her lungs. Her eyes widened as she watched his dark head descend and she realised that he was going to kiss her. He wouldn't dare, she assured herself. But this was Cruz Delgado—a man who would dare to make a deal with the devil if he believed the odds were in his favour.

'I warned you, I'll scream.' It was melodramatic, but she felt melodramatic, damn it! She gasped as he pulled her against him and she felt the heat from his body melting her bones.

He gave a wolfish smile. 'Perhaps you will. I remember how you used to scream with pleasure and claw me with your sharp nails when you came, *gatinha*.'

'Cruz—for God's sake!' In desperation she thumped his shoulder with her fist, but her blows had as much effect as a mosquito landing on a rhino's hide.

'You are so goddamned beautiful,' Cruz said harshly. He could not resist her and he was shamed by his weakness. If he kissed her, perhaps the fire blazing inside him would cool and he would be released from this mad desire that made his muscles taut and his heart pound. He clamped one arm around her waist and slid his other hand into her hair and up to clasp her nape as his mouth swooped down to capture hers.

Cruz's lips were hard, demanding, as he forced Sabrina to accept the mastery of his kiss. She was unprepared for the savage hunger that ripped through her.

She was transported back in time to when she had been eighteen; a girl on the brink of womanhood, a virgin who had given not only her body but her heart and her soul to Cruz. It had taken her ten long years to reclaim them.

The memory of how badly he had hurt her gave her the strength to fight him. But he remembered how to pleasure her and he knew how to undermine her defences with the bold sweep of his tongue as he traced the shape of her lips before thrusting between them to explore the moist interior of her mouth.

Sabrina felt herself tremble and knew Cruz must sense she was close to total capitulation. But rather than increase the pressure of his mouth he softened the kiss and took little sips from her lips, butterfly soft and so utterly beguiling that she sagged against him and kissed him with a sweetness and curiously evocative innocence that caused Cruz to abruptly lift his head.

Deus! He had not come to Eversleigh Hall with the intention of making love to Sabrina. His eyes shot to the big mahogany desk and for a few seconds he was tempted to sacrifice his hope of finding the map, and probably his sanity, he acknowledged derisively, to satisfy the rampant desire raging through his veins.

He had not expected to feel this overpowering attraction to a woman he had known briefly when she had been a girl. Their affair had lasted for less than a year and after she had returned to England he had determinedly put her out of his mind. When he had arrived at Eversleigh Hall this evening he had assumed he would be immune to Sabrina Bancroft. The reckless craving that consumed him was a humiliating reminder of his weakness ten years ago when he had fallen under her spell after one glance from her storm-grey eyes.

Right now, Sabrina's eyes had softened to the colour of woodsmoke, the colour of her desire; Cruz remembered that sensual look and felt his body tighten in response. He swore silently to himself. He had been a fool once, but he would not make the same mistake a second time.

His mouth curled into an insolent smile. 'Your willingness to co-operate is encouraging. All I want now is the map, and I will leave you to enjoy your *party.*'

The mockery in Cruz's voice ripped apart the seductive web he had woven around Sabrina. She pulled out of his arms, hot-faced and trembling with anger. It was bad enough that he believed she actually *liked* playing hostess to Hugo Ffaulks and his bunch of immature friends. But worse was the realisation that Cruz had only kissed her in order to make her lower her guard so that she would give him a map that he was convinced was hidden somewhere at Eversleigh Hall.

Oh, God! What was wrong with her? She hadn't seen him for ten years, but within ten minutes of meeting him again she had all but invited him to hitch up her skirt and take her right there on the desk. Erotic images swirled in her head and her shame was compounded by Cruz's husky chuckle that told her he had seen her gaze flick towards the desk. Without pausing to think, she lifted her hand and struck his cheek with a resounding crack that shattered the silence in the library. *'Get out.'*

His eyes glittered. 'I don't advise you try that again,' he said in a measured tone that despite its softness sent a shiver down Sabrina's spine.

'Just...go,' she whispered.

When he'd driven from London to Surrey, Cruz had not anticipated making the return journey without the map in his possession. But his visit to Eversleigh Hall had not gone to plan. He grimaced at the understatement. Now he was at an impasse. Either Sabrina genuinely did not know about the map that Earl Bancroft had shown his father, or she was refusing to tell him where the earl kept it.

A sudden loud crash from outside the library broke the stand-off, and with a muttered oath Sabrina hurried across the room and opened the door.

'John,' she called to the butler, 'what on earth was that noise?'

'I'm afraid it was Sir Reginald, Miss Sabrina. Some of the guests knocked him over.'

Bemused, Cruz followed Sabrina into the hall and saw the suit of armour that he had noticed when he'd arrived at the house lying in pieces on the parquet floor. A group of young men who were clearly the worse for drink were attempting to fit the pieces back together. One of them staggered towards Sabrina.

'Sorry about your knight, Sab...rina,' he slurred. 'I want you to know that this is the best birthday party ever.'

'I'm glad you are enjoying yourself.' Sabrina spoke crisply as she tried to sidestep around Hugo Ffaulks, but his reactions were quicker than she'd anticipated and he slid his arms around her waist.

'I enjoyed you coming to my bedroom this morning. Will you wake me up the same way tomorrow morning, Sabrina?'

Sabrina missed the cynical expression on Cruz's face. 'You can have breakfast in bed tomorrow if you wish, Hugo.' She struggled to hide her impatience as she reminded herself that the money his parents had paid for the party would cover the hall's outstanding electricity bill.

Still trying to extricate herself from the young man, she glanced along the hall and saw Cruz by the front door. She flushed when he deliberately dropped his gaze to Hugo's hands on her bottom.

'My apologies for disturbing you,' he said mockingly. 'Have fun for the rest of the night.'

Damn him to hell! Sabrina thought furiously as she watched him stride out of the house. She wrenched herself free from Hugo. She couldn't understand her burning desire to run after Cruz and slap the arrogant smile off his face. Usually she was mild natured, but he made her feel so angry that her body was actually shaking, and, when she glanced down, the sight of her pebble-hard nipples jutting beneath her dress was humiliating evidence that it was not only anger that Cruz aroused in her.

When he'd kissed her she had felt alive, truly alive, for the first time in ten years. Oh, she was safe from falling in love with him. She'd have to be certifiable to make that mistake again, but during those moments of passion in the library she had wanted him so badly that even now her breasts ached and she could still taste him on her lips.

She would have to get herself under control before she saw him again. And she was in no doubt that she *would* see him again. She knew from bitter experience that when Cruz wanted something he would not rest until he had it in his possession.

Ten years ago he had wanted her. Now he wanted a

map that he insisted her father had hidden at Eversleigh Hall. She was certain that Cruz would be back, but next time she would be prepared for his sizzling sexual charisma and she would not melt the moment he looked at her, she promised herself.

CHAPTER FOUR

THE EXCEPTIONALLY SMOOTH single-malt whisky served at the Earl's Head loosened tongues and encouraged local gossip, Cruz discovered. Following his unproductive visit to Eversleigh Hall he had returned to the village pub, where he had earlier booked a room for the night, and ordered a double measure of Scotch with a splash of water, no ice.

'There's no better cure for life's problems than a drop of amber nectar,' the old man sitting at the bar—a farmhand, Cruz guessed from his rough clothes—commented.

'Too true,' Cruz muttered as he pushed his empty glass towards the barman and asked for a refill, plus the same for his companion. Two-thirds of the bottle of whisky later, Cruz had learned some interesting facts about the Bancroft family, including that the pub had been named after one of the current earl's ancestors, who had been accused of fraud and treachery during the reign of Elizabeth I and beheaded for his crimes.

Treachery clearly ran in the family genes, Cruz thought bitterly. Henry Bancroft had cheated his father out of his rightful share of the Estrela Vermelha diamond, and tonight Sabrina had denied any knowledge of the map of the abandoned mine. But Cruz was certain she was lying. When he had questioned her she had hesitated for a fraction too long and her eyes had darkened to the colour of wet slate.

He drained the whisky in his glass and nodded to the barman to refill it. What could he do? He could hardly shake the truth out of her, he brooded. Somehow he needed to gain access to Eversleigh Hall so that he could search for the map that it seemed likely her father had hidden in one of the house's secret places.

He thought of his meeting with Sabrina and felt furious with himself. It had been a mistake to kiss her, but he had been unable to resist her cool beauty and he despised himself for his weakness. Although it had not been all one-sided, he consoled himself. Sabrina's ardent response proved that she still wanted him and the knowledge was a useful weapon that he would be a fool not to use.

Cruz pulled himself from his thoughts when he realised that the farmhand was speaking.

'I wouldn't be surprised if Lady Sabrina up at the hall didn't try to forget her problems with the help of a bottle of highland malt.'

'What kind of problems?' Cruz asked curiously.

'Money.' The farmhand shook his head. 'The estate has become more and more run-down since her father took over from the old earl many years ago. Henry Bancroft never spent much time at Eversleigh. He was always going abroad for business reasons. It's said that he trades in diamonds, but no one has seen the earl for well over a year and there's a rumour in the village that his daughter has reported his disappearance to the police.'

Cruz remembered Sabrina's curious statement—*my father is incommunicado at the moment*.

'My guess is Lady Sabrina is struggling to cope with running the house and estate.' The farmhand downed his whisky and allowed the generous stranger who was such a good listener to fill his glass again. 'I used to do a bit of work up at the hall myself, but all the staff have been laid off, apart from old John Boyd and his wife who have been in service there for as long as anyone can remember, and some young girl who looks after the stables.' He sighed. 'The trouble is these old country houses are expensive to maintain. It'll be a shame if Eversleigh is sold.'

'There may not be anything left of it to sell,' the barman said as he put down the phone and came over to them. 'That was Miss Bancroft. There's a fire up at the hall, and she phoned to ask if some of her guests can spend the night at the pub.' As he finished speaking the loud wail of a fire engine's siren sounded outside on the main road.

How bitterly ironic it would be if the house went up in flames before he'd had a chance to find the map of the diamond mine, Cruz thought grimly. Aware that he was over the alcohol limit to drive, he said urgently to the barman, 'Can you call a taxi to take me to Eversleigh Hall?'

'I'm glad to report that the fire is under control. The blaze was almost certainly caused by a smouldering cigarette dropped onto a carpet or chair,' the fire officer explained to Sabrina. 'I understand there was a party taking place here tonight. Perhaps one of the guests drank too much and fell asleep holding a lit cigarette.'

'I'd asked people not to smoke in the house.' She grimaced. 'I can't believe how quickly the fire spread and how much damage it has caused. It looks as though most of the top floor of the east wing and the roof have been completely destroyed.'

The fireman glanced up at the dark sky as rain began to fall. 'I suggest you call a local building firm to come and rig up tarpaulins so that the damaged part of the house will be protected from the weather until you can see if any of the furnishings are salvageable.' He gave her a sympathetic smile. 'I imagine some of the paintings are originals and irreplaceable, but at least they'll be covered by your contents insurance.'

Sabrina felt a sensation like concrete solidifying in the pit of her stomach as the fireman's words sank in. Three months ago she'd had to cancel the contents insurance policy on Eversleigh Hall because she had been unable to afford the premium. It had been a difficult decision but there had been other more urgent bills to pay for, such as a new boiler for the central heating system that had packed up on the coldest day of the winter. Since then she had been meaning to renew the policy but unforgivably it had slipped her mind.

At least Hugo Ffaulks and his friends had been safely evacuated and had gone to stay at hotels in the village. But the fire spelled the end of her fledgling party business at Eversleigh Hall, and probably her family's association with their ancestral home, Sabrina thought bleakly. She could not even afford to pay for tarpaulins to cover the damaged section of the house, let alone the building and restoration costs.

She heard a car door slam, and her heart crashed against her ribs when she saw Cruz striding towards her.

'Sabrina.' His husky accent lingered on each syllable of her name. He splashed through a puddle, uncaring that filthy black water stained his pale grey trousers. 'Are you all right?' he demanded, clasping her shoulders.

'I'm fine.' Her voice was muffled against his chest as he pulled her towards him, and for a few seconds she closed her eyes and allowed his strength and vitality to seep into her.

'It looks as though only the newer part of the house was affected by the fire, and luckily the older and more historically important section is undamaged,' he commented.

Of course the house and, more importantly, the map that he believed was hidden somewhere inside were Cruz's only concern—not her, Sabrina told herself as she stepped away from him and ruthlessly crushed her pang of hurt.

She frowned when she saw a ginger figure flash past and bolt into the fire-damaged part of the house. 'George! Come back.'

'Who is George?' Cruz found he was talking to himself as Sabrina tore across the lawn before disappearing into the fire-blackened house.

'George, where are you, sweetheart?' Sabrina called, vainly trying to peer through the blackness. The part of the house where the fire had done most damage was known as the annexe. It had been built in the early nineteen hundreds, and, as Cruz had commented, was of less historic importance than the main house. The flames had been extinguished but the rooms were still full of thick smoke that made Sabrina's eyes sting. 'George.'

'Is George the guy who was looking forward to being

woken by you in the morning?' Cruz's deep voice cut
through the darkness and Sabrina jumped when he appeared at her side.

'What…?' Comprehension dawned as she remembered that when Cruz had paid his first visit to Eversleigh Hall earlier in the evening, the party had been in
full swing. 'No,' she said distractedly, 'that was Hugo.
George is—'

'Another of your juvenile lovers?' Cruz suggested.
'How many do you have? You should not play with boys,
gatinha. You need a man to satisfy you.'

'How would you know what I need?' She bristled at
his outrageous arrogance.

'I know that the boyfriend I saw you with at the party
is not strong enough for you. On the surface you are
the cool and composed lady of the manor, but beneath
your serene smile there is, not ice, but heat and simmering sensuality. You need a man who can tame your
fiery temperament and who would be prepared to put
you across his knee if necessary.'

Sabrina's choking fit had nothing to do with the
smoky atmosphere. 'You are the most chauvinistic *dinosaur* I've ever had the misfortune to meet,' she splut-
tered. 'We haven't seen each other for ten years and you
have no idea what I want.'

'You want me,' he said with infuriating self-assurance. 'Did you think I didn't feel the quickening of
your heartbeat when I kissed you earlier, or that I did
not notice the flush of sexual desire that stained your
creamy skin so prettily?' His voice deepened and his
husky accent caused the hairs on the back of Sabrina's
neck to stand on end. 'It's still there, Sabrina, and we
both recognised it in the library. I could have had you

on the desk and you would have been with me all the way. I bet you have never met another man who excites you as much as I do.'

Sabrina was thankful that the darkness hid the wave of heat she felt spreading across her cheeks. 'This is an utterly ridiculous conversation and an even more ridiculous place to be having it.' She swung away from Cruz and yelped as she stubbed her toe on a door frame. 'Damn it, I can't see a thing.' She blinked as a light suddenly flared and she saw that it came from Cruz's mobile phone. 'There's George,' she cried as she glimpsed the glitter of green eyes.

'George is a *cat*?' Cruz swore. 'I can't believe you risked your safety for a cat.'

'He was probably terrified by the fire and he's looking for somewhere to hide. Quick—grab him before he runs off.' Sabrina heard a yowl, followed by a torrent of Portuguese that she guessed from Cruz's tone it was lucky she did not understand. 'Have you got him?'

'It would be more to the point to say that he has got me,' Cruz muttered as he viewed the ball of orange fur that had attached its teeth to his hand with considerable dislike.

'Oh, my poor darling.' Sabrina's soft-as-butter voice went some way to soothing Cruz's damaged pride, until he realised that she was speaking to the cat. The animal responded to the sound of his mistress and released its grip on Cruz's flesh before leaping into Sabrina's arms.

'I don't think he's injured,' she said as she carried George outside and inspected him anxiously.

'Lucky cat,' Cruz muttered, wrapping a handkerchief around his hand to try and staunch the blood pouring from the teeth marks left by the creature from hell.

'Thank you for rescuing him. Oh…' Sabrina was shocked to see blood pouring from Cruz's hand. 'George only bites when he's upset. It just goes to show how traumatised he must have been, poor angel.' Seeing Cruz's glowering expression, she added hurriedly, 'You had better come into the house and let me clean the wound.'

The main part of the house, including the kitchen, had not suffered any fire damage. Sabrina set George down on the floor and fed him a handful of cat treats before she took the first-aid box from a cupboard. 'Wash the bite area thoroughly,' she instructed. 'Cats have a high level of bacteria in their mouths and bites can easily become infected.'

'Wonderful,' Cruz said drily. As he held his hand under the tap he gave George a dark look and was fairly certain than the deep sound coming from the cat's throat was not a friendly purr. He turned his attention to the breakfast trays set out on the counter. 'Had you planned to serve your guests breakfast in their rooms?' He counted the trays. 'It must take you all morning.'

'I have John, the butler, to help me, although the arthritis in his knees means he can't manage the rooms on the top floors. A girl from the village comes to help on party weekends. Breakfast in bed is part of the party package offered at Eversleigh.'

Sabrina saw the puzzled look Cruz gave her and bit her lip. The shock of the fire was sinking in and she was struggling to contain her emotions. 'You may as well know the truth as it will be public knowledge soon,' she said heavily. 'I can't afford to pay for the upkeep of the house and estate and I might have to sell up. It's been on the cards for a while, but tonight's fire means that selling Eversleigh Hall looks unavoidable.' The words sounded like a death knell, and misery settled heavily in the pit of Sabrina's stomach.

Cruz dried his hand on the paper towel that Sabrina gave him and allowed her to apply antiseptic solution to the bite wound. 'I assume the maintenance costs of a huge mansion are expensive.' He recalled his conversation with the farmhand in the pub. 'Has your father run out of money?'

'There is money in his account but I can no longer access it to pay the hall's bills since—' Sabrina hesitated '—since Dad disappeared. He's been missing for over a year and his bank accounts and assets have been frozen. I've employed a missing persons' agency to search for him but so far they've found no trace of him. If he isn't found after a number of years, he will be presumed dead, but in the meantime I've used all my savings and spent everything I earn on the house and, to put it bluntly, I'm broke.'

'I imagine a house this size must be worth a lot of money,' Cruz said casually.

'The house and estate, which consists of three hundred acres of prime Surrey land, have been valued at ten million pounds.'

Cruz's brows rose. That much! Eversleigh Hall was worth more than he had expected. It had occurred to him that he could buy the house so that he would have the opportunity to look for the map of the diamond mine. But a house as old as Eversleigh was bound to be a money pit, and there was a chance that the map did not exist. He was a gambler but he wasn't a fool.

'It will probably take some time to find a buyer,' he commented, thinking that in the meantime he needed to persuade Sabrina to allow him to search the house for the map. 'Not everyone can afford, or would want the responsibility of owning, a historic stately home.'

'I already have a buyer lined up. A hotel chain approached me a few months ago and made an offer for the estate. The Excelsior Group plan to build a golf course in the grounds and turn the house into a luxury golf and spa resort.'

Her shoulders slumped. 'Once I give the go-ahead for the sale it should only take a matter of weeks. Sometimes I've even wondered if I would be happier to be free of the worry of trying to maintain the estate. But this is my home and I have happy memories of living here with my mother before she left us. My father was never interested in Eversleigh but I always hoped that one day Tristan would run the place properly.'

Cruz frowned at the unwelcome news that the house could be sold so quickly. 'You said your father's assets are frozen because he is officially registered as a missing person. Surely Eversleigh Hall is listed as one of his assets, so how can it be sold without his knowledge or permission?'

'The house is owned by a group of trustees made up of Dad, me and my brother. Only two of us need to agree to the sale.'

'And Tristan is in agreement?'

'Tris is unaware of the financial situation,' she admitted heavily. 'I've tried to spare him the worry because he is studying for his final exams at university. He'll be upset to lose our ancestral home, but he's a realist and he'll understand that we have no choice but to let Eversleigh go.'

Sabrina was shocked to feel tears sting her eyes. She rarely cried, but the impact the fire would have on her life, if—as it seemed almost certain—she would have to leave the only home she had ever known, was starting to truly sink in. Feeling as vulnerable as she did, the last thing she felt able to cope with was Cruz.

Sabrina used the excuse of putting the first-aid box back in the cupboard to move away from Cruz. Being so close attending to his injured hand, she was supremely conscious of his lean, muscular body. Vivid memories rose to the surface, the feel of him on top of her, his weight pressing her into the mattress as he thrust into her over and over again.

Just thinking about him making love to her induced a molten sensation between her legs, and a quick glance downwards showed the outline of her nipples was clearly visible. She reminded herself that the peach silk robe she had pulled on over her matching nightdress when the fire alarm had sounded was perfectly respectable, but she was aware of Cruz's intent scrutiny and fought the urge to cross her arms over her breasts. It was imperative that he leave before she made an idiot of herself, and she walked over to the kitchen door, hoping he would take the hint and follow her.

He was unfairly gorgeous, she thought as she took advantage of him looking at his phone to study his chiselled features. Wealth and success had given him an air of sophistication that he had not had ten years ago, although he had never lacked self-confidence, she acknowledged. She flushed when he suddenly looked up and caught her staring at him.

'It's late,' she said abruptly, glancing at the kitchen clock. 'I'm sure you can appreciate that it has been a stressful night. I want to go to bed so I'll have to ask you to leave.'

Cruz flashed a smile that stole her breath. 'Not a chance.'

She stiffened. 'What do you mean?'

'I mean that I am not going to allow you to stay here on your own while the house is unsecured. Every burglar and criminal in the area will have heard about the fire. They won't even have to break in—they can simply walk into the fire-damaged part of the building and access the rest of the house, including your bedroom.'

'Rubbish! You can't tell me what you'll *allow* me to do.' Sabrina's temper simmered. 'Anyway, there is very little crime in the village, and the local police constable said he will post one of his officers at the front gate tonight.' She placed her hands on her hips when Cruz did not move off the kitchen stool where he was sitting. 'I'm not going to argue with you.'

'Good idea,' he said blandly. 'Save your breath, *gatinha*, and show me to a spare bedroom.'

He slid off the stool and walked towards her, his eyes glittering with a fierce possessiveness that touched something deep inside Sabrina. Despite his size he moved with a noiseless grace and the predatory intent of a panther stalking its prey. 'Unless you would prefer me to share your room?' He stopped in front of her and ran his finger lightly down her cheek. The caress was as soft as a butterfly's wing brushing against her skin, yet her senses leapt and she felt as if he had branded her with his touch. 'Although I can't guarantee that either of us would get much sleep,' he murmured.

She swallowed hard, fighting the treacherous longing of her body. *Why not forget her worries for one night and lose herself in the guaranteed sensual pleasure of making love with Cruz?* whispered the voice of temptation in her head. But all he was offering was sex, she reminded herself. It hadn't been enough for her ten years ago, and she sensed it would not be enough now.

'You are unbelievable,' she told him tightly.

He grinned. 'So I've been told.'

Sabrina recalled the recent stories she had read in the newspapers about the hotshot Brazilian diamond tycoon who had taken the London social scene by storm and seemed to be intent on sleeping with every beautiful blonde he met. A sharp barb of jealousy stabbed her through the heart. To disguise her swift intake of breath she swung round and marched out of the kitchen door, aware, because she was so intensely aware of Cruz, that he followed her across the hall and up the stairs to the second floor. Frustration surged through her that she could not make him leave, but she recognised the determined gleam in his eyes and knew that she would lose an argument and probably her dignity in the process.

'You can use the bedroom at the far end of the corridor,' she told him in an emotionless voice, and did not glance at him as she walked swiftly along the hallway towards her room on the opposite side of the house.

But the trauma of the fire, the likelihood that she would have to sell her home, and more shockingly the images in her mind of Cruz naked in bed just down the corridor, kept her awake until the pearl-grey glimmer of dawn peeped through the chink in the curtains.

Eversleigh Hall had never looked more beautiful, Sabrina thought the next morning. She had ridden Monty up to the North Downs Way, classed as an area of outstanding natural beauty, and from her viewpoint the fire-damaged section of the house was hidden. In the early morning sunshine the sandstone brickwork gleamed palely gold, and she could see the elegant knot garden, the tall poplar trees and the deep blue of the lake.

Her heart ached. How could she bear to part from the place that meant so much to her? How could she end the Bancroft family's five-hundred-year ownership of the hall? But what choice did she have? She had run out of money and ideas, and her hopes that her father would be found alive and well were fading.

Monty pawed the ground restlessly, bored by the prolonged inactivity. Sabrina patted his neck. 'Come on, boy, let's go home,' she said in a choked voice. The woeful state of her finances meant that selling her horse seemed unavoidable.

Cruz was waiting for her in the stable yard. It was the first time since he'd come back into her life that Sabrina had seen him in daylight and her heart slammed against her ribs as her eyes were drawn to his black hair gleaming like raw silk in the sunshine.

She dismounted and let Monty loose in the paddock while she dealt with Cruz.

'You're up early,' he commented. 'I thought you might be tired after the events of last night.'

'Nothing happened between us…' She broke off and flushed hotly. 'Oh, you meant the fire.' Idiot, Sabrina told herself furiously. She didn't want Cruz to guess that she had been kept awake for most of the night by erotic fantasies of him making love to her. 'Dawn is my favourite time to ride, when the sun is pale pink in the sky and the dew on the leaves sparkles like diamonds.'

Outwardly, Sabrina was the archetypal ice princess, Cruz thought as he studied her cool beauty. Her pale blonde hair was tied in a long plait that fell to halfway down her back and her intelligent grey eyes surveyed him with an unflattering lack of interest. Only the faint tremor of her sensual mouth and the delicate rose flush on her porcelain skin gave a clue to her inner fire.

His arousal was instant and uncomfortably hard. Damn her witchery, he thought grimly. He could not take his eyes off her. Last night she had looked glamorous in her scarlet evening gown, and when he had returned to the house after hearing about the fire he had been turned on by the sight of her in a silky robe. This morning she was no less sexy wearing jodhpurs that fitted her like a second skin, teamed with a soft grey cashmere sweater that echoed the colour of her eyes and clung with loving attention to the firm swell of her breasts. The sound of her cut-glass accent catapulted Cruz back to the present.

'I trust you slept well?'

He recalled the previous night tossing and turning beneath the sheets and sweating like a teenage boy with a surfeit of hormones. 'I didn't stir all night,' he lied. 'I have to go back to London, but I've arranged for a local building firm to come to the house and make it secure.'

'That's unnecessary. There's no need for you to get involved,' she said stiffly.

'You have no money,' Cruz reminded her. His eyes rested on the stubborn set of her lips and he wondered how she would react if he were to crush her mouth beneath his and kiss her into submission. She would probably slap his face again, he decided with a mixture of amusement and reluctant admiration, remembering her explosion of temper in the library the previous evening.

'On the subject of your financial difficulties—I have

a proposition to discuss with you. Not now.' He did not give her a chance to speak. 'I'm due at a meeting at eleven.' He handed her a business card. 'This is my London address. Meet me there at six tonight if you are interested in finding out how I might be able to help you.'

Pride snapped Sabrina's spine straight. 'I don't need your help.'

'Don't be late.' Cruz swung his jacket over his shoulder, but instead of walking away he stepped closer to her and wrapped her long plait around his hand. 'And wear your hair loose tonight, Sabrina, to please me.'

Sabrina's chest heaved as she sucked oxygen into her lungs. 'Why on earth would I want to please you?'

He grinned before dropping a brief, hard kiss on her lips. 'Because you need salvation, *querida*, and I might just be the answer to your prayers.'

CHAPTER FIVE

SHE WOULD RATHER walk barefoot over hot coals than meet Cruz at his London home, Sabrina thought grimly as she watched the taxi that had come to collect him drive away from the house. As for him being an answer to her prayers! She gave a snort of derision.

Her heart lurched when in the distance she saw a car turn into the main gates of Eversleigh Hall and she thought for a moment that Cruz was coming back. The sound of a blowing exhaust pipe was a clue to the visitor's identity.

'Tris!' Sabrina forgot her worries as she gave a cry of pleasure and ran to meet her brother. 'I wasn't expecting you this weekend,' she said when Tristan uncoiled his lanky frame from his old car. She inspected him with loving eyes. 'I'm sure you've grown.'

He grinned. 'When are you going to stop saying that? I'm not a kid any more, I'm twenty-one.'

Tristan might be a good six inches taller than her, but he would always be her little brother and she would probably always try to mother him, Sabrina thought ruefully. She had taken on the role when their mother had left. Tris had only been seven. *'When is Mother coming back?'* he'd asked tearfully as they had stood at the nursery window and watched Lorna Bancroft drive away from Eversleigh.

Fourteen-year-old Sabrina had swallowed hard. *'She isn't. But we'll visit her at her new home in France in the summer holidays.'*

'But who will look after me for the rest of the time? Father is always going away, and I don't like the new nanny.'

'I will,' she had promised her brother. *'I'll always take care of you.'*

Cruz had not understood how much she had missed her brother. She had rushed back to Eversleigh Hall after the miscarriage because it was where she felt most secure. Tris had been her only source of comfort in those dark days when she had grieved for her baby. Having lost her own child, she had poured her maternal feelings onto her brother, and, even though he was now a strapping six-footer about to graduate from university, Sabrina still felt protective of him.

'What the hell happened to the hall?' Tristan's shocked voice pulled Sabrina's mind from the past. She followed his gaze to the burnt-out wing of the house and quickly sought to reassure him.

'There was a fire, but fortunately only the annexe was affected.'

Her brother gave her a worried look. 'You're all right? What about John and Mary?'

'No one was hurt.'

Tristan slung his arm around her shoulders. 'Well, that's the main thing. As long as you're okay, the damage can be repaired, and the insurance will cover the cost of rebuilding.'

Sabrina's heart sank. 'Tris, I need to talk to you about Eversleigh.'

He gave her another of his quick smiles. 'Let me tell you my news first, before I burst. I've passed the selection process to be a commercial pilot and been offered a place at an aviation school that provides airline-pilot training.'

'Oh, Tris, that's fantastic.'

'Of course, I'll need to get a first-class degree, but I'm on track to do that. The training is expensive though. I've been careful with my allowance, but I can't afford the flight school's fees. Dad promised he would invest in my career. Have you heard from the old man lately? I'll need the money soon so that I can start the training programme in the summer.'

Tristan was looking up at the burnt-out roof of the annexe and did not see Sabrina's troubled expression. She had not wanted to worry her brother while he was taking his final exams and had played down their father's disappearance, saying that Earl Bancroft was on an extended trip abroad. She couldn't keep the truth from Tristan for much longer, she realised, but she was certainly not going to ruin his excitement at being accepted for pilot training by revealing that there was no money to pay for it. This was it—she'd have to sell Eversleigh. It was the only way that would allow Tris to fulfil his boyhood ambition, the only way to raise the aviation school's fees. Wasn't it?

She remembered Cruz's parting comment.

I might just be the answer to your prayers.

She'd have to be desperate to turn to him for help. But she *was* desperate, she acknowledged grimly. What was Cruz's proposition that might help her? Was it a way to keep Eversleigh Hall and pay for Tristan's pilot tuition? Would it do any harm to find out?

Lost in her thoughts, she followed Tristan into the house and forced a smile when he put his hands on her waist and swung her round.

'Every time I come home I realise how much I love Eversleigh,' Tris said softly. 'I plan to have a career as a pilot, but one day I'll become the next Earl Bancroft and I'll settle here and take care of the place properly. After all, the estate is our heritage and it's my duty to look after it for future generations.'

Sabrina's heart clenched. Tristan's words echoed her own sentiments about Eversleigh. They were guardians of the historic house and she could not bring herself to tell her brother that they might be forced to sell it to a hotel chain. Ironically, if the estate was sold, there would be plenty of money to pay for Tristan's pilot training. If only her father would reappear, Eversleigh would be saved and she might even be able to get on with her own life without the burden of responsibility and worry that had haunted her for months.

Tristan stayed for lunch before driving back to university. 'You said you wanted to discuss something about Eversleigh,' he remembered as he was leaving.

'It's not important. Concentrate on your exams,' Sabrina told him. She lifted her face so that he could kiss her cheek and recalled how when he was a young boy she had often leaned down to kiss him and ruffle his hair. She loved her brother dearly and would do anything for him—even if it meant asking Cruz Delgado, the man who had once broken her heart, for help.

* * *

Cruz sipped his vodka martini and savoured the hit of alcohol at the back of his throat. He glanced at his watch—not the first time he had done so in the past half an hour—and gave a wry grimace. He did not usually drink this early in the day but he was annoyed to admit that he felt tense, wondering if Sabrina would arrive.

He looked out of the window of his serviced penthouse apartment opposite Kensington Palace. In the distance he could see the Serpentine Lake in Hyde Park sparkling in the clear light of the spring evening. The street below was lined with exclusive top-of-the-range cars. This was the most affluent part of London and the five-star hotels and chic boutiques were as discreetly elegant as their high-class clientele.

Kensington was a long way from the *favela* in Belo Horizonte, but in his dreams Cruz still walked the labyrinth of narrow alleyways that stank of rotting rubbish. A few times he had seen a body lying in the gutter, a victim of warring drugs gangs, or maybe just a poor fool who had been in the wrong place at the wrong time. He had learned from a young age to look over his shoulder and check around every corner before stepping out. Fear and hunger had been his constant companions.

His thoughts returned to Sabrina. Would she turn up tonight, lured by his hint that he could help with her financial problems? His jaw hardened. He was a gambler and his instincts for a sure bet told him she would come because she would do anything to safeguard her beloved Eversleigh Hall.

But would she agree to his ultimatum? His lip curled into a cynical smile. Sabrina would be a fool to refuse him. This afternoon, he'd discovered just how close

Eversleigh was to bankruptcy because Earl Bancroft had bled the estate and used the money to fund his trips abroad and invest in numerous ill-advised business ventures. Coldness gripped Cruz's heart and he felt a sense of satisfaction that once he had been reliant on Earl Bancroft to pay his wages but in a reversal of fortune Sabrina would have to come to him for help to save her family home. The shift of power intrigued him and he wondered how she would react to him knowing that he had the upper hand. Surely the ice princess would have thawed—if she came?

He took another sip of his drink and stiffened when he heard the muted peal of the doorbell followed by the low murmur of voices as the butler invited the visitor into the apartment. Cruz recognised the cultured feminine tones and a ripple of anticipation ran through him. He swung round from the window as the sitting-room door opened and the butler ushered Sabrina into the room.

Most women who wanted something from him—and that was most women, he thought sardonically—would have dressed seductively in sexy, revealing clothes. Sabrina's plain black dress with its demure neckline and three-quarter-length sleeves was starkly simple, but as Cruz studied her he realised that the dress was exquisitely tailored to show off her slim figure. The silky material flowed over her body, moulding her high, firm breasts and following the contours of her narrow waist and hips.

He lowered his gaze to her legs encased in sheer hose and her black stiletto shoes that emphasised the shapely curve of her calves, before he lifted his eyes to her fine-boned face, beautifully made up and with the merest touch of pale pink gloss on her lips. The double string of pearls around her neck shimmered with a soft sheen that reflected her creamy skin and her pale blonde hair was swept up into a businesslike chignon. Sabrina looked what she was, a member of the English aristocracy with an impeccable pedigree; elegant, refined—untouchable.

For a moment Cruz was a young man again, a poor miner from a *favela*, entranced by an English rose but knowing she was out of his reach. Sabrina had been his once, he reminded himself. Ten years ago he hadn't been able to forget the difference in their social status. Now he was determined that she would be his again, but things were different. He was Sabrina's equal. He had made his fortune but she had lost hers and she needed his help. This time when they became lovers he would be in control and Sabrina would have to play by his rules, he decided as he strolled towards her.

The muted click of the door signalled to Sabrina that the butler had left the room and she was alone with Cruz. She was aware of her heart thudding hard beneath her ribs and fought the panicky feeling that made her want to run out of his apartment. She was not Cruz's prisoner, she reminded herself, she was his guest and she could leave whenever she chose.

She was well acquainted with Kensington and had frequently shopped at the exclusive boutiques, but since her father's disappearance her life had changed dramatically. A year ago she would have travelled up to town in the Bentley driven by the chauffeur. Now the Bentley was in the garage waiting to be auctioned, the chauffeur had a new employer, and she hadn't dared splash out on a taxi and had caught the Tube across London to Cruz's luxurious apartment. But she did not care about the loss of the little luxuries she had been used to. All she cared about was saving Eversleigh and helping her brother fulfil his dream of being a pilot.

She watched Cruz walk towards her and drew a swift breath as she acknowledged how handsome he was. His black trousers were superbly tailored and his pale blue silk shirt was open at the throat to reveal his darkly tanned skin. Sabrina noticed a flash of gold on his wrist and recognised his watch was an exclusive and exorbitantly expensive brand.

The situation felt surreal. It was hard to believe that the suave, sophisticated man standing in front of her was the poor miner who had been her first lover ten years ago. In Brazil, the only clothes she had seen Cruz wear were ripped jeans and tee shirts, but she hadn't been bothered by his lack of money. She had fallen in love with his olive-green eyes and his wide smile, his springy, silky black hair that curled onto his brow and his fit, muscular body that he had used with dedicated skill to ensure her pleasure before he had taken his own.

Memories of him making love to her bombarded her mind and she quickly lowered her lashes to hide her thoughts from him, but she could not control the betraying thud of her pulse at the base of her throat when Cruz lifted his hand and removed the clip from her chignon so that her hair unravelled and fell in a heavy swathe down her back.

He met her fulminating look with a bland smile. 'You need my help and I suggest you drop your defiance,' he drawled. 'Your hair is like silk.' He wrapped a few strands around his finger. 'Always wear it loose when you are with me.'

She longed to tell him to go to hell, but the memory of her brother's excitement when he'd announced that he had been accepted for pilot training made her take a deep breath and she schooled her features into an expression of cool composure. 'What is your proposition that you invited me here to discuss?'

'All in good time,' Cruz said urbanely as he strolled over to the bar. 'Would you like some champagne?'

It might calm her nerves, Sabrina decided as she accepted the long-stemmed glass Cruz offered her. She noted that the champagne was an excellent vintage and once again she felt a sense of surrealism that the Cruz she had known ten years ago had drunk beer from a bottle, but now he seemed completely at ease with his millionaire lifestyle.

He waited for her to sit down before he lowered his tall frame onto the sofa facing her and stretched his arm along the backrest. The action caused his shirt to tighten across his chest so that Sabrina could see the delineation of his pectoral muscles. Although he presumably no longer worked down mines his physique was even more toned and powerfully muscular than when he had been a young man. Images filled her mind of his naked, bronzed body and she licked her suddenly dry lips and took a gulp of champagne.

'I have shown the top gemologist at my jewellery company Delgado Diamonds some photographs of the Estrela Vermelha,' Cruz said. 'He estimates its value to be in the region of one and a half million pounds, but of course he will need to assess the diamond properly and I suggest that you have your own independent valuation carried out.'

Sabrina wondered where the conversation was leading. 'It was valued at one point four million pounds for insurance purposes. But why are you interested in what the diamond is worth?'

'Because I want it, and I am prepared to buy it from you.' Cruz's expression hardened. 'I wish to give my mother the Estrela Vermelha as tribute to my father. Vitor wanted to give his family the chance of a better life away from the slums, but in doing so he lost his own life and was cruelly snatched from my mother, sisters and I.'

The sudden huskiness in his voice evoked an ache of sympathy in Sabrina and without thinking she leant forwards to put a comforting hand on Cruz's knee, before it occurred to her that she was the daughter of the man he blamed for his father's death and perhaps he hated her as much as he hated Earl Bancroft. Flushing, she shoved her hand into her lap, and in the tense silence she brooded on Cruz's offer to buy the diamond. Her disappointment was acute even though she had told herself not to get her hopes up. She had clung to the possibility of a respite for Eversleigh, but now she knew there was none and it was hard to bear.

'I can't sell you the red diamond,' she said flatly. 'My father is its registered owner and it is listed as one of his personal assets, which, as I have already explained, I am unable to use as a means of raising capital.'

So that was that. She put her glass down on the coffee table in front of her, gathered her handbag and stood up. 'I'm truly sorry about your father's accident,' she blurted. 'I wish I could sell you the diamond, but I can't and I have nothing else to offer you.'

'That's not quite true.' A curious nuance in Cruz's voice made Sabrina hesitate as she was about to walk over to the door. 'There is something else I want and I am willing to pay the same amount that I offered for the Estrela Vermelha.'

She turned to look at him, her finely arched brows drawn together in a frown. 'I've told you I have nothing, apart from Eversleigh Hall.'

He stood up and towered over her. He appeared relaxed but his eyes glittered with a fierce gleam that caused Sabrina's heart to slam against her ribs. 'I don't want an ancient pile of bricks. I want you, Sabrina.'

Shock rendered her silent for several seconds as she registered his words and absorbed their meaning. She stiffened as he trailed his eyes over her in a frank appraisal, as if he was mentally stripping her naked, she thought furiously. Even worse was her treacherous body's reaction to the sensual promise in Cruz's gaze. Her breasts ached with a delicious heaviness and every nerve-ending on her skin tingled.

I want you. No doubt he had said those words to the countless attractive blondes he was reputed to have had affairs with. The tabloids were full of stories about the hotshot Brazilian diamond tycoon's playboy lifestyle, and she would just be another notch on his bedpost, Sabrina realised bitterly. But she would be an expensive notch because Cruz was offering to pay her to sleep with him as if she was a hooker he had picked up off the streets. His suggestion was deeply insulting and she hated him for it, but she despised her body even more for responding to his smouldering sensuality.

Her heart ached as she remembered a much younger Cruz with smiling eyes, who had taken her virginity so tenderly and whispered soft words in Portuguese while he'd made love to her with sweet passion. She had loved him so much, but by offering to buy her sexual favours he had given her the ultimate proof that she had never meant anything to him.

Years of practice at disguising her feelings meant that her expression revealed nothing of her thoughts. 'Am I to understand that you are offering to pay me a million pounds to have sex with you?' she said coldly. 'Did you really think that I would *prostitute* myself? Let me make something absolutely clear. I would *never* demean myself by sharing your bed, however much money you offered me. You have become a wealthy man, but you need to learn that there are some things your money can't buy.'

Ice replaced the fire in Cruz's blood as he met Sabrina's disdainful grey gaze, and he struggled to control his anger. Once more, he recalled Lord Porchester's party.

'Delgado's a self-made millionaire...you can always pick out the nouveau riche by their lack of breeding.'

He jerked his thoughts back to the present. For a few moments Sabrina's disdain had made him feel unworthy and ashamed of his poor background. *Deus*, he should not feel ashamed because he hadn't been born with a silver spoon in his mouth. He owed his fortune partly to luck at discovering top-grade diamonds in the Montes Claros mine, but for years before that he had slogged his guts out to provide for his mother and sisters.

His jaw hardened. How dared Sabrina, who had only ever known a life of privilege and luxury, tell him in her cultured accent that she would not demean herself to have sex with him? In fact she had jumped to the wrong conclusion when she had accused him of offering to pay her for sex. What he had been going to suggest was that she would allow him to move into Eversleigh Hall so that he could search for the map of the diamond mine and in return he would pay for the cost of the repairs to the annexe and the ongoing expenses of maintaining the estate.

It was true he had hoped that if he and Sabrina lived under the same roof they might rekindle their affair. He desired her more than any other woman, and he knew she wanted him. God knew he had enough experience of women to be able to recognise the telltale signs of attraction. He had been prepared to woo Sabrina. He'd been looking forward to an enjoyable chase before she finally and inevitably succumbed to the chemistry that existed between them.

But she had scraped his pride raw and now the rules of the game had changed. She might look at him as if he were something unpleasant on the sole of her shoe, but he would have her in his bed and he would make her beg for him to possess her and give her more pleasure than she had ever known with any other man, Cruz vowed to himself.

She had to get out of Cruz's apartment immediately, Sabrina decided, before her tenuous hold on her emotions cracked and she did something unforgivably stupid like agree to any demands he made if only he would take her in his arms.

Without saying another word she walked swiftly across the room, but her sense of relief as she gripped the door handle turned to panic when Cruz caught hold of her arm and swung her round to face him.

She flashed him a steely glare, which he returned with an amused smile.

'I'm fascinated by the contrasts in your personality,' he drawled. 'As I've said before, you give the impression of being cool and controlled, but beneath your ice there is fire and passion and a depth of sensuality I've never known in any other woman.'

She did not want to hear about his other women. 'Take your hands off me.'

'Don't push my patience, *gatinha*. I am your only hope of saving your precious Eversleigh Hall. I know you have applied to various banks for a loan and been turned down.'

Her temper simmered. 'How can you possibly know personal information about me?'

'Information isn't difficult to obtain if you pay the right people.' When she did not reply, he continued in a hard voice. 'What I'm offering is a simple exchange. My money, which you can spend on maintaining your family's ancestral home, and in return you will be my mistress for six months.'

'Six *months*!'

He shrugged. 'That's somewhere in the region of one hundred and eighty nights, for which you'll get paid one and a half million pounds. Not a bad return surely, *querida*?'

The Portuguese endearment transported Sabrina back in time to when Cruz had called her darling as if he had meant it. She searched his hard-boned features for any sign of softening but found none. 'Why do you want to humiliate me?' she whispered. 'Once we created a child together and you asked me to be your wife. Did our relationship ten years ago mean so little to you?'

'It meant little to you,' he said harshly. 'If it had meant anything you would have accepted my marriage proposal. But you would have preferred our child to have been born illegitimate than to marry a man you considered below your social class.'

'That's not true.' She was shocked by his accusation. 'I never thought you were below me. My decision not to marry you was because I had seen how unhappy my parents' marriage had been. My mother once told me that the only reason she had married my father was because she had fallen pregnant with me. I didn't want history to repeat itself.'

'The argument about marriage became obsolete after you suffered a miscarriage,' Cruz said flatly.

His comment confirmed what Sabrina had already guessed—that he had only asked her to marry him because he had wanted his child.

'I'll find a way to save Eversleigh that doesn't entail having to have sex with you,' she told him fiercely.

'If I only wanted sex I could obtain it for a lot less than I am willing to pay you.'

She frowned. 'What else do you think I can provide?'

'Class,' he said succinctly.

'You've got a hang-up about class. A person's position in society doesn't matter.'

'It shouldn't matter, but it does.' Cruz's expression became cynical. 'It doesn't matter how much money I have in the bank, or how many yachts or penthouse apartments I can afford to buy. I will always be regarded as an outsider by the aristocracy because I wasn't educated at one of the top public schools and I can't trace my family tree back hundreds of years to show that my ancestors were linked to royalty like you can, Lady Bancroft.'

Sabrina gave him an impatient look. 'Having a title means very little these days.'

'It is an invaluable commodity in business, and especially to a business like Delgado Diamonds. My jewellery company is aimed at the top end of the market. My boutiques in Dubai, Paris and Rome have received acclaim, but the success of the company will be measured by sales at the flagship premises that I am about to open on Bond Street.'

'What do your business plans have to do with me?'

'Delgado Diamonds needs to attract a certain class of wealthy clientele, people who demand exceptional design and craftsmanship and will think nothing of spending thousands of pounds on an item of jewellery. The old-school aristocracy won't be interested in a jewellery company owned by an ex-miner who grew up in a slum in South America,' Cruz said bluntly. 'But if I am seen to be in a relationship with an earl's daughter who belongs to one of the oldest and most prestigious families in England, I'll become acceptable in high society, particularly as I intend to move into Eversleigh Hall with you. It will be the perfect opportunity for me to search for the map of the diamond mine that belongs to me.'

Cruz's lips curled into a sardonic smile as he studied Sabrina's stunned expression. He lifted his hand and slowly ran his knuckles down her cheek and the white column of her throat and was exultant when he felt the frantic beat of her pulse. Despite her proud words he knew she would be his whenever he chose to take her. He was tempted to sweep her into his arms and carry her through to the bedroom so that their bodies could communicate on a fundamental level that did not require words.

The shadows in her grey eyes stopped him and he felt a faint tug of regret that they were on opposing sides of a battlefield. It was safer that way, he reminded himself. She was the only woman who had ever made him lose control, unmanned him with her sweetness and fire and mind-blowing passion, but he would not succumb to such craven weakness again.

'As well as having been born into a high-ranking family you are a respected historian specialising in antique furniture restoration, and, according to my private investigator, you have undertaken commissions at the Wallace Collection and the Victoria and Albert Museum. You are also a well-known patron of the arts and no society dinner party is complete without your name on the guest list.'

Sabrina drew a sharp breath. 'I can't believe you instructed someone to pry into my private life.'

He shrugged. 'The first rule of business is to thoroughly research the subject you are interested in, and, in this instance, I am interested in you.'

'Because of my so-called pedigree,' she snapped.

'You belong to the rarefied world of the English upper class. I can get sex anywhere,' Cruz stated coolly. 'What I desire from you, Sabrina, is your heritage and breeding. You will be my very public mistress and your connections to the aristocracy will open doors that would otherwise be closed to me.'

Sabrina held her breath as he trailed his knuckles over the upper swell of her breast and she felt her nipples pucker in anticipation of his touch. She jerked away from him and this time he did not prevent her from opening the door. 'Hell will freeze over first,' she told him grimly.

His mocking voice followed her down the hallway. 'I'll give you three days to come to me, *querida*. If I haven't heard from you by seven p.m. on Tuesday evening I will withdraw my offer and you will have lost your chance to save Eversleigh Hall from the developers.'

CHAPTER SIX

THERE WAS NOT a chance in hell that she would agree to Cruz's outrageous ultimatum, Sabrina thought angrily, when she arrived back at Eversleigh Hall. But she had to face the stark truth that she could no longer afford to keep the house and estate, especially as it seemed increasingly possible that her father might not be found.

The fire and the huge costs of repairing the annexe had made a bad situation even worse. The best thing she could do would be to sell Eversleigh to the Excelsior hotel chain. But she hadn't discussed it with Tristan yet, she argued with herself. She had hoped he could finish his exams before she broke the news that he might lose his home and heritage. In retrospect she knew she should have explained the situation to her brother months ago, but she had spent so many years caring for him after their parents' divorce and she still felt an instinctive need to try to protect him.

Ten years ago Cruz had not understood how worried she had felt about leaving her brother in England. He had accused her of wanting to return to her comfortable life at Eversleigh Hall, but, in the end, the arguments about where their baby would be born had been immaterial. Seventeen weeks into her pregnancy she had started to bleed heavily. Cruz's mother had driven her to the hospital because Cruz had been at work at the mine. By the time he had arrived at her bedside Sabrina had had to tell him that he was no longer going to be a father.

She had called her baby boy Luiz. A lump formed in her throat. Memories of the miscarriage had become less painful over time, but seeing Cruz again had brought it all back. She had been consumed by grief and guilt that the miscarriage was somehow her fault and had sought refuge at Eversleigh, resuming her role of parent to her brother as a way of helping her through the mourning process. For a long time she had hoped that Cruz would come to her and they would be able to grieve for their child together. But weeks and months had passed and she had not heard from him.

He had not wanted her once she was no longer carrying his child. He did not want her for herself now, Sabrina thought bitterly. He had made the insulting proposition that she could sell her body to him for the price of the red diamond. But even more insulting— and hurtful, damn it—was his admission that he had only chosen her to be his mistress rather than any of the blonde bimbos who flocked round him because of her breeding. He made her sound like a prize heifer!

As she passed the portraits hanging in the hall she paused by a painting of the daughter of a previous Earl Bancroft who had lived in the time of the notorious womaniser King Charles II. According to a family story retold through generations, Lady Henrietta had become a mistress of the king in return for him settling the huge debts her father had left when he died, thereby saving Eversleigh Hall from being sold and allowing

Henrietta's younger brother to inherit the earldom and the estate.

Heaven help her. Perhaps whoredom was in her genes! Sabrina thought wryly.

Her mind kept on replaying her confrontation with Cruz and she had no appetite for the chicken salad the housekeeper had prepared for her. The TV failed to hold her attention, and she switched it off and went into her studio where she carried out restoration work on Eversleigh Hall's collection of antique furniture. But the detailed work of applying gold leaf to a Georgian cabinet that she had spent weeks restoring seemed a waste of time when there was a strong chance that the cabinet would have to be sold with the house.

In the library that her father had used as his study she began to search the drawers in the desk for the map Cruz had spoken of. It was unlikely that Earl Bancroft would have put something that he presumably valued highly in such an obvious place, but it had occurred to her that if she could find the map it was possible she could make a deal with Cruz.

Half an hour later, Sabrina had found nothing of interest apart from a couple more bills that she had been unaware of and that required paying immediately. Lying at the bottom of the last drawer she opened was a photograph of her parents on their wedding day. The cracked glass in the frame summed up her parents' marriage, she mused. Neither her mother nor father looked happy, but the old earl, Sabrina's grandfather, had insisted that his grandchild could not be born out of wedlock.

Her parents must have had a brief spell of marital harmony which had resulted in Tristan being born. But her father had soon grown bored of family life. De-

serted by her husband for long periods, Lorna Bancroft
had started an affair with a groom who worked at the
Eversleigh estate.

As Sabrina replaced the photo in the drawer she
mused that her parents' shotgun marriage had not been
a good advertisement for wedded bliss. It was why she'd
turned down Cruz's proposal, but she was surprised to
learn he believed she'd refused because she'd thought
he wasn't good enough for her.

Was her rejection of him years ago the real reason
for his humiliating proposition that she could sell herself to him for the price of the red diamond? Back then,
Cruz had been far more bothered than she had by what
he had perceived as the difference in their social status
and he'd refused to move to England and live at Eversleigh Hall with her in case he was labelled a gold-
digger. Now that their financial situations were reversed
and she could be seen as a gold-digger if she accepted
money from Cruz, Sabrina had a new insight into how
he must have felt when he had been a poor miner in a
relationship with an earl's daughter.

She still had not called! Cruz checked his phone for new
messages and felt a mixture of frustration and disbelief when Sabrina's name did not appear in his in-box.

He put his phone back down on the boardroom table
and forced himself to concentrate on the details of the
launch party for his new Bond Street store that the
event planner was explaining. Opening a Delgado Diamonds shop in the heart of London was the biggest
gamble he had ever taken. As he'd explained to Sabrina,
the success or failure of his whole jewellery company
depended on whether the new store would attract the

super-rich clientele who could afford to live and shop in exclusive Mayfair.

This was what he had been working towards for years, ever since he had created Delgado Diamonds. For months he had focused on little else, but for the past three days he had barely given a thought to his business expansion plans, his mind preoccupied with Sabrina. Not just his mind, Cruz acknowledged with savage self-contempt, recalling his erotic fantasies about her.

He had been certain she would accept his offer of financial help in return for becoming his mistress. She had reacted furiously when he had set out his terms, but he had given her a few days for her temper to cool and he'd been convinced that she would agree to his demands, which would allow her to safeguard Eversleigh Hall. He knew how much the stately home meant to her and he could not understand why she was delaying her inevitable capitulation.

He glanced at his watch. Five hours left until the deadline he had given her expired. Would she come to him? His gut twisted as he faced the possibility that she would thwart him. He drummed his fingertips on the polished table and acknowledged that he couldn't take the risk that Sabrina might decide to sell Eversleigh Hall to a hotel chain and deny him the chance to search for the map of the diamond mine.

'Would you like to accompany me to the party venue to make sure you are happy with the arrangements, Mr Delgado?'

Cruz forced himself to concentrate on the matter at hand and smiled at the young woman from Party Perfect who was organising the launch party.

'I'm sure that you and your team have done an excellent job, Miss Simms.' He stood up and slipped his phone into his jacket pocket. 'Something urgent has come up and I'll be busy for the rest of the afternoon, but I'll be back in time for the party at eight this evening.'

It was the third day! Sabrina could not dismiss the thought and she was finding it hard to concentrate on the intricate restoration work on the Georgian cabinet. She now understood why Cruz had given her an ultimatum of seven o'clock this evening to decide if she would sell herself to him. Several of the daily newspapers had carried full-page advertisements announcing the opening of Delgado Diamonds' flagship store in Bond Street, and Cruz had been a guest on a morning television programme, speaking about the lavish party he would be hosting that evening to celebrate the launch.

The flirtatious female interviewer had clearly been smitten by Cruz's charisma, Sabrina remembered irritably. Many women would leap at the chance of an affair with a millionaire diamond tycoon, but she refused to sacrifice her self-respect by becoming his mistress, even to save Eversleigh Hall. *But what of her brother's hopes of training to be a pilot?* her conscience questioned. Could she, *should* she agree to Cruz's demands for Tristan's sake?

The sound of her phone pulled her from her thoughts, and she answered a call from the horse dealer who explained that he had found a buyer for Monty. Her heart plummeted at the news, even though she desperately needed the money from the sale.

If she sold herself to Cruz, she would not need to sell her horse, whispered the voice in her head.

But although Cruz had offered to pay her over a million pounds, the sum would only cover the renovation work after the fire and leave her with enough money to maintain the estate until Earl Bancroft returned or was declared dead. Sabrina knew she would still have to live to a tight budget, which would not include the upkeep of a horse. It was a bitter irony that if she sold Eversleigh to the hotel chain she would be able to afford Monty, but she would not have anywhere to keep him and she would not have a home herself. While her future was so uncertain, it seemed kinder to sell Monty to a new owner who could give him a secure home.

Her mind was in turmoil and she gave up trying to work on the cabinet and went to get changed into her riding clothes. Monty greeted her with the snuffling noise he always made when he saw her, and when Sabrina led him out of his stable he nuzzled his nose against her shoulder. Hopefully it would not take him long to get used to his new owner, she thought bleakly. Monty whinnied with delight when she led him into the jumping ring. He loved to jump, and Sabrina was determined to enjoy her last precious ride on him.

'Come on, boy,' she whispered in his ear as they approached the first fence. She held her breath as she felt the power and strength of the horse beneath her, and then the two of them were flying through the air as Monty cleared the fence with inches to spare.

As Cruz climbed out of his car he noted that the bright red Ferrari looked gaudy and out of place parked on the driveway in front of Eversleigh Hall. A Rolls-Royce or a Bentley would suit the elegant grandeur of the stately home far better than a brash sports car. He grimaced as he once again recalled the comment he'd overheard Lord Porchester make about him being one of the *nouveau riche*. Porchester hadn't minded borrowing money from him, Cruz thought sardonically. And if Sabrina had any sense she would accept his offer of financial assistance that would enable her to keep her family's home.

He'd caught sight of her riding her horse as he drove along the lane leading to the Eversleigh estate, and instead of walking up to the front door he made his way around the side of the house, heading towards the stables.

She was a superb horsewoman, Cruz acknowledged as he leaned against the paddock fence and admired Sabrina's skill and perfect timing as horse and rider sailed over a six-foot wall made out of polystyrene bricks.

'That was impressive,' he commented when she rode up to him and dismounted. She was wearing her riding gear again. When she bent over to pick up the horse's reins, Cruz watched the stretchy material of her jodhpurs tighten across her pert derrière and felt his body tighten in response.

Santa mãe! How could he want her so badly? What spell had she cast on him that had decimated his ability to think of anything but her and his consuming longing to feel her soft body beneath him?

She unfastened the strap beneath her chin and as she lifted off her riding helmet her blonde hair cascaded down her back like a river of silk. Cruz almost groaned out loud. When they had been together he had loved her hair, loved the way it felt against his skin when she had straddled him and leaned forwards so that the long golden strands brushed his chest.

His jaw clenched. Once he had loved her, and for a

while he had even managed to kid himself that she was in love with him. What a fool he had been to think that a woman of Sabrina's class and refinement would give up her life of privilege and luxury for a poorly paid, poorly educated miner.

'Why are you here?' Her cultured voice pulled Cruz from the past. 'You told me I had until seven o'clock this evening to give you my answer.'

Sabrina led Monty back to the stables and was supremely conscious of Cruz walking beside her. She despised the way her heart had missed a beat when she'd noticed him watching her ride. In black trousers and shirt, his eyes hidden behind designer shades, he was devastatingly handsome and a dangerous threat to her peace of mind.

Katie, the teenage groom, was waiting in the yard and took Monty into his stall to unsaddle him.

'Do you only keep one horse here?' Cruz glanced at the five empty stables.

Sabrina nodded. 'When I was a child all the stables were occupied. My mother had a couple of hunters and a horse for dressage, and my brother and I learned to ride on ponies.' Her voice faltered. 'Soon there will be no horses at Eversleigh. Monty is to be sold.'

'Tears, *gatinha*?' Cruz caught hold of her chin to prevent her from turning away and captured the sparkle of moisture clinging to her lashes with his thumb pad. He noted the dark shadows beneath her eyes that looked like bruises on her porcelain skin. Her lower lip quivered almost imperceptibly before she firmed it and her air of vulnerability made his gut twist.

Abruptly he released her and thrust his hands into his pockets. 'You can cry over a horse, yet you did not cry when you lost our child,' he said harshly. 'But I know you regretted your pregnancy and perhaps you did not find the loss of our baby so terrible.'

Sabrina stared at his hard face and the arrogant line of his mouth and a fierce rage simmered inside her. 'Not terrible?' she choked. 'The day of the miscarriage was the worst day of my life. I was utterly heartbroken when I lost Luiz.' At Cruz's look of surprise, she went on to explain, 'We'd discussed baby names. When I was miscarrying they scanned me at the hospital and could see that we were expecting a boy. Although he never lived in the world, he lived inside me for seventeen weeks and I wanted him to have a name.'

She felt a couple of spots of rain and glanced up to see ominous dark clouds had covered the sun. But she ignored the imminent storm as the storm inside her became an unstoppable force. 'How can you suggest that I wasn't affected by the miscarriage? I was devastated.'

'If you were, you hid it well.' Cruz's tone seemed to imply that he did not believe her. 'You did not appear grief-stricken—and I should know. After I was born my parents tried unsuccessfully for many years to have another child. My mother suffered several miscarriages and each time she lost a baby she was beside herself with grief. My overriding memory of my childhood was hearing my mother sobbing,' he said grimly.

'After a few months she would be happy because she was pregnant again, but each of her pregnancies ended in more tears and heartache and there was nothing that I or my father could do to comfort her. My mother believed it was a miracle when she eventually gave birth to my twin sisters, fourteen years after she'd had me.'

Sabrina stared at him. Ten years ago he had not spoken about what had happened to his mother, and his revelation now gave a new insight to why he had been overly protective during her pregnancy. 'I appreciate that your mother must have been distraught every time she suffered a miscarriage. Everyone deals with things differently and at the time we lost Luiz I was in a state of shock and I couldn't cry. But that wasn't because I didn't care.' She was shaking with anger now. 'How dare you judge me because my reaction to losing my baby was different from your mother's? And how dare you say that I had regretted falling pregnant? If you believe that, it proves that you never really knew me, and you certainly didn't care about me. All you wanted was our child.'

Her voice rose as her words spilled out in a furious torrent. 'Nothing has changed. You didn't want me then and you don't want me now. The only reason you're willing to pay me to be your mistress is for my social skills and because you think my connections with the aristocracy will boost sales for your jewellery company. Well, I am not for sale!'

She whirled away from him and ran across the yard, heading towards the nearest shelter from the rain that was now falling hard. By the time she reached the hay shed her jacket was soaked and she wrenched open the buttons and tugged her arms out of the sleeves.

'*I don't want you?* That's a laugh,' Cruz's voice growled close to her ear.

Sabrina spun round and gasped as he snaked his arm around her waist and hauled her against his muscular and very aroused body. She looked up at his face and saw no evidence of laughter on his hard-boned features, only a savage determination that made her heart lurch.

'Does this feel like I do not want you, *gatinha*?' he demanded. He gave her no chance to reply as he captured her mouth with his and kissed her with a fierce hunger, crushing her lips as he sought to crush her resistance with his urgent desire.

CHAPTER SEVEN

HE FILLED HER SENSES, and beneath his hands her body became alive, every skin cell and nerve-ending quivering with pleasure at his touch. But Sabrina still felt blazingly angry at how badly he had misjudged her at the time of the miscarriage. When she was eighteen she had put Cruz on a pedestal and thought he could do no wrong. But now she was older and wiser and she knew he was a mortal man with strengths but also weaknesses.

She was determined not to be overwhelmed by him as she had been in the past. His physical strength was superior to hers, but she was not going to submissively let him have things all his own way. His mouth was creating havoc as he trailed his lips over her cheek to her ear and his sharp teeth bit her tender lobe. She repressed a shudder of longing and renewed her attempts to resist him, but her wild struggling had a counter-effect, she discovered, as she felt his rock-hard arousal push against her thigh.

His arms were like bands of steel around her, making escape impossible. He slid one hand down and splayed his fingers over her buttocks, urging her into even closer contact with the solid ridge of his manhood straining beneath his trousers. Sabrina gasped as he circled his hips against her pelvis, and in a corner of her mind she registered that he could not be faking his desire. Cruz was on fire for her and she was melting in his heat.

His other hand tangled in her hair as he angled her head and kissed her mouth again, forcing her lips apart so that his tongue could plunder her inner sweetness. He kissed her as if he could not have enough of her, as if he had fought a battle with himself and lost.

'I wish I did not want you,' he muttered when he finally wrenched his mouth from hers to allow them both to drag oxygen into their lungs. 'You are like a drug in my veins, so bloody addictive that I can't resist you even though I know I should for the sake of my sanity.'

His words made no sense to Sabrina. How could she be a threat to Cruz's sanity? It was the other way round, and it was imperative that she found the strength of will to resist him. He still had one hand clamped on her bottom, and he moved his other hand to the front of her shirt. Her heart gave a jolt when he began to unfasten the buttons, but she did not stop him, couldn't, if she was brutally honest.

Excitement spiralled inside her as he pushed her shirt off her shoulders to reveal her plain white bra. She wished she were wearing sexy underwear in black satin and lace, but then Cruz traced his fingers over the outline of her nipple visible through the stretchy material of her bra and she caught her breath as a shaft of exquisite pleasure shot through her.

'It doesn't help that you are so damned responsive,' he said harshly. He reached around her back to unfasten her bra and tugged the straps down her arms, baring her breasts to his hot gaze. His voice thickened. 'How the hell am I supposed to resist you when your body tells me that you are as hungry as I am?'

Sabrina shivered when he cupped her naked breasts in his hands, but it was not cold that made her nipples harden into burgeoning points but anticipation and uncontrollable sexual excitement. Cruz gave a husky laugh as he flicked his thumb pads across her nipples and heard her swiftly indrawn breath.

'I remember you used to love it when I caressed your breasts with my hands and especially my mouth. Do you still like that, *gatinha*?' He gave another low chuckle when he realised that she was incapable of replying. 'Let's find out, shall we?'

Dimly she knew she should stop him and bring an end to this madness, but she was enraptured by the feel of his warm hands on her flesh, seduced by his soft words of promise. He lifted her into his arms and laid her down on the pile of square hay bales. The hay felt scratchy beneath her shoulders but she forgot the slight discomfort as Cruz knelt over her and lowered his head to her breast. He drew her nipple into his mouth and suckled her hard. The pleasure was so intense that she gave a keening cry and curled her fingers into his shoulders to urge him to continue his exquisite torment.

He needed no persuading, pausing only to transfer his mouth to her other nipple. 'Oh, God!' she groaned as deep shudders of pleasure racked her body when he flicked his tongue back and forth over the tender peak. She could feel the fire building low in her pelvis as he continued his merciless ravishment of her body. Reality faded and she was aware only of the sweet smell of hay, the sound of the rain drumming on the roof of the shed and Cruz's uneven breaths as he took his mouth from her breast and claimed her lips in a deep, drug-ging kiss that ravaged her soul.

This was the Cruz she remembered from the past. He might wear expensive clothes now, instead of jeans, and drink champagne rather than beer, but the essence of him hadn't changed and her senses recognised the familiar musk of male pheromones and the subtle scent that was uniquely him.

She ran her hands over his soaking-wet shirt and tugged open the buttons before pushing the material over his shoulders. His bronzed chest was satin over-laid with black hairs that felt like silk beneath her fin-gertips as she traced the ridges of his powerful pectoral and abdominal muscles.

He was so beautiful. And so massively aroused! De-sire flooded through her when he bore his weight down on her so that her breasts were crushed against his bare chest and she was supremely conscious of his erection pressing into the junction between her thighs. Their clothes were an unwanted barrier. The fire inside her burned hotter and became an inferno of feverish need, and she sensed from the fierce intensity of Cruz's kiss that he had passed the point of no return.

He tugged the zip of her jodhpurs down but struggled to pull the clingy trousers over her hips.

'These were not designed for easy access,' he growled impatiently.

The sound of his voice broke through the sexual haze surrounding Sabrina's brain and forced her to acknowl-edge a vital fact.

'I'm not on the pill,' she muttered.

Cruz did not seem to hear her as he managed to slip his hand inside her jodhpurs and stroked a finger over the damp panel of her knickers. Instinctively she arched her hips and a shudder of longing ran through her when he eased the panel aside and touched her eager flesh. But her common sense could not be ignored. She would never risk another unplanned pregnancy and she pulled at his hand to make him stop his intimate exploration.

'We can't. I'm not protected.'

This time he heard and he lifted his head and stared down at her, his eyes glittering with frustration before he swore savagely and rolled away. He lay on his back on the hay bales and held his forearm across his eyes—almost, Sabrina thought, as if he was ashamed of what emotions they might reveal. But he could not disguise the ragged sound of his breathing or the heaving of his chest as he dragged air into his lungs. Outside, the rain fell harder and somehow the thunderous drumming on the roof and the feeling that they were trapped in the hay shed made the prickling atmosphere even tenser.

'Cruz…' She flinched as he leapt to his feet and could not disguise her shock when she saw his tortured expression.

He gave a bitter laugh. 'So now you have discovered the truth. How does it feel to know that you have the power to bring a grown man to his knees? *Of course I damn well want you.*' He threw the words at her as if the confession had been ripped from his soul. 'I wanted you ten years ago and nothing has changed. I desire you more than I have ever desired any other woman. You are my nemesis, *gatinha.*' His lip curled in self-mockery. 'No doubt you are gloating at my weakness?'

'*No,*' she said shakily. His self-contempt touched something inside her and she stretched her hand towards him. 'Cruz, I…'

He swore again and snatched up his shirt, thrusting his arms into the sleeves with such violent force that the material ripped. *Deus*, was that pity he had heard in Sabrina's voice? Cruz felt humiliated by his inability to resist her and his anger made him want to verbally lash out at her.

'However much you might wish to deny it, you want me as badly as I want you. We are both gripped by this madness, and neither of us will know any peace until we have sated our desire for each other.'

He strode over to the door and turned to look at her, his mouth curling into a mocking smile as he noted her flushed face and rumpled hair before he dropped his gaze deliberately to her breasts. 'Your body betrays you,' he drawled, and laughed softly when she grabbed her shirt and held it in front of her to hide her swollen, reddened nipples.

'You have two hours left before your deadline expires and you lose your only chance to safeguard your home. Think of the benefits. As my mistress you will enjoy six months of the best sex you've ever known. I don't believe any other man has turned you on as much as I do,' he taunted.

'Go to hell!' Infuriated beyond endurance, Sabrina grabbed an old horseshoe that was lying on the floor and flung it at Cruz. But he had already walked out of the door and the iron shoe clattered on the flagstones of the stable yard.

She watched him stride across the yard until he had disappeared from view and then flopped down on the hay bales, breathing hard as if she had run a marathon. No one but Cruz Delgado had ever made her feel so

furiously angry. And he had been right, damn him—
so turned on!

Her hands were shaking too much to be able to fasten
her bra and she gave up and pulled on her shirt, winc-
ing as the material scraped over her acutely sensitive
nipples. The ache of unfulfilled sexual desire slowly
ebbed from her body but the image of Cruz's tormented
expression lingered in her mind.

*It was not true that he had only asked her to be his
mistress because her aristocratic background would
be useful to his business.*

Cruz wanted her in his bed and he had actually admitted that he desired her more than any other woman.
The realisation that he wanted her for herself above any
other reason gave her a feeling of liberation and her
self-confidence soared.

During her childhood, and especially her teenage
years, she had felt rejected by both her parents and the
feeling that she was somehow not good enough had
made her anxious to please people. She had striven to
be a perfect daughter and a perfect sister to her younger
brother, even though it had often meant sublimating her
hopes and desires out of a sense of duty to her family.

Rarely had she put herself first or thought about what
she wanted, Sabrina realised. But Cruz's admission
freed her from her insecurities and she acknowledged
that what she wanted and desired more than anything
was *him*.

He had stated that neither of them would have any
peace until they had sated their desire for each other,
and she could not deny it was the truth. She had never
forgotten him and she recognised that subconsciously
she had compared every man she'd dated to Cruz. *Dear*

God! After ten years he was still in her system, she thought with a flash of despair. She had allowed herself to be held back by the past for far too long. But if she agreed to be his mistress in a sex-without-strings affair she hoped she could walk away from him at the end of six months, having gained closure, and finally be able to move forwards with her life.

The vintage champagne cost eight hundred pounds a bottle and the caviar was Iranian beluga. Only the absolute finest—and most expensive, Cruz thought sardonically—delicacies were good enough to be served to the exclusive guests attending the exclusive party to celebrate the launch of Delgado Diamonds' new premises in Bond Street.

The flagship store was spread over four floors and had been designed in a contemporary and ultra-luxurious style. The party was taking place in the main salon where the lacquered walnut-panelled walls and Italian marble floors provided a stunning backdrop for exquisite crystal chandeliers suspended from the double-height ceiling, which gave the room a feeling of lofty grandeur.

Cruz sipped his champagne and looked around the room at the guests who were milling between glass display cabinets admiring jewellery presented on black velvet cushions. Discreet lighting added to the ambiance of the room, and the soft hum of muted conversation was barely disturbed by the faint clink of glasses borne on silver trays by the waiters.

He had come a long way from the *favela* in Belo Horizonte, and the mine at Montes Claros. He wondered what his guests would think of him if he revealed that

once he had spent his days underground digging diamonds out of rock. Few people knew the truth of his
background and he preferred to keep it that way. He was
not ashamed of the fact that he had clawed his way out
of poverty, but he was finding it hard enough to be accepted into high society, and it was better that he was
regarded as a man of mystery than a beggar from the
gutter, he thought cynically.

He pictured Sabrina when she had visited his Kensington apartment looking the epitome of elegance in
a black cocktail dress and pearls. In his head he heard
her cool voice crisply informing him that she would not
demean herself to have sex with him. She had forgotten
her high ideals when he had kissed her at the stables
earlier today. His body tightened involuntarily as he
remembered her soft moans of pleasure when he had
flicked his tongue across her turgid nipples. When he
had tumbled her down in the hay she had lost her airs
and graces and turned into the sensual wildcat she had
been in Brazil.

He shifted his position in an effort to ease the nagging ache in his groin and cursed his impatience that
had made him come on to her with an embarrassing lack
of finesse instead of his usual laid-back charm. *Why
was he even bothering to pursue her?* he asked himself.
At least half the women at the party were sending him
signals that they were available and he knew he could
have any one of them in his bed with minimum effort
on his part. But the only woman he wanted was not
here and he could only look forward to another night
of sexual frustration.

A ripple of activity over by the door caught his attention and he assumed a guest had arrived late to the

party. He could not see past the burly bodyguard, but inexplicably he felt the hairs on the back of his neck prickle.

For some reason, the proverb 'clothes maketh the man' slipped into Sabrina's mind, but it was a new dress that was making this particular woman feel slightly more confident—and at this moment she needed all the self-confidence she could get!

Strictly speaking, the midnight-blue silk crepe gown with narrow diamanté shoulder straps wasn't new. She had bought it last year when she had still been able to afford to buy haute couture but had never had the opportunity to wear it until now. As she entered the main salon of Delgado Diamonds' opulent Mayfair store she breathed a sigh of relief that her name had been on the guest list and she had avoided an argument with the security guard, or, even worse, the humiliation of being escorted from the premises.

Although that could happen if Cruz had decided to withdraw his offer of financial assistance for Eversleigh Hall in return for her agreement to be his mistress. The gold clock on the wall told her that it was an hour past the deadline of seven p.m. that Cruz had given her.

He was standing at the far end of the salon and the enigmatic expression on his chiselled features gave no clue to his thoughts. Taking a deep breath, Sabrina sauntered towards him, but her heart was thudding in her chest and she fought an urge to run back out to the street away from Cruz's cynical gaze and the curious glances from the other party guests.

She forced herself to keep walking forwards, conscious that the click of her stiletto heels on the marble floor sounded overly loud in the silence that had settled over the room. Her eyes darted to either side of her and she recognised several arts correspondents from national newspapers who were presumably here to report on the party. If Cruz publicly rejected her the whole country would be able to read about it.

Instead of dwelling on that potentially embarrassing scenario she focused on him. He was devastating in a formal black dinner suit and a snow-white shirt that contrasted with his darkly tanned face and throat. She halted in front of him and forgot every word of the speech she had rehearsed on the way here.

Cruz's eyes were hooded as if he wished to hide his thoughts from her, but the rigid set of his jaw betrayed his tension. Sabrina felt the fierce pull of attraction between them and exhilaration swept through her. Words were unnecessary, she decided as she stepped closer to him, so close that their hips touched and her body burned in his heat.

Despite her three-inch heels she had to go up on tiptoe to wind her arms around his neck and pull his head down level with hers. She felt his shoulder muscles clench as she covered his mouth with hers and kissed him.

At first he did not respond and she felt a rising sense of panic as she acknowledged that she was going to look very foolish if he pushed her away and called the security guards to escort her from the building. In desperation she nipped his lower lip with her teeth and a violent shudder ran through him. She was startled, her lashes flew open and she saw a feral hunger in his eyes as he took control and stole her breath with a kiss that plundered her soul.

He kissed her fiercely, feverishly, as if for the past ten years he had missed her as much as she had missed him. He roamed his hands up and down her spine, seemingly unconcerned by the fact that they were making a very public spectacle, and as Sabrina sank deeper into the velvet darkness of desire she lost all awareness of her surroundings and there was only Cruz.

When at last he lifted his mouth from hers she swayed on her feet and stared at him dazedly, unaware of the storm of emotions that darkened her eyes to the colour of wet slate.

'You're late,' he drawled. Sabrina knew he was not referring to her late arrival at the party. How could he sound so cool and seem so unaffected? she wondered as she soothed her ravaged lips with the tip of her tongue. It would be easy to feel overawed by him as she had been ten years ago, but she was no longer an innocent girl and her mouth curved into a sensual smile.

'But worth waiting for,' she murmured.

'I'll hold you to that promise later tonight.' He spoke softly so that the journalists who had crowded around them did not hear him, but Sabrina heard the warning in his words and for a moment her nerve nearly failed her as she faced up to the fact that she had sold her body and possibly her soul to a man who ten years ago had stolen her heart.

Triumph surged through Cruz as he ran his eyes over Sabrina. She looked stunning and desire flooded hot and fierce through his veins. The launch party of Delgado Diamonds represented the pinnacle of his success, but he felt frustrated knowing that it would be several hours before he would be free from his responsibilities and could take her to bed.

He liked the fact that she had developed from a shy teenager who had been a virgin when they'd met ten years ago into a sexually confident woman with the self-assurance to come on to him. But when he studied her closely he saw a vulnerable expression in her eyes and noticed the almost imperceptible tremor of her lower lip that caused him to feel a faint pang of regret.

Ten years ago she had broken his heart, and with a sudden, uncomfortable flash of insight he recognised that he had given her the ultimatum because he wanted to punish her for leaving him. What kind of man planned to use sex as a means of retribution? he asked himself with self-contempt. The past no longer mattered. He felt no emotional connection to Sabrina now, and he would never again confuse lust with love. His attraction to her was purely sexual, as he assumed hers was to him. There was no reason why they should not enjoy a physical relationship and in six months he would walk away from her, his sexual hunger sated, and hopefully with the map in his possession. He was jerked from his introspection when one of the journalists spoke.

'Lady Sabrina, can you confirm that you are in a relationship with Mr Delgado?'

Sabrina tore her eyes from Cruz, wishing she knew what he was thinking behind his shuttered expression. She glanced at the reporter. 'I thought I just did,' she said drily.

It was inevitable that pictures of them locked in a passionate kiss would feature in many of tomorrow's papers. There was a ripple of laughter and she became aware of her surroundings once more: guests dressed in formal evening clothes, white-jacketed waiters serving canapés on silver platters, a buzz of conversation as the party resumed.

She had attended countless such events and felt on familiar ground as Cruz guided her around the room and introduced her to the other guests. She was acquainted with many of them. Cruz was right to think that the English aristocracy was a tightly knit group, partly because historically marriages between the landed gentry had been encouraged. At least two of the guests were Sabrina's distant cousins.

She found herself relaxing as she sipped champagne and chatted about a new art gallery that had opened in Chelsea and the excellent production of *La Traviata* at the Royal Opera House. Cruz revealed a broad knowledge of the arts and current affairs and Sabrina noted that he cleverly steered every topic of conversation around to his jewellery company.

She was continually aware of his presence by her side, of his hand placed lightly in the small of her back that seemed to burn through her dress and scorch her skin. As the evening drew to an end and the guests started to leave the party her tension grew, and on the short drive to Kensington in Cruz's chauffeur-driven limousine her silence earned a comment from him.

'You're very quiet suddenly.'

She chewed her lip. 'I suppose you are wondering why I changed my mind about…' She struggled to continue as the reality that she had agreed to have sex with him for one and a half million pounds sank into her brain.

'About selling yourself to me,' Cruz drawled. He

shrugged. 'It's not a mystery. I knew you would do anything to save your beloved Eversleigh Hall—' his tone hardened '—even if it means having to demean yourself by sleeping with me.'

'I'll pay you back the money as soon as my father returns. And if he doesn't…' her voice faltered '…if he is declared dead I will be given access to his bank accounts and I'll be able to reimburse you out of my inheritance.'

She stared at the angles of Cruz's sculpted profile illuminated by the street lamps and felt as though she were looking at a stranger. 'Saving Eversleigh wasn't my only reason,' she said huskily. 'Meeting you again has made me realise that there are unresolved issues between us from ten years ago. There are things we need to talk about, in particular how we both felt after I miscarried our baby…' she hesitated '…and how we feel about each other now.'

'I've told you how I feel.' Cruz sounded bored of the conversation. 'I want to have sex with you and I am prepared to pay for the privilege of having you as my mistress for the next six months.' His glittering gaze pierced the shadowy darkness of the interior of the car and raked across Sabrina's pale face. 'We made a business deal,' he reminded her. 'What happened between us in the past is irrelevant.'

'What about the future?' she asked in a low voice.

He frowned. 'If you are asking me if we might have a future, then my answer is a categorical no. I'm not looking for a long-term relationship with you or anyone else.'

Until two minutes ago Sabrina's thoughts had been focused on the night ahead. She hadn't cared about the future—at least that was what she had convinced herself. But Cruz's unequivocal statement that he would not want a relationship with her beyond her six-month stint as his mistress was unexpectedly hurtful. Of course there was no possibility that she would fall in love with him, she told herself firmly. She had been there, done that and her heart bore the scars.

The car pulled into the underground car park, and as Cruz ushered her into the lift she felt a rising sense of panic that maybe she was making the biggest mistake of her life. She debated telling him that she had changed her mind and could not go through with their *business deal.*

She had to do whatever it took to safeguard Eversleigh for future generations of the Bancroft family, whispered the voice of her conscience. And her brother's future career as a pilot was dependent on her being able to raise the aviation school's fees.

While the lift made its smooth ascent to the top floor she could not tear her eyes from Cruz. He had undone his bow tie and the top few buttons of his shirt and she could see a sprinkling of black hairs that she knew covered his chest and arrowed down over his flat stomach. Her mouth felt suddenly dry as she pictured the fuzz of body hair running below the waistband of his trousers and becoming thicker around the base of his manhood.

The light-headed feeling she was experiencing had nothing to do with the one glass of champagne she'd had at the party, she acknowledged ruefully. Her body felt as though she were on fire and the core of her need was centred low in her pelvis. She tried convincing herself that the reason she was so intensely turned on was because she hadn't had sex for two years—and that one occasion, with a guy she had dated for a few months, had been unfulfilling. But as her eyes moved back up Cruz's lean, hard body and connected with his sultry gaze she knew she was kidding herself.

She wanted him more than she had ever wanted anyone or anything in her life.

She had not come to him for the sake of Eversleigh or her brother's career or from a sense of duty to protect her family's long history. For the first time in her life she was choosing to put her needs first and the sense of freedom she felt was wildly exhilarating.

Cruz's sexy mouth promised heaven and she instinctively moistened her lips with the tip of her tongue as she imagined him kissing her. The lift halted and the doors opened directly into his penthouse apartment.

'If you've changed your mind, say so now,' he advised.

Her heart was thudding unevenly, but she said steadily, 'I haven't changed my mind.'

To her surprise she saw dull colour flare along his cheekbones, and she suddenly realised that he wasn't as in control as he wanted her to think.

'Then come here.'

She went unhesitatingly, and he swept her up into his arms and strode purposefully down the hallway of the apartment into the master bedroom.

CHAPTER EIGHT

HE KNEW WHY Sabrina was here, Cruz reminded himself. She would do anything to safeguard her family's ancestral home and as she couldn't sell him the Estrela Vermelha she was prepared to sell him her body. He felt an unexpected flicker of regret that he'd had to coerce her into being his mistress, but his common sense told him it was better to have a business arrangement that negated the risk of emotions becoming involved.

In the car she had said that she wanted them to talk about their past relationship. Why did women always want to discuss their emotions and everyone else's? he thought irritably. Sabrina had not been interested in his emotions ten years ago. She had rushed back to England and left him alone to grieve for their baby, and she hadn't spared him a second thought.

Talking was definitely not on his agenda, Cruz decided. Mindless sex without emotional baggage was a far better option, which would allow him to stay in control. A control that was already being tested, he realised, aware that he was harder than he could ever remember being as he set Sabrina on her feet and her breasts brushed against his chest. He had planned on a slow, skilful seduction intended to drive her to the brink so that she begged for his possession.

His pride still stung when he remembered her telling him that she would not demean herself by having sex with him. He wanted to show her that she was just another blonde in his bed. But he had never felt this hungry for any other woman, he acknowledged grimly.

His heart had given a peculiar lurch when she'd arrived at the party dressed to kill in a gown that looked as if she had been poured into it and with her hair flowing like a river of pale gold silk down her back. All evening he'd felt an ache of anticipation in his gut. But now that the moment was here, *Deus*, he felt like a teenager on a first date. He wanted to please her, he wanted sex to be perfect for her—he wanted to show her what she had been missing all these years since she left him.

The subtle fragrance of her perfume teased his senses and he felt an almost painful tug of desire in his groin. He needed to take control before he succumbed to his primitive instincts and took her hard and fast as his body was clamouring to do.

Her lips were slightly parted as if she was expecting him to kiss her, as if she wanted him to. He resisted and walked over to the bed, quickly stripping down to his underwear before he stretched out on top of the satin bedspread and propped himself up on one elbow.

'You look very beautiful in that dress, but I want to see you naked. Take it off,' he commanded.

Sabrina's stomach muscles clenched as she stared at Cruz's handsome face and then dropped her gaze to his bare chest covered in whorls of dark hairs. Her attention was drawn lower to the very obvious bulge beneath his boxer shorts. He was gorgeous! She could not take her eyes from the outline of his massive arousal and she felt a flicker of doubt, knowing she'd not had sex for a long time. She hoped he would take things slowly, but the molten sensation between her thighs was proof that her body was way ahead of her and was already preparing to accommodate him.

She wished he'd held her in his arms and undressed her, but he was paying her a lot of money to please him, she thought ruefully as she reached behind her to unzip her dress and drew the shoulder straps down her arms. The dark blue silk pooled at her feet and her body burned as Cruz ran his eyes over her sheer black lace strapless bra and matching knickers.

'Very pretty,' he murmured. 'Did you choose your sexy underwear for me, *gatinha*?'

She thought of denying it, but what would be the point? Her mind flew back to a few hours earlier when she had made her preparations to become Cruz's mistress. After soaking in a bath scented with fragrant oil, she had smoothed moisturiser onto every inch of her skin before dressing in exquisite lingerie.

'Of course,' she told him in a husky voice that she barely recognised as her own.

The sound of his swiftly indrawn breath made her feel powerful in a way that she had never experienced before. Tonight she wasn't Sabrina the serious historian, or Sabrina the dutiful daughter. She was a temptress, desired above all other women by the sexiest man on the planet.

'I always sleep naked, and while you are my mistress I expect you to do the same,' Cruz drawled. 'Take your bra off.'

She sensed a power struggle between them and rebellion flared inside her as she looked at him sprawled
on the bed like a sultan who had commanded his favourite concubine to pleasure him. But there was no escaping the truth that she had sold herself to him. Pride
whipped her head up. If he wanted a whore he would
damn well get one!

She deliberately held his gaze as once again she
reached behind her and unfastened her bra. The cups
fell away to reveal her firm breasts adorned with dusky
pink tips.

'Very pretty,' he repeated, but this time his voice was
husky with need and his Brazilian accent was as sensual as molten chocolate. 'We made an arrangement, Sabrina, and earlier tonight one and a half million pounds
was transferred into your bank account. Now it's your
turn to fulfil your side of the deal.'

She wondered if he was deliberately trying to make
her feel like a tramp. But she discovered that she did not
care. She wanted him so badly that her body throbbed
with a deep drumbeat that pulsed insistently between
her legs, and her desire intensified when he slipped off
his boxers and revealed the swollen length of his manhood. The sight of his potent virility made her feel weak
with longing.

Cruz settled himself comfortably against the pillows
and folded his arms behind his head. He trailed his eyes
over Sabrina's delectable body. Her lace knickers were
provocative rather than practical and barely covered the
triangle of downy blonde hair at the top of her thighs.

'I want to see *all* of you,' he ordered.

Sabrina felt no embarrassment as she stripped for
him. The feral glitter in his eyes made her feel intensely

desirable and she hooked her fingers in the top of her panties and pulled them slowly down her legs, revealing herself to him inch by inch and almost purring with feline pleasure when he gave an audible groan. She knew she looked good. Her body was toned, with a slender waist and full, rounded breasts that jutted proudly forwards.

Her eyes didn't leave his as she sauntered round to the empty side of the bed. A spark of rebelliousness prompted her to ask coolly, 'Is there a particular position you want me to adopt?'

'Don't push your luck, *gatinha*.' Cruz watched her lie down beside him. 'You look like a vestal virgin preparing to offer yourself up for sacrifice,' he mocked. 'We can start with the missionary position by all means. But you will have to open your legs—or I'll do it for you,' he warned softly when she did not move.

'Cruz…' She choked out his name, appalled that it seemed he really did intend to take her body without finesse, but she was even more appalled by the searing lust that swept through her at the prospect of surrendering herself so utterly to his possession.

Casting a fulminating look at his hard-boned face, she spread her legs a little.

'Wider.'

She hesitated fractionally before obeying him. With her legs now open in a vee shape she felt exposed and she smelled the sweet musk of her arousal and knew Cruz could smell it too. Her heart was beating unevenly, but deep down a part of her revelled in his masterful commands. She didn't want to think, or question her decision to sell herself to him. She was tired of responsibility and duty and always trying to do the right thing

for other people and she wanted Cruz to take charge
and give her hot, hard sex.

She wished he would roll on top of her and penetrate
her with his powerful erection. She wanted him to touch
her intimately and probe her with his fingers, and she
instinctively arched her hips in mute supplication.

He laughed softly. 'Patience, *gatinha*. Anticipation
is part of the pleasure, don't you think?' She made an
inarticulate sound and he laughed again and unfolded
her hands from her breasts before he bent his head and
lazily flicked his tongue across one pink nipple so that
it swelled and tightened. He repeated the action to her
other nipple and drew the hard tip into his mouth, eliciting a husky moan from her.

Triumph surged through Cruz. Sabrina's response
was exactly what he intended. His jaw hardened. She
might find having sex with him demeaning, but she
wanted him all the same.

He continued to play with her nipples, suckling each
in turn while at the same time rolling the other between
his fingers and eliciting helpless little whimpers from
her. Oh, yes, she wanted him. He lifted his head and
looked down at her flushed face. Her eyes were wide,
her pupils dilated as she silently implored him.

It pleased him that she was so desperate. From the
moment he had seen Sabrina again at Eversleigh Hall
he had planned his revenge, and discovering that she
had financial problems had given him the leverage to
force her into his bed. Cruz suddenly felt sickened by
himself. What the hell had he been thinking? He would
never force a woman to do anything against her will.
But he was not forcing Sabrina, he reminded himself.
She was here of her own free choice and she had made

it clear that she was prepared to have sex with him to safeguard her home.

'Cruz.' She murmured his name like a prayer, and the pleading note in her voice touched something deep inside him.

'Is this what you want, *querida*?' he whispered against her lips as he trailed his hand over her stomach and thighs that were parted for him, and slid a finger into her silken folds.

Her reaction was instant. She jerked her hips upwards, offering her body to him and giving a guttural cry as he pushed deeper inside her.

'Yes…*oh*…yes.'

Sabrina almost came when Cruz finally touched her where she desperately wanted him to. She was so wet for him that foreplay was unnecessary. She wanted him inside her now, *now…*

She gave a sob of frustration when he withdrew his finger but her momentary panic that he was enjoying teasing her faded as she watched him rip open a condom packet and deftly sheath himself. His eyes glittered with purpose and something else she could not define. Cruz wanted emotionless sex, she reminded herself. So it could not have been regret that she'd glimpsed in his olive-green depths. It must have been the shadow cast by the bedside lamp. Her thoughts scattered as he leaned over her and kissed her mouth passionately but with an unexpected tenderness that completely unravelled her.

He was Cruz, her Cruz, and she had missed him so much. With a soft sigh she stroked his cheek and moved her hand up to run her fingers through his springy black hair while he took the kiss even deeper, drugging her senses with his sensual exploration of her lips.

He kept his mouth on hers as he positioned himself over her, and she instinctively bent her knees as he pressed forwards and entered her with a powerful thrust that drove the breath from her lungs. He felt the slight resistance of her body and paused, his voice thick with remorse as he muttered, 'Did I hurt you?'

'No.' Sabrina forced herself to relax, allowing her internal muscles to stretch around him. 'It's been a while since I last did this,' she admitted with faint embarrassment in her voice. Feeling him begin to withdraw, she clutched his shoulders and urged him down onto her. 'Don't stop.'

Cruz had no intention of stopping. Sabrina's confession that there had been no other man in her life recently had decimated the last vestiges of his restraint, and he groaned and thrust into her again, driven by an intensity of need that shocked him because it was utterly beyond his control. It was just sex, he reminded himself. Very, very good sex—but he had known it would be. The sexual connection he felt with Sabrina went beyond anything he'd felt for any other woman. He set a rhythm that she quickly matched, and with deep, measured strokes he reclaimed her and possessed her utterly.

He felt the first ripples of her orgasm and heard her gasp as the spasms grew stronger and her muscles clenched around him, inciting him to increase his pace as he drove them both higher. Cruz's sole aim was to ensure her pleasure, and he tormented her nipples with his tongue, lapping each swollen peak in turn until she suddenly gave a cry and arched like a bow beneath him.

For a few seconds he held her at the edge, testing the limits of his self-control, and then drove into her again, deeper and harder, and felt the explosion of her

climax. She wrapped her legs around his back and her
fingers gripped his buttocks. The sensation of her fingernails raking across his flesh was beyond his endurance. Pleasure surged through him in an unstoppable
force, causing him to lose control spectacularly. Eyes
closed, his head thrown back so that the cords in his
neck strained, his groan was wrenched from his soul
as his body shuddered with the exquisite ecstasy of
sexual release.

For a long time afterwards neither of them moved.
Sabrina felt Cruz's heart echo the jerky rhythm of her
own thunderous pulse as she held him tightly to her. She
breathed in the sweet musk of his sweat-sheened skin,
loving the warmth of his body and the weight of him
pressing her into the mattress. She could have stayed
like that, joined with him, for ever. But then he rolled
off her without saying a word.

His silence stretched her nerves. She felt hot all over
as she replayed her wanton response to him in her mind.
Perhaps he was shocked by her shameless enjoyment
of sex, unaware that she had only ever behaved with
such wild abandon with him? She remembered the deal
they had made. He was paying her for sex but perhaps
he thought that *she* should pay *him* for servicing her so
thoroughly? She risked glancing at him and discovered
that he had fallen asleep.

He looked younger and the grooves at the sides of
his mouth had disappeared. His dark lashes fanned on
his cheeks and his black hair fell across his brow so
that Sabrina longed to run her fingers through its silky
thickness. In his relaxed state he looked like the younger
man she had known ten years ago and she wondered
how she had ever had the strength back then to have left

him. The painful truth was that he had not loved her and it had been that certainty that had sent her rushing back to Eversleigh, she thought bleakly.

Nothing had changed. He did not love her now. But he had gone to great lengths to make her his mistress despite the fact that he could have any woman he wanted without having to fork out one and a half million pounds. She had been half amused, half irritated at the way the majority of the female guests at the party had openly flirted with him. But Cruz had only had eyes for her, and when he had made love to her just now his primitive hunger had thrilled her because she had known he was powerless to resist the blazing sexual chemistry that sizzled whenever they were near each other.

She bit her lip. At eighteen she had been too young and unsure of herself and too devastated by the miscarriage to fight for him. But making love with him just now had shown her that she still had feelings for him and that maybe—her heart jolted as she tested a startling idea—maybe she had never fallen out of love with him.

So why not fight for him? She would not be the first woman in history to use sex as a way to a man's heart; she thought of her ancestor Henrietta Bancroft who had been the king's mistress.

Her strongest weapon was Cruz's desire for her, but he had insisted that he wanted sex without emotion so that was what she would let him think he was getting. Dared she go through with her plan knowing that six months from now he might walk away from her and break her heart? Her heart had been doomed from the minute he had turned up at Eversleigh Hall, she thought ruefully. If nothing else, she would have six months of amazing sex to remember him by.

The sound of his regular breaths reminded her of when they had been lovers in Brazil and she had lain awake watching him while he slept. She gave in to the temptation to trace her forefinger lightly over his mouth and when he did not stir she moved her hand lower to his chest, following the path of dark hairs that arrowed over his stomach. He took a deeper breath, and she held hers, but he remained asleep and after a moment she continued her exploration, carefully lifting the sheet away from his hips.

He was still semi-aroused, and even in that state the size of his manhood made her breath catch. He was so beautiful, his body honed to perfection and powerfully muscular. Utterly absorbed in her study of him, she could not resist running her fingers over the proud tip of his penis.

His response—to full, hard arousal—was immediate.

'*Deus*, Sabrina, I hope you are prepared to finish what you've started,' Cruz growled.

Her smile made his gut clench. She was an evocative mix of seductive minx and curious innocence that reminded him of the virginal eighteen-year-old who had gifted him with her maidenhood. His thoughts became focused on what she was doing with her hands and he drew a sharp breath when he watched her open a condom and roll it over his throbbing erection.

'I'm prepared, and now so are you,' she murmured. She sat astride him and leaned forwards so that her long blonde hair tumbled in a silken curtain over his chest. 'What is your wish, master?' she said in a teasing voice.

Evidently she had decided to enact the role of concubine. Cruz knew he should respond in the same light
tone and join in with her game, but he couldn't. Desire was a ravenous beast inside him that demanded
appeasement. How could he be this desperate for her
so soon after he'd had sex with her the first time? He
despised himself for his inability to resist her, but she
leaned further forwards and deliberately stroked her
nipples across his chest, and he felt the pressure building inside him until he feared he would explode.

'Kiss me,' he ordered harshly.

When she complied he took her lips, took everything
she offered and claimed possession, driving his tongue
into her mouth to elicit a sensual exploration that he
sensed shocked her with its blatant eroticism. He slid his
hands down her spine and shaped the twin globes of her
buttocks before he gripped her hips, lifted her high and
brought her down onto his erection so that she gasped
as her vaginal muscles stretched to accommodate him.

He knew she was surprised by his barely leashed
savagery but she did not falter as he encouraged her to
ride him. She quickly learned the rhythm he set and the
expression on her face became intent as she absorbed
thrust after devastating thrust of his solid shaft into
her velvet heat.

Faster, faster, Cruz gritted his teeth as he fought to
control the primitive urges of his body. He needed her
to come now before this went spectacularly wrong, and
he was relieved when she gave a sudden sharp cry and
he felt her convulse around him. His relief was short-
lived as with a sense of disbelief he realised that he
could not stop his own release. With a muffled oath
he reversed their positions and rolled her beneath him,

gave one final, powerful thrust and was hit by a tidal wave of pleasure that went on and on as his seed flooded out of him.

Last night had not been his finest hour, Cruz brooded the following morning. He sat down at the breakfast table but had no appetite for food as his mind replayed his total and humiliating loss of control caused by Sabrina's witchery. He did not understand why she affected him so strongly. With every other woman he'd had sex with he had never had a problem curbing his desire. He could make love for hours, and there had been many occasions when his brain had been occupied with his latest business project while he had gone through the motions of assuring whichever woman was in his bed that she was amazing.

His temper did not improve when Sabrina strolled into the room wearing a short black silk robe that barely covered her thighs. Last night he had ordered her to strip naked and the memory of how she had enjoyed playing the sexual tease evoked a heated sensation in Cruz's groin. She had turned into a wildcat in his arms, but this morning she was a picture of refinement with her blonde hair caught in a knot on top of her head, revealing the slender column of her elegant neck.

As she sat down opposite him at the table he made a show of glancing at his watch. 'Good morning. Although it's nearly afternoon.' It was an exaggeration but he was irritated that she had evidently had no problem sleeping, while he had stayed awake for most of the night trying to comprehend his craven weakness for her. 'I was about to come and wake you.'

She shrugged. 'I had a bath.'

And she smelled heavenly. Cruz inhaled a waft of rose-scented bath oil and body lotion that she had used to moisturise her skin, and felt a certain part of his anatomy spring to life. 'Would you like coffee?'

'I'd prefer Earl Grey tea if you have it.'

He poured her a cup of anaemic-looking liquid before helping himself to strong black coffee. 'I suppose you are used to a privileged lifestyle where you can get up at whatever time you like instead of having to join the morning commute to a job,' he said tersely.

'Actually my alarm goes off at six a.m. at home. I lecture at a university on two days a week, and if I am commissioned to work on a restoration project I have to travel to London or further afield to a museum or stately home.'

Sabrina frowned. 'I certainly don't swan around at Eversleigh Hall playing the lady of the manor. Running the estate takes up a lot of my time, and anyway I have to get up early to exercise Monty.' Her heart gave a pang as she remembered that her horse would have been collected by his new owner and the stables at Eversleigh would be empty.

Cruz's voice drew her attention back to him and she thought how mouth-wateringly sexy he looked with the top buttons of his shirt open and a shadow of dark stubble on his jaw. Her breasts were a little sore this morning from where his rough jaw had scraped her skin. She forced herself to concentrate on what he was saying.

'When I checked my emails this morning I opened several invitations to social functions addressed to both of us.' Cruz's mouth curled into a cynical smile. 'Many of the newspapers have reported on our romantic liaison, and it would appear that your links with the aristocracy are working in my favour. Perhaps I should marry you,' he said sardonically. 'Having a high-class wife would clearly offer me even more benefits and business opportunities.'

Sabrina's heart missed a beat but her outward response was to raise her finely arched brows. 'I assume you are joking,' she replied in her cultured voice that made Cruz long to ruffle her *sangfroid*.

He watched her take a ripe peach from the fruit bowl and cut it into slivers with a silver knife before she bit into a slice with her perfect white teeth. Juice trickled down her chin and she licked the syrupy liquid with the tip of her tongue. Cruz felt sweat on his brow. *Deus!* Was she deliberately trying to turn him on? He took a gulp of coffee, forgetting that he had just poured it and it was scalding hot. The shock of burning at the back of his throat caused him to jolt and he spilt coffee down the front of his shirt. He swore beneath his breath.

'I know what your reply would be if I had made a serious proposal of marriage,' he said grimly. 'You would turn me down just as you did ten years ago.' His eyes narrowed on her face. 'Or would you?' he mused aloud. 'You didn't want to marry me when I was poor, but now that I am a multimillionaire perhaps you would consider me a better catch. Why settle for one and a half million pounds when, if you were my wife, you could get your claws on my entire fortune?'

Sabrina pushed her half-eaten peach away. For some reason Cruz was being deliberately insulting. She did not know why he was in a foul mood, but perhaps he had tired of her already and was regretting paying her to be his mistress. She knew full well that he hadn't been serious about wanting to marry her.

'Your lack of money wasn't the reason I turned you down. *It wasn't,*' she insisted when he gave a disbelieving laugh. 'It was because you had asked me to marry you for the wrong reason.'

'You were expecting my baby.'

'Exactly. You wanted your child, not me.'

'Deus.' He slammed his hand down on the table. 'We both had a duty to do the best for our child.'

'I don't believe a shotgun wedding is in the best interests of a child, and I should know because I am the product of such a marriage. Most of the time, my parents couldn't even be civil to one another.'

'You were eighteen, I'd got you pregnant through my carelessness the one occasion I failed to use protection and I was trying to do the right thing,' Cruz said frustratedly. 'Why don't you be honest and admit that you felt trapped when you fell pregnant?'

'I did not resent my pregnancy,' Sabrina insisted. 'But it changed things between us. You were angry that I refused to marry you, and you stopped making love to me, I assumed because you found my pregnancy a turn-off.'

'It wasn't that.' Cruz was stunned by Sabrina's revelation. He recalled the nights when he had lain next to her in his small bed at his parents' cottage and fought his overwhelming desire to make love to her. 'My mother had explained that it wasn't safe for us to have sex once you were pregnant.'

Sabrina remembered that Cruz had said his mother had suffered numerous miscarriages, which might have made her believe in the old wives' tale. 'Pregnancy is not an illness. Millions of women continue with their ordinary daily activities during pregnancy, including having sex. If you had talked to me rather than your mother we might have avoided many of the misunderstandings that came between us,' she said bitterly. 'Don't you think it's ironic that we are finally talking about our relationship ten years after it ended?'

She jumped up from the table and marched into the adjoining bedroom, feeling frustrated that so much had been unsaid between them ten years ago. But perhaps if she had stayed in Brazil instead of rushing back to Eversleigh Hall they might have stood a chance of resolving their differences. In hindsight she could see that she had been as much to blame as Cruz for the breakdown in communication between them.

She heard him follow her into the bedroom. 'Talking wasn't part of our relationship, was it?' She sighed. 'The truth is that we barely knew each other when I became pregnant. Up until then we had just had sex, a lot of sex, but sex wasn't enough to build a relationship on ten years ago and it isn't enough now.'

'Well, fortunately I don't want to build a relationship.'

Something in Cruz's tone sent a ripple of warning down Sabrina's spine and she glanced over at him to see him shrug out of his coffee-stained shirt and screw it into a ball.

Sabrina had almost sounded convincing when she had said that the reason she had refused to marry him was because she had been affected by her parents' unhappy marriage, Cruz brooded. But he knew it wasn't the truth. He was convinced that she had rejected him because he had not been rich and successful. She had decided that he was not good enough for her and she had made him feel that his love wasn't good enough.

It seemed to be a recurring theme, he thought grimly. He had adored his father, but deep in his heart he felt that Vitor had cared more about finding a flawless diamond than he'd cared about his family. Although Cruz blamed Earl Bancroft for his father's accident, the painful truth was that Vitor's obsession with diamonds had contributed to his death. Cruz had been left to care for his mother and sisters, and he had tried, *Deus*, he had tried so hard to comfort his mother. But she had been inconsolable, and once again Cruz had felt that whatever he did and however hard he worked to support his family, it was not enough to lift his mother from her grief.

His jaw hardened. Sabrina had ripped his heart out when she had left him years ago, but there was no chance that she would hurt him again.

'When you lost the baby it gave you the excuse to return to your precious Eversleigh Hall and a luxurious lifestyle that you were never going to have with a miner from a *favela*,' he accused her harshly. 'Ten years ago you thought that all I was good enough for was sex. Now our situations are reversed and all I want from you is sex, a lot of sex,' he mimicked her words. 'That's what I paid you for.'

Sabrina's eyes clashed with his glittering gaze as she watched him walk towards her. 'What do you think you're doing?' It was a stupid question, she acknowledged. Cruz's sculpted features had hardened with sexual intent that sent a quiver of anticipation through her. It had been the same when they had first met in Brazil, she thought ruefully. They had ripped each other's clothes off at every opportunity and had explosive sex.

'Cruz…' She held out her hand as if to ward him off, but she knew as well as he did that it was a token protest. Excitement licked like wildfire through her veins as he unbuckled his belt and in a few deft movements rid himself of his trousers, shoes and socks and lastly the black silk boxers that had been unable to disguise his powerful erection.

He flicked open the belt of her robe, stripped her and scooped her into his arms. In two strides he reached the bed and dropped her onto the mattress. She really could not let him dominate her like this, Sabrina told herself, but he thwarted her attempt to slide across the bed by pushing her flat on her back and with firm hands took hold of her ankles, hooking her legs over his shoulders.

'I'm not interested in the past,' he told her. 'All I'm interested in is finding the map of the diamond mine that I'm sure your father hid somewhere in Eversleigh Hall. You sold yourself to me and I will hold you to your agreement to be my mistress for six months, whether you like it or not.' He smiled down at her flushed face. 'But you do like it, don't you, *gatinha*? From your response to me last night I bet you have never found another man who can satisfy you like I can.'

Sabrina wanted to deny his arrogant boast, but she couldn't, damn him. Desire coiled in the pit of her stomach and she arched her hips as he lowered his mouth to her feminine heart. His warm breath stirred the tight blonde curls between her thighs and she shuddered with longing. But he made her wait with her legs spread wide, waiting for him to run his tongue up and down her moist opening before he finally gave in to her husky plea and bestowed a shockingly intimate caress that drove her swiftly to the edge of ecstasy.

He used his fingers to keep her there while he sheathed himself and then he penetrated her with a slow, deep thrust that filled her, completed her. She wrapped her arms around his back as he began to move, driving into her with a steady rhythm that devastated her. Cruz remained in complete control while she writhed and moaned beneath him, and Sabrina, remembering her decision the previous night to fight for him and try to win his heart, wondered despairingly if he even had a heart.

CHAPTER NINE

THEY DROVE TO Eversleigh Hall that afternoon. Sabrina remained silent for the journey, feeling mortified as she remembered how she had lost all her inhibitions and come apart utterly when Cruz had made love to her. Thankfully he had headed into the en-suite immediately after he had withdrawn his body from hers and by the time he had emerged after taking a shower she had managed to hide her shattered emotions behind a mask of cool composure.

'I want to start searching for the map immediately,' he told her as they walked into the house. 'We won't be able to spend much time in Surrey because I have work and social commitments in London and various other European cities.'

Sabrina frowned. 'Surely you don't expect me to get involved in your business dealings? Why can't I stay here while you travel abroad?'

'The point of paying you to be my mistress is that you will be available whenever I want you,' he said silkily.

She bristled at his arrogant assumption that he could simply take over her life. 'I thought I had explained that I have a job at the local university, and I also do freelance work restoring antique furniture. My career is important to me and my commitment to my role as a lecturer is non-negotiable.'

'Perhaps I should remind you that you are not in a position to negotiate anything. For the next six months your only commitment is to your role as my mistress. I will also need you to show me the secret hiding places where your father might have put the map.'

She flushed at his reminder that she had sold herself to him. It occurred to her that if the map was found quickly, Cruz would presumably return to his diamond mine in Brazil and hopefully he would leave her in peace. 'I'll give you a tour of the house,' she said coolly, somehow managing to disguise the riot of emotions inside her. 'We'll start in the library.'

Sabrina swept past him, and Cruz cursed beneath his breath. She did not have to look so wounded, damn it. He had given her the means to save her precious stately home so why the hell did he feel so goddamned guilty? He followed her into the library. 'Which days do you work at the university?'

'Tuesdays and Wednesdays, but I didn't work this week because it is a reading week for the students.'

He shrugged. 'Most of our social engagements are at weekends, and it is likely that we will stay at Eversleigh during the week, meaning that you will be able to fulfil your lecturing contract.'

Sabrina shot him a startled look. Cruz almost sounded as though he understood that her career meant a lot to her. It was all she had that alleviated the burden of responsibility she felt for Eversleigh, she thought bleakly. She had a flashback to the first night he had paid an unexpected visit to the hall. When he had kissed her she'd felt as though he had brought her back to life after she had merely existed for the ten years that they had been apart. She suddenly wished that they could have met again simply as two people who were attracted to each other instead of them playing a strange game of blame and revenge.

She walked over to where he was standing by the window and followed his gaze over the immaculately kept gardens and the view of the beautiful Surrey countryside.

'I'm not surprised that you wanted to rush back here rather than live with me in a run-down miner's cottage in Brazil,' he commented. 'It must have been an incredible place to grow up.'

Sabrina was silent for a moment, thinking of her lonely childhood. Cruz believed that her life had been perfect. When they had been lovers he had been sensitive about what he had perceived as the difference in their social status. She wished she could make him understand that having money did not equate to happiness.

'I realise I was lucky to live in a big house and I attended the best schools. But although I had material things, I didn't have what you had.' He gave her a sardonic look and she knew he was thinking that she lived in a luxurious stately home while he had grown up in a Brazilian slum. 'Your parents loved you and made you feel part of a family,' she reminded him. 'My brother and I were mainly cared for by nannies. My father was rarely at Eversleigh, and even before my mother left us she was busy with her own life.'

She moved across the room and slid open one of the wooden wall panels. 'This is a priest hole where Catholic priests used to hide hundreds of years ago when they were persecuted for their faith. Tristan and I called it the choker,' she explained when Cruz put his head inside the cramped, dark space. 'One particularly unkind nanny who came to look after us used to lock us in here as a punishment. When the panel is closed no light can get in. I didn't care so much, but Tristan used to be terrified.'

'Why didn't you tell your parents that the nanny was guilty of physical and mental child cruelty?'

'My mother had moved to France, and my father spent most of his time in Brazil.' Sabrina gave a rueful smile. 'The nanny didn't stay at Eversleigh for long. Tristan put a grass snake in her bed and she left the next day. He did it because the nanny had upset me,' she explained. 'Tris had never seen me cry before. When I was a young child I learned not to show my emotions because my father couldn't abide what he called snivelling and self-pity. But the nanny had said that my mother had moved away because she obviously didn't love me...' her voice faltered '...and I realised it was the truth.'

She shut the panel and looked at Cruz. 'You often point out that I had a privileged upbringing but the reality is that I felt lonely and unloved during my childhood. I never felt a close emotional bond with my parents.'

Cruz was shocked by Sabrina's revelations about her upbringing. The picture she had painted did not match the image he had of her as a spoiled princess who had wanted for nothing and who had believed that he was not good enough for her ten years ago. Was it possible that he had misjudged her? He pushed the unwelcome thought away.

'Am I supposed to feel sorry for you, poor little rich girl?' he mocked. 'In the *favela*, the shack where I lived as a boy had two tiny rooms and no electricity or running water. I never even saw a green space or a flower. The piece of rough ground where I used to play with the other slum kids had an open sewer running next to it, but after a while you get used to the stench,' he said grimly.

His jaw hardened. 'My father worked in the diamond mine because he wanted to earn money to give his family the chance of a better life. But he paid with his own life because your wealthy, privileged father sent him into an area of the mine that he knew was dangerous.'

Sabrina's temper flared. 'You are so sure that my father was responsible for the accident, but he isn't here to defend himself and so I must. I don't believe he would have deliberately put the men who worked in his mine at risk. I admit he wasn't the best father to me and my brother but he was, *is*,' she corrected herself because she had to believe the earl would return to Eversleigh, 'an honourable man. I'm desperately sorry that your father died, but perhaps there is another explanation for his death.'

'What explanation could there be?' Cruz demanded.

'It must be wonderful to have your supreme self-assurance and the belief that only you can be right,' she said bitterly. 'You refuse to listen, and it was the same ten years ago. You were adamant that we should marry when I became pregnant, even though we didn't really know each other.'

Cruz struggled to control his anger. He *knew* she had refused to marry him because he had lacked money or a title and it infuriated him that she could not be honest. 'It was my responsibility to take care of you and our child.'

'The fact that we can't have a discussion without it turning into a row proves that if we *had* married it would have been a disaster. We can't talk to each other,' she said flatly.

'I've always thought that talking was overrated.' The hard gleam in Cruz's eyes as he walked towards her sent a frisson of mingled desire and despair down Sabrina's spine. 'There are far more enjoyable ways in which we can communicate that don't involve talking. The first night I arrived at Eversleigh we both imagined having sex on this desk.'

He began to unbutton his shirt, revealing his hair-roughened chest. Sabrina felt her body's instinctive response and she knew without looking down that her nipples had hardened and were jutting provocatively through her blouse. She closed her eyes to block out his mocking expression.

'Now seems a good time to fulfil at least one of our fantasies,' he drawled.

If he touched her she would be lost, and not just physically, she acknowledged painfully. If he insisted on sex because he had paid for the privilege, his cold cynicism would destroy her fragile defences, and she could not risk him guessing how she felt about him.

Pride and a stubborn determination learned during her childhood, to keep her emotions hidden, brought her chin up. 'I would have thought that your first priority is to find the map of the diamond mine that is so important to you. Anything else,' she said in a faintly bored tone, 'can wait, can't it?'

Did anything touch her? Cruz wondered savagely, aware that every muscle on his body was taut with rampant desire that was humiliatingly out of his control.

Sabrina was the archetypal lady of the manor, crisply elegant in beautifully tailored cream trousers and a pale pink blouse, the pearls at her throat reflecting the translucence of her skin. He knew he could have her bent over the desk and she would be with him all the way. Their sexual compatibility was one thing that had never been in doubt. But her eyes were as dark as storm clouds and he glimpsed a shadow of vulnerability in their grey depths that stopped him from pulling her into his arms.

With an effort he stemmed the hot tide of lust surging through his veins, but curiously as he moved away from her he found himself wishing that he could simply hold her until the shadows in her eyes disappeared.

'As you say, searching for the map is my top priority. In Brazil, Diego is keen to know if we will have to close the diamond mine, or if we can extend operations into a previously abandoned section of the mine that I am convinced exists.'

'How is Diego, these days?' Sabrina seized the opportunity to turn the focus away from the sexual tension that was almost tangible between them.

'Diego is—Diego.' Cruz smiled wryly as he thought of his close friend from the *favela*. One thing he was certain of was that Diego Cazorra would never allow himself to be affected by a woman, however beautiful she might be.

'I thought he owned the diamond mine in partnership with you.'

'Diego is in charge of the day-to-day operating of the mine and I concentrate on selling the diamonds we find on the international market. Three years ago I established Delgado Diamonds, and Diego has several business projects of his own and is a successful gold prospector.' Cruz looked amused. 'The Cazorra philosophy is to work hard and play harder.'

A knock on the door was a welcome interruption and Sabrina turned her attention to the butler. 'The builders have arrived to give a quote on the cost of repairing the fire damage to the annexe, Miss Sabrina,' John informed her.

'I'll come and talk to them,' she murmured and hurried out of the library, flushing hotly as she heard Cruz call after her mockingly.

'We'll wait until later to try out the desk, *gatinha*.'

Another social function—the third that week, Cruz reflected as he fastened the cuff links on his white dinner shirt. Tonight's party was a black-tie event taking place at a five-star hotel not far from Eversleigh Hall. The charity fundraising dinner would be followed by a private fashion show by one of the leading design houses, and the models would be wearing jewellery for the evening provided by Delgado Diamonds.

Business at the new Bond Street store was booming, and, since the launch party a month ago, profits had outstripped all of Cruz's expectations. He knew his very public affair with Sabrina was responsible for the huge media interest, both in them as a couple and in his jewellery company. Sabrina's connections to the British aristocracy had given Cruz acceptance into the most exclusive social circles. And he could have no complaints about the way she was fulfilling the other part of their deal, he acknowledged.

For the past month she had played the role of his mistress faultlessly. She accompanied him to parties elegantly dressed in haute couture, and she was always a charming and interesting companion with a broad knowledge of current affairs and a genuine enthusiasm for her specialist subjects of history and the arts. They either stayed in Kensington or at Eversleigh Hall, although they did not sleep in Sabrina's bedroom.

Cruz had taken one look at the candy-pink walls and the large collection of teddy bears piled on the bed and commented that the room looked as if it had been decorated for a child.

'My mother helped me choose the colour scheme when I was ten,' she had admitted. 'The room reminds me of her, and I don't want to get rid of my bears. After Mum left, they and Tristan were my best friends.'

The image of Sabrina living virtually on her own in the huge house with only a nanny to look after her had evoked a strange tug in Cruz's heart, but he had ignored the unwelcome sensation. He'd chosen another bear-free bedroom for them to share and added a few toys of his own, namely a mirror fitted to the ceiling above the bed, and a pair of diamond-encrusted handcuffs, which he had persuaded Sabrina to wear the first time and she had asked him to use on several occasions since.

Whoever had coined the idiom 'be careful what you wish for' had known what they were talking about, he mused. When Sabrina had agreed to be his mistress he had insisted that all he wanted was sex without emotion—and that was exactly what she gave him every night.

Their enormous four-poster bed at Eversleigh Hall was their sensual playground where they shut out the world and indulged in long hours of lovemaking that left them sated until the morning, when hc would reach across the mattress for her and she would slide into his arms, as hungry for sex as he was.

But afterwards she always moved back to her side of the bed. It was as if there were an invisible barrier between them, and with each passing day, and night, Cruz felt a growing sense of frustration that had nothing to do with his sexual appetite. He found himself wishing that she would remain in his arms after they'd had sex, even though he had always been irritated by previous lovers who had wanted to cuddle and cling to him, or, even worse, wanted him to talk to them.

There were no such problems with Sabrina. She would reply if he initiated conversation, and she was perfectly pleasant and cordial, but her air of detachment made him want to shake a response from her. Even in bed, when her desire matched his and she responded to him with a fervency that drove him to the edge of his sanity, he sensed that she held some part of herself back from him.

He should be pleased, Cruz told himself, that when their business deal ended five months from now and he no longer required her to be his mistress, he would not have to worry that she might make a scene when he walked away from her. In fact, she probably would not even notice that he had gone.

He turned towards the door as she emerged from her dressing room, and the faint tug on his heart became a hard ache. The full-length, strapless evening gown, the colour of deep red wine, fitted her like a glove and showed off her tiny waist while the ruched bodice pushed her breasts high and gave her a deep cleavage that Cruz knew would draw the eyes of every male at the party.

'You look exquisite,' he murmured, hoping she did not hear the raw note of longing in his voice. He picked up a slim leather box from the dressing table and walked over to her. 'I have something for you to wear that I think will suit your dress perfectly.'

Sabrina caught her breath as Cruz opened the lid to reveal a single strand of square-cut diamonds that even though she was no expert she could tell were of exceptional quality. The diamonds glittered with a fiery brilliance as he lifted the necklace out of the box and held it against her skin.

'Turn round and lift up your hair.'

Pleasure shivered through her when she felt his fingers lightly brush against the back of her neck as he fastened the necklace. He looked unbelievably gorgeous in his formal dinner suit and she wished the evening were over and she could undress him slowly, tease him a little so that he promised punishment in return. Perhaps he would order her to lie face down on the pillows and use the diamond handcuffs to secure her hands to the ornate Victorian bedhead. She felt a familiar molten sensation between her legs. Cruz had revealed a depth of sensuality to her nature that she had not known existed and she was certain she would never experience with any other man, she thought bleakly.

'What do you think?'

'What?' She was startled out of her reverie and prayed he had no idea of her wayward thoughts. 'Oh… it's beautiful.' She touched the diamond necklace that circled her throat. 'This must be the loveliest piece in the Delgado collection and I'll enjoy showcasing it for you tonight. I'm sure it will attract plenty of interest from potential buyers at the party.'

'It's not a Delgado piece. I commissioned the necklace using stones from my own personal collection, and it's not for sale, it's a gift for you.'

Her heart gave a jolt. 'I can't possibly accept something so valuable.' She spun round to face him and saw an indefinable emotion briefly cross his sculpted features. 'You have already given me the means to safeguard my home,' she said huskily. 'I don't ask or want for more.'

'You didn't want to save Eversleigh for yourself. You wanted it for your brother, didn't you? I am aware of how titles and estates are passed down the generations of a family through the male line.' Cruz cut her off before she could argue. 'I also discovered from Tristan when he visited last week that he is about to begin the very expensive training course to become a commercial airline pilot. Your brother was under the impression that the course fees were paid out of your father's bank account, but you and I know differently, don't we, *querida*?'

'You didn't tell Tris the truth, did you?' she asked sharply.

'Of course I didn't. But I wish you had been more honest with me. You allowed me to think that you wanted to continue living a life of luxury at Eversleigh Hall, but instead I find that you are responsible for running the house and estate and you do everything from mopping floors to mending farm fences.'

She shrugged. 'What difference would it have made if you had known the situation here? I still needed money to keep the estate solvent until my father returns.' Her grey eyes met his olive-green gaze, and she said quietly, 'There was only one reason why I sold my body to you.'

She meant Eversleigh of course, Cruz told himself. He raked a hand through his hair. 'If I'd known you were offering yourself as a martyr for your family I would have… I don't know…been kinder, more caring.' Dull colour ran under his skin when Sabrina stared at him.

'Caring is an emotion, but all you want from me is sex. You can't change the rules halfway through the game.' She threw her pashmina around her shoulders. 'It's time we were going, or we'll be late.'

Cruz inhaled her perfume, a subtle blend of white orchids and jasmine, as elegantly beautiful as the woman wearing it, and he was tempted to haul her into his arms and tell her that it was his game and he could change the rules whenever he liked. But Sabrina had already stepped into the hallway and she stooped down to scoop a ball of ginger fur into her arms.

'Darling George, I won't be gone for too long,' she crooned to the cat. 'I hope you don't miss me, sweetheart.'

'I'm sure he'll survive on his own for a few hours.' Cruz told himself it was ridiculous to feel jealous of a cat. He and George had come to a truce of sorts, in that he tolerated the cat, and the cat gave him a smug look every time it jumped into Sabrina's lap.

'You are so heartless,' she complained when he firmly closed the door to deny the cat access to the bedroom. 'I love George.'

'Lucky George,' Cruz murmured.

As he followed Sabrina down the stairs he realised that he could not allow this unsatisfactory situation to continue. He had set the rules of their relationship and he could change them, but first he needed to be clear about what he wanted from his infuriatingly aloof mistress.

CHAPTER TEN

IF SOMEONE HAD told him when he had been growing up in the *favela,* forced to search through piles of rotting rubbish for something to eat, that one day he would be bored of champagne and caviar, he would have found it hugely funny, Cruz brooded.

He kept his thoughts to himself and smiled at the silver-haired woman beside him who seemed to have been talking for hours. Lady Aisling's husband had business connections in China, and networking was always useful. The chance to socialise with powerful business leaders was the reason Cruz had coerced Sabrina into being his mistress. One of the reasons, he acknowledged self-derisively as his gaze was drawn to her. She looked stunning in her figure-hugging velvet gown, and she was clearly charming the socks off Lord Aisling.

Sabrina's beautiful face was animated and she exuded an air of warm friendliness that drew people to her. Why did she never smile at him the way she was smiling at Lord Aisling, or the waiter who stopped to offer her a tray of canapés? She showed more affection to her goddamned cat than to him, Cruz thought darkly. But as she had reminded him, emotions were not included in their deal.

Lady Aisling's voice pulled him from his thoughts. 'Charles and I are driving down to Chichester tomorrow to spend a few days on our yacht. Do you have any plans for the bank holiday weekend, Mr Delgado?'

'Actually I've arranged to take Sabrina to my house in Portugal.'

'This is the first time you have mentioned your plans to me, darling,' Sabrina said sweetly while her eyes flashed daggers at Cruz.

'I wanted to surprise you—darling.'

'Oh, you have,' she murmured in a syrupy tone that didn't fool him for a minute.

He deemed it sensible to keep out of her line of fire for the rest of the evening. The party was a lavish affair, the food was divine and the vintage champagne superb, but Cruz could not throw off his black mood. He had everything he had ever dreamed of as a boy: money, several beautiful houses in various parts of the world and, perhaps more important than anything, financial security that enabled him to take care of his mother and sisters. He also currently went to bed every night with a stunning blonde who had proved herself willing to satisfy his every sexual whim, so why the hell wasn't he happy?

'How long do you plan for us to spend in Portugal?' Sabrina demanded after the party had ended and they were travelling back to Eversleigh Hall in the chauffeur-driven Bentley.

'A week or two.'

'A week or *two*! May I remind you that I have a job? My lectures at the university—'

'Have been rescheduled for next month,' Cruz told her blandly. 'I phoned the principal and explained that I needed to arrange for you to have special leave. Mrs Peters thought it was very romantic,' he added drily.

'Presumably you didn't disillusion her and tell her that the only reason you require my presence in Portugal is to provide you with sex?' Sabrina snapped. She felt furious that Cruz thought he owned her, although technically for the next five months he did, she conceded.

At the end of their business arrangement he would walk away from her. The thought hurt more than it had any right to. Each time they made love she found it harder to hide her emotional response to him, but she knew she must, because Cruz was not interested in her emotions. All he wanted from her was convenient sex while he was at Eversleigh to search for the map that had so far proved elusive.

She glanced at his chiselled profile and thought that he did not look particularly happy. Her heart lurched. Had he grown tired of their arrangement and bored of her? He had been in a curious mood all evening, and several times during the party she had caught him looking at her with an unfathomable expression in his eyes.

'Tell me about your parents,' he said unexpectedly. 'You gave the impression that they hated each other.'

It was the first time since she had become his mistress that he had shown any curiosity about her personal life. 'I don't think they felt such a strong emotion as hate,' Sabrina said slowly, 'but they grew to dislike each other intensely. My mother told me that they had only dated a few times when she fell pregnant with me. I was very much an accident, but my grandfather, who was the earl at that time, insisted that my father

married my mother, and threatened to disinherit him if
he refused. My father stood at the altar with a figura-
tive gun aimed at his head. It was hardly a good start,
and the marriage deteriorated rapidly when Dad started
spending most of his time in Brazil.'

'I don't understand how you can compare our situation ten years ago with your parents,' Cruz said harshly.
'No one forced me to propose to you.'

'You only asked me because I was carrying your
baby. There was a good chance that if we had married we would have ended up arguing constantly like
I remember my parents doing, and like we seem to do
now. We don't discuss things,' Sabrina muttered. 'You
lay down the law and expect me to comply. The trip to
Portugal that you've decided on is a prime example of
how you are determined to have your own way and you
ride roughshod over my feelings.'

Cruz raked a hand through his hair. He was unused
to being verbally crucified and he did not like the experience. 'That was not my intention.' Honesty forced
him to acknowledge there was some truth in Sabrina's
words.

'I suppose I might seem controlling sometimes,' he
said grudgingly. 'After my father died I became responsible for my mother and sisters. Graciana and Jacinta
were just ten years old and they missed their *papai* ter-
ribly. My mother crumbled without Vitor. She relied on
me to earn money to keep the family and make all the
decisions about my sisters' upbringing. In effect I became a substitute father to the twins.'

Sabrina reflected that some aspects of their lives
mirrored each other's. 'It was the same for me when

my parents divorced and I felt that I had to take care of my brother,' she admitted.

The car drew up outside Eversleigh Hall and as they walked into the house she murmured, 'Do you realise that was the first time we have talked about the past without it turning into an argument with accusations on both sides?'

Cruz had been thinking the same thing. He recalled Sabrina had said that if they had talked more ten years ago maybe there would have been fewer misunderstandings between them. But when he had first met her he had been younger and less self-assured than he was now. He had been tormented with insecurity that he was a poorly paid manual labourer while Sabrina came from an aristocratic family and was used to a luxurious standard of living. It was true that they had not talked much, but he had shown her how he felt about her every time they had made love, he thought defensively.

When Sabrina had fallen pregnant he had not risked initiating sex because he had believed it could be dangerous for her and their unborn child.

He put his hand on her arm as she was about to walk up the stairs. 'Will you join me in the library for a nightcap?' He saw her look of surprise. Usually he liked to have a drink while he checked his business emails before he joined her in bed. 'I'm beginning to realise that you were right when you said that we needed to talk about what happened ten years ago,' he said roughly.

He poured whisky into two glasses, added lemonade to one, knowing it was how Sabrina preferred it, and handed her drink to her before he joined her on the sofa.

'I accept that I was perhaps overly protective of you while you were pregnant,' he admitted. 'Growing up in the *favela*, my experiences of women in pregnancy were mostly bad and led me to believe that childbirth was potentially life-threatening for both mother and infant. Recently there have been improvements in health and social care for the poorest of Brazil's population but twenty years ago it was a different story. My mother almost died during one of her pregnancies. I remember when I was about twelve years old Mamãe miscarried late in her pregnancy. She lost so much blood and I thought she could not possibly survive.'

'It must have been a frightening experience for you.' Sabrina was appalled as she tried to imagine the terrible scene Cruz had witnessed when he had been a boy. 'Were you concerned for our baby during my pregnancy?'

'I was terrified for you and the child. When I came up from the mineshaft and was told that you were in hospital and had been bleeding heavily, it was like I had fallen back into a nightmare, only it was you instead of my mother whose life was in danger, and my own child not a sibling whose life was over before it had begun.'

A lump formed in Sabrina's throat. 'I thought you were angry with me. You hardly spoke after the miscarriage, and you avoided looking at me.'

'I felt guilty.' Cruz's jaw clenched. 'If you had died, it would have been my fault. You had told me you felt unwell that morning and I should have stayed with you instead of going to work. But I needed to earn money. In a few months there was going to be a new mouth to feed, and I was determined that my child would never go hungry like I often did when I was growing up.'

'I wish you had told me how you had been affected by your mother's experiences. It would have helped me to understand why you acted the way you did when I became pregnant.' Sabrina bit her lip. 'I'd hoped you would come to Eversleigh after me. I was unaware that your father had died.'

'I assumed when I didn't hear from you after Vitor's death that you didn't want anything more to do with me.' Cruz looked at her intently. 'If you had known about my father would you have come back to Brazil?'

'Of course I would have done. It makes me sad to think that you were on your own trying to help your mother and sisters through their grief while you were grieving for your father.'

Something tight and hard inside Cruz softened a little. He finished his Scotch and caught Sabrina's hand in his. 'Let's go to bed.' He watched her eyes turn smoky with a desire that matched his own. 'I arranged the trip to Portugal because you were right about us needing to lay the past to rest. My villa is beautiful and secluded, but more importantly it represents neutral territory that holds no painful memories for either of us. Maybe at Quinta na Floresta we will find the courage to be honest with each other so that we can both move forwards with our lives.'

Cruz's villa was situated in the stunning Sintra National Park on the west coast of Portugal. On the half-hour journey from Lisbon in his open-topped sports car they drove past miles of golden beaches on one side, and verdant forest on the other.

The feel of the warm sun on her face and the wind blowing her hair helped to ease Sabrina's tension. It was the first time she had been away from Eversleigh for months, and, although she loved her home, she realised

that the responsibility of running the estate had become
a burden. Since the plane had landed in Portugal she
had felt a sense of freedom and excitement at sharing
a holiday with Cruz. Sun, sea and plenty of sex were
guaranteed! But she also hoped that on neutral territory they would be able to set aside the hostility and resentment that had simmered between them in England.

'The landscape is breathtaking,' she commented.
'It's amazing that dense woodland grows so close to
the coastline.'

'This area of Portugal is known historically as the
place where the land ends and the sea begins. The national park boasts some of the most spectacular scen-
ery in the world.'

She gave a sideways glance at Cruz and thought that
he looked pretty spectacular in his designer shades,
with his dark hair tousled by the wind as the car raced
along the coastal highway. 'What made you choose to
buy a house in Portugal? Was it because Portuguese is
the national language in Brazil?'

'The language was one factor. I brought my mother
here to visit her sister and she felt immediately at home.
Mamãe speaks very little English, but that's not a problem for her here. I wanted to base myself in Europe and
I fell in love with Quinta na Floresta.'

Cruz turned the car onto a long gravel driveway and
Sabrina caught her breath when the house came into
view. 'When you said you owned a villa I wasn't expecting a palace.'

He laughed. 'It was actually a palace originally, built
by a bishop back in the sixteenth century. The building
has been updated many times over the years but many
of the historic features remain. The olive grove is over

two hundred years old and there are forty acres of vineyards. I plan to retire here one day and spend my days inspecting my grapes and drinking fine wine.'

'I can understand why you would never want to leave,' Sabrina murmured as she climbed out of the car and looked at the house. The walls were painted cream and the shutters at the windows were soft olive-green, contrasting with the terracotta roof tiles. Exotic trees and shrubs with vividly coloured flowers stood against the dense blue sky. Encircling the house was a wide moat and access to the front door was over a pretty white stone bridge.

Cruz led the way across a cool marble-floored entrance hall, off which there were numerous elegant rooms decorated in muted pastel shades. As they passed a glass-roofed garden room Sabrina glimpsed the deep blue of a swimming pool beyond the French doors. She followed him outside and discovered that the villa had been built around a central courtyard. At its centre was an ornamental pool and magnificent fountain that sent jets of water shooting high into the sky.

'I love how the spray is cooling on your skin,' she said, stepping closer to the fountain. 'This is just lovely. It's so peaceful here, as if the rest of the world doesn't exist.' She leaned forward, intrigued by the pattern carved all around the central stone plinth of the fountain, and her heart missed a beat. 'It says... *Luiz*.' Deep inside her she felt as though a knot were being tightened.

'I commissioned the fountain to be built soon after I bought the house, as a memorial to our son.'

'But—how did you know that I had given him the name Luiz?' she said huskily.

'I *didn't* know you had named the baby.' Cruz's eyes narrowed on her suddenly pale face. 'You showed no emotion after the miscarriage and you seemed impatient to return to England. I assumed you wanted to forget everything that had happened and get on with the plans you had made before we met. Although our son had never lived, I knew I would never forget about him and in my heart I called him Luiz.'

The knot inside Sabrina pulled tighter. 'I will never forget him either. Sometimes I wonder what he would be like if he had lived. I wish…' She broke off and swallowed in an effort to ease the ache in her throat. She felt Cruz move closer to her, but she dared not look at him, afraid she would see anger on his face, blame that she should have taken better care of their child when he had been developing inside her.

'What do you wish?'

'It doesn't matter.' She could not bring herself to tell him that she wished she could turn the clock back to the day four months into her pregnancy when she had made the fateful decision to ride her horse. She would never know if it had been the reason for the miscarriage but her sense of guilt would always haunt her.

Lost in her thoughts, Sabrina watched the droplets of water from the fountain cascade through the air and sparkle like diamonds in the sunlight. She felt moisture on her face and knew it was tears, not spray, that she wiped from her cheeks with trembling fingers.

'The fountain is a beautiful memorial to our son,' she said huskily.

Cruz stared at Sabrina's drawn features. She looked fragile, as if being reminded of the child they had lost had hurt her. If she had not wanted their baby as he had supposed, would she look so shattered? Her raw emotions as she stood in front of the fountain were palpable and made him question his belief that she had not been as devastated as he had by the miscarriage ten years ago.

She gave him a tremulous smile and he felt a tug on his heart when he noticed the shimmer of tears in her eyes. 'I'd love to explore the villa.'

'I'll give you a tour of the house later. I told my mother I would bring you to meet her as soon as we arrived.'

'Does your mother live here?'

'Not in the main villa. She has her own house that I had built for her in the grounds and my sisters share another house. Jacinta and Graciana are looking forward to meeting you.'

Time and grief had left their mark on Ana-Maria Delgado and Sabrina hardly recognised the white-haired woman who greeted her in halting English. Cruz's twin sisters had been little girls when Sabrina had last seen them, and she remembered that they had been shy and unable to speak any English. She was surprised when Cruz introduced two beautiful, articulate, multilingual young women who were studying at university. Jacinta explained that she planned to be a doctor, and Graciana hoped to graduate as a lawyer.

'It is because of Cruz that we can look forward to good careers,' Graciana told Sabrina over dinner at the twins' house. A large crowd sat around the table. Cruz's aunt and uncle and several cousins had been invited to the meal. 'We owe our brother so much,' Graciana explained. 'After Papai died Cruz worked tirelessly to

support us and our mother. But more than simply providing money so that we could enjoy a good standard
of living, he took care of all of us and he acted like a father to me and Jacinta.' She grinned at her older brother.
'Sometimes he can be *too* protective. He interviews our
boyfriends so thoroughly that he frightens them off.'

'Would you rather I allowed you to date unsuitable
men?' Cruz queried. His tone became serious. 'That
will never happen, *bonita*. I would protect my little sisters with my life if necessary.'

Jacinta laughed. 'Graciana and I realise it will take
a brave man who will not be overawed by our brother.'
She waited until Cruz had turned his head to speak to
another of his relatives before she said in a fierce voice
to Sabrina, 'Cruz is an amazing, wonderful person and
he deserves a very special woman who will love him
as much as his family loves him.'

Fortunately the arrival of dessert—a Brazilian sweet
milk pudding called *pudim de leite*—turned attention
away from Sabrina. She glanced around the table at
Cruz laughing with his sisters and cousins and thought
of her solitary mealtimes in the grand dining room at
Eversleigh Hall. She had plenty of friends who often
came to stay, and of course Tristan was good company
when he was home from university. But she had never
experienced the bond that existed between Cruz and his
family and she felt like an outsider who did not belong
in his close-knit circle.

The twins clearly adored him, and Cruz's love for
his mother and sisters was evident in the warmth of
his voice. He looked more relaxed than Sabrina had
ever seen him and she felt a stab of envy every time he
laughed and joked with his family. She remembered

how, in the early days of their relationship ten years ago, they had shared laughter and friendship as well as passion and her heart ached for everything she had lost. Not just her child but the man she had loved—and would always love, she realised—but who had never loved her.

If he had cared for her at all he would have tried to persuade her not to leave Brazil. He would have fought for her as he had fought to look after his mother and sisters. Cruz had worked so hard for his family and he was still determined to protect them. Sabrina blinked away the tears that suddenly blinded her. To all appearances she had a privileged life and wanted for nothing, but what she wanted more than anything was to be cherished and protected, to be *loved* by Cruz, who she had discovered was a truly wonderful and honourable man.

'Your sisters are a credit to you,' she told him later when they strolled past lemon and olive groves on the way back to his villa. 'Jacinta told me that when she and Graciana were younger you worked long hours but you always made time to help them with their homework so that they gained the required grades for them to go to university.'

'I wanted them to have the chance of good careers. Growing up in the *favela* where there was poor schooling made me realise that education is the means of escaping poverty. That is why, with Diego, I have established the Future Bright Foundation, which provides college funds for young people from the slums.'

The scent of lemons perfumed the night air. Sabrina took a soft breath, afraid to disturb the sense of companionship she felt with Cruz as he told her things about his life that he had never spoken of before.

'Tell me more about your career,' he invited. 'What made you decide to become a historian?'

She smiled. 'I grew up literally surrounded by history. Parts of Eversleigh Hall date back to the fifteen hundreds. I was always fascinated by the Bancroft family's connection to the estate, and history seemed a natural subject for me to study. I specialised in furniture restoration partly because the house has a large collection of antiques that needed to be restored.'

'Do you have any other ambitions, or do you plan to devote your life to Eversleigh?'

The question forced Sabrina to acknowledge that she had given so much of her time to the stately home and she had not considered what she wanted to do in the future, either in her career or her personal life. She might as well face it, she did not have a personal life, she thought dismally. She was twenty-eight, and if she did not take control of her destiny there was a good chance that another ten years would slip past without her achieving any of her dreams.

'I enjoy lecturing and I'd like to do more work at the university.' She hesitated. 'I would also like to have a family,' she admitted. 'Many of my friends are settling down and having children.'

Cruz shot her an intent look. 'I'm surprised that you want children. Ten years ago you did not seem happy when you became pregnant.'

They walked into the villa and Sabrina halted in the entrance hall and turned to face him.

'I *was* happy when I found out I was expecting a baby, but I also felt scared and alone. I was eighteen,' she reminded him, 'living in another country away from the familiar things I was used to in England, and I admit that I missed Eversleigh Hall and especially my brother. But when I tried to explain how I felt you didn't seem to care or understand, and you don't understand me any better now,' she said flatly.

She swung away from him, but Cruz caught hold of her arm. 'Then let me try to understand you. It's true that we didn't communicate enough back then. I had no idea that you felt scared of being pregnant because you never told me, and I now realise that my failure to talk about my mother's problems during her pregnancies caused misunderstandings between us.'

He pulled her into his arms and stared into her stormy grey eyes. 'We came to Quinta na Floresta so that we could discuss what happened in Brazil years ago. But I am more interested in looking forwards. Neither of us are the people we were then. We have developed, changed...' he gave a wry smile '...grown up. What if we stop thinking about the past, and instead spend our time here getting to know each other better, with no preconceptions?'

CHAPTER ELEVEN

SOMETHING STIRRED INSIDE SABRINA. It was too fragile to call it hope, but it was so infinitely precious that she was almost scared to breathe. 'Is that really what you want, a chance for us to learn more about the people we are now?'

'Yes.' His warm breath feathered her lips as he slanted his mouth over hers and kissed her with fierce passion and an unexpected tenderness that tugged on her heart.

'I'd like that, too,' she said huskily. Her smile stole Cruz's breath and he silently acknowledged that he had longed for her to smile at him unguardedly and without the shadow of mistrust in her eyes.

'We will make time to talk,' he promised. 'But when we make love we understand each other perfectly.' He lifted her into his arms and carried her up the stairs. 'Let me prove how well I understand your desires, *querida*.'

In the master bedroom slivers of pearl-grey moon-light slanted through the blinds and cast stripes across the bed and on Sabrina's body as Cruz undressed her. His hands smoothed over her skin as he slid her dress down her hips, awakening every tiny nerve-ending on her body to urgent life.

She would not have unrealistic expectations that Cruz's suggestion for them to get to know one another properly would lead to him wanting a meaningful relationship, she told herself firmly. But her thoughts scattered when he removed her bra and cupped her breasts in his hands, rubbing his thumb pads over her nipples until they hardened and reddened in anticipation of him taking each peak into his mouth.

He gave her a quick smile and she sensed that he was holding back. His words confirmed the idea. 'I want to caress every inch of your body, kiss every centimetre of your skin and discover every pleasure point as if this is our first time making love with each other,' he told her raggedly. 'I want to make it perfect for you.'

She cradled his face in her hands, loving the rough stubble on his jaw scraping her soft palms. 'You always make love to me perfectly.'

He would not be rushed, however much she pleaded and implored in a voice breathless with desire. His touch was soft as gossamer as he stroked the undersides of her breasts before moving lower to slip between her thighs where he discovered that her knickers were damp with the slickness of her arousal.

'You are so beautiful,' he murmured as he eased the panel of her panties aside and ran a finger up and down her moist opening until she parted for him like the petals of a flower and he probed her, delicately at first and then more intensely, swirling one digit and then two inside her.

'Cruz…' She clutched his shoulders to steady herself, feeling her legs tremble, and murmured her approval when he bared her and laid her on the bed. She began to unbutton his shirt but he straightened up and swiftly removed his clothes himself.

She pouted. 'I wanted to undress you.'

'Not this time, *querida*. This is all about me giving you pleasure.' The sensual promise in his voice sent a quiver of excitement through her and she gave a voluptuous sigh when he knelt over her and kissed her mouth in a deeply erotic kiss. He moved down to her breasts and teased each nipple in turn with his tongue before he trailed a line of kisses to the apex between her legs and bestowed a shockingly intimate caress that made her lift her hips towards the powerful ridge of his erection.

She ran her hands over his chest and traced the ridges of his abdominal muscles, ignoring his protest as she moved lower and curled her fingers around his arousal. A shudder ran through him as she began to move her hand up and down, faster and faster until he groaned and rolled away from her to quickly sheath himself.

He entered her slowly, carefully, taking his time to allow her to absorb his length, and at the same time he claimed her mouth in a kiss that simmered with sensuality yet was so evocative that Sabrina thought she would die from the pleasure of it. When he began to move she met each deep thrust with such unguarded delight that Cruz's intention to make the loving long and slow was lost in the maelstrom of fierce passion that had always blazed between them.

With each steady stroke he took them both higher, increasing their mutual pleasure until the world no longer existed and there was just their own world of exquisite sensations building, building to a crescendo. Sabrina locked her ankles behind his back and drew him deeper inside her, taking each powerful thrust and wanting more, wanting it to never end and yet desperate, so desperate for the explosive climax that she knew was just ahead of her.

He caught her as she fell, and they tumbled into the abyss together wrapped in each other's arms, hearts pounding; two bodies in total accord, two souls connected. It was a long time before their breathing slowed and Cruz rolled off her, but he gave her no chance to slide across the bed and firmly drew her against him so that her head rested on his shoulder.

She smiled sleepily and kissed his satiny skin. There were things she wanted to say, things she was afraid to say, she acknowledged ruefully. Cruz had stated that he wanted to look forwards rather than dwell on the past, but Sabrina sensed that the shadow of the accident at the diamond mine and the fact that her father might have been responsible for Vitor Delgado's death still hung over them.

'What would you like to do today?'

Sabrina looked across the breakfast table at Cruz and her heart gave a familiar flip. Dressed in faded jeans and a tight-fitting white tee shirt, his black hair falling across his brow, he was as handsome as ever. But this was a different, more relaxed Cruz. He was a charming and entertaining companion and she loved spending leisurely days with him, relaxing by the pool at his villa or exploring the local area when they visited the beach or walked in the national park.

During the past two weeks that they had been at Quinta na Floresta they had talked more than they had ever done ten years ago. It was different now, she mused. They were older, and she knew it was important to Cruz that they were financially equal, although she had never cared that when she had first met him in Brazil he had been a poor miner.

'The beach, I think,' she decided. 'And maybe we could visit that little market where they sell the hand-painted pottery.'

He looked amused. 'At this rate we're going to have trouble taking your collection of crockery on the plane when we fly back to England.'

'I suppose we will have to go back soon.' Some of the pleasure went out of the day. 'Diego will be impatient for you to carry on searching Eversleigh Hall for the map, and I have work commitments.' The thought of leaving Portugal seemed unbearable, especially as the future was uncertain. They talked about every subject under the sun, the glaring exception being their relationship. 'The last two weeks have been fun.'

'For me too,' he assured her. An indefinable expression darkened his eyes. 'We can spend a few more days here in our private world,' he said softly. 'After we've visited the market, we'll have lunch at our favourite seafood restaurant before coming back here for a siesta.'

Sabrina threw him an impish smile. 'I thought a siesta is meant to be when you take a nap during the hottest part of the day.'

Cruz's sexy grin sent a tingle down to her toes. 'Well, you will be lying down, *querida*, but I can't promise that you will be sleeping.'

They spent the morning at a secluded beach that was only accessible by climbing down a steep, rocky path, which might have explained why they had the place to themselves.

'This is heavenly,' Sabrina murmured as she lay on

a beach mat, enjoying the deliciously lazy feeling of the sun warming her skin. She opened her eyes as a shadow loomed over her, and gave Cruz an unguarded smile that stole his breath.

Growing up in the *favela*, he had never believed in a heaven, although he'd been well aware that there was a hell. But today was a perfect day, in a perfect place, and most perfect of all was Sabrina. He bent his head and kissed her, and her ardent response stirred his hunger. 'I need to go for a swim,' he said as he reluctantly lifted his mouth from hers.

'Are you too hot?' she asked innocently. Her gaze dropped to the bulge in his swim-shorts. 'Oh, I see that you're very hot.'

'Tease all you like, *querida*,' he growled. His eyes gleamed wickedly. 'But expect to be punished later.'

After lunch they strolled through the market and Sabrina stopped at a stall that sold exceptionally good watercolour paintings. 'The picture of the horse looks like Monty.' She gave a wistful sigh as she studied the painting of a chestnut-coloured horse with a dark brown mane.

'Thank you,' she murmured when Cruz paid for the picture and gave it to her. She glanced around at the other market stalls. 'Is there anything here that you want?'

He ran his eyes over her skimpy denim shorts and long, tanned legs and he felt his body stir. 'There is only one thing I want, *gatinha*. It's time we went home for that siesta.'

Cruz had parked his car in a side street behind the market. As he and Sabrina walked towards the silver Lamborghini, a football flew through the air and thudded onto the car's gleaming bonnet. A group of young boys tore up the street to reclaim the ball, but they stopped dead when they saw Cruz inspecting his beloved sports car for a scratch.

'Sinto muito!' One of the boys stepped forwards. He was skinny, with a mass of black hair and big dark eyes. His gaze darted to Sabrina's blonde hair and back to Cruz, and he must have assumed that they were tourists. 'Sorry!' he repeated in English. He stared at the Lamborghini and gave an irrepressible grin. 'Nice car, meester!'

Sabrina expected Cruz to react angrily. His car was his pride and joy, but he laughed and kicked the football towards the boy. 'Are you any good at football? I bet I can score a goal before you can.'

The gang of boys chased after Cruz down the street while Sabrina leaned against a tree and watched the impromptu football match. He would have been a great father if their child had lived, she mused. Her heart ached as she imagined Cruz playing football with their son, who would have been a similar age to the boys.

He returned to the car ten minutes later, followed by the gang of boys, who looked suitably impressed when he started the powerful engine.

'I was a football-mad kid like those boys,' he told Sabrina as he drove back to the villa. His fingers tightened on the steering wheel. 'Sometimes I wonder what our son would have been like. If he'd have liked to play football, and shared my love of sports cars.' He gave her a wry smile. 'Maybe he would have been fascinated by history.'

She heard the sadness in his voice and her own sadness was mixed with a sense of guilt that had always haunted her, the belief that the miscarriage had been her fault.

By the time they arrived at Quinta na Floresta Sabrina's head throbbed with tension. Cruz looked at her closely, wondering why she suddenly seemed so remote after they had spent an enjoyable day together. Since they had come to Portugal he had discovered that the real Sabrina was very different from his previous opinion of her. Although she had grown up in a luxurious stately home, she had simple tastes, rather than wanting a champagne lifestyle as he had supposed. He had known she was intelligent, and she had revealed a dry sense of humour that he appreciated. She was the only woman who he had found that he genuinely enjoyed spending time with out of the bedroom.

He wished he could persuade her to tell him what was troubling her. 'Do you want to swim in the pool?'

'If you don't mind, I'd like to lie down for a while. I've got a pounding headache,' she admitted.

'You've probably had too much sun. Go to bed,' he said gently.

'I'm sure I'll feel fine after a nap.' Sabrina hurried up to their bedroom, needing to be alone with her thoughts. In her mind she heard the regret in Cruz's voice when he had spoken of their lost son and she felt as if a knot inside her were pulling so tight that it might snap.

She must have fallen straight to sleep because when she opened her eyes the room was rose-tinted with rays of sunset filtering through the slats. The clock showed that it was eight p.m. and she wondered if Cruz was waiting for her to go down to dinner. The idea of food made her stomach churn, but she told herself she would feel better after she'd splashed cold water on her face and caught her hair up into a loose knot.

The house was silent as she walked downstairs. Her feet instinctively took her outside to the courtyard where the soft splash of the fountain stirred the still air. The sun was a scarlet ball sinking in the sky and golden light lingered on the inscribed words around the fountain's base. Luiz, Luiz…the name formed a never-ending circle with no beginning and no end, just as there would be no end to her love for her little boy.

Her baby would always live in her heart.

The knot inside Sabrina broke and released a torrent of pain that she had held inside her for what seemed like a lifetime. She cried for the child she had lost and her excited hopes of motherhood that had been cruelly destroyed. Most of all she cried for all the empty years of loneliness without Cruz that she had endured and all the years ahead that stretched endlessly before her.

The pain kept coming in great waves that engulfed her and she sank down onto the wall of the fountain and buried her face in her hands as her shoulders shook with sobs.

Cruz found her there. He had been drawn to the courtyard when he'd heard a curious noise as a wounded animal might make; a sound of pain so raw that the sound of it had felt as if an arrow had pierced his heart.

Santa mãe! For a few seconds he could not comprehend what his eyes were seeing. Sabrina was sitting by the fountain, hunched over so that her head was almost resting on her knees, and the terrible, heart-rending cries were coming from her.

'Sabrina, are you ill? Tell me, are you in pain?' He put his hands on her shoulders and gently urged her to lift her head. The sight of her tear-streaked face shocked him. He had never seen her cry before and he recalled her telling him that her father had disapproved of displays of emotion.

She lifted her hands to her face to try and hide the evidence of her raw emotions, but Cruz wrapped his arms around her and held her tightly while her body shook with the storm of weeping.

'What is wrong, *querida*?' His voice roughened as he wondered if she was seriously ill.

Sabrina took a shuddering breath. 'You thought I didn't care about the miscarriage because I didn't show any emotion. But I did care, I wanted our baby. When I lost him, I felt numb inside but I couldn't cry because…' Her voice trembled and she could not go on.

'Because you had learned as a child not to show your emotions,' Cruz finished for her. 'You always had to be strong for your brother and you felt you must never let anyone see you crying.'

'I rushed back to Eversleigh so that I could cry in private. I didn't stop to consider that you must be grieving for our child.' She wiped away her tears but they were immediately replaced by more. 'I know that you blamed me for the miscarriage.'

'Of course I didn't blame you,' he said gently. 'My mother's tragic losses had shown me that pregnancies don't always go to term.'

'I shouldn't have ridden my horse.'

He captured her chin and tilted her face up so that he could look into her eyes. 'My PA ran a half-marathon when she was four months pregnant and went on to have a healthy baby who arrived a week late. A reasonable amount of physical exercise is said to be good for expectant mothers. You were *not* responsible for losing our baby.'

Sabrina felt some of her tension lessen as she absorbed Cruz's words and realised that he truly did not think that she had jeopardised her pregnancy.

'You believed I rushed back to Eversleigh because I had decided that you were not good enough for me, but it wasn't true. I never cared that you didn't have much money,' she told him fiercely. 'When we met you were kind and interesting and you made me laugh a lot, and those are the important things. I admired you for being hard-working and risking your safety in the mine to earn money to support us. I left because I thought you blamed me for losing our child, and I couldn't bear it because I...' Her voice faltered as she realised that she was giving away too much of herself.

'Because you what, *querida*? Why did you leave?'

If they were going to stand any chance of having a relationship in the future they had to resolve the misunderstandings from the past. She took a swift breath. 'I was in love with you,' she said quietly.

Cruz's sculpted features showed no reaction, and after a moment Sabrina continued. 'You didn't understand why I refused to marry you. But I had seen my parents' marriage disintegrate into bitterness and resentment and I was afraid of that happening to us. I didn't want you to feel trapped in marriage because I had conceived your baby. After the miscarriage I thought you no longer wanted me, but leaving you was the hardest thing I have ever done and it broke my heart to say goodbye.'

She sighed. 'I wish we could turn the clock back. I

wish we had been more open with each other ten years ago, but now it's too late.'

Cruz felt a pain in his chest as though his heart were being crushed by an iron fist. *Now it's too late!* He swallowed convulsively. *Deus*, it was the most heartbreaking statement he had ever heard because he knew it was true. Sabrina had said that she had loved him ten years ago. He noted she had used the past tense. But what else could he expect? He could not hope that Sabrina still loved him. Not after the appalling way he had treated her.

He stared at her tear-stained face and the pain inside him intensified as he acknowledged how he had misjudged her in the past, and since they had met again. When she had left Brazil he had thought she had rejected him because of the difference in their social status. But he now believed she genuinely had not cared that he'd earned low wages working in the diamond mine. She had admired him and she had loved him, but he had allowed his damnable pride to come between them.

The bitter irony was that he realised he had deserved her when he'd been poor. But now that he was wealthy, and financially they were equal, he absolutely did not deserve her. Sabrina's beauty was more than skin deep. She was a beautiful person, compassionate, caring and loyal to her family. It was for her brother's sake more than any other reason that she had desperately wanted to save Eversleigh Hall.

And what had he done? Cruz asked himself with savage self-contempt. He had offered her the money she needed to maintain the stately home, but in return he had demanded that she must become his mistress in a despicable deal that shamed him utterly and made a mockery of the fact that Sabrina had once admired him. There was nothing admirable about the way he had treated her and he knew that even if he spent the rest of his life apologising to her he could never deserve her now.

CHAPTER TWELVE

SABRINA FELT DRAINED after her emotional breakdown.
She got unsteadily to her feet and would have stumbled
but Cruz caught her and lifted her into his arms, carrying her into the house and up the stairs to their bedroom
as if she weighed nothing. Neither of them spoke but
she sensed that he had been shocked by her revelation
that she had loved him ten years ago.

When he had demanded that she became his mistress he had made it clear that he only wanted her for
sex, she remembered. But while they had been in Portugal they had, at his suggestion, spent time getting to
know each other and she had felt hopeful that their affair might develop into a meaningful relationship. His
unfathomable expression gave her the sinking feeling
that she had blown it.

He set her down on the end of the bed and headed
into the en-suite bathroom, and moments later Sabrina
heard the bath filling. She was so tired she could have
fallen asleep in her clothes, but she allowed Cruz to undress her and help her into a foaming bath that smelled
divinely of jasmine-scented bubbles. He took care of
her as if she were a child, sponging her body and wash-

ing and rinsing her hair with such gentleness that more tears filled her eyes.

When the water started to cool he wrapped her in a fluffy towel and dried her. He slipped a silky night-gown over her head before he led her out onto the balcony where one of the household staff was finishing placing dishes of food on the table.

'You need to eat,' Cruz insisted when they were alone again. Sabrina doubted she could swallow food, but he had gone to such effort, and to please him she forced herself to eat some of the herb omelette he served her. To her surprise she felt better after she'd eaten a few mouthfuls. The experience of being cared for was new to her and she was reluctant to say anything that might shatter the fragile bond she felt with him.

After they had finished the meal he led her back into the bedroom and pulled back the covers for her to slide into bed. The sheets felt deliciously cool against her skin, and as she watched him strip off his jeans, tee shirt and boxer shorts she felt a familiar throb of desire low in her pelvis.

Cruz lay down beside her and drew her into his arms, but to her disappointment he turned her onto her side. 'You need to sleep,' he told her in a curiously taut voice. 'We'll talk in the morning.'

For a reason she could not define the promise filled her with unease and she stayed awake long after she heard his breathing settle into a steady rhythm.

She was unaware that Cruz's will power was tested to its limits as he remained awake and forced himself to resist the temptation to make love to Sabrina. He bitterly regretted that he had coerced her into being his mistress, and the price of his shameful behaviour was the knowledge that she would never be his.

Sabrina was woken by a persistent noise that as the fog of sleep cleared from her brain she recognised was her phone. The clock revealed that it was nearly ten a.m. and she discovered that she was alone in the bed. Tristan's name flashed on the phone's screen and she quickly answered the call.

'Tris—is everything okay?'

'Good news. Dad's come home,' Tristan announced. 'He turned up at the British Embassy in Guinea a week ago without money or belongings and told them he had been seriously ill after contracting a tropical disease. He had been staying in a remote village and as a result of a high fever he had lost his memory for months. He arrived at Eversleigh yesterday and he's impatient to see you. Apparently he has an idea for making money for the estate and he wants to put you in charge.'

It was typical of her father to make plans that involved her without pausing to consider that she had her own life, Sabrina thought ruefully. But she was relieved that he was safe and well. She was used to the earl's eccentricities and although he had not been the best father when she had been growing up, she was fond of him.

Cruz was outside on the balcony. He appeared to be deep in his thoughts and although he smiled when he saw her, Sabrina noted that his smile did not reach his eyes. She relayed Tristan's message. 'I'd like to go home to see Dad,' she said. 'We were due to go back to Eversleigh in a few days anyway.'

Cruz did not immediately reply and his shuttered expression gave no clue to his thoughts. Sabrina felt a strange sense of unease as she had done the previous night when he had said that they would talk in the morning. Something about him had changed. Was it coincidence that he seemed tense this morning after she had confessed that she had loved him in Brazil? His words confirmed her fears.

'It will be better if you go back to Eversleigh and see your father on your own.'

'I thought you would want to ask him about the map.'

'I no longer care about finding the map.'

She stared at him. 'But the map was the reason you moved into Eversleigh Hall.'

'That's what I told myself,' he said in an odd voice that sounded as if he was mocking himself. 'I have decided to give my share of the Montes Claros mine to Diego. He will have geological surveys carried out to find out if there are old, deeper mineshafts, and if he finds more diamonds I wish him well. But the mine holds too many bad memories and I want to sever my connections to the past.'

He sounded so grim, and so final. Sabrina bit her lip. Was she part of the past that Cruz wanted to leave behind?

'If you don't want me to go to Eversleigh I'll stay here...or go with you to wherever your next business meeting is as I agreed when we made our deal,' she offered tentatively.

'Ah, yes, our deal!' He looked at her broodingly and she was startled by the flicker of pain she thought she glimpsed in his eyes before his expression hardened. He swung round and looked out over the balcony at the gardens. Sabrina had the idea that he would rather look anywhere than at her.

'It's over,' he said tersely. 'I am releasing you from

our arrangement and you no longer have to be my mistress.'

Shock stole her breath so that she could not speak. But even if she could, she did not know what to say. Pride prevented her from asking him *why*, and she would not plead with him to allow her to stay. It was clear to her that by revealing that she had loved him ten years ago she had overstepped a boundary. He had not wanted her love then and he did not want it now.

Her throat ached with tears, but she swallowed hard, determined not to break down in front of him. She dug deep into her reservoir of mental strength and managed to answer him with cool composure. 'In that case I had better go and pack.'

Cruz did not turn round but he sensed that Sabrina had walked into the bedroom and minutes later he heard the sound of a suitcase zip. He clenched his hands on the balcony rail until his knuckles felt as if they would split open. This was what he had to do, he reminded himself. He had to let her go because she deserved to meet someone far better than him. He was so bitterly ashamed of how he had treated her that he could not even bring himself to look at her because surely he would see disgust in her eyes where once there had been love, if only he had not been too blind to see it.

It had been raining ever since Sabrina had arrived back at Eversleigh Hall three days ago. The depressing weather echoed her mood as she stared out of the window and watched the geraniums being battered to death.

'You don't look very happy,' Earl Bancroft commented. 'What's the matter with you?'

'Nothing.' She blinked away her tears before she turned to face her father.

'Tristan told me you were dating Cruz Delgado again. Do you think that was wise after he broke your heart years ago?'

'Probably not,' she said dully. 'Anyway, I won't be seeing him again.' Ever. The knowledge felt as if a knife had been plunged through her heart. She forced herself to concentrate on her father, who looked in remarkably good health. 'I'm glad you are okay. I was worried about you.'

'Were you?' he said casually. 'You should have known I'd turn up sooner or later.'

'Tris mentioned that you have plans for Eversleigh Hall.'

'Ah, yes. I've had the brilliant idea of turning the estate into a wild animal park.' The earl ignored Sabrina's startled expression. 'You know the sort of thing, lions and tigers in enclosures, and monkeys. I thought of basing myself in Africa so that I could arrange for animals to be shipped over to England.'

'So, who will organise the animal park here at Eversleigh?'

'You will, of course.'

She stared at her father, feeling exasperated by his assumption that she would remain at Eversleigh for ever, like a lonely Victorian spinster, she thought bleakly. 'Have you ever thought that I might have other plans for my life?'

Earl Bancroft looked intently at his daughter. 'I have a feeling that you would like your plans for the future to include Delgado.'

Sabrina did not deny it. 'When I left Brazil and came

back to Eversleigh ten years ago, why didn't you tell me that there had been an accident at the mine and Cruz's father had been killed?'

Her father sighed. 'I felt guilty that I hadn't tried harder to convince Vitor not to go into the deepest section of the mine. I knew the roof supports were unstable and I had arranged for them to be reinforced, but the work was delayed.'

'Did you send Vitor back to look for more diamonds that might have been as valuable as the Red Star?'

'Good heavens, no! I pleaded with him not to go back, but he was obsessed with finding a diamond that would make him rich. They call it diamond fever, and Vitor had it badly. After his death, I decided to sell the mine. When I came back to Eversleigh that summer I didn't tell you about the accident because I knew you were suffering after you had lost a baby. You were so thin and pale, drifting around the house like a ghost. I was relieved when you decided to go to university that autumn and it seemed best not to mention what had happened in Brazil.'

The earl gave her a speculative look. 'Cruz is a decent man, from what I've heard. He and his business partner, Cazorra, have pushed for improvements to safety in Brazil's mining industry, and they pour money into a charity they set up to help children living in the *favelas*. I guessed that you fell in love with him ten years ago. Is there a chance that the two of you will get back together?'

Sabrina turned her head towards the window so that her father would not see her tears as she remembered Cruz's unyielding expression when he had sent her away from Quinta na Floresta. 'No, there is no chance,' she whispered.

* * *

'Why didn't you tell me the truth about Papai's accident before now?' Cruz spoke in Portuguese. He leapt up from the sofa in his mother's house and dragged oxygen into his lungs as he tried to come to terms with her shocking revelation. 'Why did you allow me to think for all these years that Earl Bancroft had forced Vitor to go back into an unsafe area of the mine?'

'I was afraid that if I told you what had really happened, you would think less of your father.' Ana-Maria wiped tears from her face. 'Vitor was a good man but he became obsessed with finding another valuable diamond like the Estrela Vermelha. His obsession became almost like an illness. He would not listen to me or to Earl Bancroft, who pleaded with Vitor not to go into the deepest part of the mine until the roof supports had been strengthened. Your father ignored the earl's advice and lost his life as a result.'

'*Deus.*' Cruz dropped his head into his hands. 'I wish I had known.'

'You blamed the earl and believed that Vitor was a hero, and I saw no reason to tell you the truth,' his mother admitted. 'You had idolised your father when he was alive, and I wanted you to carry on feeling proud of his memory. I realised I should tell you how the accident had really happened when you brought the Bancroft girl here and I saw your face when you looked at her. But I did not say anything these past weeks because Sabrina broke your heart once and I was worried she might do so again.' She hurried after Cruz as he strode towards the front door. 'What will you do now?'

His jaw clenched. 'Obviously I need to apologise to

Sabrina for my unfair accusation that her father was responsible for Vitor's death.'

Deus, he had so much to apologise to Sabrina for, Cruz thought grimly. He kissed his mother's cheek and walked out of her house, craving solitude while he tried to come to terms with what she had told him. It was true he had idolised his father, and with hindsight he realised that he had *wanted* to blame Earl Bancroft for Vitor's accident rather than accept that Vitor's obsession with diamonds had ultimately resulted in his death.

He had allowed his skewered view of events that had happened ten years ago to affect his opinion of Sabrina, Cruz acknowledged grimly. When he'd taken the time to get to know her properly, he had discovered that she was as lovely as the girl he had fallen for years ago. He'd sent her away because he was consumed with guilt at the way he had treated her and he believed he did not deserve her.

But she had loved him once.

Perhaps she could fall in love with him again?

His heart was hammering and his steps slowed as another thought rocked him to his core. Was he allowing his guilt at how he had behaved with Sabrina to stop him from fighting for her? He had told himself he was doing the honourable thing by letting her go. But he was a coward, Cruz told himself contemptuously. All his life he had fought for the things that mattered to him. He had escaped poverty and fought to take care of his family. So why the hell wasn't he fighting for the person who he now realised mattered to him more than anything in the world? Yes, he was ashamed of how he had treated Sabrina, and if she rejected him it would be nothing more than he deserved. But he could not, *would* not, allow his guilty conscience to hold him back from going after her.

Sabrina was thankful that her father quickly lost interest in his idea of creating a wild animal park but her relief was short-lived when he announced that he was thinking of starting an alpaca farm. The truth was she did not care what happened to Eversleigh Hall, which, a few months ago, would have been unthinkable. For the past ten years she had devoted all her time and energy to her family's stately home, but she had poured her emotions into Eversleigh to hide from the fact that she had never stopped loving Cruz.

Unable to concentrate on her latest furniture-restoration project, she walked listlessly around the estate. The hawthorn bushes along the lane were covered with tiny white flowers that smelled divine, but the beauty of the Surrey countryside in early summer failed to lift her from her black hole of misery. Out of habit her feet took her in the direction of the stables. She was even imagining that she was hearing things, she thought despairingly. But her heart gave a jolt when she recognised a familiar whinnying from the other side of the beech hedge.

As she walked across the yard she told herself she must actually have lost her sanity, and her eyes were deceiving her. But there was no mistaking the chestnut-coloured head that appeared over the stable door. Monty greeted her with the snuffling sound she had missed so much, and when she lifted a trembling hand to pat him, he nuzzled his face into her neck.

Nothing made sense. How could her beloved horse be back at Eversleigh? Something at the back of the stable caught her attention and she discovered it was a package addressed to her. She opened it with trembling fingers and stared at the painting of a horse that Cruz had bought for her from the market in Portugal. She had forgotten to pack the picture when he had sent her away from Quinta na Floresta.

How had the picture got here…? Unless…

She jerked her head round and made an inarticulate sound when she saw Cruz standing in the yard. Her brain registered that he looked utterly gorgeous in black jeans and a polo shirt topped with a tan leather jacket. She closed her eyes, but when she opened them again he was still there, still real, still the keeper of her heart as he would always be.

Her voice shook. 'Why are you here?'

His smile held faint irony. 'I think I've proved that I can't keep away from you, Sabrina, *meu amor*.'

My love! She only knew a few words of Portuguese but she told herself she must have misunderstood him.

'I wanted to deliver Monty in person. I know how much you love him,' he said softly. 'I tracked down his new owners and persuaded them to sell him. Now he is yours for ever.'

She bit her lip. 'I don't understand. You told me you don't want me to be your mistress.'

'It's true, I don't.'

She stifled a gasp of pain. 'Then why did you go to the effort of finding my horse?' She dared not hope that his gesture of returning Monty to her meant anything. But as she stared at his face she saw deep grooves beside his mouth and an expression of wretched despair in his eyes that she knew was mirrored in hers.

'Cruz…' Her feet had been rooted to the ground but

suddenly she was able to move and she ran to him, not caring that she was giving away the secret she had tried to keep hidden from him for the past weeks. She was tired of pretending that she felt nothing for him. Ten years ago she had been too unsure of herself to fight for the man she loved, but she was determined to fight for him now, even if it meant risking his rejection.

Tears streamed down her face as she flung her arms around his neck. 'I'm sorry I left you years ago.'

'*You're* sorry?' Cruz groaned. 'You have nothing to be sorry for. I'm the one who should apologise for wrongly accusing your father, and especially for the way I treated you.'

Sabrina eased away from him so that she could look at his face, but he pulled her hard against his chest and wrapped his arms around her, holding her so tightly that she felt the uneven thud of his heart.

'My mother told me the truth about my father's accident,' he explained. 'Your father did not send Vitor back to search for more diamonds. Papai chose to go back into the mine against Earl Bancroft's advice. His obsession with finding diamonds made him ignore the risks and it was because of his decision that he left behind a grieving widow and two little girls without a father, and left a son so full of anger and bitterness that I behaved in a way that shames me,' he said roughly. 'I came to Eversleigh Hall to demand the map of the diamond mine from your father, but instead I met you and from the moment I saw you I was determined to have you in my bed again.' His voice was laced with self-contempt. 'Hardly the most noble ambition, but at the time I believed I had a right to want revenge for my father's death and I was angry that you had left me ten years ago. Believe me, *querida*, when I say that I deeply regret forcing you to become my mistress.'

Sabrina shook her head. 'You didn't force me.'

'I used your love for your home to blackmail you into selling yourself to me.'

'I chose to be your mistress for one reason only,' she said fiercely. 'It wasn't to save Eversleigh or to help my brother.' She met his gaze fearlessly. 'It was because I wanted *you*, the only man I have ever desired...and the only man I have ever loved and will love for the rest of my life.'

'Sabrina,' Cruz said hoarsely. But she hadn't finished. She had found the courage to open her heart and now she could not hold back her emotions.

'I wish you hadn't made your fortune, because then I could prove to you that I love you for who you are, a wonderful man who took care of his family and worked hard to support them, a man who will never forget the hardship he endured as a child and has set up a charity to help other children living in poverty in the *favelas*. I would be proud to marry you if you were penniless because love is more precious than anything.'

She looked at him with her heart in her eyes. 'I wish I had been brave enough to accept your marriage proposal ten years ago. I wish I had stayed in Brazil with you.'

'I wish I hadn't let you leave. I should have told you that the reason I had asked you to marry me was because I loved you.' He gently stroked her hair back from her face. 'I won't make the same mistake a second time, *meu amor*.'

There was a catch in Cruz's voice as Sabrina's words swirled in his heart and healed the ache that had been with him for so long that he was almost scared to believe that her beautiful smile was for him and him alone.

'I love you so much it hurts,' he said rawly.

'Cruz…my love.' Sabrina could hardly speak through her tears, but there was no need for words as he claimed her mouth, kissing her with passion and a bone-shaking tenderness that revealed the true depths of his love for her.

'*Eu te adoro*, I adore you.' He whispered the words over and over again, in between taking soft sips from her lips, beguiling her with his tender adoration. She made a small sound of protest when he lifted his mouth from hers, but then caught her breath as he dropped down onto one knee in front of her and took a small square box from his jacket pocket.

The solitaire white diamond ring sparkled in the sunshine that had emerged from behind the clouds. The square-cut precious gem was flawless, perfect, just as Sabrina was perfect, Cruz thought. 'Will you marry me, *meu anjo*, my angel, and be my only love for the rest of our lives?'

'Willingly, and so very happily,' she said, blinking back more tears as he slid the ring onto her finger. 'But we won't love each other exclusively.' Her voice shook a little. 'We will always love our first baby, Luiz. And hopefully there will be more children for us to love. I'd like at least four,' she told him with a teasing smile that Cruz knew would hold his heart prisoner for ever.

'Only four?' He swung her up in his arms and strode into the hay barn, pausing to secure the latch on the door so that they would not be disturbed.

'I don't think we should wait to start trying for a family.' Sabrina pulled off her tee shirt and bra and felt a delicious shiver of anticipation run through her as she watched Cruz sling his jacket on top of a hay bale, followed by his shirt, and move his hand to the zip of his jeans.

'Indeed,' he murmured, 'and when do you think would be a good time to start trying, *gatinha*?'

'Right now.' She stepped out of her skirt and panties and smiled when he drew an audible breath.

'How do you feel about holding our wedding here at Eversleigh Hall, followed by a honeymoon in the Seychelles…' he paused for a heartbeat '…and making our home at Quinta na Floresta? There are stables for Monty, and your cat can move in too, if you insist.'

'Of course we must take George with us.' Sabrina linked her arms around Cruz's neck and felt his very hard arousal push between her thighs. Her eyes gleamed wickedly. 'I love him almost as much as I love you.'

'I'm glad you said almost—' Cruz pushed her flat on her back on a hay bale and grinned at her gasp of surprise as he surged into her '—because I plan on being the number one male in your life for ever, *meu amor*.'

'For ever sounds perfect,' she agreed.

* * * * *

LET'S TALK

For exclusive extracts, competitions
and special offers, find us online:

f facebook.com/millsandboon

⊙ @millsandboonuk

🐦 @millsandboon

Or get in touch on 0844 844 1351*

For all the latest titles coming soon, visit
millsandboon.co.uk/nextmonth

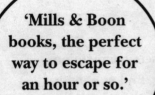